In the Dark

Volume 2

Jin Shisi Chi

ISBN 978-1-7365009-6-5 (Paperback edition)

ISBN 978-1-7365009-7-2 (ebook Edition)

Translation by Beans

Editing by D. Gareau

Proofing by E. Flo

Cover Illustration by Carm

Cover Design by Beans

This edition is arranged with Baoding Manyu Culture Media Company through Wuhan Loretta Media Agency Co., Ltd.

First Edition printed in 2021, USA

Published by Peach Flower House, LLC™ 2021

PO Box 1156

Monterey Park, CA 91754

Visit www.peachflowerhouse.com

Note: Character names are written in the order of the original Chinese naming style: family name first followed by the given name.

Table of Contents

Panic on the Road

Both Lu Weiwei and Zuo Ruoqi had escaped the critical stage thanks to the first aid treatment they received, and both were staying in the hospital for recovery. Although Xiao Gu's corpse still had suspicious aspects, no other evidence could prove that she was murdered. The Prosecutor's office stepped in while the case was still in the hands of the investigators. It was clear Xiao Gu killed Chang Ming, and Peng Yixuan's case was likely going to be settled as intentional homicide. The girls and officer Xie Lanshan all witnessed Peng Yixuan chasing Zuo Ruoqi with a knife in hand while still on the ship; they could all prove as witnesses that the young girl was intentionally breaking the law and had once threatened to murder all of her fellow school-mates on the ship.

The mass kidnapping case was now in the headlines across the country. With Yao Yao's corpse finally discovered, the truth behind that mysterious disappearance many years ago came to light. The drug trade case was associated with the Starex group; despite not having direct evidence to convict Peng Cheng of being involved, it was still a massive blow to the family's reputation. The professionals from the Prosecutor's Office all agreed that Peng Yixuan was not yet 14 years of age when she killed Yao Yao, thus per the law, they could not use the case in court as a prior criminal record. But the minor protection law could not be used as a breeding bed for underage criminals. Peng Yixuan's evil nature remained unchanged even upon adulthood. A judge could still assess her act of killing Yao Yao and disposing of the young girl's corpse as a misdemeanor case in court.

This decision was not only within the limits of the law but also a satisfactory verdict the public wanted to see, earning applause from people all over the country.

Hanhai City certainly broke the municipal's record with the amount of illegal substances they confiscated during the case. However, Chang Ming's death halted further investigations on this front and summoned Sui Hong personally to Hanhai City. The Special Forces Captain prepared himself to assist the city's homicide and violent crimes unit, in addition to customs security, aiming to dig deeper into the source of these drugs.

Captain Sui was an easy-going and friendly man. Despite carrying a Superintendent 3rd Class badge, he lived in the most modest public bureau housing. Upon his arrival at the bureau, he summoned his two subordinates to hear a detailed report of the case.

In front of their captain, the two stood straight and upright as if their backs were steel boards. Chi Jin was quite proud, and Ling Yun was quite excited. Whether it was the kidnapping or the drug trade, the Blue Foxes played a pivotal role in both cases and proved their worth to the city.

Sui Hong turned to look at Ling Yun, then coughed a few times with his hands over his mouth. Yet he directed his words at his other subordinate, whose gaze he didn't meet. "I heard you were quite the hero here in Hanhai City, but had a rough time getting along with the inspectors in the homicide unit?"

Chi Jin's face heated up when he wasn't awarded his expected praise. The young man was a fierce and independent wolf before anyone, except Sui Hong, whom he admired like a loyal subordinate. He turned his face and gave Ling Yun a leery look.

"I-I didn't tattle-tell on you." Ling Yun felt his goosebumps rise with Chi Jin's stare and waved his hands in denial, then gave a wimpy remark, "Captain asked so I can only tell him the truth..."

"I just don't like how laid-back and unorganized they are," Chi Jin said with a hard expression, his words mingled with a hint of displeasure and frustration.

"I know why you have beef with the people in Hanhai, it's because of Xie Lanshan, right?" Sui Hong stood up and walked towards Chi Jin, his expression stern, and said, "You still think that Xie Lanshan was the one that let Mu Kun escape that time, don't you?"

Chi Jin clenched his teeth, his cheeks popping up slightly. He didn't say another word. Ling Yun pressed his lips tight, also afraid to speak.

Sui Hong let out a gentle sigh and gave a pat to Chi Jin's shoulder."But I can tell you with confidence that it's impossible. Are you telling me that you can't even trust my words?"

Chi Jin panicked at the question and quickly explained, "That's not it, Captain... I... I'm just not convinced."

Sui Hong gave another cough and asked, "Not convinced about what?"

Chi Jin's refusal to give any kind words toward Xie Lanshan displayed strongly; he said with an icy voice and expression, "Why was Xie Lanshan chosen to go undercover for the Golden Triangle operation when I can do it too? In terms of physical and combat requirements, I'm clearly no less than him!"

Sui Hong was taken aback for a moment before he raised a hand and gave a knock on Chi Jin's head. The young officer reached a hand behind his head, staring at his boss in shock, confusion, and even pouted. The latter scolded in laughter, "Now you're being ridiculous! You had just enrolled in the police academy and hadn't learned a thing when A'Lan was sent off on his mission. How could we send you out like that?"

Chi Jin pondered for a moment and realized that was indeed the case. He then noticed Sui Hong coughing a few more times and quickly pulled out a small bottle of Nin Jiom Cough Syrup from his pocket, then handed it to his boss. "Captain, please take care of your body. The weather's getting cold."

Before Sui Hong could take the small bottle, Ling Yun grabbed it from his comrade's hand and said, "Oh hey, my throat's also been itching lately, let me have some—wow! The bottle's all warm too, so much effort for one little thing."

"Give it back, go pour your own cup of water if your throat's itchy!" Chi Jin glared sharply at Ling Yun, but the latter ignored the threat and continued playing with the bottle. Chi Jin grew even more upset and reached out a hand to take the bottle back.

"Alright, that's enough." After separating the fighting monkeys, Sui Hong laughed as he coughed. "You two did well on this case. Even though we've temporarily lost connections to track down the mastermind, I'm sure they will make a move soon now that we've confiscated so much red ice. As long as we keep our eyes on it, I'm sure we'll eventually be able to catch them. Anyway, let's forget about the cases for now. How about we decide how we're going to celebrate tonight?"

Ling Yun responded immediately, "Dinner's on you, cap'n! Let's go to karaoke after dinner and sing all night!"

Sui Hong nodded. "Dinner's on me. What do you guys want to eat?"

Ling Yun once again chimed in, "No more Japanese food, like usual. I'm not too big on it. I like pork and roasted ham; I found a good place for them, cap'n, so you're coming with me tonight."

Ling Yun continued on about wanting to have some team-building activities while the three walked toward the reception area of the bureau. As soon as Sui Hong opened the door outside, he was met with a surprising guest—Song Qilian.

Song Qilian also noticed the man, but didn't walk toward him. She stood still behind the twilight and simply watched him in silence.

Sui Hong walked towards her and invited, "I'm treating my teammates tonight to dinner. If you're free tonight, you're more than welcome to join us, Qilian."

Song Qilian didn't respond. She stood dumbly as she stared at Sui Hong, still and silent like a tree. A while later, her eyes finally turned slightly and showed that she was indeed still alive. She said, "I'd like to speak to you about A'Lan."

Sui Hong noticed her reddened eyes, the grief and determination in her gaze, and responded sternly after a moment of silence, "Sure, follow me."

Chi Jin noticed the change in his Captain's expression at the name A'Lan; this strange reaction also grappled his heart.

He stood frozen even after Sui Hong and Song Qilian's figures disappeared into the central park.

"What are you doing?" Ling Yun pulled onto his teammate and said, "Cap'n is talking to his girlfriend, no eavesdropping."

"Nonsense! She's just a female friend, not his girlfriend." Chi Jin turned and corrected him irritably.

"Are you a porcupine? Just stabbing back at anyone you see around you? I was just joking." Ling Yun intended on teasing his teammate and reached a hand to tug on Chi Jin's ears, then dragged the man away.

For a second, Chi Jin really intended on following his boss without hesitation but couldn't bring himself to pull such a low act like eavesdropping. So the two young men in their early 20s left after a brief fight.

It was a typical fall evening after an autumn rain, the aftermath of the typhoon prepared the earth for winter. The park was still empty at this hour, but it was close to the time when elderly women would come out to dance in the plaza.

Sui Hong stood face to face with Song Qilian at the corner of the central park. Trees and flowers surrounded the area, and it was rather quiet; an ideal place to have a conversation.

Sui Hong had already guessed the reason for the woman's visit, so he wasn't surprised when Song Qilian took out the DNA test results between Gao Zhuyin and Xie Lanshan.

"What can this possibly prove?" Sui Hong returned the report to Song Qilian and said, "Perhaps they've never been blood related in the first place—"

The voice of a woman on the verge of a breakdown interrupted his words.

"Then how do you explain the birthmark? And what about his drastically changing personality? He stayed by the side of the most dangerous drug lord in the world for six years.

How was he able to return without a single injury on his body?"

Sui Hong closed his eyes as he listened to Song Qilian's tearful questioning and accusations. He knew since the beginning that he would never be able to hide the truth from this woman.

"My grandfather has knife scars all over his arm. I once asked him about it; he told me it was inevitable to brawl with drug dealers during undercover missions and sometimes he had to even cut himself with a knife to avoid being forced to use drugs. He said that virtually all frontline undercover agents had to go through this horrific situation, but why didn't Xie Lanshan have to suffer through this?" Song Qilian took out the wooden sculpture she hid inside her bag and held it up with a shaking hand before Sui Hong. She cried in despair under this tranquil autumn sky and said, "Please, I'm begging you, please stop lying to me. This is the person I've been in love with since I was twelve. I can't possibly mistake him... Something must have happened to him during his undercover days... right...?"

Sui Hong clenched his fists without a word.

"You must know the truth," she said. Judging from the man's reaction, the woman knew she was closing in and risked it all with a harsh threat. "If you don't tell me, then I'll take all of this evidence to your director!"

Song Qilian turned and was ready to leave, only to be grabbed around the waist by Sui Hong from behind.

"Qilian, no! You'll ruin him!"

This was the first time Song Qilian had seen this man lose his cool. She met with him a handful of times before Xie Lanshan went undercover; Captain Sui of the municipal's main Narcotics Special Forces was always a man of elegance and fortitude who never lost his cool, even in the face of a shattering world. Yet the same man right now had his eyebrows

7

pressed together, eyes red, and lips trembling. Even his fists were shaking as he said, "Xie Lanshan... comrade Xie Lanshan..."

Since names were casually used among officers in the bureau, nicknames were also common. Older officers would often be referred to with more seniority, while younger ones were treated like juniors. Closer colleagues would even have their own nicknames among each other. Typically, the phrase 'comrade' was used ironically and almost never during casual occasions. Song Qilian could feel a hard blow to her chest as she heard Sui Hong say that word: her heart skipped a beat in fear.

As she had expected, a rare and warm tear rolled down Sui Hong's voice as he said, "Comrade Xie Lanshan gave his life in the line of duty."

It was a month before the multinational anti-drug operation and for Xie Lanshan to accomplish his final mission. He noticed something off on the streets and was lured into a dark alleyway by gangsters attempting to violate a young girl—only to walk right into a trap.

Sui Hong said, "It was already too late by the time we found him. His face... was deformed by the beating."

Song Qilian was right; how could a frontline undercover agent return from a mission without even a scratch on his body?

Xie Lanshan was lying completely naked on the autopsy table. His face suffered around fifty harsh blows by a heavy metal rod, to the point where his eye sockets and chin were completely concave in a horrifying manner. This terrifying deformity erased all of his former handsome glory. The man fell asleep with this bloodied and deformed face, along with a body full of various injuries. Perhaps he hadn't been able to get a good night's sleep like this in many years. Even the doctor, who had witnessed countless life and death moments, quietly shed a tear of pity at the awful scene...

"Then where is... A'Lan's body?" Song Qilian already had tears welling up in her eyes when she asked and she covered her mouth to stop herself from crying out too loudly.

"Because we still needed to keep Xie Lanshan's identity, we couldn't bring his corpse back to China or announce his death. I buried him beside a Buddhist temple in a rural village in Myanmar with no gravestone."

Song Qilian tried to imagine the scene of Xie Lanshan's sacrifice but discovered tragically that she couldn't even draw out an image of the man's face as an adult after uncovering the truth. The only thing that consumed her mind was the Xie Lanshan from ten years ago. He was a kind-hearted and strong young man who smiled at her during those halcyon days, like a pure and saintly statue on the throne of a deity. Xie Lanshan had always been like that; despite being a man of few words who smiled little, every rare instance of his smile was like the gentle sunlight during a cold winter day.

Song Qilian suddenly realized something and asked in panic through her tears, "Then who's this Xie Lanshan right now?"

Sui Hong let out a small sigh. "The U.S. military was involved in secret research. It involved combining a precise RNA injection and a craniotomy in a process of transferring memories between animals; of course, because of many ethical issues, the research ground to a halt. The research was still young, with very little information about potential side effects. Nobody even knew if it would succeed for humans. But the multinational operation to hunt down Mu Kun couldn't afford to fail at the last minute—coincidentally, we discovered a criminal in prison at the time who looked almost exactly like Xie

Lanshan. It was almost as if the stars had aligned for the experiment to succeed."

"Prison..." Song Qilian almost couldn't believe her ears with these shocking reveals. "What kind of criminal?"

"He was..." Sui Hong struggled to explain, his expression twisted in pain and regret. After some hesitation, he finally confessed. "A criminal on death row. To be more precise, he was a serial murderer who had countless lives staining his hands."

Song Qilian interrupted Sui Hong's explanation with the most despairing cry; this shrill cry continued until it turned into a pained laugh. After shifting between crying and laughing, she howled in agony, "Didn't you always call him the subordinate you're most proud of?! He trusted you and admired you, how could you do something like this?!"

"This was my decision. The higher-ups aren't aware! I couldn't possibly sit by and watch my comrade and subordinate sacrifice his life in a foreign land. I really want..." The man's voice trembled as another tear rolled down his face. "I really wanted for him to live, even if it was a one in a million chance, even if it was in this unethical and incomprehensible form... I still wanted A'Lan to live on."

"I'm going to tell your director, I'm going to tell him everything word for word—" Song Qilian was on the verge of a breakdown. She turned and got ready to run.

But Sui Hong once again stopped her.

"Qilian!" Sui Hong pulled onto Song Qilian's arm and growled hoarsely. "Think about it, there is no amnesty law for death sentences in our country, so if anyone were to expose this, A'Lan... no, the Xie Lanshan right now would immediately be put on his deathbed."

Song Qilian couldn't stand it anymore and slowly dropped to her knees while still clinging onto Sui Hong's arms. She had mentally prepared herself for all sorts of scenarios after receiving the DNA report, imagining every possibility. Yet she could never have imagined the bloodied and horrific truth. She regretted everything. Why couldn't she have pretended nothing was wrong? Why did she instead choose to search for the truth?

"But have you ever thought... that if one day, he discovers the truth..." Song Qilian was kneeling on the ground, her blood and flesh all washed out in the form of tears. She was now nothing but an empty shell on the ground, exhausted. Suddenly, she realized that her current despair and shock was nothing compared to the amount of trauma Xie Lanshan would face when he discovered the truth. She lifted her head and stared at Sui Hong, then questioned him numbly, "How could you let Buddha accept that he became a demon without knowing?"

(ii)

Sui Hong asked for Song Qilian to keep the secret for him, but she refused. She threatened to expose the truth and forced Sui Hong to give her all the information about the criminal that he had.

He had no choice but to concede and handed her a heavy file envelope while still attempting to convince her that the Xie Lanshan right now was no different from the man he was in the past. He was still a courageous and immovable soul, like the mountain; all of his good nature and character still bloomed inside him.

Song Qilian didn't listen to another word the man said and left in tears.

The files revealed to Song Qilian that the man who had Xie Lanshan's memories was a man named Ye Shen. He was formerly a manager at a French investment bank; the man in the photo had long hair tied up in a unique manner, dressed finely, and had an elegant smile on his face—but this same man also had the blood of at least five people on his hands.

A family of six died tragically in a serene rural village. Police discovered a type of poison called paraquat in the wells of the village, but that wasn't the cause of the family's death. A culprit brutally murdered the family with a knife while they were suffering from poisoned water. Photos of the crime scene were gruesome; the youngest victim was a boy only eight years of age. What kind of demon would murder an eight-year-old without batting an eye? Song Qilian shivered.

The corpse of the wife was never found; however, the entire tub was filled with the fresh blood of the women. Also discovered at the scene of the crime was a ripped piece of human skin from the wife, so she was presumed dead.

The case was from over ten years ago; Ye Shen was only fourteen. Song Qilian covered her mouth and let her tears fall. This was a natural-born murderer.

Even more shocking was that many years later, a girl by the name of Zhuo Tian had once called the cops for help. This was how the police caught Ye Shen red-handed—as he was about to brutally murder the young woman. Ye Shen didn't deny any of the crimes he was accused of, but aside from a floor filled with blood and a butterfly-shaped piece of human flesh, the police could not find the girl anywhere in his residence.

Recalling now, Song Qilian noticed the strangeness of everything; Xie Lanshan didn't have dimples, but Ye Shen did. More importantly, Xie Lanshan was not interested in men.

The young Liu Chang stood nervously behind her, his eyes wide in shock, unable to comprehend his mother's grief.

The doorbell rang before she could finish going through the

files. Song Qilian was still drenched in pain and sorrow, so Liu Chang rushed to open the door in place of his mother.

Outside the door stood Xie Lanshan. He had promised this mother and son duo that he would continue teaching the little boy how to swim, yet he didn't see Liu Chang show up after waiting close to an hour at their designated meeting place. Xie Lanshan attempted to contact Song Qilian; he called and messaged her but never received a response. He knew they would never miss an appointment and was worried, so he paid the house a visit.

Xie Lanshan didn't get any response after ringing the doorbell multiple times. Just as he was about to leave, thinking nobody was at home, the door suddenly opened. Liu Chang only opened the heavy wooden door behind the metal security gate; the young boy stared at the man behind the openings between the gate slats.

The safety of these two was of utmost importance. Xie Lanshan relaxed his racing heart and kneeled to face the boy's gaze, asking gently, "We promised to meet. How come you didn't show up?"

Liu Chang mumbled, "Momma won't let me go. She said I'm not allowed to go near you in the future."

This shocked Xie Lanshan. "Why is that?"

Liu Chang also found it baffling. Even at his young age, he could tell that his own mother had clear romantic feelings for this uncle Xie, and the boy also quite liked the man himself. The little boy made a slight gesture, deep in thought for a moment, before reaching his hand up to the door handle, ready to open it up for the man.

"ChangChang!" His mother's cry stopped him. Liu Chang jumped in shock and he sheepishly pulled his hand back. He gave Xie Lanshan outside the door an apologetic look, confusion written all over his face.

Xie Lanshan saw Song Qilian appear behind the boy. The woman stood frozen, with no intention of opening the door for him.

It was the tail end of fall reaching into winter; the weather was numbing to the flesh. Xie Lanshan had already been waiting for an hour out in the chilly wind, limbs numbing as time passed. Hoping to enter the house for a cup of hot tea, he raised a hand and knocked on the door again. He turned to the woman inside with a playful grin on his face, laughing. "Trick or treat."

But Song Qilian still didn't open the door. She couldn't and refused to understand this "human brain transplant procedure." Regardless of whether it was the flesh, the identity, or the soul of A'Lan, she found at that moment she could no longer recognize this man.

That was when Xie Lanshan noticed the tear stains on Song Qilian's face. His first instinct was that Liu Mingfang once again came to harass the single mother and child. He asked, concerned, "Qilian, why are you crying?"

Realizing she could no longer find traces of her former lover on this man's face, Song Qilian pulled her son into her embrace and cried out, "Please don't come to find my son anymore, I'm begging you, please don't come to me anymore..."

In front of her face full of hatred and fear, Xie Lanshan stood frozen and watched as Song Qilian avoided him like a monster.

"Just what exactly happened?" This hurtful and distant reaction from his former lover painfully stabbed Xie Lanshan's heart. His eyes reddened as he mumbled, "I don't understand..."

Even though he had only known for a brief period of time, Liu Chang didn't hide his fondness for uncle Xie, struggling within his mother's grip to pull out.

"Sorry... I'm really sorry..." Song Qilian apologized through her tears. She had decided already; to protect her son from a monster, she would write a letter to the Provincial Bureau's Director, Sui Hong's direct boss, to expose the bloodied truth of Xie Lanshan's identity.

And Xie Lanshan himself was completely oblivious to this destructive decision.

"There's nothing to apologize for. I'm just glad to see that you and ChangChang are okay. I'll take my leave then." Even after being pushed out of the door, he didn't feel he needed an apology. His heart might hurt, but he only wished for her to be happy.

He bent down and left a snow-white lily by the woman's front door. Out of courtesy to pay an unprompted visit, he had brought a flower with him. He always remembered that white lilies were her favorite flowers.

After considering that the woman's reaction might have stemmed from something that she couldn't talk about so easily, Xie Lanshan turned back after taking a few steps away from the door. He gave Song Qilian a familiar and warm smile, then said, "I just want you to remember that no matter what happens, I am always ready to give my life for your sake."

(iii)

Even though Song Qilian's sudden change in attitude was hurtful, the most important job right now was to investigate the girl called Zhuo Tian that appeared in his dreams.

Xie Lanshan and Shen Liufei grew closer over the last few months, and the former was able to rip open the file bag that Xiao Qian had delivered last time with Shen Liufei in the same room.

The files suggested that this Zhuo Tian girl had criminal

records of being imprisoned for drug usage and had been sent off to rehab centers. From the witness accounts recorded, she quit school at a young age and ended up getting involved with gangs, later becoming a druggie.

With the help of Shen Liufei, the two completed some further investigations based on these reports. Surprised to find out that the process went smoothly, they successfully were able to get in contact with Zhuo Tian's father.

Old father Zhuo lived thousands of kilometers away so they could only contact him by phone. He spoke with a heavy accent and explained that his daughter stepped into the world of drugs through shady friends, which eventually led her down the path of selling and living off illegal substances. She refused to listen to her parents, who tried to stop her. The last they heard from their daughter, the young girl had claimed she was going to stop doing drugs after she completed a big business deal in Thailand with her boyfriend.

The young girl in the photo appeared young and pretty, nothing like what they would imagine a drug dealer to look like.

After the call with her father ended, Even Xie Lanshan's surprise was evident. He asked, "A drug dealer at her age?"

Shen Liufei was the first to contact Zhuo Tian's father and added, "Remember the last case; that third-year high school girl by the name of Qiu Fei was also dealing drugs in secret. Isn't it the primary focus of your job now to figure out how to deal with the ever-changing forms of narcotics and illegal substances while handling a new generation of younger drug dealers?"

Xie Lanshan saw some truth in this statement. Piecing it together with what they now knew about the young girl, it wouldn't be surprising for a female drug dealer from the Golden Triangle to die in his hands, as she did in those dreams.

Shen Liufei added calmly, "If you don't believe me,

perhaps we should consider paying Zhuo Tian's father a visit and speak to him in person."

Xie Lanshan turned and stared at Shen Liufei. There were still many truths to be uncovered about this girl dressed in white who haunted his dreams, but Shen Liufei returned his gaze openly, like an exposed net waiting to capture anything that came up. Those earnest eyes convinced Xie Lanshan.

After a while, Xie Lanshan let out a deep breath of air. He walked up and buried his face in Shen Liufei's shoulder, repeating quietly beneath his breath, "Thank you."

"For what?"

"Thank you for letting me know that I'm not a monster." This nightmare involving Zhuo Tian had made him doubt himself and his identity perpetually; among those doubts were some suspicions that he felt too nonsensical to even speak of. The weight on his shoulders finally lifted after a belated peace of mind; Xie Lanshan sank into Shen Liufei's embrace and almost wanted to laugh at his own silly thoughts.

"Of course you're not a monster." Shen Liufei let the man go but kept his warm, affectionate gaze on him. The artist's lips lifted into a faint smile, and he placed a gentle kiss on Xie Lanshan's forehead. "You're a good cop, you're Xie Lanshan."

Shen Liufei lived modestly and naturally wouldn't put too much effort into decorating the interior of a rental house. Autumn was a season of solitude, especially during the hours of dusk. The room seemed emptier and more lifeless than usual as Xie Lanshan glanced outside the window; the skyscrapers stood tall like trees in a forest, the neon lights glistened against the dark background. People's voices echoed from afar, but a unique sense of quietness engulfed the streets that made the city seem like a different world for a brief moment.

"Now that you found your answer, I have another suggestion for you. I think it's time for you to admit that this is part of the PTSD symptoms you've developed from your undercover mission, and it's time for you to completely forget about all of those traumatic memories that still haunt you. We've uncovered the truth behind Yao Yao's case, but the red ice case is still a mystery. We don't have that much spare time for you to patch up your wounds, so you should focus on doing your job as a cop." Shen Liufei turned and walked into the kitchen. He bent down to open up the fridge and then asked Xie Lanshan, "What do you want for dinner? I'll cook."

Years of living under harsh conditions as a law enforcement officer had trained Xie Lanshan to survive on cold food and rations. He could count the number of times in a year he had a warm meal with one hand, so he could hardly believe that one day he would have a pretty lover that cooked for him. It was a memorable taste that reminded him of a New Year's Eve where his old man was off duty. Freshly cooked New Year's dishes filled the table, the aroma of home wafted in the air. He finally pushed down those unsolved mysteries in his memories temporarily and allowed them to collect some dust. His gaze fell on Shen Liufei's back and down to that slim waistline, then said, "I have a suggestion too."

Shen Liufei stood up and turned in confusion. "What is it?"

Xie Lanshan lifted an eyebrow playfully. "Your house is too cold and big. Why don't you just move in with me anyway since this is a rented place?"

Shen Liufei's expression remained unfazed. "Are you inviting me to live with you?"

The fact was that Xie Lanshan had already been staying over at Shen Liufei's place for a couple of days with the excuse of recovering from his injuries, but the cop felt it was quite inconvenient. First of all, the place was too far from the Municipal Bureau, and second, this wasn't his own house—it was quite embarrassing to live like an in-law freeloading off of the artist. Xie Lanshan gave a sly smile toward Shen Liufei; the glint in his eyes shined a suggestive color. "Your five sons back home miss you a lot. I can't possibly keep them at a foster home all the time, either."

"Depends on how serious you are. I'll think about it." Shen Liufei lifted the corner of his lips as he closed the refrigerator door; his cold face finally warmed up slightly.

"Absolutely serious." Xie Lanshan hooked a finger on the corner of his underwear and pulled it down a few centimeters. He then turned and said with a grin, "Try me, if you want."

Xie Lanshan was usually the deep sleeper between the two. Perhaps it was the long-term headaches that lowered the quality of his sleep over time, or perhaps it was the stress of working on the frontlines over these years, but he finally seemed to have found a place to rest peacefully. Shen Liufei got up at midnight and walked into the study on his own. He placed a file into the ashtray and burned it to dust.

He made a fake copy of Zhuo Tian's files. Of course, the girl's basic information could easily be found if Xie Lanshan had searched himself, but the most important piece of information about the girl was fake. He knew that Xie Lanshan would trust him and not conduct a second investigation.

The night of cooling autumn was much chillier than usual. Those deep, dark eyes reflected the little sparks of flame and warmth in the ashtray. Shen Liufei stared at it for a moment until his cellphone rang.

The person on the other side of the Pacific Ocean asked, "What do you plan on doing? Expose this secret to his superiors or take care of it yourself?"

Shen Liufei didn't answer immediately. He leaned on his chair and lifted his chin up. His fingers tapped along to the jumping sparks of fire in the ashtray. He finally spoke up after the paper fully transformed into a pile of ashes.

"He's a good cop. I plan on giving up now."

(iv)

He wasn't able to give Liu Chang the swimming lesson over the weekend, but that didn't mean he could afford to miss a therapy session during the workday. Xie Lanshan arrived much earlier than his appointment time and sat before Song Qilian's desk, questions and suspicion still building up within his mind.

There was a heavy and large express mail envelope on Song Qilian's desk. He knew that was the report from his therapy sessions. Song Qilian told him that the report wasn't for his boss in the Municipal Bureau; she was sending it directly to the Provincial Branch.

"The Provincial Branch?" Xie Lanshan felt his heart jump but still attempted to put on a playful smirk. "Don't praise me too much, I'll get embarrassed."

Just as soon as he spoke up, he noticed something was off. Song Qilian's eyes reddened and her face grew deathly pale; her expression was a grave mourning.

Xie Lanshan had his guesses on Song Qilian's sudden change in attitude, but he assumed most of it was from Liu Mingfang. He went through all kinds of possible scenarios in his mind but could never have imagined that the package didn't contain his psychological report—in fact, it was Ye Shen's personal files and all the documents about the brain transplant surgery. The blade of the guillotine would drop as soon as these files were delivered to their destination.

"I'll be sending out your report today, so you're free to leave now." Song Qilian avoided making eye contact with Xie Lanshan and tried hard to hide the pain in her gaze. She pressed the package beneath her palm and prepared to send it out like a bullet shot from a gun.

She then looked at Xie Lanshan's face, her gaze filled with lingering affection, disgust, and fear. She bid him goodbye, but she knew it was a forever farewell.

"Goodbye, A'Lan."

And then she kicked him out of the office. Xie Lanshan didn't rush back home and instead pulled out an old cassette tape from his pocket, stopped his footsteps as he stared at it, then turned around and walked upstairs.

Aside from the therapy centers in the city's hospital, there were two psychiatric offices that handled more severe cases of mentally ill patients. The offices and hospital rooms were located on the top levels of the building; regular and severe mental patients all lived in locked units behind heavy metal doors.

Xie Lanshan arrived in search of someone. He would walk around the hospital after his own therapy sessions sometimes, and last time he came he had promised an old woman suffering from dissociative identity disorder that he would find a tape of Teresa Teng's songs for her.

Xie Lanshan knew these patients weren't all severely ill, but due to lack of professionals in the hospital, the management simply locked them all up for easier control. He had an epiphany one time as he saw the nurses walk in and out of the ward: *why couldn't these patients listen to some music?*

The doctors sure couldn't understand this gesture. To them, letting these mentally ill patients run around in the open area was already a great deed of benevolence from the hospital. There was no need to put in the extra effort in such trivial matters. But Xie Lanshan insisted on helping. He said that his own mother was a patient at another psych ward, and could confirm: music and dance helped improve both the emotional stability and cognitive abilities of these patients.

The doctors had no reason to argue with this police officer and could only agree to let him do as he pleased on the matter.

After finally finding a working cassette player, he placed the tape inside and played the start button. Soon, Teresa Teng's beautiful voice rang out in the room, *"Blooming flowers and beautiful scenes are all fleeting..."*

Xie Lanshan allowed the old lady to step on his feet as he led her to dance to the beautiful beat of this music. The old lady's cheeks became a cherry red from a bright grin, the people around them laughed joyfully. Perhaps it was the lure of the Queen of Mandopop, or perhaps the scene of an old woman dancing with a handsome young man was too comical, or perhaps it was just a senseless laughter. Regardless, all the patients soon joined in the joyride and grinned.

Song Qilian followed the sounds of laughter upstairs and immediately saw Xie Lanshan leading an old woman to dance out in the open area.

Xie Lanshan's smile was beaming and beautiful, his expression and posture elegant as the music consumed his mind. Even that old woman suffering from mental illness seemed to have regained her youthful vitality for a fleeting moment. Both of them danced gently to the shock of everyone around. A colleague walked beside Song Qilian and asked her as they eyed Xie Lanshan, "That's your friend, right?"

Song Qilian nodded slightly, still dazed.

The colleague seemed to have spoken to Xie Lanshan a few times and said, "This old lady asked for Teresa Teng's tape last time he came. I thought he was joking with her when he agreed to bring one back. It's hard to find old cassette tapes like this now, so I told him to just record something random on a blank cassette tape for her. But he said no, he made a promise and had an obligation to keep it." The colleague seemed to be puzzled at why Xie Lanshan would put so much effort into a request from a mentally ill patient. "You know, she might not even recognize it if you find something similar. Why did he need to search for such a rare item just for a request like this? But I have to say, his smile is beautiful!"

Song Qilian smiled. She listened to the music quietly and watched Xie Lanshan. Other patients began joining in to dance with Xie Lanshan, laughing as they danced and almost lost their balance.

Before the end of a song, a commotion from upstairs suddenly interrupted. All the medical personnel rushed upstairs and called out anxiously, "There's an emergency! Serious emergency!"

A patient went on a violent rampage, broke out of the nurses' barricade, and rushed up to the roof, ready to jump off the building.

Xie Lanshan ran up to the roof along with the doctors and nurses, asking about the condition of the patient. The person in question was a 40-something-year-old male patient who was suffering from severe schizophrenia. He used to be an obsessive martial artist when he was younger, so he was not an easy target to restrain when he fought back in full force. His daughter had come to pay him a visit today, but seemed to have accidentally triggered something during their conversation. The man acted up immediately and knocked out a handful of nurses on standby.

"They all want to poison me, the sovereign!" The man was already climbing on a dangerous metal pole sticking out from the rooftop, the pole precariously wobbling.

"The sovereign?" Xie Lanshan asked a nurse beside him, "What kind of hallucinations is he seeing?"

"He thinks he's Emperor Wu from the Han Dynasty." The nurse shook their head, wanting to laugh but couldn't. "And, he said that all the doctors here are his eunuchs, the nurses are his palace maids."

The man waved a hand and called out, "It is I, the true Son of Heaven, The Great Emperor Wu of Han! Answer me, subjects! Hast thou lured in the Huns and plotted to take the life of our imperial sovereignty?!"

"Well, at least his history is pretty decent." The nurse who was used to dealing with delusional patients finally burst out laughing; it certainly was a comical scene if they could ignore the dangerous environment. Xie Lanshan quickly analyzed the situation at hand. The building on this side of the hospital was under construction, and the fire truck had already arrived down below. However, the lower level was still a dangerous field of broken metal poles and broken concrete. Even if the man could survive a fall from this height, he would suffer severe injuries that not even air cushions might save him from.

Xie Lanshan attempted to take a step forward, only to see the man back up frantically. The young cop gestured as if he was lifting an invisible long robe and dropped to one knee, a single phrase rolling out of his mouth, "This humble servant pays respect to his imperial majesty."

This shocked the doctors and nurses, but the man was very pleased by that line and momentarily settled down.

"By your majesty's decree, your servant has initiated a counterattack against the Huns. Your army has now returned with an honorable victory in hand, offering 20,000 enemy lives." Xie Lanshan said as he carefully made his way forward, one step at a time, toward the middle-aged man. It takes a real maniac to follow the footsteps of a madman; the young cop's expression was stern, his mouth pressed to a sharp line as if he really believed he was playing a role—this was a life or death matter now, not a comedic skit.

While the madman was pleased and consumed with this poetic and overly formal nonsense, Xie Lanshan grabbed onto his arm and forcefully dragged the man back to safety.

He leaned against the wall and panted heavily. He saw the daughter cry as she hugged her father, then brushed off the dust on his knee, and gave a soft smile.

Song Qilian also followed up to the roof and waited in the back for the patient to be saved. As soon as the roaring claps rang out around her, she silently left the scene.

The old woman was still listening to the same song downstairs. Just as the song lyrics, *When will you return?* played, Song Qilian felt tears rolling down her cheeks uncontrollably.

That man would never return, but it also felt as if he had never left.

When she returned to her office, a colleague asked if she had any packages to deliver. The mailman had arrived.

Song Qilian shook her head. That package on her desk was quietly placed in her drawer.

(v)

Young love was a passionate and burning sensation that could light a person on fire, fueling all kinds of energy from inside and out. If Xie Lanshan said they were moving in, they were moving in; he restlessly helped Shen Liufei prepare to move out over the weekend.

The young cop was busy, covered in sweat even in this cold weather. He rolled up his sleeves to do the heavy lifting, but seemed to enjoy the job. Shen Liufei was on the other side casually feeding the goldfishes in his fish tank—the fish being gifts from his female students again—while Xie Lanshan worked. It had been a while since the last day of the Crane Museum's public art classes, but the girls had not given up on sending their instructor fan letters to this day. The gifts finally evolved from plants and flowers to living creatures.

The two round goldfish in the circular tank swam joyously. One fish was black with red patterns, while the other was a beautiful gold color. Both had a little crown on their heads—they were apparently a rare kind of their species. Xie Lanshan asked, "Where did they get the idea of gifting you goldfishes from?"

"It was because I copied Klimt's Goldfish painting during the last lesson." Beneath the twilight, Shen Liufei's handsome profile shined as he lowered his head to feed the goldfishes. "I can keep them in memory of the class."

Like how Xu Beihong had once copied Rembrandt's painting and Feng Zhenlin copied Matisse; Xie Lanshan had once seen this painting Shen Liufei copied. Three naked women spanned the canvas, their luring shapes boldly on display. According to Shen Liufei, the main focus of this painting was merely the naked female body, nothing else.

Xie Lanshan wasn't too interested in art and instead shifted his attention to some old English books and vinyl records that were organized into a cardboard box. He asked for the owner's permission to look at those, only to receive a sharp glance from Shen Liufei. "Those can be tossed away."

"Your interests sure are strange." Xie Lanshan dug through the cardboard box and picked out the heaviest Art History book to flip through. A photo dropped as he opened the book. In the photo was a beautiful woman holding a young boy of about 8 or 9 years old in her arms.

Xie Lanshan's first instinct was that this was Shen Liufei's mother and held the photo up beside the man, trying to see the similarities between the two. He mumbled, "How come you look nothing like your mom—"

Shen Liufei swiftly took the photo away before he could finish and placed it in his shirt pocket without a second word.

Xie Lanshan rubbed his chin and studied Shen Liufei's profile; this cold and blank face was still difficult to read as usual. But he was a little upset. He was upset at the artist's stern refusal, at him keeping a distance.

Xie Lanshan suppressed the frustration in him and said almost jokingly, "You said you were going to tell me about it eventually, but it's been so long already. Still can't tell me about her?"

Shen Liufei turned to Xie Lanshan and said in a calm voice, "She was a gentle and kind woman, almost to the point of being too passive. She was an obedient wife and depressed mother."

"And?"

Shen Liufei didn't seem interested in continuing this conversation, and the doorbell rang at that moment.

Xie Lanshan opened the door to see a young man standing outside with a basket of fresh fruits in hand. The man grinned widely at Xie Lanshan and said in a pleasant voice, "Hello neighbor, can I ask for your help?"

The man wore black frame glasses that pressed on his flat nose, but his eyes were beaming with life. From first impression, he seemed rather courteous with the way he dressed. The man handed Xie Lanshan the basket of fruits and introduced himself as Qiao Hui, a resident of unit 803 in this same residential building. He scratched his head sheepishly and said he was planning to confess to his crush tonight, so he thought of an idea to create a giant light display on the building at 8 PM to spell out "I love u" for her. The "love" in the middle would be stylized into an actual heart-shape, but all residents in the building would need to take part by turning on or off their lights at the designated time. Despite the cheesy method, it was certainly a thoughtful and romantic gesture.

Because of the location and high price of the units, there weren't very many people living in this residential building, so it wasn't too difficult to organize this sort of event. Qiao Hui had already received permission from the manager of the building for his idea, and the manager agreed to help him control the lights of the empty units. However, Qiao Hui would need to knock on occupied individual units to request permission for help on his project.

Shen Liufei's unit was the topmost unit of the letter "I" according to the layout plan. Qiao Hui said they only needed to roll open the curtains and light up their room for five minutes. That would be enough time for him to make his confession.

Xie Lanshan had the heart to support a good deed, and Shen Liufei didn't seem to have any objections. The artist walked over and nodded courteously after receiving the basket of fruits.

"Thank you, thank you so much! You guys are the last unit. Everyone else was quite supportive too and have all agreed to help!" Qiao Hui beamed gleefully and bowed in appreciation. He pointed at a business card inside the fruit basket and said, "I'm the primary oral and maxillofacial surgeon at Puren Hospital. If you're ill, please don't hesitate to come find me anytime!" After realizing the words came out a little too morbid, he smiled and said, "Of course, better if you don't need to come to visit."

. . .

The young man left cordially after the visit; the door closed as Qiao Hui's figure disappeared. Xie Lanshan wanted to continue the conversation from earlier. Yet he knew his boundaries and instead leaned on the sofa while taking out an apple from the basket. He rubbed the fruit on his shirt a little before biting crisply into it, then said with the juicy flavor of fresh apple in his mouth, "Huh, a doctor like him must not be in his early 20s anymore. He's surprisingly romantic for someone his age."

It was a sharp turn in conversation, but Shen Liufei noticed Xie Lanshan had more to say after this. The artist turned and leaned down without a second word, gripping onto Xie Lanshan's neck like he was reigning in a horse.

The bitten apple rolled onto the ground. Xie Lanshan attempted to fight back. He lowered his head and bit hard on Shen Liufei's arm. Shen Liufei frowned but didn't loosen his grip and leaned in closer until he pushed the cop down. A muffled thunder rolled outside as the two bodies embraced and tugged each other until both men fell to the ground.

It was clear that Shen Liufei was trying to offer bodily pleasure to avoid answering more questions, and it was unfortunately a very effective method. Xie Lanshan was a little displeased with the action, but the rain of burning and passionate kisses quickly soothed the unease.

The doorbell once again rang at the wrong time. Xie Lanshan cursed out loud in the midst of their heat, then crawled up and mumbled while he answered the door begrudgingly, "Isn't it just a damn confession?"

Yet Xie Lanshan's eyes widened the moment he opened the door.

The man standing outside looked to be a few years older than Shen Liufei, but was still a very handsome man. To be more precise, Xie Lanshan could say that he'd never seen any man who looked as fine as this person in his life.

The visitor seemed to recognize him; his eyes glowed in a slightly incomprehensible light for a moment before an elegant smile lifted on his face. "Hello, Officer Xie."

Xie Lanshan was surprised. "Do I know you?"

Shen Liufei stepped out from behind, his expression stunned.

It was only a split second of flicker in that expression, but Xie Lanshan caught every little change in his eyes.

"This is a friend of mine from the States, Duan Licheng; he used to be a neurosurgeon for the U.S. military." Shen Liufei didn't introduce Xie Lanshan to the other; his gaze fell onto the man outside the door. There was no hint of joy from reuniting with an old friend on his face as he said sternly, "I didn't think you would come back so soon."

Xie Lanshan wanted to invite Duan Licheng into the house, only to be told by Shen Liufei to leave. "The doctor and I have some things to discuss, you should go back first."

Xie Lanshan was still a little dumbfounded. "But it's about to rain outside."

Seeing Xie Lanshan stand dumbly, Shen Liufei handed an umbrella hanging by the door to him and added another line in consolation, "Wait for my message."

This attitude was drawing a clear line between the two; Xie Lanshan realized that Shen Liufei had something to hide from him, but he wasn't the type to get upset about it. The cop didn't even bother picking up his jacket that fell to the ground and left without any complaints.

"You know, they say that finding love and good sex isn't hard in life, it's more valuable to find someone who understands you. I used to think this was some cheesy romance line, but now

I see some merit in it." Xie Lanshan turned to Shen Liufei before leaving, hand still on the doorknob. "I don't believe my love for you is merely from uncontrollable hormones."

Almost as soon as he stepped out of the building, the heavens deemed to prank him and poured a heavy rain shower on him. A young woman got out of a taxi and ran with her head down, trying to escape the rain as soon as possible. She was dressed in a lotus pink coat with a black long dress beneath it, completed with a diamond-shaped black purse around her shoulders. She didn't watch the road as she ran and slipped, falling right into Xie Lanshan's chest.

Xie Lanshan helped the woman up, but the woman's sharp nails scratched on his arm and left a long cut deep enough to draw blood. The fish tank Xie Lanshan was carrying also dropped to the ground; one fish fell into the sewers as the other struggled for a while on the wet ground before it stopped moving.

"Sorry, I'm so sorry..." the woman looked up and saw Xie Lanshan. Her eyes widened in surprise immediately. "Oh, it's you!"

The young woman looked to be in her early 20s, cleanly dressed and had beautiful, long, black hair. Despite not knowing her name, Xie Lanshan recognized her. She lived in the same residential building as Shen Liufei and he would often run into her in the elevator, so the two were somewhat acquainted.

"Your fish... Why don't you give me your contact information so I can buy a new one to repay you? Please?" The young woman clapped her hands together and looked at him apologetically. She insisted on getting Xie Lanshan's contact information to repay him for the perished fishes, but she was simply using this as an excuse to hit on the handsome man.

Xie Lanshan knew her intention but didn't expose her, only responding with a smile, "Unit 2103, my friend." He gave her Shen Liufei's address.

The two parted as the rain poured harder. The young woman stared with a racing heart at Xie Lanshan's tall silhouette, afraid that she would forget the four numbers he gave her. She couldn't find a pen at first and resorted to pulling out her liquid eyeliner to write the number down on her palm. She turned and walked back to her house, humming a song in a good mood.

Xie Lanshan sprinted down under the eaves to shelter himself from the rain after being drenched from head to toe. The rain also stopped at a convenient time, leaving only the fresh smell of wet mud around.

He looked at his watch—it was 20 minutes until 8. He wasn't in a rush to go home and remembered that stupidly romantic doctor from earlier, then decided to stay a little longer to witness the dramatic confession.

At exactly 8 P.M., Shen Liufei's residential building lit up all at once.

But Xie Lanshan quickly discovered that the heart in the middle was missing one piece—one unit didn't light up their room as they had promised.

(vi)

Old mentor Tao of the Hanhai City Municipal Bureau was hospitalized. Tao Jun had always been a tough man who refused to rest up when he had a minor injury. It started off with a migraine and fever that he paid little attention to until his son insisted the old man get a check-up at the hospital. There, he discovered it was a dangerous brain tumor.

The doctor suggested staying in the hospital to monitor the tumor for a few days and perform surgery to remove it if the tumor didn't spread.

The condition wasn't too awful, but as soon as Tao Jun was hospitalized, the entire violent crimes unit swarmed into the hospital room. So many people quickly filled a double room in the hospital that there was no open space for even a small plant to grow.

Tao Jun was warmed by the visit but still kept his harsh tone as he said, "Are there no cases to work on? Why are you all here?"

Tao Longyue retorted, "Better to not have any cases. You think we should all work with heavy burdens on our shoulders all the time? World peace is a great thing!"

Tao Jun turned his head and saw Xie Lanshan sit beside the bed, eyes lowered and seemingly elsewhere mentally. He reminded the young cop, "Vice Chief Liu will be in charge of the violent crimes unit while I'm out, so you better not cause any more trouble for him."

Xie Lanshan lifted his gaze but didn't respond.

Tao Jun glared at him and asked harshly, "Do you hear me?"

Xie Lanshan didn't want to talk about Liu Yanbo and changed the topic, "Who's in charge of your surgery, are they reliable?"

"Of course, the most reliable we can get!" Tao Longyue had met the primary doctor in charge of his dad's case and answered, "The neurosurgeon just came back from the U.S., what's his name? He's based!"

Xie Lanshan frowned slightly and pondered when a low and soothing man's voice called from outside the door—

"That's an exaggeration."

The soles of the leather shoes clicked crisply on the ground; the public security officers blocking the doorway immediately dispersed to allow a man to step into the room. White lab coats were not the most flattering for many, highlighting the body shape of the person donning the coat. It tended to be loose-fitting, like a bedsheet for most people, but on this man in particular, even a bland lab coat looked like shining armor for an elegant and handsome knight.

Xie Lanshan recognized this face and Shen Liufei's, who followed the handsome doctor into the room. The two men looked close—like brothers—as they stepped inside.

A nurse knocked on the door and timidly reported that a patient next door was demanding to stay in a private ICU room: the commotion was getting out of hand and was becoming even more pressing than a serious medical issue.

Duan Licheng asked, "What's the illness?"

"Nothing too serious, but..." the nurse hesitated, then stood on her tiptoes to whisper something into Duan Licheng's ears. The troublemaker patient was someone of high social status.

"There aren't many beds in the hospital and I've always discouraged opening up extra ICU spaces without a good reason," Duan Licheng responded sternly and calmly. "I don't care what his background is, I treat all my patients equally. The turnover rate of empty hospital beds here is well below average, so I plan on reforming the policies starting from these ICU rooms today. Non-critical patients currently staying at the hospital will be forced to leave as soon as possible."

Tao Longyue shot a glance toward Xie Lanshan. Despite always complaining about Shen Liufei's Americanized way of work that lacked discipline, strangely, the Captain found himself bowing down to Duan Licheng's non-negotiating and almost draconian style of handling jobs.

Xie Lanshan felt his stomach churn in disgust. Shen Liufei had agreed to move in with him, but the former seemed to have vanished from the world over the last three days and didn't even call him.

The chatter inside the room completely stopped, as if a spark of fire from candlelight extinguished the moment Duan Licheng walked in. The room turned deathly quiet. As the only female officer in the violent crimes unit, Ding Li's round eyes fixed on the doctor who walked in and practically transformed into pink hearts.

In contrast, Xie Lanshan's eyes were burning dry.

With his sharp senses as an experienced cop, Tao Longyue noticed the strange air between the two men. He nudged Xie Lanshan with his arm and whispered, "Keep it low-key, don't let the old man catch your eyes. Remember, he's got a tumor in his head—don't piss him off and make it explode."

Tao Jun struggled to move a little on the bed in frustration; he wasn't used to being so relaxed for extended periods of time.

The old man was from a more conservative generation. It was possible that he could knock himself out from anger if he were to find out about Xie Lanshan's new romantic interest. Xie Lanshan retracted his gaze and lowered his head.

After paying Tao Jun a visit, Shen Liufei left early. The baggage of Xie Lanshan's heart was full of frustration, but he couldn't question the artist in front of Tao Jun. During this brief internal dilemma, Shen Liufei had already walked out of the door with Duan Licheng.

Tao Longyue offered to treat everyone to dinner and wine tonight, vaguely implying that he had exciting news to share. But everyone in the violent crimes unit already knew that his proposal to Su Mansheng was a success.

Xie Lanshan had visited the bar twice with Tao Longyue before. It wasn't an easy place to find and was small compared to other bars, but the owner was friendly and the atmosphere was less crowded than other places. At the center of the bar was a pool table that was free to play for customers, so anyone could go play a few rounds.

Xie Lanshan noticed Shen Liufei and Duan Licheng the moment he stepped into the bar. It was an honest coincidence that the two groups had chosen to hang out at the same place after hours.

Shen Liufei sat in the corner and also noticed Xie Lanshan when he lifted his head. The two exchanged glances across the bar in a spark of mixed emotions before Shen Liufei looked away first.

Tao Longyue instinctively realized something was a little off and said to Xie Lanshan, "I think Shen Liufei and Doctor Duan have things to discuss. How about we move to the other side?"

"The more the merrier, don't worry." Xie Lanshan lifted a smile and walked back to his seat with the server.

Ding Li and Xiao Liang also showed up at the bar party. Everyone joined in to play dice games in pairs of two and took a shot as punishment for losing a round.

Xie Lanshan was teamed up with Ding Li, who had never played the game before and lost virtually every round. Of course, Xie Lanshan couldn't possibly let this young girl be forced to take all the punishment shots and offered to drink for her.

The man had a fairly decent alcohol tolerance, but tonight his face glowed red at the touch of alcohol. A few more drinks and his eyes were clouded with delusions, his face crimson like he was already wasted.

Tao Longyue noticed that Xie Lanshan didn't have his

mind on the game as they played and kept looking in Shen Liufei's direction on the other side. Afraid that alcohol would completely wash away his buddy's senses, the Captain quickly took his full wine glass and downed the drink before Xie Lanshan even realized.

Shen Liufei seemed to have gotten into an argument with Duan Licheng. The two men both got up and walked away from their seats toward the restroom.

Xie Lanshan popped up from his seat and followed. The two men ended their conversation just as Xie Lanshan rushed over. The young cop saw Duan Licheng wrap an arm around Shen Liufei's neck tightly in an intimate manner, but the two men in contact stood firmly and stared at each other with hostility.

Finally, Shen Liufei said coldly, "I don't need you to remind me what I need to do. I've already told you, I've given up."

"You sure have changed." Duan Licheng released his arm and shot a glance back at Xie Lanshan. He then turned on Shen Liufei with a knowing smile and said, "You'll find out soon enough that you made the wrong decision."

Every word was like a cryptic message that seemed to hint at an answer related to Xie Lanshan. The young cop tried to decipher them to no avail, feeling more frustrated and annoyed.

Duan Licheng walked past Xie Lanshan as he stepped back to his seat and knocked on the young cop's shoulders by accident.

"My bad, Officer Xie." He gave Xie Lanshan a faint smile before lifting his head toward the pool table. "How about we play a few rounds together?"

· · ·

Everyone in the bar was standing up at this point; some had already made their way around the pool table to watch the match between these two handsome men.

The rules followed the 15-ball rotation, simple and easy to follow. Duan Licheng opened the game with an elegant and comfortable gesture. Yet as soon as the cue ball rolled out, the audience all clicked their tongues; the white ball shot into the pile of pool balls, every sphere inside exploded and rolled out like chaos. This was still Xie Lanshan's turn.

It was almost as if the man was declaring his loss before he even began. Duan Licheng didn't seem to mind and leaned down toward the pool table, gesturing with his cue stick before he straightened his back and held out a hand to signal Xie Lanshan's turn.

Of course, Xie Lanshan didn't give his opponent an opportunity to strike back. He held up his cue stick like a professional, bent his back down at a handsome angle, and then narrowed his eyes like a leopard ready to lock in on its prey. His careful control of the cue ball sharply sent a handful of target balls down into the pockets. Ding Li cheered on from the side. "Nice going, big bro!"

Xie Lanshan didn't even bat an eye at the young girl and instead kept his sharp gaze on his opponent, Duan Licheng. Duan Licheng had been leaning on the side nearby Shen Liufei ever since he stepped away from the pool table, occasionally rubbing the tip of his cue stick with chalk, seemingly unbothered by his imminent loss.

Just as Xie Lanshan was shooting down the last ball, he saw Duan Licheng suddenly turn and lean in close to Shen Liufei. The doctor pressed his lips to his earlobe and gently bit down—

But of course, the doctor's smiling expression and gaze were locked on Xie Lanshan. It was a clear provocation.

Like a woken beast, Xie Lanshan's veins popped on his

forehead the moment he hit the cue ball. He purposely put in more force than needed, causing the numbered ball to jump out of the pool table and fly directly toward Duan Licheng's face. Thankfully, the doctor reacted quick enough to dodge the ball before taking a hit right to his handsome features.

Even Shen Liufei was shocked and scolded in a harsh tone, "Xie Lanshan."

Duan Licheng smiled and said generously, "Officer Xie had been working hard to protect people on the frontlines these past years; it's not a big deal for him to vent some stress."

Taking the first hit graciously, a single line from him successfully stumped Xie Lanshan and made the cop look extra petty.

"Xie Lanshan, what's going on with you?" Tao Longyue didn't want to offend his old man's primary surgeon and rushed over, whispering into his buddy's ear, "I've never seen you act so aggressive, even when Liu Mingfang tried to tease you in the past."

His own action surprised even Xie Lanshan. The painful headache came just in time as he reached a hand over his forehead, nausea slowly consuming him. "I think... I had a little too much booze."

Before Tao Longyue could respond, he wobbled out of the bar.

(vii)

After a cold breeze to the head, Xie Lanshan felt his headache easing up. He didn't want to return home just yet and began wandering the streets. The weather was cooling, the trees by the street side already trimmed with virtually no leaf left on the naked branches. If one were to stand in the middle of the street and look directly forward, it would look as if two rows of balding old men were standing beside them on the streets—what an unsightly image.

Xie Lanshan suddenly felt that following the rules all the time in life would turn people into these trees on the side of the roads, dull and lifeless.

He raised a hand, ran his long fingers through his hair, and felt quite relieved after a brief ruffle. *Forget about Song Qilian and Shen Liufei's attitudes*, Xie Lanshan thought to himself as he removed his jacket and tossed it over his shoulders. With a smile on his face, he snaked his way along the street like a drunk man, leaving a trail of flowery dance steps on the road.

There weren't many people on the road, but all eyes were on him. Xie Lanshan didn't mind the attention and even bowed to the strangers, as if he was at a curtain call on stage.

Xie Lanshan was beat by the time he returned home and washed his face with cold water in the bathroom, hoping to wake himself up. His forehead heated up even more after a splash of cold water on his face. Xie Lanshan touched his cheek and looked into the mirror, feeling his vision blur as he attempted to make out the sincerity and kindness on this face, the darkness and madness—

Suddenly, the soapbox on the counter captured Xie Lanshan's attention. The sink was only decorated with soap and toiletries, but it was clear that someone had moved them. Even though his headache was still acting up, it didn't hinder his cognitive abilities and analytic skills—no detail could escape those sharp eyes of his. Xie Lanshan quickly realized that the person who had been watching him in the dark had snuck inside his house.

He walked out of the bathroom and into his bedroom,

immediately noticing that his bed and pillow had been messed with as well. A faint smell of tobacco lingered by his bedside.

Myanmar Twin Tower.

This was a rare brand of cigarettes that had a unique luring and sweet smell. Xie Lanshan had only ever associated this smell with one person—Mu Kun. The drug lord didn't use drugs despite being engaged in the drug trade, but this was the brand of cigarettes he always smoked.

The light in the bedroom suddenly went off.

The smell of the smoke disgusted Xie Lanshan and perpetuated his headache. He began searching through his own household and picked up a knife when he passed by his kitchen. The window curtain swayed gently, as if a silhouette was lingering behind it; every dark corner in the house looked suspicious. Xie Lanshan carefully trudged forward, his gill muscles twitched in high alert while sweat rolled from his palm, loosening his grip on the knife handle. This horrifying feeling felt familiar—like the last time he was at the boxing bar. He was convinced that Mu Kun was inside his house.

The main door suddenly creaked open, then swayed back and forth. A faint ray of light peeked out from the small gaps of the door like a lamp luring in a moth. Xie Lanshan remembered that he locked the door when he walked in, but now it was open.

He fixed his gaze on the shadow cast from the faint light outside the door, slowly tracing out a figure of a person.

Someone was there.

Danger was only inches away, but Xie Lanshan strangely found himself calming down. He held in his breath and quietly made his way toward the door. Xie Lanshan had always known the day would come when Mu Kun found him.

He charged forth the moment the door pushed open, but

pulled back the knife in hand just as he was about to slash down.

The light in the hallway was faint and yellow, the shadows of two men intertwined under the glow. Their eyes met, and Xie Lanshan asked Shen Liufei, "What are you doing here?"

"Visiting my sons." The artist's voice was nonchalant, as if he didn't realize his life was in danger mere seconds ago. Shen Liufei tried to switch on the light inside the house as he walked in, but the house was still dark. He turned on the flashlight on his cellphone and checked the main power switch. He then turned and glanced coldly at Xie Lanshan. "You didn't pay your electricity bill?"

Crisis averted: it was all just a false alarm. Xie Lanshan returned to the living room and leaned back on the sofa, then responded lazily, "I was staying at your place not too long ago, so I forgot."

Shen Liufei scanned the house briefly before he walked toward Xie Lanshan. "Where are the cats?"

"The little neighbor girl is watching over them for me for a few days." After relaxing himself from high tension, Xie Lanshan could feel his head throbbing once again. He closed his eyes and rubbed on his temple, then said almost coldly, "No sons today, you can go back now."

This was one of the rare times Shen Liufei received this kind of cold shoulder from Xie Lanshan, but he didn't seem to mind. Instead, invited himself in and sat down right next to Xie Lanshan. Shen Liufei reached a hand and placed it on the latter's forehead, then remarked lightly, "Your forehead is burning up."

Xie Lanshan harshly pushed the artist's hand away. He had his own pride and was insistent on refusing any sort of kind gesture; he couldn't hide the sourness in his eyes as he glanced toward Shen Liufei. The latter's gaze fell down on the coffee table as he carefully rearranged the items with the flashlight from his cellphone. The man clearly didn't think of himself as a guest, nor did he seem to mind the events that happened at the bar tonight.

Xie Lanshan pulled the cellphone resting on the coffee table and shone it under his chin, making an ugly face at Shen Liufei.

It would have been scarier if he was a woman with long hair. Xie Lanshan's hair was only a little longer than most men, but not long enough to cover his face, making it look more funny than scary. Shen Liufei was unfazed as usual. The unimpressed look from his gaze judged the man's childish act. Xie Lanshan also felt he was being silly and placed the cellphone down, shooting a grin at Shen Liufei.

His smile was brilliant and bright, but his gaze was both pure and alluring; the dichotomy of these expressions made him seem extra attractive.

As if his heartstrings were a kite tugged on by the wind, Shen Liufei reached out and pulled Xie Lanshan into an embrace. Then, he pressed his lips to the latter's ear and said with confidence and gentleness, "Trust me."

The last bit of lingering frustration within Xie Lanshan vanished with this warm embrace. He closed his eyes and allowed himself to drown in this rare moment of peace before he finally opened his eyes and said, "Okay."

This clear and easy response instead shocked Shen Liufei. He let go of Xie Lanshan and asked in surprise, "Just like that?"

Xie Lanshan lifted a brow and smiled. "We've already slept together. Just how much more complicated do you want our relationship to get, cuz?"

Shen Liufei also smiled—or perhaps it wasn't exactly a smile—those thin lips moved slightly, like a fleeting mirage.

"I have to correct your comment earlier; I love you, not only because of your noble soul, but because passionate hormones also define us."

His expression was relatively blank despite those passionate words and his heavy breathing. Xie Lanshan's grin grew deeper as he leaned forward and pressed his lips against Shen Liufei's mouth. "Bite me."

The next morning, an emergency call from Tao Longyue woke up Xie Lanshan from a sweet slumber in his bed. The captain said that they discovered a female corpse by the bar they were at last night.

The Girl and the Goldfish

Tao Longyue came to pick Xie Lanshan up to head over to the crime scene; Xie Lanshan kissed Shen Liufei goodbye in a rush and left the house. The iconic car was already waiting outside the residential area. Tao Longyue yawned and waved lethargically as the car door opened, clearly still not awake.

"I'll drive." Xie Lanshan kicked his buddy out of the driver's seat and took over. "Nap a bit first. I'll wake you up when we arrive."

Still hungover, Tao Longyue leaned his head back on the passenger's seat and closed his eyes.

Xie Lanshan started the engine and shot his friend a glance as he turned the steering wheel; young Captain Tao of the violent crimes unit was certainly not a traditionally handsome man, but he had a built physique and energetic spirit. Even that scar on his face was glowing like an honorable badge normally —this defeated look was certainly not fitting for the young man. Xie Lanshan was up with Shen Liufei for the entire night and still felt a bit of heat in his head, but he certainly wasn't as tired as his buddy. He laughed and asked, "Why are you so tired? Last party of freedom right before your marriage?"

"My ass!" Tao Longyue's eyes shot open as he turned to Xie Lanshan, annoyed. "We left not long after you walked out and I had to go care for the old man in the hospital that night; he scolded me the whole night because of your situation!"

This shocked Xie Lanshan. "My situation? What did I do?"

Tao Longyue sat upright. "What, didn't you know that Song Qilian gave Vice Chief Liu your therapy report?"

Xie Lanshan nodded. "I thought that report was going directly to the provincial branch."

Tao Longyue gave a slight pout. "I don't know about sending it to the provincial branch, but Liu Yanbo personally came by the hospital last night and told the old man about it."

Tao Longyue's nagging middle-aged woman's tone of voice was already giving away a hint of unpleasant news. Xie Lanshan pondered slightly and asked, "What did Qilian's report say?"

"Ah, there was a lot on there and a bunch of jargon I couldn't understand." Tao Longyue let out a long sigh as expected and said, "The point is, the report she gave to Liu Yanbo said that you didn't pass your mental stability check. There was something about how you have a severely violent nature that makes you very incompatible with investigative missions of high stress and danger levels. So, in consideration to prevent you from breaking the code of conduct and law, she suggested that you still be transferred to the traffic department."

Xie Lanshan had already guessed this based on Song Qilian's strange attitude toward him lately; he clenched tightly onto the steering wheel without a word.

Tao Longyue continued, "Liu Yanbo has always had beef with you. Remember how you caused a ruckus last time during his wife's birthday party because of Liu Mingfang? I'm sure he's ready to put you in the spotlight again with this report. When the old man asked me what exactly happened, I could only say that Qilian's grown to have a love-hate relationship with you. She knows she can't have you, so she could only slander you—"

Xie Lanshan interrupted him coldly, "Qilian's not that kind of person."

It annoyed Tao Longyue that his buddy was still a *hoes before bros* man at a time like this and raised his voice to question, "So you would have rather I said you were a criminal in training?"

Xie Lanshan didn't mind taking slander on himself and repeated firmly with his gaze still fixed on the road, "She's not that kind of person."

There was a quiet and hidden park nearby the bar where an old man discovered a half-naked woman's corpse hidden behind leaves on his morning run. The sudden scare was so shocking it almost gave him a heart attack. The scene of the crime was already locked down.

If it wasn't for the corpse, rows of police cars parked around the scene, and the bright yellow cordon tapes, it would have been a beautifully quiet autumn day. The chirping sounds of birds and falling yellow leaves would have decorated the tranquil scenery.

The young woman's face was half-buried in the dirt, her blouse ripped and dirtied while her lower body was completely exposed. On her neck was a black dog collar decorated with a metal rivet. The corpse was already rotting with an unbearable foul smell. An eerie green spiderweb-like pattern appeared beneath her deathly pale skin.

Su Mansheng was at the scene doing her initial autopsy as usual. As one of the very few female forensic doctors able to do fieldwork in Hanhai City, her professionalism and work ethic were reflected in her focused gaze and unfazed expression.

"Our initial findings suggest that the victim's time of death was three days ago. There are signs of injuries on her skull and it's very likely she was brutally violated before death."

Su Mansheng turned the woman's body over; the corner of her mouth was slit open by a sharp knife and then sewn back up with fabric needles. There was nothing but despair frozen in those bulging eyes that contrasted the forced smile slit onto her face; the contradiction of expressions made it extra unnerving to look at. Xie Lanshan was taken aback as he saw the face of the corpse. "It's her?"

Tao Longyue asked, "You've seen her before?"

Xie Lanshan nodded. "She lived in the same residential building as Shen Liufei. I've seen her a couple of times before."

"This is not the original scene of the murder, it's the location the culprit disposed of the corpse after committing the crime. Inside the victim's bag." As Su Mansheng lifted a small piece of pink fabric that covered the stomach area of her corpse, everyone simultaneously gasped—

A large butterfly-shaped piece of skin had been carved and ripped from the woman's stomach area.

Xie Lanshan was stunned as if someone had cast a spell on him; he could feel cold sweat pouring out like a waterfall from his skin, a chilling sensation crawled up his spine.

Tao Longyue noticed his friend's unnatural reaction and called out to him, concerned, "A'Lan? A'Lan?"

"My head... kind of hurts..."

A woman, fresh blood, ripped skin, a dirty and messy crime scene...

A strange sense of familiarity paralyzed Xie Lanshan's whole body. It took him a long while before he finally pulled his mind back onto the case. It puzzled him as he lied about the headache, wondering why his instinct was to lie and pretend nothing was wrong.

The corpse needed to be transported back to the bureau for a more detailed autopsy. Because Xie Lanshan recognized the victim, it didn't take long for the investigation team to confirm her identity. Work quickly consumed the team, with no room to rest.

Tao Longyue took the wheel on the way back. Xie Lanshan sat in the passenger's seat, rested his head on an arm, and looked out the window. His eyebrows had been pressed together since they left the crime scene, as if something was on his mind.

"I feel like this case looks familiar. Hey, Xie Lanshan?" Tao Longyue intended to discuss the case but didn't receive any response after calling out to his buddy a few times. He figured his colleague was having another headache episode and said, concerned, "So what's up with your body anyway? You've got this headache thing going for a while, and now it's headaches *and* fevers. Are you sure you don't want to get a good brain checkup with Duan Licheng? I'm telling you, this guy's a real genius."

Tao Longyue didn't notice the straightforward conflict Xie Lanshan had with Duan Licheng that night at the bar, so naturally, he wouldn't know about the complicated beef the two men had. But Xie Lanshan couldn't even spare a moment to think about Duan Licheng right now. He was almost certain he had seen a case similar to this murder before.

(ii)

There was no traffic on the road and it didn't take long to reach the municipal bureau. As soon as Tao Longyue and Xie Lanshan stepped out of the car, they noticed Song Qilian walking into the main building not too far away. Xie Lanshan could recognize her silhouette just from a glance. That slightly wistful and spiritless figure was very easy to spot. Song Qilian was a much more energetic and bright young woman in the past, but an unhappy marriage completely changed her demeanor. Xie Lanshan had noticed ever since returning from his undercover mission that the woman had grown only more melancholic and distant than before. Tao Longyue assumed she was here for Xie Lanshan's therapy report.

Yet Xie Lanshan also saw Liu Mingfang chasing after Song Qilian, attempting to reach an arm over her shoulders. Song Qilian pushed him aside, but the man didn't take the hint and continued to pester her.

Xie Lanshan took a few steps forward and pushed the annoying Liu Mingfang aside. He said coldly, "This is the bureau. Leave if you have no business here."

Liu Mingfang shot back, "What about the bureau? The bureau's also a public branch that serves the people. You think this is some Qing Dynasty political office where you can just sit behind a government banner and not do any work behind the doors?"

Xie Lanshan wasn't in the mood to argue with Liu Mingfang. He shifted his gaze towards Song Qilian to get a reaction; if the woman certainly wanted this annoying ex-husband to leave her alone, he would not hesitate to kick the man out by force.

But Song Qilian only stared at him dumbly before turning her head and said to Liu Mingfang, "Mingfang, please let me have a few words with him alone."

"As you wish." Liu Mingfang stood up straight with pride and walked past Xie Lanshan, purposely shoving the latter's shoulder as he walked forward. He gave the cop a look as if to say, *this is our family business—stay out of it, like an outsider.*

Xie Lanshan stood frozen on the spot; he wasn't upset, simply confused. It wasn't until Liu Mingfang walked far off that he finally opened his mouth again and said, "I didn't know you two were back together already."

"It's not like that. We just happened to run into each other on the road." Song Qilian didn't want to pursue this discussion further and changed the topic with a professional tone. "If it's about your report, I've only reported the facts. I hope you don't hold a grudge against me for it."

"Of course not." Xie Lanshan gave her a faint smile.

This smile threw Song Qilian into a daze. Xie Lanshan had always been this kind to her in the past, never giving her attitude regardless of how he felt. There was always something tranquil but soothing in that gaze of him.

"Transferring to the traffic department isn't necessarily a bad thing for you, and it's also my bottom line." Song Qilian's voice began cracking as she repeated, "I'm sorry," through her tears.

Xie Lanshan reached out a finger and pressed it gently on her lips. He brushed his finger to swipe away a tear from her face.

"It's nothing, don't worry about it," Xie Lanshan said. The smile on his face grew gentler. "Chief Liu is waiting for you still. Go find him."

Song Qilian turned to give Xie Lanshan one more look before she stepped upstairs. The man was in the same spot. It was as if he was still standing on a hot summer day ten years ago, looking back at her.

Before pursuing Song Qilian, Liu Mingfang had actually received news from his son Liu Chang—his mother had banned the child from going near that uncle Xie by his mother.

Liu Mingfang immediately realized that something must have happened between his ex-wife and her old crush, which meant that his chance to win her back was now. He had multiple accounts of cheating and domestic violence after marriage; the list of awful deeds went on. Of course, like almost every other man out there, Liu Mingfang quickly regretted his actions as soon as he divorced her. He wanted to win back her love.

With Tao Jun hospitalized, Liu Yanbo was tasked with handling day-to-day operations in the bureau. For the first time, Liu Mingfang returned home early today and waited patiently for his father's return.

Liu Yanbo heard from the nanny in his household upon his return that his son was already waiting for him in the study. He opened the study's door to find his son searching through his desk for something. He scolded the young man, "Mingfang, what are you doing?!"

"I dropped my wedding ring at home. Auntie said she picked it up and kept it in your study." While the wide desk blocked his old man's view in the room, Liu Mingfang discreetly took off the ring from his finger and shoved it inside the wooden pen holder to create this lie.

"The only things inside the drawer are important documents from the bureau. Your nanny knows that and wouldn't touch it, so hands off!" Liu Yanbo really didn't know how to deal with this son of his sometimes; he still remembered how he had to lower his head toward his subordinates last time because of Li Guochang's case. The pent-up frustration exploded as soon as he saw his son, and he couldn't help but scold the young man. "You should have learned your lesson after you got yourself caught up in such a big case last time!"

Liu Mingfang was already an adult man, but still acted like a child in front of his father. He swiftly closed the drawer on his father's desk and sat on the sofa, then smiled playfully. "Y'know, they say fish always begin rotting from the head. I'm still Chief Liu's son. Sure, I make mistakes sometimes, but you know that I'm not a bad person at heart!"

Liu Yanbo's expression remained unfazed as he walked towards his desk and found that diamond ring in his pen holder with his sharp eyes. He pulled out the ring and handed it to his son. "Is this what you're looking for?"

Liu Mingfang faked a surprise and received it gleefully. "Finally! I'm planning on winning Qilian back with this ring once more."

This one line struck the right chord in the old man's heart. He also didn't want his own grandson to call another woman his mother and immediately turned to his son. "Qilian is a fine woman, you little shit. Better not screw up again and bring your wife back!"

Liu Mingfang nodded his head and said, "Yes, yes, count on your son."

Liu Yanbo continued to nag at his unreliable son after recalling all the nasty rumors in the past and said, "I've heard that you were still contacting Li Guochang's American wife lately. Is this true?"

"Nah, we broke up after she flew back." Liu Mingfang said, "She's now a widow with a huge sum of money behind her, she's a hotcake in the dating scene now."

"I've also heard you've been getting close to some sort of antique investor lately. What's her name again, Miss T or something?"

"Man, where'd you get all this gossip, dad?" Liu Mingfang carefully checked his expression and gave a nonchalant laugh. "We're just business partners, don't think too much of it."

"As long as you two are not in that kind of relationship." Liu Yanbo sighed and sat down beside his son. "You can't just say you want to win Qilian back. You need to act on it properly like a man."

Liu Mingfang nodded his head repeatedly like a puppet. He noticed his father's expression softened up and attempted to probe by saying, "Dad, your daughter-in-law has been having some issues with her ex-crush—sorry—old classmate lately. Do you know what's up with Xie Lanshan?"

Liu Yanbo was well-aware of how lenient he had been with his son due to putting his career as a drug enforcement officer before family. He was always fighting on the front lines and spent little time with his family, so he wasn't around to properly educate Liu Mingfang. That was why he was quite envious of Tao Jun; his comrade's son was clearly much more accomplished as a young captain of the violent crimes unit, who was skilled as an investigator, and had earned many awards.

But no matter how much of a failure his own son was, he still believed that his son was better than Xie Jiaqing's offspring.

Liu Yanbo frowned and fell silent for a while before he finally said, "To be fair, in terms of raw skills and abilities, the captain of the violent crimes unit should have been young Xie. I was originally planning on promoting him myself, but..."

Liu Mingfang sniffed out something through his father's hesitation and asked, "But what?"

Liu Yanbo let out another sigh. "But even if young Xie's got the skills, he fails in the department of psychological stability. Captain Sui from the Blue Foxes personally gave me a call to say I must not promote him. He even asked me to carefully monitor his behavior and attitude, and report upwards immediately if any issues occurred."

Liu Mingfang was shocked. "But why? Didn't he return after earning huge merit from going undercover in the Golden Triangle?"

"There's a rumor that young Xie is a traitor from the drug enforcement team, that he was the one who let the Golden Triangle's drug lord Mu Kun escape. But I don't think Captain

Sui believes this rumor, judging from his attitude." Liu Yanbo lifted his eyelids slightly; a sharp glint flashed across those half-opened eyes. "Besides, that child's father—"

His voice stopped abruptly as he turned to his son, expression grave as he scolded, "Stop asking about all these things that have nothing to do with you!"

The violent crimes and homicide unit spent days working overtime and quickly discovered the identity of the female victim behind the park. The victim was Luo Xin, a 23-year-old freelancer who lived on the tenth floor of the same building as Shen Liufei. Judging by the level of decay on the corpse, the estimated time of death was last Sunday between 7 and 8 P.M. —the time that doctor named Qiao Hui was planning on giving his confession using the lights of the building.

The window that didn't light up that night was Luo Xin's residence.

The tech team made another discovery. They found a four-digit number written on the right palm, which could be a dying message left by the victim. Even though it was virtually impossible to tell what the number was after heavy rain washed it off her palm, the tech team was successfully able to recreate it: 2103.

The investigators didn't retrieve any bodily substances left on Luo Xin from the suspect, but luckily, there were still some skin cells left inside her fingernails.

Naturally, they went to check the DNA sample in the official database of the bureau, but the result stunned everyone.

The DNA belonged to Xie Lanshan.

(iii)

Xie Lanshan was imprisoned for a short while in order to go undercover in the Golden Triangle, so the public security database had rightfully recorded his DNA. Of course, nobody knew that Sui Hong had once tampered with the data in the past.

There were six questioning rooms within the Hanhai City Municipal Bureau; some were decorated to be more comfortable than others with wide spaces and bright lights, while others had metal bars on the windows, ropes on the tables, and tear gas canisters in the corner of the room. The latter were normally reserved for suspects of more serious offenses in order to stop them from attempting to escape.

This was the first time Xie Lanshan sat inside this dimly lit room with metal bars outside the window as a suspect. Like how the metal bars separated two worlds inside and out, he went from the interrogator to the interrogated. Due to his cooperation and simplicity of the case in the past, he didn't have to suffer through this kind of treatment when he had to spend six months in jail for his mission.

Along with Tao Longyue was Xiao Liang conducting the questioning. The latter still couldn't break out of his customary courteous words around Xie Lanshan. He scratched his ears almost sheepishly before his senior at the table and said, "Sorry, Xie bro, but you know we gotta walk through the process—"

Tao Longyue didn't let his personal biases distract him from work and interrupted Xiao Liang harshly, "There are no Xie bros in the room, only a criminal suspect!"

Xie Lanshan nodded and lifted a difficult smile. "Understood."

Even though Captain Tao refused to believe that Xie

Lanshan was the true culprit deep down, he still had to do his job and asked, "The surveillance showed that you left Shen Liufei's residential building at 7:10 P.M. on Sunday. So where were you at during the time of the murder, from 7:10 P.M. to 8 P.M.?"

Xie Lanshan responded calmly, "I ran into the victim not too far away from the residential building. I left quickly after a brief exchange with her."

"And then?"

"I was waiting out the rain under the eaves." There was a security camera installed on the metal bars; the red lights flashed repeatedly and gave Xie Lanshan a headache. The headache only grew worse.

"So you don't have any witnesses?" Tao Longyue frowned as the siren in his mind blared. He pondered a little and continued, "It's late fall now. Most people have already switched to more appropriate clothing for the weather. There would be no reason under normal circumstances for anyone to take off their clothes and lift their sleeves up; the scratches on your arms are clearly abnormal. Can we safely assume that the injury was caused by violent scratching and resistance from the victim when you raped and killed her?"

The words rape and murder stung his ears; Xie Lanshan let out a small breath of air. He understood Tao Longyue's attitude at work and attempted to respond as cooperatively as he could, "I was helping Shen Liufei move that day. I ran into Duan Licheng while halfway through packing and got into a fight with the doctor, so I forgot to bring my jacket when I walked out the door—"

A bright light suddenly shot right into his eyes, piercing into his pupils and covering a layering of white mist over his eyes. Xie Lanshan's head throbbed violently from this strong light—something in his head snapped at that moment. His brain was like a broken machine desperately trying to operate nonstop. The buzzing sounds consumed his thoughts.

Xiao Liang shined a strong light right into Xie Lanshan's eyes and howled, "Tell us the truth!"

This was a common method used in interrogation against suspects who were uncooperative and refused to speak. The investigator would shine a bright light before the suspect's eyes and holler to break the suspect psychologically.

Xiao Liang said, "You've been seen going in and out of Shen Liufei's mansion very often before that time, so the victim mistook you as her neighbor. You released your anger from the fight you had earlier with someone else on the victim you happened to pass by, so the victim had your unit number written on her palm before she died."

This powerful, threatening scene of interrogation wasn't just familiar, it was like a reenactment of a past event. Xie Lanshan didn't dare to open his eyes as he lowered his head and pounded on his temples to stop the buzzing noise in his ears. It was too painful. It was so painful he could feel the blood exerting pressure on his temples as it rushed up, expanded, and exploded in his head. Finally, a bloodied spiderweb surfaced under the fair skin on his handsome face.

Tao Longyue noticed the discomfort on his old friend's face and asked, worried, "What's wrong?"

Tao Longyue was speaking, Xiao Liang was also speaking, but Xie Lanshan couldn't process even a word of it. He could almost feel heavy waves pounding on his eardrums more violently with each drum; upon closer analysis, he discovered those sounds were actually human voices. They came from a foreign world, commotions made by countless strangers he'd never seen, but they all seemed to know who he was.

He managed to capture a familiar name in this cacophonous symphony. It was from a scene similar to the predicament he was in right now, and the investigator in front of him said, "Ye Shen, tell us the truth. Did you kill victim Miss Zhuo?"

The noise stopped abruptly, and the headache also healed within an instant. The man felt his soul float up from the crowded sounds around him and flew out toward the edge of the sky. Xie Lanshan opened his eyes slowly; heavy drops of sweat rolled down from the side of his forehead.

"Xie Lanshan?" Tao Longyue noticed the peculiar expression on Xie Lanshan's face and grew even more worried. "A'Lan? A'Lan, what's wrong?"

As if his soul was forcefully pulled from his body, Xie Lanshan did not speak another word, whether he faced another harsh interrogation or concerned questioning.

Young Captain Tao was in a hurry to help clear his buddy's innocence, but Xie Lanshan's silent attitude only perpetuated the current suspicion of his alleged crimes. Tao Longyue poured his heart and soul into talking to the man, yet failed to even get a word out of Xie Lanshan. He finally lost his cool and said, "I'm going out for a smoke break. You're also an investigator, so you should know that using silence to hide from your crimes will never work out. Think about it for a bit!"

Tao Longyue got up and walked toward the door in anger, then stopped right before he left and turned to yell at a dumbfounded Xiao Liang, "You come out too!"

Almost as soon as Xiao Liang stepped out, he felt his captain grab onto the back of his head and gave a hard and loud slap.

"Cap'n, why are you hitting me?" Xiao Liang rubbed on the back of his head and sheepishly scrunched up his face.

"Why are you waving around the flashlight like that? Who said that was acceptable behavior in the room!"

Judging by this attitude and words, the Captain was clearly

scolding him for being too harsh. Xiao Liang felt even more wronged and complained, "You were the one that said there's no Xie bro in the interrogation room, only a criminal suspect."

Tao Longyue walked back into the violent crimes unit office with a heavy heart. He leaned on the wall with a cigarette in hand, blowing out clouds of white smoke silently. Xie Lanshan's attitude was both infuriating and suspicious.

A sexual assault murder case with abuse after death was serious enough to stir up a social storm across the country. Vice Chief Liu Yanbo personally administered and was leading the investigation for this case. Liu Yanbo arrived at the violent crimes office and noticed the gloomy faces across the entire unit. Nobody was researching the case, so he cleared his throat loudly for attention.

The entire unit looked up to see the Vice Chief in office and called out in unison, "Chief Liu!"

Tao Longyue quickly extinguished his cigarette and turned to Liu Yanbo, asking, "Chief, what are you doing here?"

With his direct subordinate officer being detained as the first suspect of the case, it was natural that Liu Yanbo had to keep an eye on any updates. His hawk eyes locked on Tao Longyue and asked sternly, "Did you get anything out of him?"

Tao Longyue answered honestly, "I didn't get much info; he was quite cooperative at first but stopped responding halfway through."

Liu Yanbo shot a harsh glance, anger written on his face. "What's wrong, are you not going to continue just because you can't get answers out of him?"

Tao Longyue stuttered slightly as he said, "I just don't think A'Lan is the culprit. He... there's no reason for him to be..."

Ding Li chimed in from the side, "Cap'n, it's not that I don't believe in our big bro, but remember that mass murder case with the Cong family? Didn't we find the culprit Li Rui's skin cells in the victim's nails too?"

Before Tao Longyue could shoot a harsh glance at her, Liu Yanbo scolded, "Don't get too sentimental about work. Don't you remember what Qilian's therapy report for him said? It was clearly written on there that he is extremely prone to act with violence."

Tao Longyue tried to argue back and said, "But a medical report can't be used as direct evidence in court. At most it's only a supplemental reference—"

"Then why isn't he saying anything? Don't you think it's suspicious that an experienced law enforcement officer would choose to use this method to fight against criminal questioning?!" Liu Yanbo once again interrupted Tao Longyue harshly and slammed on the table. "Send out a search warrant and bring out the polygraph. We are going to make him speak up using all methods allowed within the limits of the law!"

The revered Vice Chief Liu walked in and out of the office like a storm, leaving the entire violent crimes and homicide unit staring dumbly at each other. Influenced by their colleagues and surroundings, more than half of the team had worked with Xie Lanshan for almost three years and refused to believe the man could commit such a heinous crime.

Of course, Liu Yanbo's words gave Tao Longyue some ideas; the young captain's expression darkened as he rubbed on his scar with a finger, tracing his memories. He quickly realized that Liu Yanbo wasn't purposely giving Xie Lanshan a hard time; the latter's attitude throughout the case had been very abnormal. Digging deeper into it, the man himself had been acting strange lately. He recalled the words the man said in Xiao Zhou's hospital room during Li Guochang's case, and Xie Lanshan's strangely cold and blood-thirsty gaze when Qin Ke died...

From personality, to attitude, to habits, all sorts of trivial details in everyday life began to string into a series of related events. Guessing, suspicion, and conspiracy theories—once a hint of these negative thoughts surfaced, they would spread and grow like an unstoppable virus.

Seeing Tao Longyue stand still, deep in thought, Ding Li carefully asked, "Cap'n Tao, so... what do we do now?"

Tao Longyue closed his eyes and let out a long sigh. "What else can we do? Boss gave the orders, bring out the polygraph."

"Captain Tao, may I request to speak to Xie Lanshan in private?"

Tao Longyue looked up and saw Shen Liufei walk into the office. The latter's gaze was deep and unfathomable, expression blank and cold.

Shen Liufei was only a specialist of the bureau, and it was difficult to say whether he could be considered a close friend or family to Xie Lanshan with their relationship. Letting him meet with Xie Lanshan in private would clearly violate proper conduct.

"Uh..." Tao Longyue hesitated.

"Five minutes," Shen Liufei said, "just give me five minutes."

Captain Tao nodded. To avoid stepping on Chief Liu's toes again, he had Xiao Liang discreetly take Shen Liufei to the interrogation room Xie Lanshan was staying in.

The room was like a metal cell lit by a deathly bright and pale light. After the headache that had been bothering him suddenly vanished, Xie Lanshan found himself strangely dispirited. He sat with his head hanging behind the metal bars, his gaze lifeless, as if everything in the world was monochrome. Only the moment Shen Liufei walked in did he finally see a flash of color and life in this dead world.

He lifted his head and gave Shen Liufei a smile.

Shen Liufei sat on the other side of the table and lifted his gaze to look at Xie Lanshan. He almost couldn't stand looking at the man; it had only been a day or two, but the young cop looked like a completely different person now. His hair seemed to have grown out a little more. The sweat on his face was still wet, drenched strands of hair were glued onto his cheeks. Xie Lanshan looked as if he had suffered through a long torturous episode, already severely damaged, both physically and mentally.

To everyone's surprise, Xie Lanshan spoke up before Shen Liufei opened his mouth. As if trying to ease up the heavy air around them, he smiled; his smile was beautiful like a spring field of flowers, his white teeth peeked out from a grin that didn't look like it was from a criminal suspect. He called out with that usual playful tone: "Hey cuz."

That gentle voice reached Shen Liufei's chest; the latter felt his heart skip a beat and responded softly in acknowledgment.

"Cuz," Xie Lanshan called him again and asked with a smile, "you didn't lie to me, right?"

Shen Liufei asked, "Lie about what?"

Xie Lanshan said, "About Zhuo Tian's file."

"It's not a lie." Shen Liufei looked directly into Xie Lanshan's eyes and then said after a moment of silence, "You're a good cop, you're Xie Lanshan."

Yet Xie Lanshan leaned back slightly at this response—it was a very small gesture, but it was clear enough to show his distrust and repulsion.

"Hah." He laughed so much that his eyes reddened. A single tear rolled down his cheek. He said, "But I saw it. I saw those corpses lying on the ground... it wasn't just the girl that died, there was also a child of about only seven to eight..."

Five minutes went by like a breeze. Tao Longyue stood by the door of the room and said he would take Xie Lanshan to the evidence identification center for a polygraph test.

A polygraph specialist from the bureau conducted the test. Xie Lanshan's chest, fingers, and arms were all connected to special wires for the polygraph. The test began with some simple yes or no questions to record the physical patterns of Xie Lanshan's heart rate for reference.

Once the preparations were ready, the polygraph test officially began. The specialist started off by asking the suspect's name. "Who are you?"

The polygraph test room was very quiet. Xie Lanshan lifted his eyes and looked at the conductor silently before answering, "Xie Lanshan."

"W-what's going on?!" Outside the glass window, both Liu Yanbo and Tao Longyue let out a gasp of shock at the same time.

It was only the first question, but the polygraph was already showing abnormalities; the line chart on the laptop screen began fluctuating rapidly.

(iv)

The case was exceptionally complex and severe. Xie Lanshan had been detained for 48 hours already and Shen Liufei paid a visit to Tao Jun during this time at Puren Hospital. Tao Jun's surgery went well; the old man was in good spirits, even while hospitalized for recovery, and was already whining to leave the hospital. Tao Longyue found some spare time in between investigating this murder to visit his father, but didn't speak a word about Xie Lanshan's involvement as a prime suspect of the case. He feared scaring the old man.

The sky was already dark at dusk; chilly winds blew in the

autumn weather behind the closed windows of the hospital room. Shen Liufei sat against the light by the bedside, peeling an apple for Tao Jun. He held a fruit knife in his left hand and an apple in the right, peeling the skin of the apple off swiftly in a clean motion.

Tao Jun had long been acquainted with Shen Liufei through phone calls and emails since they started discussing criminal psychology cases ten years ago. He had no idea that to whom he had been speaking across the ocean was such a tall and handsome young man. He stared at Shen Liufei a little before blurting out, "I didn't know you were left-handed."

Tao Jun had exchanged many letters with this Mr. Shen in the past. Elegant and smooth writing could often be seen in the handwritten letters he had received.

Shen Liufei lifted his head slightly to look at the old man without a word.

Tao Jun explained, "That Lil' Liang from our team is also a lefty, so if we make him write a report with ink, he'll for sure smudge the ink all over the paper." After some thought, the old man also found his question to be strange. He then added with a smile, "I guess people are different."

Shen Liufei lifted the corner of his mouth and switched the knife to his right hand to continue peeling the apple without an issue. As soon as he finished, he asked Tao Jun courteously, "Should I cut them into slices for you?"

Tao Jun shook his head. "No need for a brute man like myself."

Shen Liufei handed the apple to him and wiped his hand on the paper towel by the bedstand. He then said, "Captain Tao, I'm actually here today for a case."

Tao Jun took a bite down on the crunchy and sweet apple. "Whose case?"

Shen Liufei said, "Xie Lanshan."

Tao Jun's expression shifted as he placed the apple to the side. Shen Liufei quickly summarized the current murder case the unit was investigating without missing an important detail.

Considering Tao Jun and Xie Lanshan's relationship, it would be natural for the old man's first reaction to be disbelief. Not only that, but the old man should have been shocked and pained as if arrows pierced through his heart. Instead, Shen Liufei saw a peculiar, almost knowing kind of expression on Tao Jun's face. Quickly, this unnatural expression was replaced by a more appropriate response. A forensic sketch artist like him had a keen eye for observing negative human emotions; he concluded that this fleeting reaction he had caught was abnormal.

Tao Jun asked, "Do you believe in him?"

Shen Liufei responded with, "Do you not believe in him?"

Tao Jun was speechless; after a moment of being taken aback, he let out a gentle sigh and said, "This child's history is a bit complicated."

"You've known him longer than me. You should know better than me the kind of person Xie Lanshan is." Shen Liufei paused briefly, then said with a stern face, "I believe him."

Tao Jun studied Shen Liufei for a while with a sharp gaze and said, "Mr. Shen, are you sure this trust is not a little biased?"

Paper cannot hold fire. Even without words, the passion burning inside him could not be hidden from his eyes. Old Tao might be a stubborn and traditional man, but he was still a sharp-minded cop with years of experience. He had already sniffed out some hints last time the entire unit came to pay him a visit. Shen Liufei refused to deny it, but he wasn't in a position to fully confess their relationship. He could only look into the other's eye with his usual calm gaze.

"Ah, this is almost hard to believe. That kid had never

shown any signs of being interested in men since he was little; I still remember him carving up small wooden rabbits for Song Qilian all the time." Tao Jun let out another sigh. Then a flash of determination appeared in his eyes as he struggled to get up from his bed. "Alright, call Longyue over so we can go over this case again!"

Shen Liufei supported the old captain to stop him from getting too excited and said in a gentle voice, "I remember there was a time where I frequently consulted you about some unsolved rape-murder cases in the past."

Tao Jun frowned as he attempted to dig through his memories and nodded. "That was many years ago, they're all old cases."

"Dog collar, sewn up lips, and peeled off skin: I'm certain that I've heard about a case with the same methods like these from you before." Shen Liufei lifted a brow and helped the old man sit upright before continuing. "Please, Captain Tao, I need you to dig through your memories for me. I have a feeling that this case has some sort of connection to the old cases in the past, and that the true culprit is someone else."

"That was a case at least twenty years ago... I don't think I can remember all the details even if you ask..."

As Tao Jun squinted his eyes to recall the details, Tao Longyue walked into the hospital room. The latter was taken aback slightly when he saw Shen Liufei, but immediately realized that his old man must know about Xie Lanshan's situation now.

"If everything goes smoothly, A'Lan should be out of custody soon and regain his innocence," Tao Longyue announced to the two men in the room. "While Xie Lanshan was being detained and questioned, we've discovered another young female corpse. The victim's death was identical to Luo

Xin, so it's very possible that this is a serial murder case by the same culprit."

Shen Liufei didn't get the answer he had hoped for from Tao Jun regarding the old case from twenty years ago, so he returned to his residence. He sat in his study and began searching for information on his laptop.

He had always been very interested in violent crimes against female victims, so like a stamp collector, his notebooks contained thousands of these cases over the years. The sources ranged from the police, lawyers, news, to other related professionals in the industry, and were all organized neatly in his files. Photos of these murders were often gory and horrifying, and the stories behind them were all tragedies. Those women who had been raped, tortured, and beaten mostly died. Some disappeared, others grew up to become criminals that brutally harmed the next victim in the same way they had suffered.

It wasn't easy to face these horrific human tragedies. Even Shen Liufei had to pause briefly after opening up a new file to take in a deep breath of air.

He remembered what Fu Yunxian said to him; there's something in your heart that will spread and rot.

It was easy to say that it was an illness of the psyche, but Shen Liufei had no way to treat it or avoid it. He could only rely on venting it out on boxing stages time and time again until the injuries and sweat on his body evaporated the darkness inside.

After searching through his old files for a while, he pulled out a photo kept inside a book resting beside him. It was the same photo that Xie Lanshan saw: a young mother holding her son.

With immense gentleness, he caressed the face of the woman in the photo before suddenly closing his laptop. The only light source vanished—the room returned to darkness.

Shen Liufei sat for a long while in the dark before he reopened his laptop and relied on his memories to search for an old case similar to this skin-peeling murder.

He found it before dawn struck.

It was an old case that occurred twenty-five years ago around the Cangnan region. The culprit's method of murder was the exact same as Luo Xin's case and spanned over four years, claiming the lives of eleven young women. Because the internet was still in its infancy back then, on top of the case being old and solved, most people didn't know about this case—including the majority of investigators at the bureau.

Perhaps because of its age, the case wasn't recorded in much detail; the only thing he found was that the criminal suspect was never caught because he had committed suicide before the police found him.

Shen Liufei clicked open the Cangnan murder police report file and discovered that this old cop by the name of Zhu Mingwu used to be on the same investigation team as Tao Jun. Even though they hadn't worked together for long, he could almost be considered Tao Jun's mentor.

He arrived at the bureau in the afternoon and was told by Ding Li that Xie Lanshan had already left. "To where?"

"Dunno. Maybe he went home. Vice Chief Liu told him to go on a break and farm or something, that it's not appropriate for him to be involved with Luo Xin's case as a criminal suspect."

As if she knew that the two men's relationship was a little more than just colleagues, Ding Li smiled kindly and gave some extra words of apology for Shen Liufei to take back to Xie Lanshan, "Mr. Shen, please tell our big bro Xie that it's not that we don't trust him, we just gotta do our work and Chief Liu is still watching us."

Shen Liufei gave Ding Li a look and then shifted his gaze

to Xiao Liang and the rest of the crew hiding behind the young woman. He saw an emotion called suspicion in their gazes. In all fairness, it wasn't abnormal for law enforcement officers to suspect all criminal suspects before they settled the case. These kinds of emotions came like a gust of wind but were hard to get rid of; like drawing thin silk from a cocoon, these dangerous thoughts were weapons that could strangle a person.

Xie Lanshan's attitude throughout the session had been very reluctant to speak, which was unusual.

The lights in the house were off when Shen Liufei walked in. It was the hour where lights of the city glistened neon outside the window. Xie Lanshan's house was silent like an abandoned unit, but the sparks of light that shone through the glass spread on the grey flooring like dancing heartbeats.

There was nobody in the living room or the bedroom. Shen Liufei followed the sounds of water flowing from the bathroom and opened the door.

He saw Xie Lanshan sitting on the floor with his head hanging down. Due to the dimming lights of dusk, the man's face was half covered in clean light while the other was hidden within the dark shadows.

There were shards of glass everywhere in the bathroom, making it look as if the entire room was covered in mercury from afar. Shen Liufei only realized upon walking closer that Xie Lanshan had smashed the mirror on the wall. Still drenched, his hands were draped over his knees, shards of glass still stuck on his knuckles. Fresh blood dripped down between his fingers.

The blood mixed in with the water that overflowed from the bathtub, tainting an entire floor of redness that flowed by Shen Liufei's feet.

Shen Liufei stepped over the broken glass on the floor

beside Xie Lanshan. The latter lifted his head and stared blankly at the guest with his bloodshot eyes.

Shen Liufei brushed his fingers gently through the man's hair and along his face, then asked softly, "Does it hurt?"

This question seemed to have pulled the man back from hell to the mortal world. Xie Lanshan suddenly resisted like a madman and rushed forward to grab onto Shen Liufei's neck. Shen Liufei dodged the attack, but the man was already standing in front of him. Unable to move, Shen Liufei had no choice but to throw a punch. This wasn't the first time he'd thrown a punch, but it was the first time he put such force in his fist. Xie Lanshan was like a beast ready to kill and conquer. They brawled and rolled on the shard-filled and chilling floor until Shen Liufei was forced to the defensive—Xie Lanshan had pressed a piece of the broken mirror against the man's throat.

Their chests moved up and down in sync. Xie Lanshan pressed his entire body onto Shen Liufei and stared at the latter below him. There was blood in the corner of his lips; his eyes were buried in a dark shadow, but it almost looked as if he had an arrogant smile on his face.

"Do you still trust me now?" Xie Lanshan pressed his hand closer. The glass shard in his hand was now touching the skin on Shen Liufei's throat. There was a tattoo there, a dazzling lotus flower or tail of a phoenix—the image moved on his skin under high pressure in a dangerous situation, as if it was alive.

The glass forced Shen Liufei to lift his chin slightly. His cheekbones were also injured by the glass shards on the floor. Fresh blood rolled down his handsome face. Xie Lanshan leaned in closer and asked once again, lips almost touching the other. "Am I still worth your trust?"

Shen Liufei raised an arm and grabbed onto the hand with the glass shard, then pulled it toward his own throat—thankfully, Xie Lanshan pulled it back just in time. The shard still pierced into his skin, but the injury wasn't deep, only creating another cut.

"How else do you want me to prove it to you?" Shen Liufei's attitude remained unfazed, his gaze calm and deep, but his voice stern.

The aggression in Xie Lanshan's eyes finally vanished.

After a short but passionate wet business in the bathroom, the two returned to the bedroom. Shen Liufei treated the wounds on Xie Lanshan's hands, carefully pulling out those glass shards that were stuck deep inside his flesh like mini flagpoles.

Law enforcement was a dangerous job; cops were used to injuries on duty and all had their own first aid kits at home. Xie Lanshan sat on his bed while Shen Liufei kneeled before him and helped treat his wounds.

Xie Lanshan couldn't help but chuckle as he saw the serious face of the artist.

Shen Liufei looked up and asked, "What's so funny?"

Teasing the other had become a habit as Xie Lanshan lifted an eyebrow. "Having such a trophy wife is the dream of all husbands in the world."

The wounds were wrapped up, but Shen Liufei squeezed Xie Lanshan's hand as if to punish him. The artist stood up and responded calmly, "Love yourself a little more. Your life doesn't just belong to you now."

Xie Lanshan had barely gotten any sleep during the last two days in custody. He could barely keep his eyes open right now with no spare effort to remember that he was still a crime suspect. Xie Lanshan fell into Shen Liufei's embrace and buried his face in the latter's waist, then wrapped an arm around him like a child.

"There was always someone who would remind me since I

was little how a person should live and the power they should have," Xie Lanshan said as he touched the bullet hanging on his chest. He felt the corner of his eyes heating up and closed them. "It was my dad who told me this in the past, but now that person is you."

(v)

Even though Liu Yanbo refused to let him investigate this case, Xie Lanshan didn't plan on staying on the sidelines for long with his reputation on the line.

Zhu Mingwu was Tao Jun's mentor; by that relation, he would also be Xie Lanshan's mentor by proxy. When Tao Jun was doing criminal investigations with Zhu Mingwu, Xie Lanshan was still a hot-headed young man. Old officer Zhu had switched twice across different municipalities during that time, so he must be an old man of at least 60 by now. Time was like a sharp blade that carved deep wrinkles on his aged face.

Zhu Mingwu had retired and moved to another city with his son already, living a rather carefree and peaceful life with his grandchildren. Xie Lanshan was forced to be on a break and Shen Liufei also requested for a temporary leave of absence to pay the old man a visit, hoping to investigate this case before Tao Longyue and his team came over.

They left almost as soon as the plan was decided. Xie Lanshan walked out the door in the morning and rushed to the train station, waiting with an empty stomach at the waiting lounge in the station. He sat with his head tilted and leaning on Shen Liufei's shoulder, "Hey cuz, I'm hungry."

Shen Liufei pretended to not understand and turned to look at Xie Lanshan. He reached out a hand and grabbed the other's chin. "Still? Did you know how much I fed you last night? You almost couldn't even drink it all, and you're still hungry now?"

This man sure loved to speak such scandalous words with a straight face. Xie Lanshan felt his face burning up and leaned his head in, using this opportunity while the station was still empty to steal a kiss from Shen Liufei.

The small peck quickly deepened until they reluctantly

parted. Shen Liufei stood up and said, "Wait here, I'll buy you some food."

Xie Lanshan's mood was lifted and couldn't help but praise how good of a wife he had in his mind. He leaned on the chair and closed his eyes to rest. That was when a small and pretty little girl walked up to him and called out shyly, "Big bro."

Xie Lanshan opened his eyes and knelt down to face the little girl at eye-level, smiling in response to her.

The little girl was holding a teddy bear almost half of her size as she asked, "Another big bro asked me to ask you a question."

Xie Lanshan said, "What is it?"

"He wants me to ask you," the little girl clenched her teddy bear tighter, long eyelashes flickering as she said, "did you find the 'Apostle' yet?"

His heart sank into the bottom of an icy lake; Xie Lanshan's expression shifted almost instantly. He knew he wasn't having hallucinations that night at the bar—Mu Kun was really back.

"What else did he say?"

"He said that he found it already and if you want to know who the 'Apostle' is, go find him."

Cold sweat rolled down his back. He suddenly heard muffled ticking sounds coming from the plush bear the little girl was holding, like some sort of countdown. Xie Lanshan had deactivated bombs before and was extra sensitive toward these types of sounds.

He felt a vein on his forehead pop and quickly asked the little girl, "Who gave you the teddy bear you're holding?"

The little girl held up the bear proudly in front of Xie Lanshan and gave a bright grin with a missing front tooth, then said gleefully, "It's from that big brother that asked me to tell you all of that!"

Xie Lanshan once again felt the scathing malice reeking out of Mu Kun. The drug lord never cared much for life, and would dare to shove a bomb in a little girl's arms.

Even with a racing heart, Xie Lanshan tried to remain calm and spoke softly to the little girl, "Can you show me your teddy bear?"

"Ok, here you go." The little girl had an innocent naiveté in her voice as she lifted the bear and handed it to the taller man in front of her.

Xie Lanshan immediately noticed the weight of the plush bear was off. He traced the seams of the bear and ripped through the fluffy exterior, then reached a hand inside to search the cotton within.

"How could you do this!" The little girl cried out loud after seeing how such a handsome man treated the bear.

A young mother who was picking up her train tickets had just noticed her daughter ran off when she heard the little girl's cries. Afraid her daughter would run into a bad person, she ran over and cried, "Nan Nan!"

"Stay away!" Xie Lanshan ordered harshly. The bomb was still ticking; there were less than ten seconds left on the countdown.

Some other pedestrians gathered beside him thinking it was a grown man bullying a child. Xie Lanshan howled once again, "There's a bomb, all of you, back off!"

The men and women on the platform station began screaming and dispersing away from Xie Lanshan.

Xie Lanshan quickly analyzed his surroundings; the train station was crowded and there wasn't enough time for him to deactivate the bomb. Thankfully, there was a bright blue explosion-proof tank not too far away from him. Xie Lanshan rushed out and shoved the teddy bear carrying the bomb inside the tank, then closed up the cover of the tank.

Even if the tank could decrease the impact of the explosion, the damage would still be inevitable. Xie Lanshan turned around to see the little girl stumbling over for her teddy bear, then rushed over to protect her. He covered her ears and shielded the child with his own body.

Yet after a few minutes, that expected explosion didn't happen.

It wasn't until the explosion tank was moved to a safe space and the armed police forces made their way to the scene, that they discovered it wasn't a bomb inside the bear—it was just a timer.

The armed police were clearly unhappy with this charade and thought Xie Lanshan was purposely joking with the lives of the passengers.

Xie Lanshan could feel his soul leave his body as he hung his head in silence. Shen Liufei had to flash the man's police badge to explain that they were investigating a crime.

Seeing they were colleagues also fighting crime, the armed police let them go without another word. After confirming there were no other bombs threatening the safety of the station, the armed police left. Only the station security was baffled by this and asked, "Who could have made a prank like this? This is serious and can be prosecuted under the law!"

Finally, Xie Lanshan lifted his head and studied the security officers around him, then said coldly, "I want to check the surveillance."

. . .

A row of ten screens lit up. They first pulled up the footage of the time when Xie Lanshan and the little girl were waiting on the platform. It wasn't too difficult to investigate with everything laid out in front of him; Xie Lanshan's gaze scanned sharply like lightning across the screen. He discovered a man wearing a hat, sunglasses, and high-collared coat that approached the little girl. The man handed her a plush bear and said something to her, then turned around and left.

The man carefully hid his appearance and didn't show his face throughout the entire exchange. As if he knew where the blind spots of the security cameras were, he vanished and appeared like a ghost, and then quickly disappeared for good. Even if the man was burnt to the ashes, Xie Lanshan could still tell from a glance that the man was Mu Kun.

This whole charade was a setup Mu Kun used, teasing like a cat. The man knew Xie Lanshan too well; he knew how the young cop would react in this situation. He was meticulous, as if he also predicted the chill that would run down the spine, the cold sweat that would roll down Xie Lanshan.

Six years of being undercover was not an experience he wanted to look back on. The horror that Mu Kun represented was a feeling that only grew heavier by the day, with no signs of ever vanishing. Xie Lanshan felt disgusted, like he had been violated; he pointed at the paused screen and said to the train security guards beside him, "Go catch this guy, he's an extremely dangerous drug lord."

Despite being under the same law enforcement system, Xie Lanshan wasn't a direct boss of these people. The security guards felt they had already given him leeway with not pestering him about a false alarm in public; they had no idea the man would dare to order them around now. A young and inexperienced security guard was annoyed at this attitude and said, "You're clearly mingling with our everyday work now. We can't go, arrest someone, just because they gave a child a teddy bear, besides, you were the one that thought it was a bomb—"

A strange spark of fire arose within Xie Lanshan. He turned around and grabbed onto that guard's collar and pushed the young man to the wall.

The guard gasped; the man was at least an entire head taller than him, face almost unbelievably handsome, but eyes extremely terrifying. He looked nothing like a cop.

The older security guard also jumped and started yelling. Xie Lanshan didn't move or speak, only staring coldly at the young man before him, his gaze deep like a black pond.

Shen Liufei approached him from behind, wrapped an arm around his neck, and pulled the man back toward him. The artist pressed his lips beside the cop's ear and said in a deep, luring voice, "Calm down, Xie Lanshan."

Xie Lanshan loosened his grip immediately. He admitted he was too aggressive, but for some reason, he wasn't able to control himself at that moment.

Only this man behind him could bring him peace of mind.

Because of the false alarm bomb incident, the bullet train station automatically entered anti-terrorism mode and was delayed numerous trains. By the time Xie Lanshan returned to his platform, all the passengers that had been evacuated earlier returned, annoyance written across their faces. This evacuation order lasted a whole day, making them feel as if they had wasted all that time for nothing.

The public announcement loomed above their heads, explaining that it was a mistake caused by the police during an investigation, but the threat had been removed.

The little girl in the dress was still there, waving vigorously when she saw Xie Lanshan come back as if jumping for joy.

This man was handsome and strong; even though she was too young to understand words such as anti-terrorism and bomb threats, she knew that his act of protecting her under his body was a heroic move that would only appear in movies. Yet the young mother holding her daughter had different opinions. She gave Xie Lanshan an eye roll and mumbled beneath her breath, "Cops these days sure lack discipline, making such a scene over a trivial matter..."

Xie Lanshan was tired and didn't want to explain himself. Shen Liufei handed a cup of hot coffee to him. Xie Lanshan held the cup; the tips of long fingers touched the rim of the cup as he stood in silence.

He felt as if he was losing control of himself, standing by the edge of a cliff that led down to the depths of the abyss. He was only a step away from completely falling.

He felt that he was straying further and further away from being a "good cop".

(vi)

They finally got on the train at 8 P.M. Xie Lanshan sat in a window seat, speaking very little throughout the whole trip. He spent most of his time looking out the window in silence, resting his forehead on his hand while he fell into a daze.

He fell asleep almost immediately. He dreamed of the handsome old Xie, and how his father took him out for a game of basketball with the Tao family right before a mission. Old Xie's foot was like a springboard that made slam-dunking easy, and Xie Lanshan was also quite skilled in basketball himself; the father and son duo were very much in sync during the game. The little round Tao Longyue at the time was ready to cry after the defeat. Who could have known that old Xie would never return from a mission again?

Shen Liufei saw in the reflection of the night's window a quiet face drenched in tears. It was a very thin line of tears, but it ran down as if it also burnt a trail in his heart that stung with every heartbeat. He looked at Xie Lanshan briefly before he finally called out gently, "Xie Lanshan."

The young cop always kept his weaknesses hidden, only ever allowing himself to miss his father in his dreams. He woke from his short dream and rubbed his eyes, then pulled off the bullet necklace from his neck. He placed the necklace carefully in the palm of his hand and stared at it.

Shen Liufei said, "You've been acting quite odd today. Does it have something to do with your father?"

Xie Lanshan answered honestly after taking in a quick breath of air, "When I was still undercover in the Golden Triangle, Mu Kun once told me that a traitor in the police department known as the 'Apostle' killed my dad. And that person was my dad's closest comrade." He paused slightly, frowned, and then continued, "I have someone on my suspect list."

"You mean Liu Yanbo?"

Xie Lanshan nodded. He explained that this wasn't a baseless guess, that Liu Yanbo's harsh and discriminatory attitude toward him was proof itself. Besides, there were only a handful of people alive now that could be considered a 'close comrade' to old Xie back then. Those who had sacrificed in the line of duty could not have been the culprit, and those who quit the industry had long left. The only one who was still alive and lived a better life after the mission was Vice Chief Liu.

There was another layer of meaning beneath Xie Lanshan's anxiety, one line he didn't tell Shen Liufei: He felt that if he didn't discover who the Apostle was for his old man, he would fail as his son.

Of course, Shen Liufei had some words he didn't tell Xie

Lanshan as well: Perhaps because the man was the center of this event himself and couldn't see the bigger picture, the artist felt Tao Jun was more suspicious than the consistently hostile Liu Yanbo.

By the time they arrived at their destination, it was already near midnight. The small town was nowhere as robust as Hanhai, so the two men settled in a motel near the station for the night. The next morning, they followed the address Tao Jun gave them to pay Zhu Mingwu a visit.

Old officer Zhu Mingwu looked much older in age, more so than even Tao Jun, but he also looked tougher and more hard-boiled. The old man was in good spirits. He had expected the visitors with all the files prepared on the old case after receiving a courtesy call from Tao Jun.

There were certainly very little files left of the horrifying Cangnan Rape-murder Case. Shen Liufei and Xie Lanshan studied the profile of the culprit; he was a surgeon by the name of Kong Xiangping. The man had once offered his services to rural and poorer neighborhoods in the past, so even if he was still alive today, he would have already been long retired. The black and white ID rusted with age, immortalizing the face of the devil on there. Just from his appearance, it was impossible to imagine that such a clean and sophisticated-looking man was actually a twisted demon who had raped and killed eleven young women.

Among the victims, the oldest was 28 years old while the youngest was only 8.

The old officer seemed to have read through their expression and shook his head. "This man's a demon, a horrible monster. He would lure innocent girls into his house and lock them in his basement to torture and use as sex toys. If anyone tried to fight back or attempt to flee, he would sew their mouths shut with fabric needles and peel their skin off with his surgery knife. After torturing them to death, he would toss the corpse into the wild and continue searching for his next victim. Because he was a volunteer medic in the rural town, he was very respected in the daytime by the residents in the village. For a very long time, nobody suspected him to be the culprit."

Shen Liufei continued to look through the file and asked, after turning a few pages, "If Kong Xiangping had already committed suicide by the time the police found him, where did all these hidden details about his crimes come from?"

"We saved a little girl at the time, who was also the only survivor of this horrific serial murder case." The old cop sighed. "The truth is, we discovered over twelve young women's DNAs in that basement. There were also massive amounts of feminine products, dolls, lipsticks, handkerchiefs, and more—there were even some infant supplies. This demon must have killed far more than eleven girls, but only eleven of their corpses were found."

Shen Liufei and Xie Lanshan exchanged a glance; their expressions grave at how horrific and twisted this culprit was.

Xie Lanshan quickly scanned the files and discovered that the surviving girl's profile was very simple, with only one name on file that was clearly an alias: Xiao Man. He remarked in surprise, "This surviving little girl could be the key to breaking this case today, was her information not recorded on file?"

The old man shook his head and said, "The little girl was only eleven when she was saved. The cops involved in the case back then didn't want this child to live under the shadow of such a traumatic experience for the rest of her life, so they did their best to hide her from mass media and didn't record too much of her personal information."

Shen Liufei pondered a little before asking the old officer, "What do you still remember about this little girl?"

The old man squinted his eyes as if he was reminiscing a blurry dream. After a long while, he finally returned to reality and said, "I remember when they saved that little girl from the basement that she was already on her last breath, she laid in fatigue on my shoulder. The little girl seemed to be of mixed ethnicity. Her features were very pretty and delicate at the age of eleven, and looked almost prettier than a doll."

Over twenty years later, a time so far away from this old man's life, he could still clearly remember the scene of how he saved this young girl from the hands of the devil. He continued on as if he was in a daze and repeated, "She wore a beautiful red dress..."

Knowing that Xiao Man had once been hospitalized in the municipal hospital, Shen Liufei bid the old man farewell and prepared to take his leave. Just before he stepped out of the door, the artist suddenly turned back and asked, "Do you happen to remember anything about your old student Tao Jun?"

The old man squinted once again and said, "He's reliable, hardworking, and very skilled. I know he later switched to the drug enforcement department and made quite a name there."

"What kind of person is he aside from work?"

Xie Lanshan didn't understand what prompted Shen Liufei's sudden questions.

The old man pondered once again, which took up another long while before he finally said, "There's an unexplainable stubbornness in him. I always had a strange feeling that he would one day do something that could harm both himself and the people around him."

The Red Dress

Another corpse was discovered; the time of death estimated to be earlier than the previous two victims. Three young women had died within a short period of time, all in similar and horrifying ways. On their necks hung a dog collar, their mouths were slit open and sewn back up. With the skin peeled off their bodies from all different parts, they were bloodied masses.

This serial murder stirred up a storm in the city as people now lived in fear while the violent crimes unit felt an unprecedented pressure on their shoulders. Tao Longyue had been clocking out late almost every day; he was stuck in a loop of investigations outside or meetings within the bureau, barely scraping some time on his own birthday to invite Su Mansheng out for a dinner date.

They still went to the French restaurant that Doctor Su liked at the same seat they both preferred by the bookshelf. Tao Longyue kindly pulled out the chair for Su Mansheng and suddenly recalled the day he called his teammates out for a party, then asked, "I went to call you over that day we went out to the bar, how come you didn't pick up your phone?"

Su Mansheng seemed to not have much of an appetite, her expression also a little cloudy. She closed the menu after flipping through half-heartedly, then responded lightly with her head down, eyes staring at the piece of lemon in her water, "I was reading, so I had my phone off."

"I wanted to pick you up at your house, but I didn't see the lights on." There wasn't anything suspicious about the exchange; a forensic scientist was an around the clock job. Su Mansheng often spent her free time reading books and attending seminars or lectures. However, he had noticed that the doctor's attitude had grown distant ever since she accepted his proposal. Aside from work, it was virtually impossible to contact her. This made the young captain feel as if he was involved in a long-distance relationship, doubting himself as the days went by, unsure where he had failed her.

"Maybe I was tired from reading." Su Mansheng lifted her eyes to look at him and then smoothly responded, "I fell asleep."

Tao Longyue didn't pursue the question further and called the waiter to place their orders. Both of them got the same special steak combo today; Tao Longyue asked for a medium-well while Su Mansheng had her meat a little rarer.

By the time their orders were ready, the French chef that was acquainted with Su Mansheng showed up again. He passionately asked for hugs and intimate exchanges, to which Su Mansheng responded amiably and welcomingly.

This Frenchman called Le Goff was clearly in love with Su Mansheng. Ever since she had confirmed her relationship with Tao Longyue, the chef would always shoot cold glances at the latter as if he was eyeing a mortal enemy. Le Goff shook his head right in front of Tao Longyue and placed his big hand around Su Mansheng's shoulders. He spoke with his accented

Chinese to her, "If I knew you weren't into women, I would have pursued you as I would chase after the sun."

Maintaining his dignity and class, young Captain Tao couldn't respond with a direct eye roll and instead only cursed in his head: *Great chef Le Goff my ass, more like a silly Le Goof.*

Though the man had a point. Doctor Su was cold and aloof; her demeanor and attitude towards men had always been quite intimidating. In contrast, she was extra kind and caring toward women around her to where even Xie Lanshan had assumed she was gay.

"I will do anything to earn a smile from you." Chef Le Goff openly flirted with her right in front of Captain Tao, holding Su Mansheng's hands as he gazed at her affectionately.

Tao Longyue was getting tired of this and asserted his dominance. He stood up and wrapped his arm around Su Mansheng, then said with a grin, "Chef Le Goff, I think it's time that you return to the kitchen. I also need to discuss some details about our marriage with my girlfriend."

After a heavy hit to his heart, the chef reluctantly returned to the kitchen—finally.

Su Mansheng sat back down, her expression cold as she said, "That was a little petty of you, Tao."

The appetizers came out first, fresh boiled eggs and salad with geese liver. Tao Longyue was three years younger than Su Mansheng, yet the captain had always felt a little intimidated before her. Now that he'd seen she had no intention to chitchat, he no longer dared to upset her more and ate silently with his head down.

The two ate quietly for a while until Su Mansheng said, "Where's Xie Lanshan, is he cleared from this case now?"

Tao Longyue nodded and said, "We've already proven that it's a serial murder by the same culprit. With the timing of when we discovered the second victim, it was impossible for Xie Lanshan to have committed the crime."

Su Mansheng had no interest in discussing their marriage but had her attention all on this serial murder case. She asked, "So are there any breakthroughs with the investigation so far?"

Tao Longyue shook his head and responded, "From the looks of it now, it seems like a series of indiscriminate murders. The victims are unacquainted with each other and they share nothing in common, so it's much more difficult for us to lock in on a suspects list."

The steak arrived. Su Mansheng held up a steak knife in her hands and gave Tao Longyue a smile. "Should I give you some advice?"

The atmosphere between them clearly eased up, and Tao Longyue didn't hesitate to put back on his fanboy attitude and said, "I'd love to hear from the expert."

"The edges of the skin peeled off from the victims are very clean with very even thickness, so the culprit must be a professional."

"A professional? Like a doctor?" Tao Longyue had considered this possibility, but it was difficult to narrow in on one person with so many doctors in Hanhai.

"Or a chef." Su Mansheng suggested in a jesting tone. She pulled Tao Longyue's steak over and kindly helped him cut the meat into small pieces, then said, "The second autopsy revealed that there was massive bleeding from the private areas on the three victims. There were no DNA samples we could find from their lower bodies, but combining this with the level of damage discovered on their flesh, it's highly possible that these injuries were caused by something hard and similar to a wooden rod."

"In these circumstances... The culprit could be an adult man with some sort of disability," Tao Longyue further analyzed and then came to an even more surprising hypothesis, "or, the culprit could be a woman!"

"It would be very difficult for one woman to complete the act of a murder, hiding corpses, and then tossing the corpses all in one go." Su Mansheng had finished cutting Tao Longyue's steak and went back to cutting her own as she said, "The culprit is clearly very experienced. It would be difficult for an average doctor to complete everything so meticulously. The skin that was cut off from the victim's bodies had cleanly kept muscle tissues; you can see the veins and even some of the organs through the cut."

The steak was too rare, one slice down the meat was already squeezing out red juice onto the plate like fresh blood. Tao Longyue looked at how Su Mansheng discussed the culprit's method of peeling skin nonchalantly as she cut the steak, feeling his stomach churn a little in disgust.

They took a stroll in the shopping mall after dinner, though they didn't shop. It had been a while since he had seen his girl-friend. Young Captain Tao felt relaxed and at peace for the first time in a long while and didn't want to toss himself back into the horrifying and cruel serial murder case that soon.

They passed by the female clothing section and saw a boutique displaying a beautiful, long, red dress by the window. Su Mansheng stopped and stared at the dress.

Su Mansheng was mixed-blood and always had a dazzling aura around her. If she wasn't a forensic scientist, she could have easily become an actress or model. However, she didn't seem to be interested in fame or attention, and very rarely wore bright colors outside of work. Tao Longyue pondered briefly and decided that he could ask his fiancée to dress in this beau-tiful red gown for the annual New Year's party the municipal bureau hosted. Imagining how his future wife would stun everyone with her beauty at the party, he could already feel himself beaming with pride.

Captain Tao said, "Do you like it? I can buy it for you."

But Su Mansheng didn't answer him. Her gaze was still fixed on this red dress, a strange expression appeared on her face as the corner of her lips curled into something that wasn't a smile.

Tao Longyue looked at the profile of the doctor for a moment and suddenly felt something eerie grab his heart-strings. Yet as soon as he tried to figure out what it was, Su Mansheng already retracted her gaze and turned her head back to him in her usual queenly demeanor. "No need, let's go."

The date ended early and Tao Longyue drove Su Mansheng back home. In order to solve the problem of limited parking, the parking structure around the shopping mall had been working on its expansion lately. It first took down a small park around the neighborhood, which was now surrounded by a wired fence all around.

Just as Su Mansheng got in the car, a horrifying cry for help rang out from the dirt field behind the fence, "Help me, help—"

The cry was quickly cut off as if the person suffered a devastating injury. Before Su Mansheng could call out to him, Tao Longyue already rushed out as fast as he could toward the source of the sound. He then quickly turned back as soon as he stepped out and pressed a hand to stop Su Mansheng from getting out of the car. "Stay in the car and wait for me. Be careful!"

The former park was already in shambles as construction began. There were no stars in the sky, no lights on the ground, but even through the wired fence a few meters ahead, Tao

Longyue could still see a man violently beating a young woman. The man was tall and dressed in black, face covered in a mask. The young woman had long black hair and fair skin, dressed only in a simple red dress on this cold winter night with a black dog collar around her neck.

The man attempted to wrap the dog leash around the woman's face and closed her mouth shut. The girl felt death approaching and desperately struggled out of the man's grip. During the struggle, she somehow knocked the man's mask off.

The man quickly picked up his mask to cover up his exposed face. The girl attempted to flee but was quickly pulled back by the leash around her neck. He dragged her forward as if he was dragging cattle. She couldn't win in strength; a menacing trail mark dragged through the muddied ground.

The fence was about two meters tall. Tao Longyue jumped from the ground and pulled himself over the fence as fast as he could. He glimpsed the man's profile and saw that the culprit was wearing a mask.

Noticing that someone arrived to save the girl, the man in black immediately tossed his victim aside and ran for his life. Tao Longyue chased after him until he reached the girl. He pulled out the chain covering her mouth, noticing that aside from her tear-filled face, she was alive and not severely injured. He then quickly got up and continued to chase after the man in black.

The suspect ran fast, but he was clearly not an expert. He attempted to jump over the fence but was caught off balance as soon as he landed and rolled on the ground for a good meter out. Tao Longyue pursued closely, climbed swiftly to the top of the fence, and then jumped down toward the suspect below, landing right on the man.

Fists shot out faster than words; Tao Longyue landed a heavy blow on the suspect without a greeting as soon as he took control. The man in black struggled as he suffered the blows, then grabbed a fist full of sand on the side and splashed it toward Tao Longyue's eyes. Captain Tao turned his head and dodged the blow swiftly; the man on the ground took this opportunity to crawl back up. As soon as he lifted his head, he noticed Tao Longyue's face not too far away from him.

With the help of ghostly white light, Tao Longyue saw it clearly. The man wore a human-skin mask sewn together like a quilt, only exposing a pair of dark eyes that looked like a horrible alligator peeking out from a deep mire.

Despite solving many gory and horrific cases, Tao Longyue had never seen such a terrifying scene and felt his heart jump as he laid eyes on the mask. The man seemed to have expected this reaction and gave a rough and deep laugh behind the mask. He took this brief opening and launched an attack at Tao Longyue.

Even if the man in black was tall and strong, he was still no match for young Captain Tao in terms of physical combat and quickly fell to the defensive. He took steps back and found his wrist caught in a tight grip. Tao Longyue didn't hesitate and pressed harder until he dislocated the man's wrist.

"Ah!" Su Mansheng also arrived at this point and saw the two men caught in a violent brawl. She then suddenly screamed.

The suspect was already one step away from being caught, but Su Mansheng's sudden scream distracted Tao Longyue. A slight loosening of his grip was a fatal mistake. The Captain didn't expect the suspect to react suddenly like a fish back in the water; he reached into his sleeves and pulled out a surgical knife, then stabbed right at Tao Longyue.

"Watch out!"

But Su Mansheng's cry was too late. The knife had already stabbed into the left side of Tao Longyue's abdomen. Tao Longyue didn't feel pain as the cold knife stabbed into his boiling flesh, only dazed.

Injuries already covered the man in black. As if he was afraid more cops would come, he sprinted away.

Tao Longyue suddenly bent forward and panted heavily with a hand over his injury. Within seconds, his face was already deathly pale, sweat covering his forehead. Su Mansheng rushed over to help him up, then asked, concerned, "Are you alright?"

"Didn't I tell you... to stay where you were at..." Tao Longyue pressed a hand on his injury, but fresh blood continued to stream down his fingers. He wasn't trying to scold her, but felt frustrated as he cursed, "Dammit, I was so close... so close to catching him..."

(ii)

This serial murder case was causing unrest among the citizens as rumors began surfacing on the internet. The red ice case from earlier was also an important case appointed by the national government, so the provincial branch began sending out extra resources to support the investigations. They founded a special investigation unit and even enlisted the help of members from the Blue Foxes in hopes of solving these heavy cases as soon as possible.

Tang Qinglan knew that Xie Lanshan had his eyes on her. It was a time of turbulence and she had been on the down-low; her company in name and all-female nightclub were still in business with an added investment to a certain project.

It was Liu Mingfang's project.

· · ·

Tang Qinglan invited the man into her office, but neither of them talked about business and only chatted aimlessly in the room. Liu Mingfang wanted to talk business, but this rumored Miss T certainly did not seem to trust his business plans.

"I've already done what you guys asked and searched through my dad's files about the drug enforcement cases. I can't help anymore."

He had placed his hopes on the *Ode to the Goddess Luo* to save his business, but ended up becoming a suspect in Li Guochang's case. His reputation in the industry deteriorated and he had no more connections outside; without Tang Qinglan's financial support, his company would have gone bankrupt already. Liu Mingfang might not be a cop, but he came from a family of policemen and had a good guess what Tang Qinglan's real business was. Of course, the man was too cowardly to involve himself with the drug trade and only wished for an opportunity to get out of this pit.

Yet a privileged rich child raised under a shelter did not know the consequences of mingling with dangerous businesses and people. The playing field was all but a facade that hid the real depth of the swamp, and he was already too deep into it all before he even realized it.

"I know you're not a cop, so stop worrying over nothing." Miss T smiled. "I'll just ask you to do one more thing for me and install an app on your dad's phone—"

"No, no, no, I swear it's not a joke if he finds out," Liu Mingfang refused. He could tell the woman wanted to install a hacking device onto his father's cellphone to steal intel and quickly waved his hand off in horror. "Stealing info from my dad's out of the question now! He almost got me last time I was searching through his files in his study! Sure, this old man's a little easy when it comes to his hobbies and art, but he always takes his job seriously. If I even try to mention something about a bug at home, I swear I'm going to get a harsh scolding from him. He's a former drug enforcement officer with awards and honors behind him. His sharp sense in this field isn't a joke."

Tang Qinglan rested her face on her hand and leaned in toward Liu Mingfang. Her eyebrows were thin lines of ink, lips a touch of red. She lifted an eyebrow and pressed her lips together as if she was blowing a kiss and said, "I know, he's one of the famous 'flaming triangle of the anti-drug forces.'"

The woman had very full lips, a flat nose, and eyes that were further apart than most people. She wasn't someone Chinese culture would traditionally consider a beauty, but there was something unique about the way she looked that was luring and captivating. As if dancing to the song of the siren, Liu Mingfang knew he couldn't step out now because he had also fallen into the charm of this woman.

His thoughts quickly returned as he picked out something strange in those words and said, "Is that a well-known title? Where did you hear that from?"

Drug enforcement units tended to work away from the spotlight, and this was from cases that were over twenty years ago. It was almost impossible for internal nicknames and jokes to be spread out to the public.

Tang Qinglan gave a chuckle and responded vaguely, "From your father's comrade. I'm very familiar with their history in the unit."

"My dad's comrade... who?" Liu Mingfang desperately tried to decipher the meaning behind those words.

"But he's useless now." Miss T lifted the corner of her lips and said, "If we don't use your dad... then why don't we have you do the work instead?"

"Me? I'm not a cop, I don't have any internal intel—"

Someone knocked on the office door from the outside. Before anyone inside could invite them in, the door opened on its own. A delicate face with heavy makeup peeked in from outside. It was Liu Mingfang's personal secretary, Xia Hong.

She was indeed quite a personal secretary to him. Liu Mingfang's desperate pursuit of Song Qilian back then was because he fell for the woman's refreshing and clean appearance, but drinking clear water got boring after a while. That was why he had episodes of affairs even after marriage, mostly with women who dressed more lavishly.

Xia Hong slept with her boss before and believed he had her back, so she often acted boldly and a little out of line during work. She didn't explain whether she was listening in on their conversation outside the door to Miss T, and instead turned to remind Liu Mingfang that they had dinner plans with Chief Wong later and needed to leave soon.

Liu Mingfang's nasty habit picked up again; he complained that Xia Hong looked too proper and businesslike, unlike Miss T, who had her own style looking less like a professional. It was one thing to be undisciplined in the workspace, but Xia Hong was also someone who was extremely superstitious and into the occult. She was well-versed in various fortune-telling techniques and often went on about her spiritual findings.

Compared to Tang Qinglan, Liu Mingfang grew more annoyed at Xia Hong and waved her off in annoyance. "Alright, you can wait outside for now."

There was nothing more venomous than the judging gaze between women. Xia Hong studied Tang Qinglan from top to bottom and grew more confident of herself. The latter dressed in a men's black jacket and looked objectively less appealing. Of course, Miss T couldn't compare to Xia Hong in looks, but the female CEO had an unexplainable sense of authority that Xia Hong couldn't compete with. The secretary stomped away with sourness in her mouth.

"We're not done talking yet, you're leaving already?" Tang

Qinglan got up and sat right on Liu Mingfang's lap. She wrapped her arm around his neck and pressed her lips to leave a mark on his shirt collar.

"I'm waiting to remarry my wife, I can't do these things anymore." Liu Mingfang could feel his heart race, almost unable to control himself.

"Alright, I won't keep you here if you have plans after this." Tang Qinglan escorted him out without troubling him anymore. She gave Liu Mingfang another playful wink before saying, "How about this, I'll wait for you tonight at the club."

Liu Mingfang had an eventful night. After being offered drink after drink by many pretty ladies in the club, he let his intoxicated self fall into the gentle embrace of Miss T.

As soon as he opened his eyes and reached an arm out to touch the woman sleeping next to him, he felt something wet beneath his fingers.

The man sat up on the bed in shock and saw Xia Hong's bloodied corpse lying beside him, already cold, without a heartbeat.

"What-what's going on? Weren't you the one sleeping with me last night?!" Liu Mingfang was panicking as he stared at his hand covered in blood, then turned to Tang Qinglan, who had just walked into the room.

"Turn off the camera." Tang Qinglan flashed Liu Mingfang a smile after giving her subordinates an order. "Should I call the cops right now or help you get rid of this body?"

"G-get rid of it? How?" After the distraction of alcohol wore off, Liu Mingfang finally realized he had walked right into the woman's trap. However, he also realized that there was no way for him to walk out of this with a clean hand anymore.

"How do you hide a body? You just need to hide it in a pile

of dead bodies." The woman's usual enchanting expression grew cold and distant as she said in a low voice, "But I won't help you without conditions. I need you to plant some spies for me inside the municipal bureau."

"I can't do it, I told you, I'm not a cop..." Liu Mingfang was ready to cry, unable to finish the latter half of his sentence.

"You coward, of course I'm not asking you to be the spy!" Miss T scolded harshly. The next moment, her usual playful and coquettish expression returned as the tone of her voice audibly lifted. She dragged out the last syllable as if she was singing and said playfully, "You only need to let out the bait."

(iii)

After bidding Zhu Mingwu farewell, Xie Lanshan and Shen Liufei continued their investigation, using the old man's intel at the provincial hospital that saved Xiao Man. It had been over twenty years and neither was sure if they could still find any useful evidence. They were quite fortunate. The nurse that handled the girl's case back then was now the head nurse of her department and still remembered the case clearly.

The nurse said that the harassment and beating Xiao Man went through while she was kidnapped left severe physical and mental scars. The little girl was psychologically worn down by the time she was saved and suffered extreme PTSD. Unable to obtain more information from her witness account, the hospital contacted a local orphanage and law office for abuse after treating her physical wounds to enroll her in an all-female convent.

Most children saved from such horrific kidnapping and sexual abuse were returned to their parents, but if they could not contact any parent or legal guardian, they would normally be placed in the care of a local orphanage. This news shocked Xie Lanshan, who said, "Why a convent?"

"That church also serves the community like this in certain ways, and the headmaster was the kindest and most benevolent person I knew in my life." The nurse said with a sigh, "That poor little girl, not only was she violated at such a young age, she also had to see other innocent girls like her get killed one after another. I thought that after facing the most extreme pain and evil, perhaps the only salvation for her could be found in faith and spirituality."

As one of the biggest cities at the center of three provinces, Cangnan had been developing rapidly over the last few years. The work to upgrade the governing scale of the city had been pushed forward to manage the developments. The convent was on the other side of the city, near a neighboring province. In order to save on time, Xie Lanshan gave the headmaster a call right before they left the hospital to explain their visit.

Early winter was cloudy with harsh winds. They called a cab and rushed toward their destination, passing through the robust and crowded newly developed city. Their racing hearts finally settled by the time they arrived at the convent.

The convent was a private historical monument built over a hundred years ago by a visiting Catholic priest, not usually open to the public. Beautiful trees surrounded the marbled white walls of the chapel on all sides, like a fortress in the woods. There was a small stream of water outside with some fishes still swimming in this weather. The two men walked over the stone-paved walkway to the front gate of the convent, greeted by the writing hanging outside the door:

His Holy Light brings salvation to man.

Xie Lanshan stared at the sign silently, praising the tranquil and isolated location of this convent, truly a good place to forget the temptations of the mortal world.

Xie Lanshan explained to the headmaster he was here for an investigation and to find out where Xiao Man is today.

The old headmaster was a woman nearing her 60s with an amiable face but also displayed uncontested authority in the convent. She took the two men on a tour of the community, including the school, and explained Xiao Man's life when she lived here. She said, "Xiao Man found her inner peace and faith here; by the time she was ready to leave the convent, she had already healed the wounds in her heart. I don't think there's a need to disturb her newfound peaceful life."

Shen Liufei explained, "A case very similar to what happened back then recently occurred. We must find some useful evidence through her past experiences in order to prevent more victims like her from falling prey to the criminal."

The headmaster walked toward a little girl sitting outside the chapel as they conversed. The girl looked to be about twelve to thirteen years of age. She held a drawing board and pencil in her hands, all of her attention on the drawing. She didn't speak and looked mature for her age, as if her only entertainment was to sit outside the chapel and draw quietly by herself.

According to Shen Liufei, the girl had some talent for drawing.

The headmaster communicated with her using sign language and brushed her hand gently on her hair.

The headmaster walked back to the two guests and sighed. "This child is quite unfortunate as well. She came down with a severe illness almost as soon as she was born and became deaf, then her family tossed her away."

Xie Lanshan's attention wasn't on the little girl and he continued to steer the conversation back to Xiao Man, "We don't have a clue who the culprit might be, nor whether this is an indiscriminate serial murder or something with a hidden motive. Whether or not we can solve the case in a timely manner is dependent on our investigation."

"All you guys have been talking about is solving the case. Have you not considered the mental trauma it could cause her if we bring this up again?" The headmaster was insistent on not revealing any private information. She said that the girl was well now; she didn't know where Xiao Man was living, but she also refused to remind the girl of such traumatic experiences.

"How do you know she's doing well?" Xie Lanshan caught the loophole in her words and continued to question like an unstoppable force, "Has she been keeping in contact with you? Does she contact you regularly? Has she come by to visit you lately? Lately as in within the last two months, or perhaps three months? She should be about 32 now. Is she married yet? Does she have a child?"

This kind of aggressive questioning was another way of getting answers. Xie Lanshan's expression was stern, gaze a little sharp. He stared at the headmaster's face without looking away. In the eyes of a professional investigator like him, any sign of lying could be detected with the slightest change in expression, and answers could easily be found in subconscious body language.

It didn't take long for Xie Lanshan to find his answer. He softened the tone of his voice and said, "She's paid a visit to you recently, hasn't she?"

The headmaster was no match against him and could only say, "She's going to get married soon. Can you please leave this poor girl alone and let her live a fulfilling life with her family?"

Xie Lanshan still tried to explain, "I really don't want to disturb her, but the culprit is still free."

The headmaster let out another long sigh, then finally said after a long silence, "Is there a law out there that says witnesses can refuse to testify?"

"The Criminal Procedure Laws say that anyone who is knowledgeable about the case has an obligation to testify before the law," Xie Lanshan said truthfully. "Of course, there are no legal repercussions or consequences if you refuse the obligation. Therefore, the choice is still yours."

"Then I've already made my decision. I will not speak another word." Her long robe danced gently in the wind as the headmaster turned to make her leave, saying that she still had business to take care of and left the convent.

A young nun offered to escort the guests out, to which Xie Lanshan asked if she had seen Xiao Man before.

"I've never heard our headmaster mention anyone by the name of Xiao Man," she said. It was impossible to tell whether she truly didn't know or if she was told to not reveal any information, but the young nun shook her head and said, "I can show you two around the convent a little more, but I really don't know any more about this person."

Xie Lanshan wanted to show off his charm and knock out some intel from the young nun but was stopped by Shen Liufei's judging eye.

Shen Liufei retracted his gaze from the little girl drawing outside and said to the nun courteously, "Sure, let's tour the other side."

The nun led the way a few steps ahead of them. Xie Lanshan leaned his head toward Shen Liufei and whispered, "What a pain."

Their lead stopped abruptly. Shen Liufei pressed his eyebrows together and once again turned to the mute and deaf little girl.

"What 'citizen's obligation,' it's practically useless when talking to these people." Xie Lanshan complained in a whisper out of fear that the nun would overhear them. Running into obstacles during the investigation wasn't uncommon, but they can't simply arrest anyone that doesn't cooperate. Xie Lanshan was confident he could set traps and outsmart people who were sly and tricky, but he didn't know how to deal with people who were honest and righteous like the headmaster.

As if he didn't hear any word Xie Lanshan had said, Shen Liufei suddenly asked the nun, "Do you know sign language? I saw that you guys have some special needs students here as well."

"I don't." The young nun gave an apologetic smile. "Everyone here that knows sign language is out today with the headmaster for a seminar at the city."

"I'm an artist, can I request to give that little girl some lessons?" Shen Liufei had only introduced himself as company during this visit. He eyed that solitary little girl and added with a sincere tone, "She has talent, just missing a little bit of professional training."

Xie Lanshan immediately knew what was up. After seeing the young nun step away, he quickly rushed by Shen Liufei's side and asked, "Are you trying to have her do a forensic sketch for you? Do you even know sign language?"

Shen Liufei looked at him calmly and answered, "No."

Xie Lanshan almost cried out, "Then why—"

Shen Liufei interrupted him, "The pen is the best tool of communication between artists. As for how I should approach her first, you can look up how to do simple greetings."

Xie Lanshan was ready to roll his eyes. Shen Liufei gave

him five minutes to learn the basic greetings and questions they needed to ask in sign language, either through looking it up on the internet or asking an acquaintance for help.

Xie Lanshan left the convent using the excuse of needing to use the restroom, then quickly pulled out his phone to look up some easy sign language tutorials. On the other side, Shen Liufei had already walked up toward the little girl. He saw the girl was drawing the scenery outside the chapel. After getting approval from the girl with an exchange of a gaze and some simple hand gestures, he picked up her pencil and began drawing on her board.

Just as the artist had said, the two only needed a pen to communicate. A few strokes and the two had grown close. The little girl smiled brightly.

The two sat shoulder to shoulder and began drawing together outside the chapel. Xie Lanshan returned and walked toward the girl. He kneeled down to face her and asked her in sign language: *Have you seen a very pretty and slightly foreign-looking woman lately? She rarely visits, but would always be with your headmaster when she's here.*

Xie Lanshan figured this convent was located in quite a rural area. It must not be very common to see a biracial beauty visiting the headmaster often. And for someone so beautiful that could leave an impression on an old police officer twenty years later, surely this little girl would also have an impression of her.

The little girl thought about it and nodded her head.

This made things easier. Xie Lanshan asked in sign language: *Shall we draw a picture of her?*

The little girl nodded even more enthusiastically as she turned to look at Shen Liufei with joy on her face.

. . .

The girl started to draw, but because she was still not too skilled, it was difficult to make out the individual. Shen Liufei patiently instructed her with a pencil. After at least twenty different attempts at drawing a portrait, the two men let the little girl scan through and picked out the drawing that looked the most like Xiao Man.

That five-minute intro to sign language lesson proved no use here. Xie Lanshan couldn't understand what the artists were discussing and could only sit on the side, staring dumbly at Shen Liufei's profile.

The man had a high nose bridge, long eyelashes, and a unique profile that gave off an almost androgynous attractiveness. Shen Liufei was a very distant man who seemed above mortal temptations normally, but was always extremely diligent and focused on work. Xie Lanshan was mesmerized by the man and suddenly felt it wasn't too painful to kill time right now.

Shen Liufei seemed to have noticed the affectionate glance toward him and turned to return the gaze.

As their eyes met, Xie Lanshan smiled and said something in sign language.

He managed to pick up one more line earlier in the restroom: *I love you.*

Shen Liufei didn't understand sign language, but he could understand the meaning of the gesture just from the look in Xie Lanshan's eyes. He turned his head back to the canvas, but the corner of his lips lifted slightly in response.

Just as Xie Lanshan rested his head on his hand after what felt like an eternity of boredom, the little girl finally picked up her paper, studied it around, and gave a confident nod.

Xie Lanshan stood up and asked Shen Liufei, "Is it done?"

Shen Liufei took the paper and looked at it. After a moment of hesitation, he walked toward Xie Lanshan, his eyebrows pressed together in a strange manner.

Xie Lanshan didn't rush to look at Xiao Man's portrait and asked, "Why did you have to pick the kid that can't speak out of all the kids here?"

"Her drawings have a unique vitality in them, which means that she has very strong observation skills and a keen eye for detail. So, she must have a much stronger memory and impression of people's faces than other children of her age. And because she can't talk, you can tell that the headmaster pays extra attention to her. Therefore, it's likely that she has been around Xiao Man when the woman comes to visit the headmaster."

There was some logic behind this. Xie Lanshan waited to see Xiao Man's portrait but didn't get another response from Shen Liufei, so he had no choice but to take the paper from the artist's hands. He was dumbfounded the moment he saw the drawing, and finally stuttered after a while, "Isn't... isn't this Doctor Su?"

Even though the woman in the drawing didn't look exactly like her, it was still very similar.

Just as he pondered what to do next, Shen Liufei's cellphone rang. Xie Lanshan was removed from the case, so Ding Li could only call Shen Liufei if anything came up. She said that Tao Longyue and Su Mansheng ran into that serial murderer during their date, and the Captain ate a knife right into his stomach.

Shen Liufei asked, "Is it bad?"

Ding Li answered, "Well, he ain't dead. But I think you should come back with Xie bro soon. Captain Tao saved a girl from that murderer that night. She is likely the only survivor who has seen the true face of the culprit!"

(iv)

The surviving girl likely saw the victim's face and would need Shen Liufei to help draw out a forensic sketch based on her witness account. The two men rushed back from Cangnan to Hanhai without a second word.

By the time the express bullet train left the station, the sun was already setting, painting the sky with red clouds and purple mist that surrounded the sun like a celestial flower garden. Of course, the miraculous scene would soon disappear with the withering of the large sunflower. If sin cannot grow under the light of the sun, the coming of darkness naturally instilled fear in the hearts of people.

They returned with great findings from Cangnan. Xiao Man was only a witness they originally intended to find, but the doctor in charge of all autopsies on this case as more bodies were found kept silent about her involvement with the old case. Even someone as experienced and well-trained as Tao Longyue was injured by the culprit on their date—there was not a more solid reason to suspect Su Mansheng's involvement in the case.

The sky outside the window grew more muddied as the light disappeared, scenery blurred quickly along the high-speed tracks. Xie Lanshan analyzed the case and said to Shen Liufei, "Su Mansheng's age does match up with Xiao Man's, and from the way the culprit removed the skin so precisely, it's very possible that the culprit is a forensic scientist."

Shen Liufei added, "It would be almost impossible for a single woman to accomplish such a large case all by herself. If we assume that Xiao Man is the culprit, the man that injured Tao Longyue must be her accomplice who takes her orders."

"But there's one thing I don't understand; the first female corpse was discovered 25 years ago, and the original suspect committed suicide four years later. Why did the culprit wait another twenty years after that to continue his crime?"

"I'm wondering if there is a possibility," Shen Liufei pondered a little before saying, "that Xiao Man had hoped to return to normal life upon rescue many years ago. However, some unexpected and strong stimulation from the outside triggered her to break down once again, quickly transforming her from the victim years ago to a criminal today."

"This isn't uncommon." Xie Lanshan let out a sigh. The explanation was most likely the case. He said, "Poor ol' Tao."

This was just speculation between the two men at the end of the day. They still needed concrete evidence to prove it. Xie Lanshan couldn't imagine how despaired Tao Longyue would be if Su Mansheng's verdict came out, and Shen Liufei also seemed to be deep in thought beside him. They fell into silence.

The train continued to trudge forward. The end of fall was quickly taken over by the winter weather; the sky darkened faster than usual.

After a long silence, Xie Lanshan suddenly asked, "So why did you ask Zhu Mingwu those questions right before you left?"

Shen Liufei responded nonchalantly, "Old Captain Tao could be counted as my future father-in-law now. Am I not allowed to at least learn about his interests and hobbies?"

Xie Lanshan laughed. Intelligent and like minds didn't need extra words to communicate. One glance was enough to understand each other, making the company of one another comfortable and trusting. Of course, there were also consequences; it would be difficult to hide from one another and only leave rocky feelings that could damage their relationship.

Xie Lanshan's head was a jumbled pot of everything right

now. All sorts of questions and strange thoughts consumed him; while he wanted to trust Shen Liufei unconditionally, he couldn't trust himself.

Tao Longyue was hospitalized the night he suffered the injury. Thankfully, the wound did not stab through important organs and the tough guy only had to deal with ten stitches.

Of course, Captain Tao didn't even bat an eye at his injury. As soon as he woke from his surgery, the man was already beating himself up over not being able to catch the culprit.

Tao Longyue's physician didn't like uncooperative patients like him and scolded the young captain, "I've never seen such a troublemaker like you, ready to run out of the hospital before you could even get off the surgery bed! Let me tell you here, that knife almost hit your spleen. If we had to remove your spleen, you wouldn't be able to do manual labor for the rest of your life, let alone be a cop on the frontlines!"

"How close is almost?" Duan Licheng spoke up. He had just finished another surgery and passed by to check up on Tao Longyue. Tao Longyue lifted his head up, then turned his eyes to glance at his own doctor. His physician looked almost the same age as Duan Licheng and was quite clean looking, but looked like an ugly duckling when standing next to the neuro-surgeon. Even the long lab coat couldn't save the poor man's looks.

"It's..." the doctor didn't expect Duan Licheng to be here and stuttered, unable to answer.

Duan Licheng's expression grew stringent. "Medical professionals cannot afford even a millimeter of error margin when it comes to treating our patients."

The physician said awkwardly, "I'm just concerned for his well-being, and if anything happens after he gets dispatched before the suggested time, the responsibility would fall back on the hospital."

"They can hold me accountable if anything happens. We can't delay Captain Tao's work in capturing the criminal." Duan Licheng smiled and then shot a glance at Tao Longyue, who was staring back at him like a pleading child on the bed. "Besides, it's not a severe injury. His life isn't in danger."

The primary physical left the room in defeat, but his complaint echoed down the hallway as he walked away, "Just a dude who came back from the U.S., who does he think he is?!"

Tao Longyue sat up from his bed when there were only two of them left in the hospital room and asked, concerned, "What happened to the girl that was saved, is she alright?"

"Most of it is soft tissue injuries, not severe," Duan Licheng said with a frown. "But she suffered strong psychological damage and refused further medical treatment. She would scream if anyone touched her at first, but now she's a little more stable."

"And she didn't say who the man who hurt her was?" Tao Longyue was regretful and thought he should have run faster that night. At such a young age of fourteen to fifteen, the young woman had already been violated. He couldn't imagine how traumatizing the experience was for her.

"I don't think it's a good time to ask her about these things right now," Duan Licheng said. "However, she's been talking to herself and repeating the same phrase right now."

"What is it?"

"Red dress."

Captain Tao was ready to follow up with another question when a sudden commotion arose from outside. It was a swarm of reporters who had somehow found out that the police rescued a survivor. They all arrived with the same overbearing energy outside the hospital, chanting something about how the public deserves to be informed. The case of the serial murder was grabbing too much attention from all sides. Everyone battled to get the latest scoop on the case.

The commotion was loud, almost enough to be mistaken for an earthquake from inside the hospital. Tao Longyue felt his head boiling with rage as he struggled to get out of bed.

Duan Licheng raised a hand to stop him and said, "I'll go check it out first."

"Young women are too afraid to walk outside at night now! Three victims have already been found dead, but the police still don't have a clue about the culprit's motives and the connection between these victims. The killer is still roaming free before the eyes of the police—can we say this is a grave failure of protecting the safety of our citizens from the police department?"

The female reporter leading this army was from one of the most critical news channels in the country, the Eastern Eye Witness. The news outlet was known for their sharp and direct commentaries that didn't beat around the bush. Other reporters joined in support of her, hoping to pressure the law enforcement teams to obtain more information on the case.

"We've already filed a report for medical disruption." A powerful and authoritative man's voice rang out and silenced the crowd.

Duan Licheng walked out of the hospital room toward the crowd of reporters outside. The nurses and patients who had gathered around the commotion instinctively backed off to make way for the neurosurgeon.

"Unauthorized stay at a medical center and disruptive

social gatherings on public property are severely affecting our work as medical professionals." Knowing that it was easiest to take down a whole army by attacking its commander, Duan Licheng stood before the female reporter and gave a courteous nod. He said rather provocatively, "As an organizer of such unlawful activities, you may face a sentence between three to seventeen years under the laws of this country."

The crowd completely fell silent at these words. Among them were new media and private reporters; many of them didn't even have a proper license and simply joined in to get a scoop on their own. The same crowd who surrounded the nurses and doctors confidently less than a minute ago noticed the powerful aura around this neurosurgeon and quickly backed down.

The female reporter was from one of the biggest news outlets in the country and held a license as a professional journalist. She didn't back down and instead fought back, "I'm a journalist, I have the right to request information and conduct investigations on important cases to accurately report to the public. Especially at a time like this where citizens live in fear of their safety, they have the right to know about any and all updates regarding the case."

"All lawful rights are contradictory to inherent freedom." Duan Licheng locked eyes with the reporter and spoke firmly, "In the cases of reporting an event involving the law, especially a case that is still currently under investigation, reporters must adhere to the rule of conducting interviews without disrupting the investigation process of the police. If your report exposes key evidence and intel regarding the case that directly affects the eventual arrest of the suspect, you can expect at least some sort of legal consequences, even if you don't get pinned for a criminal act."

The female reporter's face grew pale at these words, only to see the doctor handsomely give her another bow and smile before adding, "Of course, I'm sure they will be a little more lenient to a beautiful woman like yourself."

Duan Licheng turned to the rest of the crowd gathered at the hospital before he could see the flustered face of the woman and said, "You all can wait in the meeting room in the hospital. With the condition of not exposing any important details and the victim's private information, our hospital will announce the current status of the survivor and injured police officer shortly."

The candy and stick method worked; at least the media didn't return empty-handed and dispersed from the lobby.

After taking care of the noisy reporters, Duan Licheng returned to Tao Longyue's room.

Tao Longyue let out a sigh of relief and shook his head. "Journalists these days are getting out of hand. Who knows if they're even legit or just out there to get clicks."

"I actually think it's better to have more curious journalists like them." Duan Licheng smiled and said, "But of course, they must also be mindful of the method they use to gather information."

Recalling that Xie Lanshan had once mentioned he was at odds with Duan Licheng, Captain Tao had been ready to back his buddy unconditionally and stay away from this shady doctor. After this episode, however, the last bit of negative impression he had of this doctor finally vanished. He looked at Duan Licheng and asked, "You seem to be quite acquainted with Shen Liufei."

Duan Licheng nodded. "We've known each other for many years."

Captain Tao was an honest man who didn't hesitate to act friendly toward anyone he admired and admitted bluntly, "I'm not too fond of that guy, to be honest. For someone who also came back from the States, you're a much cooler guy."

Duan Licheng narrowed his eyes slightly as if he was tracing back his memories before saying, "That's because you don't know what he has been through."

Tao Longyue was surprised. "What kind of tragic backstory could a rich boy like him possibly have?"

"His current father is actually his mentor in art. The boy's talent in art caught the old man's attention, and they later moved to the States together because the old man didn't have a son of his own."

"What about his biological parents?"

"His entire family was murdered when he was only fourteen." After a moment of silence, Duan Licheng continued with a grave face, "Not even his eight-year-old little brother managed to survive, and his mother was also recorded as deceased after she went missing. He was the only one who survived the massacre because he was out of town during the murder."

(v)

The girl who was saved had long black hair and fair skin, looking to be around only fourteen to fifteen years old or even younger. Due to suffering a horrific psychological trauma, she didn't speak and only stared blankly while on the hospital bed. Aside from "red dress," she spoke no other words. It would be too cruel to force her to recall the face of the criminal suspect in this state, so Shen Liufei's forensic sketch project was also put on hold.

The girl feared anyone who touched her body, especially her lower body, so she only received very minimal physical checkups. Fortunately, her wounds healed quickly. She was cautious of all strangers aside from Tao Longyue and Su Mansheng, who saved her from the horrors of the murderer. The girl would sometimes give intermittent responses in front of the couple, and rush into their embrace in fear of being harmed by strangers again.

It was impossible to identify the victim and contact her family, which gave Tao Longyue a bit of a headache. Leaving her in the hospital could mean potentially exposing her to harassment from shady journalists, but there was also nowhere else for her to go outside the hospital.

Finally, Song Qilian gave a solution. Considering that Tao Longyue was still in recovery and a man, it would be best to temporarily leave the girl in Su Mansheng's care. After she became more stabilized mentally and felt less defensive toward strangers, they would send her off for therapy.

In order to make things easier, Song Qilian nicknamed the girl Xiao Qun. She even offered to stay at Su Mansheng's place for a while to help care for the young victim. Of course, she had some ulterior motives; she wasn't able to face Xie Lanshan as she was now and didn't want to deal with Liu Mingfang's aggressive pursuit. She needed to escape these tiresome dramas, even briefly, and calm her mind.

Tao Longyue was relieved after everything was settled and decided to stay at the hospital a little longer for his injury.

Just as he stared in boredom and loneliness at the ceiling in his hospital room, Xie Lanshan came to visit.

"Damn bro, it's already been four days since I've been laying in the same bed and you only now remembered to pay me a visit?!" Tao Longyue jumped up from his bed as soon as he saw his old friend arrive and picked up an apple from the basket to throw at the visitor.

Xie Lanshan raised a hand swiftly and caught the apple in his hand, then rubbed the fruit on his shirt and took a bite. He walked toward the injured man and sat on the bed without hesitation, then said as he ate his apple, "Just checking to see if you're dead or not."

"You still mad about how we locked you up last time? Be a man, bro, take that stick out of your asshole like this and get over yourself!" Tao Longyue raised a fist to punch Xie Lanshan on the chest, then quickly turned and looked at the latter. "No wait, you're a bottom—Shen Liufei probably pulled that out of your hole already."

Xie Lanshan almost choked on the apple and laughed, then said after he cleared his throat, "Can't you just pretend you're still an ignorant straight dude? I'm not used to you being such a damn gossiper."

There were no grudges between brothers. Tao Longyue laughed and playfully gave another punch to Xie Lanshan's shoulder.

Xie Lanshan asked about his buddy's injury, then quickly changed the topic back to the case after he confirmed Tao Longyue was fine.

"So, what exactly happened that night? How could you have let the culprit run?" The journalist had a reason to be upset, and Xie Lanshan was also surprised. Tao Longyue's physical combat skills were top-notch even among peers in the Municipal Bureau. It was one thing to let the culprit go during a chase, but how could he have possibly lost the target and gotten injured after being engaged in a brawl? The culprit sounded like an Olympic medalist in martial arts.

"Ah, you know..." Tao Longyue wanted to say that it was Su Mansheng's scream that distracted him but quickly stopped himself after realizing it was wrong to put the blame on his girl-friend. He bit down on his lip and said, "Just take it as my hubris got the best of me. I'll take this as a lesson learned and I swear next time I'll catch that bastard!"

"But weren't you and Doctor Su—" Xie Lanshan wanted to follow up, unconvinced of this explanation, only to be inter-rupted by another visitor.

Su Mansheng opened the door and walked into the room. She lifted a faint smile as soon as she saw Xie Lanshan sitting by the bed and asked, "Is Officer Xie back on the case now?"

Despite having come to an agreement with Shen Liufei to keep their speculations to themselves for now, Xie Lanshan couldn't help but be reminded of the image of the girl in red twenty years ago as soon as he met Su Mansheng's eyes. He gave her a smile and attempted to test her. "Yeah, just got back from Cangnan and Yuncheng. We went to the city hospital in Cangnan and that place in Yuncheng... What was it called again?" Xie Lanshan rubbed his chin with his fingers and then suddenly exclaimed, "That nunnery place!"

"It's not a nunnery place, it's an actual convent." Su Mansheng corrected him, "Yuncheng Holy Mother's Convent."

"Right, that, but nunneries and convents are practically the same." Xie Lanshan nodded as if he was a humble student. He then lifted an eyebrow and asked, "You've been there before?"

Su Mansheng responded without a change of expression, "Don't you know already?"

She didn't deny nor confess, which proved that she wasn't afraid, but certainly had something to hide. Xie Lanshan's smile grew deeper, but his eyes remained sharp as he said, "Only a coward would choose to harm others who are weaker than them for revenge. It's not something an honorable queen would do, it's too dirty."

Tao Longyue grew even more puzzled as he listened to the conversation and grabbed onto Xie Lanshan to question, "What the heck are you guys talking about, how come I don't understand a word?"

Su Mansheng had no intention to continue this conversation and turned to Tao Longyue. "I've taken Xiao Qun home already. You can sit back and rest up for now."

Xie Lanshan smiled and followed up with his own question, "Who's Xiao Qun?"

Tao Longyue answered, "The little girl that I saved."

Su Mansheng didn't seem like she intended to linger in the room any longer and left after saying she still needed to take care of the victim.

The two men sat in the room. The sun was already shifting west; the glow passed through the window softly like a warm ray of light that peeked out from a closing stage. One of the men's handsome faces turned against the light until he was completely in the shadows.

Xie Lanshan noticed there were painkillers by Tao Longyue's bedside and tried to say nonchalantly to his friend, "Hey Tao, take some painkillers. You might need them later."

Tao Longyue's sharp senses told him something was wrong as he asked, "What did you manage to find?"

Xie Lanshan's expression remained stern as he explained, "Your old man had a mentor by the name of Zhu Mingwu. He was involved with a huge case 25 years ago that took them four whole years to solve: the Cangnan Serial Rape-Murder. The eleven corpses of young women found back then died the exact same way the three victims have died in our case right now. Their mouths had been sewn shut, skin peeled, and they suffered horrific torture before death."

Xie Lanshan handed Tao Longyue some files on the case. The Captain skimmed through the first two pages and exclaimed in horror and anger, "This bastard sure is fucking twisted!"

Xie Lanshan continued, "But there's one thing that's different. The victims found twenty years ago were actually raped; foreign bodily fluids were found in their lower bodies, and not just injuries caused by shoving hard inanimate objects into their private areas. So, Shen Liufei and I have a hypothesis; the culprit 25 years ago had a motive rooted in twisted sexual desires, but the case now is driven by hatred."

Tao Longyue nodded in agreement but asked, puzzled, "Even people in our bureau nowadays have barely heard of the Cangnan case, so what kind of person would suddenly think of replicating the same crimes 25 years later using the exact same torturous methods? Are you saying that Kong Xiangping has family still alive today?"

"Kong Xiangping was around 40 when he committed those crimes. His parents died when he was young and he never married, so he had no family."

"Then who else could it be?" Captain Tao rubbed his chin and fell into deep thought.

"The truth is, when the culprit committed suicide 21 years ago, an 11-year-old victim girl was rescued by the police." Xie Lanshan hesitated, a difficult expression surfaced on his face. It took a long while before he finally continued, "And we both know this girl."

Tao Longyue's eyes widened and froze. Xie Lanshan added, "Look at the last page of the files."

Tao Longyue quickly flipped to the end. A folded piece of paper fell out of the file folder. He opened it up to see a portrait of Su Mansheng.

It was only during this moment that Tao Longyue finally

understood what Xie Lanshan meant and what that cryptic conversation with Su Mansheng earlier was. He was dumbfounded for about ten seconds before he suddenly raised a fist and howled, "Who the hell cares if she has a tragic backstory? I care about her, it doesn't matter! What year do you think we're living in? Do I look like I care if she's still a virgin or not?!"

"You know that's not what I'm talking about!" Xie Lanshan didn't return a hit, knowing that his friend would give this reaction. He said patiently, "I need you to answer me truthfully; where was Su Mansheng the night we were all celebrating at the bar? And that night when you fought that culprit, did Su Mansheng call out to help that killer escape?"

"Fuck you, Xie Lanshan!" Tao Longyue didn't respond to the questions and only threw more punches, completely unfazed that his injury opened up again at the violent act. He cursed and shot out fists like a madman, "Fuck you! Xie Lanshan, I swear, screw you! Shut the fuck up!"

"You dare fucking curse at me again?" Xie Lanshan was also enraged and pinned an out-of-control Tao Longyue back onto the bed, forcing the latter down with all of his might. He couldn't stand seeing his good friend suffer so painfully. His eyes also warmed up, but his voice remained stern as he said, "Calm yourself down, damn it, can you still call yourself a policeman?!"

The injury reopened and fresh blood seeped through the patient's gown. Tao Longyue attempted to crawl up, only to feel his energy draining rapidly. By the end, his vision was blurred, his lips paled, and every last bit of energy dried out.

He could only cry with an ugly face as he yelled, "Who wouldn't want to hide their traumatic past? You think Mansheng's the only one who keeps secrets? Why don't you go ask your Shen Liufei about how his whole family was murdered?"

It was Xie Lanshan's turn to be baffled—that almost brutally cold aura, the suppression that could only be released through brawls, even those hints of hesitation, the melancholy and pain that seeped within the man like salt dissolving in seawater—everything seemed to have an answer now.

After a few seconds, Xie Lanshan loosened his grip to allow Tao Longyue to crawl back up. He then turned and left the hospital.

(vi)

At first, Xie Lanshan was upset that Tao Longyue revealed Shen Liufei's story to him, feeling as if he had been lied to. But after a night of thinking it through, most of the anger had transformed into heartache by dawn. He agreed with Tao Longyue; everyone deserved a quiet and personal place in their hearts that shouldn't be disturbed by anyone else.

The temperature dropped rapidly in the latter half of November. Xie Lanshan walked out of the bathroom, fresh and clean, immediately greeted by a tempting aroma from the kitchen that quickly filled the house.

Ever since Uncle Tan had been sent back to where his crime took place, Xie Lanshan couldn't stomach any other pancakes from street vendors in town. He lived off stealing Tao Longyue's breakfast, saving both time and money with easy-to-heat food. He would never have imagined that Shen Liufei would wake up early to make breakfast for him.

The smoked beef and sunny-side-up eggs were ready to be served; only the French toast was left to be grilled. Shen Liufei poured cream into the egg and began beating it with long chopsticks. Xie Lanshan's gaze fell onto those long fingers that held the chopsticks. They were white and delicate, and every gesture had an elegant air to them.

Those certainly were the hands of an artist that emitted creativity and aestheticism. Xie Lanshan stared carefully at Shen Liufei's hands and then shifted his gaze back onto the man's face; the artist seemed to always have a layer of thin ice over his face that froze all expressions.

It was impossible to imagine such a sophisticated man could have a horrific and tragic past.

Xie Lanshan could feel his heart warm as he looked at this man carefully preparing breakfast for him. He loved picking out the finer details in everyday life that left traces of their love, even if they were as trivial as a gentle touch.

Shen Liufei turned to look at Xie Lanshan and noticed the latter was in a daze, then asked, "Are you planning on visiting Captain Tao today?"

Judging by Xie Lanshan's gloomy face yesterday, he could guess that the cop told Tao Longyue about Su Mansheng's potential involvement in the case. He also guessed that Tao Longyue was upset with the revelation and the two had likely gotten into a fight.

Xie Lanshan didn't respond and instead walked toward Shen Liufei with his arm out, then embraced the artist tightly.

The two men were around the same height. The warm sensation of their skin touching felt especially comforting. Shen Liufei was rather unfazed and asked with little emotion, "What happened?"

Xie Lanshan lowered his head and pressed his lips to Shen Liufei's earlobe as if he was going to whisper some words of love, only to bite down like a monster.

There was a hint of scolding with the bite. Shen Liufei frowned in pain, but his arms around Xie Lanshan's waist didn't loosen up and instead wrapped tighter.

Xie Lanshan finally let go after venting out his frustration.

He then turned to gently press his tongue along the injury he left on the artist's ear.

Shen Liufei remained unfazed, as if he really was unaffected by this gesture of affection. Xie Lanshan chuckled and whispered into his ear, "I'll make you mine sooner or later, your past and future. I can wait, I'm patient."

By the time Shen Liufei finished making breakfast, Xie Lanshan took out a paper bag and packed the toast and beef to eat on the way to work. He'd already exposed his hand, so now he had to wait and see how Su Mansheng cooperated. Regardless of what people thought, she was still the only person who was familiar with the details of the case two decades ago.

The winter sun was also strangely chilling as it hung above the skyscrapers of the city, almost like a full moon at day. Xie Lanshan was in a good mood. He strutted through the streets and found the unique scenery through the naked trees quite a treat.

He walked into the hospital, gaze immediately caught by a noise as soon as he stepped out of the elevator. He turned to see a young doctor run into a nurse; upon closer look, this young doctor was that same person who wanted to give a romantic confession at Shen Liufei's residence—Qiao Hui.

The latter also noticed him and gave the cop a smile as he helped the nurse pick up the medication that dropped to the ground.

Xie Lanshan walked toward the man and greeted him, "What a coincidence, Doctor Qiao."

Qiao Hui also seemed quite happy to see him and said, "I'm interning here. I just finished checking up the rooms with my director, so I have some free time right now."

The nurse picked up her medication and apologized to

Qiao Hui, explaining that it was her fault for not being careful, and ran into him despite knowing the doctor had an injury on his wrist.

Xie Lanshan lifted an eyebrow and asked Qiao Hui, "You hurt your hand?"

Qiao Hui smiled and covered his left wrist. "Twisted my wrist while I was moving."

Xie Lanshan recalled that Qiao Hui had just moved into the residential building, then after carefully listening to his Mandarin, realized there was an accent in the doctor's voice he didn't catch before. Xie Lanshan asked, "You're from the South?"

He certainly didn't look like a Southerner.

Qiao Hui nodded and said, "I studied clinical medicine back in my hometown and then came to Hanhai for my Master's."

Xie Lanshan smiled and said, "I always assumed doctors are all cool and calm, sometimes even too aloof and cold. I'm surprised to see how much of a romantic you are. How did the confession go last time?"

"Not good." Qiao Hui shook his head sheepishly and said, "She says I'm too immature and friendzoned me."

"There are many people out there, don't give up." Just as Xie Lanshan wanted to end the conversation, he looked up and saw the nurse from earlier walk out proudly from a dressing room in a new outfit.

Perhaps she had just finished her shift, but she removed her uniform and donned a beautiful bright red dress that complimented her long black hair.

Dressing up could really change a person; this average-looking young woman from earlier had become a beautiful young model in this outfit. Another nurse complimented her, "I've never seen you dress like this, you look great."

Xie Lanshan noticed that Qiao Hui turned his head. His eyes followed the young woman like a bright spotlight, his expression obsessive and filled with adoration. It wasn't until the woman left that he finally pulled himself back to reality and said to Xie Lanshan, "You're here to visit Captain Tao in room 3, right? His forensic doctor girlfriend didn't come in last night to stay with him."

"You know his girlfriend is a forensic scientist?" Xie Lanshan was a little shocked.

"We've chatted a bit. I won't keep you around too much longer." Qiao Hui smiled and left.

Remembering that Tao Longyue's injury had just been restitched, and he had to suffer some violent punching, Xie Lanshan felt a little sorry for his friend and decided to give the man a break.

He walked in with a mouthful of sweet talk, ready to call him "Taotao," "sweetheart," and other disgusting words. Putting on an annoying smile, he said, "Sorry sweetheart, forgive me."

Yet there was nobody on the bed.

(vii)

Tao Longyue returned to the scene of the crime where he saved the little girl, his stitches still intact. After such a horrific event, the construction progress for the parking structure was temporarily halted. Outside the wired fence was a layer of cordon tape that stood out brightly amongst the tall trees.

It was 11 A.M. on a weekday; the street right outside the crime scene was empty. The area was close to the Zhongxi business district, the TV station headquarters less than a kilometer away. This location where the small park used to be seemed to keep a dark secret within the busy city.

Tao Longyue walked toward the area where he brawled with the killer, hoping to find more evidence he had missed. He squatted and stared at every corner on the ground, like a diligent and sharp police dog. His injury was still throbbing in pain, but it was nothing compared to the frustration in his heart. Xie Lanshan was clear: he suspected Su Mansheng was acquainted with the culprit and perhaps even an accomplice. And, of course, the captain himself had his own suspicion.

He had searched everywhere the police had looked but found not a single piece of new evidence. Tao Longyue frowned and attempted to recall the details of that night he saved Xiao Qun.

He could have taken the culprit down that night if Su Mansheng didn't rush over with the girl, if Su Mansheng didn't cry out. He didn't have time to think about the situation that night with the knife in his stomach, but now that he could think with a rational mind, Su Mansheng's sudden panic at the time was certainly unexpected and abrupt.

Tao Longyue let out a small sigh and stood back up. He looked off into the distance, and his gaze landed on the tantalizing sign of a restaurant. It was where he went with Su Mansheng the night of the crime, Le Goff's French cuisine restaurant.

It was almost time for lunch, and Tao Longyue made his way to the restaurant.

The restaurant offered an economy lunch special on their menu, attracting many white-collared workers from around the business district during their lunch break.

Tao Longyue saw a familiar face as soon as he stepped in—

the female reporter from Eastern Eye Witness who headed the commotion in Puren hospital a few days ago. At her table sat three young people, including herself, all with a name tag from the news station around their necks. It was clear they were out for a break with colleagues during their off-hours, like any other workers.

Tao Longyue sat in a corner. The lunch special set was quite a luxurious full three-course meal. There weren't a lot of choices, but he also wasn't in the mood to choose, randomly selecting something that looked decent and waited for his food.

Tao Longyue was never a picky eater and only cared about filling his stomach. In contrast, that female journalist seemed to be a difficult customer. Almost as soon as their order was served, she called the waiter over and complained, lifting her thin eyebrows. "This foie gras doesn't taste as it does normally. Did you guys get a new chef?"

The waiter recognized this regular customer and quickly explained, "I apologize, Director Hao, but Chef Le Goff accidentally burned his hand, so he wasn't able to cook personally. However, he is still in the kitchen instructing others on how to cook."

Reporter Hao was still dissatisfied and said, "Then you should've told me earlier, this is cheating your customer."

The waiter responded with a courteous smile as he continued to shower the customer with praises and pleasant words, almost on par with a professional food critic.

Tao Longyue lowered his head to eat, unwilling to be bothered by the scene the reporter was causing. Just as he thought today was another average day, he suddenly lifted his head and widened his eyes in realization.

He injured the killer's wrist during the brawl with that man. He didn't hold back that night, so even if no bones were broken, the culprit must still have a bruise that wouldn't easily heal up.

Before he could ponder further, Tao Longyue stood up and walked toward the back kitchen. Le Goff was instructing other chefs on cooking, then saw Tao Longyue walk in as soon as he lifted his head. The chef howled, "A kitchen is a sacred place in a restaurant. Who said you can just walk in like this?"

Tao Longyue noticed the chef's left wrist was wrapped in bandages and shot back, "What happened to your hand?"

Le Goff responded with his accented Chinese, "What's so weird about a chef accidentally burning himself?"

Tao Longyue refused to believe him and took a step forward, then said coldly, "A burn? More like a sprain. Take the bandage off. I need to check."

Of course, Le Goff didn't comply. Yet before he could voice his objection, Tao Longyue already charged at him and grabbed onto his wrist, ready to forcefully check the injury.

Le Goff also worked out daily and did boxing as a hobby, so he immediately returned a punch as soon as he dodged Tao Longyue's tackle.

The two men quickly entered a brawl, fighting from the kitchen out into the restaurant. Sounds of fists exchanging chaotically rang throughout the building.

Tao Longyue might be injured and his punches were not as heavy as they normally were, but he was still professionally trained in close-range combat. He quickly got the upper hand in the fistfight and kicked a leg out during an opening that tripped the tall French chef. As the chef laid on the ground, the captain kneed the man down and fully captured him.

Le Goff was pinned to the ground; he panted heavily like an angered ox and cursed with his reddened face. Tao Longyue couldn't understand what he was saying, but he reasonably guessed it was curses in French.

Tao Longyue ripped the bandage off Le Goff's left risk, desperate to find out what happened, only to respond in shock as soon as he saw the injury.

There was no bruise that indicated a sprain—it was a real burn.

Someone already called the cops. Tao Longyue, Le Goff, and even the female reporter who suffered collateral damage during the brawl were all brought back to the Municipal Bureau.

Tao Jun was still recovering in the hospital, so Liu Yanbo personally dealt with the management of the bureau. He got the gist of the situation from subordinate reports and also knew that the culprit was replicating the Cangnan Serial Murder case from 25 years ago. He pointed at Tao Longyue's nose and scolded, "Not reporting back when you found new evidence, conducting your own private investigation, and even beating someone up during it? Do you want to be transferred to the traffic department too?"

Xie Lanshan was also being scolded by Chief Liu, standing beside his buddy with his head hanging.

Su Mansheng walked over from behind the crowd. She was here to let Xiao Qun point out the culprit. With Xiao Qun's witness account, Le Goff certainly wasn't the killer from the night of the crime.

"The news station is right next to that restaurant. Think about how many reporters and journalists are there. Especially that reporter from Eastern Eye Witness, Hao Sijing—even if you don't care about your own reputation, think about the Municipal Bureau's reputation!" Liu Yanbo rarely scolded with such a loud voice; he was extremely upset. "Even if the culprit was wearing a mask, his eyes were still exposed. Can't you even tell if he's a foreigner or not from that?"

"I... was too rash and forgot about that..." Tao Longyue kept his head down the entire time, unable to look Liu Yanbo in the eye. He pressed a hand on his injury, fresh and warm blood staining the palm of his hand. He never stayed still to let the injury heal, then let it open up once again. Tao Longyue turned his head and glanced at Su Mansheng, then said with his teeth clenched, "I really can't solve this case. Just send down the punishment. I'll take whatever is necessary."

"Stop picking fights. You think you can shoulder everything?" Liu Yanbo was furious at this little rascal and questioned, "Don't we have a direction for investigation already? Now that we know the culprit is replicating the Cangnan Serial Murder, then the key person will now be the surviving little girl Xiao Man from 21 years ago. Go and find her!"

Tao Longyue pressed his lips together and didn't speak.

"What about you?" Liu Yanbo turned toward Xie Lanshan and said, "Didn't you go to Cangnan to investigate already? What did you find?"

Xie Lanshan noticed Tao Longyue shaking in pain as if he was desperately trying to hold himself back. He didn't respond and thought it was best if Tao Longyue said it himself.

"Just what is up with you two?" Liu Yanbo noticed the suspicious hesitation between the two and questioned in rage, "Do you guys still want to keep your job or not?!"

"I know who Xiao Man is," Su Mansheng's voice interrupted.

Everyone turned to her, including reporter Hao Sijing, who was ready to leave after giving her witness account. The reporter stared at the doctor with bright and sharp eyes, like a bald eagle waiting to prey on rotten flesh.

Su Mansheng's gaze scanned all the excited faces watching her, and with an exceptionally calm tone she said, "I am Xiao Man."

The Perfect Victim

Su Mansheng entered the questioning room as a witness. Because the case involved some personal details, with Su Mansheng's permission, Song Qilian also joined the questioning as a psychologist, in case the discussion triggered more traumatic memories for the witness.

Tao Longyue stayed away from the room and allowed Xie Lanshan and Ding Li to conduct the questioning. Xie Lanshan did his best to maintain objectivity and professionalism when speaking to Su Mansheng to avoid triggering terrible memories. He asked, "Can you still remember the situation when you were locked in the basement many years ago?"

Su Mansheng seemed almost unaffected by her past trauma; no sign of emotions surfaced as she answered honestly and calmly. She recalled the culprit had a very obsessive fascination with women who had long black hair and wore red dresses. He would collect these girls as if he was collecting dolls and lock them up in the dirty and smelly basement in his home. Then, after a period of torture and sexual assault he would kill them all one by one.

Xie Lanshan asked, "How long were you trapped inside that basement?"

Su Mansheng said, "A month, three months, or more. I can't remember."

Xie Lanshan asked, "How many other girls were locked inside the basement with you at the time?"

Su Mansheng answered, "There were seven at most. Some were adults of about 20-something-year old and younger teenage girls. I was probably the youngest there—but of course, all of the girls died."

Xie Lanshan continued, "Aside from Kong Xiangping, who had committed suicide before the police could arrest him, were there any other criminal suspects in Cangnan during that time?"

Su Mansheng seemed to hesitate a little before responding, "No."

Xie Lanshan caught that moment of hesitation and pressed his eyebrows together slightly, then asked, "Do you remember how Kong Xiangping died?"

Su Mansheng didn't stutter this time and responded coolly, "When Officer Zhu took me out of that house, I saw that man lying in the bathtub. He had slit his wrists. There were three white candles lit beside the bathtub with a bloodied doll, and the whole floor was covered in his blood. I heard from Officer Zhu later that Kong Xiangping was heavily intoxicated before he committed suicide, perhaps scared that his evil deeds were about to be exposed."

The session went by smoothly. Su Mansheng was very cooperative and confessed anything she remembered, admitting she didn't remember some details. Like a steadily twirling spinning top, she spoke as if it was someone else's story, completely unaffected and emotionless. According to Song

Qilian, this was an abnormal response from a professional standpoint.

Right before wrapping up, Xie Lanshan asked her one last question, "Why were you the only one left alive when everyone else died?"

A strange expression flashed across Su Mansheng's face for an instant. It took her a while before she recovered. She said in an airy tone, "Because I conceded to him and served him. I chose to yield to him when he violated me, time and time again."

Xie Lanshan didn't return to the violent crimes unit office after he left the bright and clean questioning room. Instead, he found a window nearby and stood dully as he smoked in silence. Song Qilian walked out along with him and noticed the usual lively face was painted with a layer of melancholy. She knew he was worried about Tao Longyue and wanted to console him, but couldn't get the words out of her mouth.

Xie Lanshan turned around first and noticed Song Qilian standing behind him. He quickly extinguished the fire on his cigarette and smiled. "Sorry for smoking around you."

Song Qilian shook her head and walked up to Xie Lanshan, also leaning on the window beside him and feeling the cold winter breeze through the opening.

After a few minutes of silence, Xie Lanshan lowered his gaze and said apologetically, "Sorry, I'm a cop. There are some questions I needed to ask."

Song Qilian knew he was afraid that the mention of the past case harmed Su Mansheng and said, "You've done well enough already."

Xie Lanshan turned to look at Song Qilian and grinned with an eyebrow lifted. "That's certainly a compliment from you, don't forget that I'm a violent patient who didn't pass his psychological assessment."

Xie Lanshan didn't intend to scold her by bringing it up; it just slipped without thinking. Yet Song Qilian felt her body heat up suddenly, her face and eyes red as she whimpered, "Sorry, I didn't know that report would cause so much trouble for you."

Xie Lanshan's gaze strayed outside the window, past the Municipal Bureau's track field, through the layered trees, the buildings of the city, and finally past the smoky clouds in the sky. Recalling the deceased Zhuo Tian and that nameless 8-year-old boy, he shook his head and sighed. "Maybe you were right all along."

His voice was a little wistful, gaze soft and almost clear. It suddenly reminded Song Qilian of Xie Lanshan, her Xie Lanshan.

"A'Lan, I..."

The words never made it out. Song Qilian noticed that the hint of sorrow and warmth deep within Xie Lanshan's gaze vanished—the man's lips curled up, his eyes glowed. She followed the direction of his gaze and noticed Shen Liufei at the receiving end of that passionate and adoring look.

About two hours later, Su Mansheng left the Municipal Bureau with Xiao Qun after she completed all procedures.

Someone blocked her off as she stepped out of the door.

Reporter Hao Sijing had been waiting by the front gate of the Hanhai City Municipal Bureau. She was a thirsty journalist that craved these sorts of explosive news stories. She used her powerful network within the industry to uncover details about the Cangnan Serial Murder case, and upon reading it through, decided that she could not let such a big exclusive scoop slide.

She chewed on her already stale mint chewing gum, then spat it out into the wrapper as soon as she saw Su Mansheng and tossed it on the ground. She first stood in front of the little girl and pointed a cellphone camera in front of her face, asking directly about the situation of her assault. Su Mansheng naturally pulled Xiao Qun back behind her and stood in front of the camera.

Hao Sijing's eyes lit up, and she continued talking, "You're the only survivor of the Cangnan Serial Murder case, Xiao Man, right? You were only eleven at the time. How come you were the only one that survived after all those adult women died?"

Su Mansheng walked away with Xiao Qun's hand in hers, uninterested in answering the same question she had just been asked earlier.

It almost seemed like the victim developed a superiority complex, and this aloof attitude angered Hao Sijing. The reporter became more determined to dig down to the core of this case. She pestered and asked, "So can I assume that you survived because you were an accomplice, that you helped that twisted culprit in harming those girls back then?"

Su Mansheng turned around to look at the reporter. Her pressed lips trembled slightly, expression resolute and powerful.

The little girl Xiao Qun wasn't fully recovered from her traumatic experience, still unable to speak due to shock. She clung to Su Mansheng's side—the shared trauma connected the two like magnets. She might be small and weak, naïve and young, but she also stared with anger at this awful and toxic reporter.

Hao Sijing noticed the gaze and leaned in to pat the little girl's hair, attempting to explain her good intention, "Don't worry little girl, I'm just doing work—"

Su Mansheng lifted the corner of her lips coldly and interrupted her, "You're just forcefully probing into other people's private lives to satisfy your own selfish and toxic desires."

"Say what you want, but I believe you still have secrets. I believe what I said earlier was already infinitely close to the truth of the story." Hao Sijing smiled arrogantly and declared war on the cold queen before her. "I will request my higher-ups create a special program for this case and slowly dig out all of your skeletons."

The reporter walked away with her head held high. Su Mansheng let Xiao Qun slide into the passenger's seat as she drove them away from the Municipal Bureau.

About two streets away from the bureau, Su Mansheng suddenly turned the steering wheel and parked her car on the street side. Like a snapped rose, a heavy shadow suddenly covered all the light in her eyes. She lowered her head and buried her face in the steering wheel.

Xiao Qun stared at her in confusion from the side. Su Mansheng remained in that position for a long while, her shoulders trembled slightly—unsure if she was crying or laughing.

From Su Mansheng's witness account, red dresses were an important clue to solving this case.

Among the three corpses discovered, none of the victims wore a red skirt. So even though Xiao Qun had also repeated the same words, the police had never considered this as a common characteristic and important piece of evidence shared by the victims.

Because he was once a suspect of the crime, Xie Lanshan paid particular attention to the first victim, Luo Xin's outfit and appearance. He said with a frown, "I remember the first victim was wearing a pink blouse and a black long dress, not a pure red dress."

Shen Liufei pondered for a little and said, "Can we consider this possibility instead? Perhaps the culprit didn't decide to commit the crime because he saw the victim wearing a red dress; instead, he happened to become acquainted with the victim dressed in that outfit by chance. Then, after a brief period of stalking, he finally committed the crime—and that's why the victims were all dressed differently when they were killed."

Xie Lanshan received an epiphany from this hypothesis and quickly followed up with, "Three murders within such a short period of time shows that the culprit didn't spend too much time stalking and investigating his victims. Therefore, the chances of it all being an indiscriminate murder are significantly reduced. If we investigate the last time the victims wore a red dress out and the people they came in contact with in that outfit, we could narrow down the suspects."

Shen Liufei nodded and said, "Especially Luo Xin, the first victim of the crime. She was a freelancer that rarely left her residence; she would not be in contact with many people often."

The mist dispersed, and a direction of investigation suddenly became clear. Liu Yanbo ordered, "Pull up all surveillance footage from the building Luo Xin lived in and track down every person she came in contact with the day she wore a red dress. Let's see if we can catch anything suspicious!"

Shen Liufei's residential building was heavy with surveillance cameras, thus it wasn't difficult to pull out footage from days before the crime. The camera was right outside Luo Xin's door, making it clear to see when she left her house and what she wore.

In order to save time, the footage was replayed at 16x speed. Ding Li could feel her head spin. Xiao Liang felt completely at a loss. Only Xie Lanshan and Shen Liufei focused their attention on the screen, carefully observing every detail. Xie Lanshan's eyes were already sharp, but Shen Liufei was still sharper as an experienced forensic sketch artist. The latter suddenly called out, "Here, pause for a second, please."

They rolled back the footage. Two days before the crime in the evening, they saw a young man carrying a fruit basket walk out of the elevator toward Luo Xin's residence.

Xie Lanshan called out, "It's him."

Puren Hospital intern doctor Qiao Hui. In order to confess to his female friend that night, he had already spent days going up and down to pay visits to his neighbors to help out with the lighting.

The young woman's door opened to Qiao Hui's knocking, but because of the angle of the camera, it was difficult to tell what Luo Xin was wearing inside her house. The two seemed to chat happily for a little while before Qiao Hui handed the basket of fruits to Luo Xin and left.

The young man hadn't walked off too far away, and Luo Xin poked the upper half of her body out the door. She lifted the fruit basket and said something to him with a grin, perhaps thanking the young man for the fruits.

Her long black hair draped down her back, complimenting the bright red dress she wore. In the dim light of the security camera, she shone like a bright torch of fire.

Xie Lanshan cried out, "Rats!"

He recalled the way Qiao Hui stared at the nurse that day in the hospital.

(ii)

Someone suddenly assaulted the young woman as she clocked out of work. A heavy item, like a wooden stick, struck her head from behind and she quickly lost consciousness.

In violent pain, the woman opened her eyes—to discover her mouth had been sewn shut. A dog collar hung around her neck. The leather collar had a strong rotten stench while the metal rivet painfully stabbed her skin.

The man standing before her pulled out a surgical knife and looked at her from above.

The woman shook her head desperately, wanting to beg for mercy but unable to speak. Every time she attempted to open her mouth, the thread that had sewn her mouth together would rip through her flesh, melding the taste of blood and saliva in her mouth painfully.

Qiao Hui kneeled down and shushed the girl. He wore medical vinyl gloves and gently caressed the woman's face as he said, "Stay put, don't call out. Cries will attract the police. I was almost caught last time because of it."

The woman turned her head in an attempt to dodge this sickening touch. Tears rolled down her face in fear and disgust. She couldn't fathom how such a sophisticated and kind young doctor could be such a monster.

From Qiao Hui's perspective, white-bark pine trees surrounded the area like an otherworldly forest. This was a developing high-end residential area that advertised itself as "the forest in the city," built near the large lake by the city border. The developers even planted more trees and flowers to create a green paradise within the urban cityscape.

The location was also very close to Puren Hospital. Qiao Hui loved bringing his victims to places like small parks, parking lots, or other abandoned buildings. There were too many unnoticeable corners within the city. Its people passed through helplessly like ants.

The young woman already suffered a heavy blow to her head and did not have enough energy to fight back. Because the leash was tied around her hands, she couldn't crawl up and could only attempt to wiggle her way out. Qiao Hui found this useless and unsightly attempt laughable. He kicked the woman down violently and then looked into her eyes passionately.

The image of this young woman dressed in red once again

appeared in his mind. He chuckled, glares of red flashed within his eyes—women with long black hair and a red dress were vibrant, like blooming canna flowers, dancing in flames.

Qiao Hui kneeled down and obsessively stripped the woman's clothes, violently exposing the woman's body. He held his sharp and clean surgical knife, picked out the cleanest piece of skin from the woman's body, and prepared to peel it off.

Loud dog barking suddenly rang out from outside the white-bark pines, quickly followed by sounds of rushing footsteps and motorbike engines.

Qiao Hui's expression froze; he had been discovered!

As soon as he confirmed that Qiao Hui was the culprit, Xie Lanshan immediately called the Puren Hospital and asked the nurses to contact that young woman he saw last time. But the young woman's cellphone was turned off, completely out of touch almost as soon as she left the hospital. After analyzing the locations of the crime scene in previous incidents, the Municipal Bureau narrowed down potential places and sent out rescue dogs.

The impending death forced the young woman to cry desperately for help as she forced open her sewn mouth and cried out with a bloodied taste on her tongue, "Help! Help me!"

"Over there!"

A black bike rushed out of the green forest; the spot of red at the front of the bike shone like a spark of fire amidst the darkness.

Qiao Hui immediately abandoned the girl and ran off; Shen Liufei accelerated his bike and sped to chase after him.

Qiao Hui could only run into the forest toward the lake. Yet there was a bike blocking his path in front and dogs chasing after him from behind. He was soon trapped on all fronts, forced to retreat to the lake. The young doctor clenched his teeth and lifted his leg, then jumped right into the water.

Xie Lanshan wanted to jump into the water when he saw Qiao Hui dive. Almost as soon as he ripped his shirt off, Shen Liufei grabbed him around the waist from behind.

Xie Lanshan's tensed-up body struggled instinctively as he tried to argue, "He's going to escape!"

Shen Liufei tightened his grip on Xie Lanshan, his deep voice a gentle shackle that rang out, "It's too dangerous."

The lake was too large, streams rushed down too fast. The sky was already dark. It would be too dangerous to jump into the water right now.

After they sent the injured girl back to the hospital, the water police arrived and attempted to fish up Qiao Hui's corpse. Of course, they didn't end up finding anything, and perhaps this devil was given another chance to live and escape.

Another corpse was discovered as they were chasing after Qiao Hui—Liu Mingfang's secretary, Xia Hong.

Xia Hong's death was identical to the previous three victims; her mouth was sewn shut, skin peeled off, her lower body violated, and a black dog collar was around her neck. The autopsy confirmed Xia Hong's death to be five days ago when Tao Longyue was brawling with Qiao Hui in the parking lot, the night when the culprit escaped.

Judging from the killer's signature, this was clearly a case that belonged to the serial murderer. Liu Yanbo would personally handle the investigation of the case from here on out, suggesting that Xia Hong was perhaps the next victim that Qiao Hui preyed on after he failed that night. Yet aside from Xia Hong, it could be concluded from the surveillance of Puren Hospital that the other two victims of this serial murder had once visited family or friends in a red dress.

The Municipal Bureau first sent out a wanted notice for

Qiao Hui and then made a public announcement for women to be extra careful when walking outside by themselves. Of course, no secrets could be kept forever. A handful of journalists exposed the key information that all female victims shared the same characteristic of having long black hair and wearing a red dress on the internet. Some gossipers even connected this case to the old Cangnan Serial Murder and further perpetuated the media storm. People fear the unknown, so the horrors that came with the murder case dwindled as the culprit was exposed. The focus of the case shifted from Qiao Hui onto Xiao Man.

The details of the Cangnan case leaked onto the internet and exposed Su Mansheng's identity. It first began with independent reporters riling up news for clicks, but it quickly snowballed into a violent tsunami on social networking websites.

Strangely, while people could forgive and be more lenient toward the young Xiao Man, they would not let go of the adult Su Mansheng, who was also working in public security. For a brief period, the story from over twenty years ago became almost like a myth through the mouths of people. Some people even brought up the potential of an 11-year-old Xiao Man developing Stockholm syndrome and falling in love with the killer. Others reasonably questioned how such a young girl could survive under the hands of this twisted killer—or perhaps, could she have possibly been an accomplice?

All eleven victims from the Cangnan case had their skin peeled off, their mouths cut open, and then sewn back together. There was only one exception, and Xiao Man didn't seem perfect enough to be considered a victim of the case.

They only needed to arrest the culprit to close the case, but something still didn't sit right with Xie Lanshan. If Qiao Hui was simply replicating the Cangnan Serial Murder, he would certainly follow the known details and sexually violate the victim, peel the skin, and sew their mouths. But it had been 25 years already; just where did he obtain the key information about the red dress that even the police weren't aware of until now?

Xie Lanshan and Shen Liufei found the woman that Qiao Hui wanted to confess to that night at their building, only to discover that this woman's appearance was completely different from the red dress and long hair requirement that Qiao Hui obsessed over. The young woman had short hair, was slightly portly, and had a large face with big eyes. She dressed in comfortable jeans and spoke refreshingly with a slight Northern accent.

She became acquainted with Qiao Hui while she was volunteering at Puren Hospital. The young man fell in love with her at first sight and restlessly pursued her. Qiao Hui was a medical student with good grades, tall, and rather good-looking, so she wanted to try pursuing a relationship with him at first. Yet after a few dates, she noticed that something was off about the man. The girl said that she had already rejected him the week before Qiao Hui hosted that dramatic confession.

Xie Lanshan asked her, "You guys haven't known each other for that long, so what about Qiao Hui did you find was off?"

"I feel like he's a momma's boy, or to be blunter, I think he's got an Oedipus complex." The girl was still a little uneasy after learning that Qiao Hui was the culprit of the horrific serial murderer on the news and sighed. "He looked quite modest and kind. I wouldn't have thought he was such a shady and horrific monster."

Xie Lanshan was shocked. "He has a mother? Have you seen her before?"

The girl shook her head and said, "No. She might not be his mother, it might be an older female he's acquainted with. He always refers to her as just a 'family member'. There was one time when I went out shopping with him and passed by a jewelry shop; he suddenly said that he wanted to buy a present for his mother. He bought a crystal necklace in the end. He's already around 24 or 25, so his mother would be at least around 50 now, but the style of the necklace he bought looked a little too cutesy for her age. It looked a little like a cartoon character, and he even carved his name on the back of it—either way, it was just really weird."

Shen Liufei followed up and asked, "So what made you think about the Oedipus complex part?"

The girl pondered a little before saying, "I guess it's not as serious as that, but more like he seemed super obedient to his mother and especially didn't want to upset her. He was quite sincere to me and had really creative ideas, like how he tried to light up a building to confess to me. I was honestly pleasantly surprised at first, and asked him why he was so good to me. He said that he's never actually asked a girl out before and that I was the first."

Xie Lanshan nodded slightly and said, "That's not too uncommon. Some people don't tend to be involved in relationships that early." If he wasn't working right now, Xie Lanshan would have shot a glance at Shen Liufei when he added, "Or maybe he just hasn't met the right person yet."

The girl said, "It's not, but then he explained to me right after and said that his family is very strict, insanely strict. They don't allow him to fall in love with girls, not because they were afraid he would get into a relationship at an early age, they just don't allow him to be in one. He said that he used to have a crush on a girl when he was in high school, then got into big trouble after his family found out. Oh right, he said that his family also forced him to follow in his father's footsteps and become a doctor. It was when he said this I confirmed that the person who told him all of this was his mother."

Xie Lanshan and Shen Liufei both noted the particular line about "following in his father's footsteps".

The girl continued, "He said he didn't want to become a doctor because he always thought the human body was disgusting when he was little. He even said that girls with long hair in dresses were also gross. His expression was really hateful when he said that; it almost scared me. That's when I told him without hesitation that I won't meet up with him again."

The two men left as soon as they finished the interview. Shen Liufei drove Xie Lanshan's car while the latter sat on the passenger's side. The day was still young, crowds of people filled the streets as the light of dusk shone from the sky.

Both of their minds were still on the case. Shen Liufei turned his head slightly to see Xie Lanshan's eyebrows furrowed, lips pressed together in deep thought, and said, "Are you still thinking about that whole 'following his father's footsteps' line? You're suspecting that Qiao Hui is actually Kong Xiangping's son?"

The two men didn't need more words between them; Xie Lanshan also turned to return the gaze and noticed the artist was as aloof and distant as usual. Noticing that Shen Liufei's gaze was focused on the road, Xie Lanshan joked, "If you weren't driving right now, I would jump and give you a kiss."

It might sound like a joke, but there was still some hope hinted at in between those words. He stared, begging for the driver's lips, but Shen Liufei's expression remained unfazed. Xie Lanshan's bit of excitement was let down as he complained, "Man, my cuz sure doesn't care—"

Before he could finish, Shen Liufei turned the steering wheel and abruptly parked the car by the roadside.

He swiftly undid his seatbelt and leaned over to hold Xie Lanshan down and pressed their lips together for a deep kiss.

This kiss satisfied the little desire in Xie Lanshan's heart as he wiped his lips almost reluctantly. Shen Liufei drove the car back onto the road, face still cool and blank. He began analyzing the case as if nothing had happened, his tone and voice calm and smooth. "Do you remember what Zhu Mingwu said? He said that they found infant supplies in Kong Xiangping's house. His theory back then was that the culprit may have also harmed infant girls, but now it looks like those may be for his son."

"If Qiao Hui really is Kong Xiangping's son, he would only be about 3 or 4 years old 21 years ago." The age matched up, but Xie Lanshan was still suspicious and said, "But before Qiao Hui was exposed, I've recorded Su Mansheng's witness account and can confirm she did not mention anything about another child in that basement."

Shen Liufei paused for a moment before saying, "There's one possibility."

Xie Lanshan already knew what he wanted to say and finished the unspoken words, "The police didn't find any feminine products in Qiao Hui's house, so he obviously doesn't live with this 'mother' of his. Perhaps this woman isn't even his own birth mother and someone he simply recognized as a motherly figure."

From this analysis, Su Mansheng was still a suspect in the case—even more so than before. It was likely that she could have befriended or developed some strange relationship with a four-year-old boy at the age of eleven.

"But the case is still strange." Xie Lanshan let out a sigh after thinking about the pain and struggle Tao Longyue must be going through and said, "If Su Mansheng was truly the mastermind behind this case, just what triggered her to commit such a crime over twenty years later?"

"I suspect that Luo Xin isn't the first victim of this serial murder," Shen Liufei said coolly after some thought, "Schopenhauer said there are only three forces behind human action: the wish for one's own happiness, wishing ill on others, and wishing for the happiness of others. The only difference is the ratio of each force's presence within a person—even if the person is a pure evil murderer."

The night fell as street lights lit up. The streets were filled with white-collared workers who just got off work, a typical rush hour scene.

Xie Lanshan recognized this wasn't the route back home and asked, "Where are we going?"

Shen Liufei stopped at a red light and answered, "To Tao Longyue's place. Don't you have a ton of questions to ask him?"

The car stopped in front of Puren Hospital. Before Xie Lanshan unbuckled his seatbelt and walked out of the car, he suddenly remembered that day when Shen Liufei wrapped an arm around his waist to stop him from jumping into the river. He turned around toward the driver and said sternly under the dim light, "You should just drive my car from now on."

Shen Liufei lifted an eyebrow, not sure what this line meant.

"Four wheels are safer than two wheels," Xie Lanshan said earnestly. His eyes glowed under the streetlight in an almost adoring manner as he said, "I can't stand your wild biking, it's too dangerous."

"I was only rushing to chase after the culprit..." Shen Liufei attempted to give an excuse, only to find his heart soften as he stared into the man's eyes. He lifted the corner of his lips and said, "Sure."

Xie Lanshan was in a good mood and dropped one last line

before stepping out of the car, "If we weren't on the streets right now, I would jump over and do you right this moment."

These words became much more suggestive as soon as he recalled the sudden kiss earlier.

Yet Shen Liufei's expression remained blank as he lifted a hand and gave a punishing slap on Xie Lanshan's butt, saying, "Let's get the job done first, then you're next on the list."

(iii)

Xie Lanshan cut the small talk and went straight to the point in the hospital room, asking Tao Longyue, "Did you ever tell Qiao Hui that Su Mansheng is your girlfriend and a forensic scientist?"

Xie Lanshan thought that since Qiao Hui was the serial murderer, he wouldn't possibly go visit the Captain he had physically brawled with not too long ago. Therefore, it's very possible that he found out about Su Mansheng's occupation from the woman herself. In other words, they've been long acquainted.

Realizing that his girlfriend was still being suspected, Captain Tao yelled, furious, "Are you fucking done yet? The case is over once Qiao Hui is arrested! What's your reasoning for chasing after Mansheng like this?"

"Because I'm a cop and I believe there are still suspicious points in this case!" It was impossible to communicate with this man, but Xie Lanshan knew that his childhood buddy was not unreasonable. Xie Lanshan suppressed his anger and patiently analyzed for his friend, "You've been a cop for years, can't you tell that there's still something fishy about this case? Qiao Hui is likely just a puppet and there must be another mastermind behind this."

Xie Lanshan shared the result of his investigations today

with Tao Longyue, then explained his reasoning based on the evidence. He felt that Su Mansheng's reaction in the questioning room was too calm, her story too smoothly told, and that she must have kept some secrets. The optimistic interpretation was that this resulted from the trauma of her horrific past, but the flip side of the coin was the possibility that she could have been involved, or that she was the true mastermind behind this serial murder.

Yet no matter how reasonable he tried to explain his logic, the anger on Tao Longyue's face remained. In face of Xie Lanshan's continuous questioning of whether or not Qiao Hui had spoken to him before, the Captain only responded stiffly, "I don't know."

This shocked Xie Lanshan. "You don't even know if you've talked to him before?"

Tao Longyue's attitude remained cold as he continued, "That's right, I don't know. I also don't know why Shen Liufei didn't tell you about how his family got murdered!"

"You're being absolutely fucking unreasonable right now. Listen to yourself!" Xie Lanshan finally realized that no words could get through to him and felt a burning rage. He then left the room, slamming the door shut.

Tao Longyue was also pained by his growing tension with his buddy lately, but he really couldn't help himself and only knew how to spew out hateful words. After giving some more thought about the information Xie Lanshan brought in today, he crawled up the bed, clutching his pained stomach, and quietly left the hospital.

He first stopped by a market nearby and picked out some of Su Mansheng's favorite foods. He then left, satisfied with his haul of vegetables and meats; it looked to be enough for a full course meal on the dinner table.

He called a cab and made his way toward Su Mansheng's

house. Almost as soon as he stepped into the residential area, he noticed all neighbors had their eyes locked somewhere, colorful expressions on both familiar and unfamiliar faces.

Tao Longyue ignored them and walked toward the building Su Mansheng lived in. He immediately noticed upon stepping up the stairs that Su Mansheng's front door had been splashed with bright red paint. Painted on the wall beside it were lopsided large words:

Whore. Criminal. Murderer.

Those words reeked of malice, and Tao Longyue grew furious. He took his jacket off and was ready to wipe away the undried paint, but the door suddenly opened.

Ever since netizens began hunting down Xiao Man, it had forced Su Mansheng to take a vacation. It seemed as if she hadn't left her house these last few days; her face wistful and pale.

She also saw the words on the wall but didn't throw a fit like Tao Longyue. She only turned around calmly and said, "Come in."

Tao Longyue asked, "These words..."

Su Mansheng said without turning her head, "Family of Luo Xin, the first victim, came here already. They might have believed what was being said on the internet and wanted justice for their daughter."

The house was locked up like a prison with no windows open. Xiao Qun curled up in a corner and stared blankly at the woman walking in. It wasn't until she saw Tao Longyue follow in behind her that her expression lightened up with joy.

Tao Longyue was also happy to see Xiao Qun, and waved the bags of groceries in his hands as he said, "I'm here to cook dinner for our two lovely ladies today."

Xiao Qun still couldn't talk and instead nodded viciously, then ran up to give Tao Longyue an embrace. While Su

Mansheng walked out to the living room, the little girl pulled onto Tao Longyue's sleeve and gestured, then pointed at the woman from behind with stuttering words, "She... talk to herself... scary..."

As if she heard the little girl, Su Mansheng turned around abruptly. A pale face and reddened eyes glared at Xiao Qun, scaring the girl away.

Tao Longyue tried to give Su Mansheng a call before he stopped by, but her cellphone was turned off. The phone was on do not disturb mode, resting on the coffee table. Tao Longyue knew that Su Mansheng had been receiving countless harassment calls lately. It pained his heart. He asked, "Is that reporter still pestering you?"

With Su Mansheng's silent acknowledgment, Tao Longyue cursed out loud in anger, "That woman sure is the scum of journalists!"

The woman Tao Longyue spoke of was Hao Sijing from the Eastern Eye Witness; the most difficult and harsh among the harassers. Hao Sijing had been wanting to write a groundbreaking news piece, so desperate that she was even willing to expose Su Mansheng's information to force the woman to speak out in public. Tao Longyue didn't doubt that professional journalists were behind these internet call-outs. Of course, now that it had stirred up a storm among the netizens, it was too late to cover it up.

Captain Tao had been living even more prudently than Xie Lanshan these last few years and barely used the kitchen. His claim to cook was only a poor bluffing attempt; it was questionable whether the food could be eaten at all.

He frantically prepared the ingredients in the kitchen, sweat dripping down his body. Xiao Qun stood beside him and helped, looking more capable than the main cook himself.

An adult man cooking with a young girl in the kitchen was

certainly an interesting scene to watch. Su Mansheng stared from outside and finally let out a bit of a smile.

The dishes ranged from too salty to tasteless; the vegetables weren't fully cooked and could barely be eaten, the steak over-cooked to the point it was virtually rubber. It was still the first time he served the girls. Captain Tao gloated about his cooking, forcing the two ladies in the house to experience his master chef's hands.

The dinner table was filled with laughter. Su Mansheng didn't have much of an appetite, but her pale face grew a little livelier.

Captain Tao offered to wash the dishes after the meal. He turned back to see Su Mansheng standing not far away, eyes on him as he worked. Despite knowing she was trying to hide it, he could still see the worry and bleakness in her eyes. Her usual queen-like demeanor vanished completely.

Tao Longyue felt his heart sting. He placed the clean dishes down and escorted Su Mansheng back to her bedroom. He asked her in concern, "You don't look well. Should I stay the night with you?"

Tao Longyue really wanted to speak to her, heart to heart and with reason. He noticed the abnormal attitude of his girl-friend and could no longer turn a blind eye to it.

Yet before he could even speak up, Su Mansheng suddenly pinned him down on the bed. It was rare for her to be so aggres-sive. She pressed her body on him, showering passionate kisses all over his face and lips.

Tao Longyue was shocked at first, but quickly returned the kisses. Amidst their loving exchange, he attempted to turn over and regain his position on top, only to be kicked by Su Mansheng on his injury and pressed back down.

She pinned him down almost violently and bit him aggressively. Her hand grabbed onto Tao Longyue's hair before she reached down under her pillow.

Suddenly, she felt something cold and wet beneath her pillow. She turned to look and noticed it was a bloodied piece of human skin.

Su Mansheng's gaze grew cold and violent. She carefully placed the piece of skin back in its place and let go of Tao Longyue, then ordered, "It's getting late, you should go back. I still need to take Xiao Qun out tomorrow to Qilian's place for therapy."

Tao Longyue noticed she was hiding something. The truth was right before him; he tried to grab her hand and suggested, "I think you're the one that needs to go see a therapist."

But Su Mansheng pulled her hand away.

Tao Longyue took a step forward at her obvious uncooperative attitude and asked bluntly, "Why did you hide the fact that Kong Xiangping had a son?"

"It's been twenty years. Can I not forget some details of the case?" Su Mansheng responded sternly, but her gaze kept floating around, as if worried her lover would discover her bloodied secret.

"Qiao Hui had long been in contact with an adult woman, even gifting a necklace carved with his name on it to this 'mother' of his," Tao Longyue said, "Tell me, just how did this man know about your personal details without ever being acquainted with us?"

"I don't know," Su Mansheng responded with that same unbothered attitude, "I don't even know him."

"If it's you, please turn yourself in." Tao Longyue's eyes reddened, his heart throbbing in pain as he said, "If it's not you, then you also haven't let go of your trauma as you thought you did. You need further help—"

"Just leave!"

Su Mansheng refused to communicate and screamed out in pain. She pushed Tao Longyue out the door, then dropped to the ground and cried out, her head buried in her hands.

That night, Su Mansheng locked her bedroom door. A strange knocking sound rang throughout the night; Xiao Qun was too afraid to sleep from the noise. She sat on her bed with her arms around her head until the morning.

The first ray of light was a beautiful rose color from the sky that gently passed through the window and landed on the face of the girl. Xiao Qun carefully walked out of her bedroom to peek out, noticing that Su Mansheng's closed door finally opened.

A strong, curious heart led the young girl to peek inside. Su Mansheng's room was a mess; her desk and chair were out of place, all sorts of clothes and items covered the floor as if she was searching for something. Xiao Qun noticed that there were some letters on Su Mansheng's bed. Age took a toll on the yellowed pages that were finally dug up from storage. Someone still hand writes letters in this day and age? She became more curious.

"What are you looking at?" A scolding voice came from behind.

Xiao Qun turned her head and met a pair of cold eyes, then took a step back in fear.

Su Mansheng stood behind her with damp hair and a wet face. The gentle light of dawn quickly brightened up from behind; shadows on her face grew darker as she stared with her hollow eyes.

Xiao Qun's first impression of Su Mansheng was unique. She thought the woman looked like a female warrior wielding a long sword in one hand and a shield in another, kind and solemn, beautiful and brave. She felt safe around this woman, but also felt a little envious of her. Yet at this very moment, she was afraid of the same woman from the bottom of her heart.

"You should get ready." Su Mansheng noticed her abnormal attitude from Xiao Qun's fearful face, almost shocked at her own change as well. She closed her eyes and tried to soften up her voice and expression, then said, "We'll go see Doctor Song in a bit."

Xiao Qun was shocked to see that a crystal necklace hung from the woman's long neck, shaped in a cutesy cartoon design.

Su Mansheng took Xiao Qun to Song Qilian's clinic for her scheduled session, and the girl seemed to be recovering very well. While psychological trauma still severely affected the little girl's reading and writing skills, her cognitive abilities were recovering. She could now speak simple words and phrases and could communicate through eye contact, small gestures, and body language to make up for her troubled speech. Song Qilian's report for her had shown that she was responding very well during their therapy session. With the help of medication, Song Qilian was confident that Xiao Qun's speech function affected by trauma would fully recover soon.

Song Qilian first let the nurses take Xiao Qun out of her office and kept Su Mansheng behind to teach her how to help the little girl's recovery at home. She welcomed the forensic scientist to sit in her office.

Song Qilian had seen the internet call-outs on Xiao Man and all sorts of evil words. She sighed and said, "You've done a lot already. Not only did you need to handle your own situation, but you have to care for a child that is a stranger to you."

Su Mansheng didn't find Xiao Qun's existence an extra burden. Rather, she felt as if she was finally making up to her young self of many years ago by helping this poor soul who was harmed the same way as her. She said, "We shared the same wounds. I see my past self in her."

"If the past Xiao Man wants to talk to someone, I'm always ears for her," Song Qilian said.

Su Mansheng looked at her and said sharply, "Did Tao Longyue ask you to do this?"

Song Qilian nodded her head. "If you think I'm too young and inexperienced, I can refer you to a more experienced specialist in our hospital. But if you just want to speak to someone as a friend, my door is always open for you. Of course, I will maintain my professional integrity and keep your secrets confidential."

Seeing how Su Mansheng remained unfazed, as if she was purposely maintaining a tough front to protect her true self, Song Qilian smiled. She said to the forensic scientist as a friend, "Did you know? Tao Longyue was completely intoxicated when he came to me and cried in desperation. I've known him for over a decade and had never seen him so helpless before; he was always bright and hot-blooded, courageous and straightforward. You're very lucky to have a man like this shed tears for you."

These words touched the softest part of her heart, tingling those unmoved chords. Su Mansheng's expression softened up as she turned to Song Qilian. "You're also quite fortunate yourself, having a man like Xie Lanshan who would willingly give his life to protect you."

"He's willing to do so out of our long years of friendship, but I'm no longer the person he loves." Song Qilian couldn't hide her pained emotions as she heard this name. That stinging pain seemed to poke out from within her, numbing her limbs and senses. Tears welled up in her eyes as she looked at Su Mansheng earnestly and said, "I don't want you and Tao Longyue to follow down the same path I did. If you love him, then trust him like how he loves you, and face the challenges with him together. Don't be like me and wait until it's too late to even regret your actions."

Su Mansheng seemed to shake as her voice quivered. "It's not that I don't trust him, I'm..."

Words stopped abruptly, but Song Qilian could tell that this woman before her had finally stepped out of her damaged past. That little jail cell she had trapped herself in and the world out of finally opened up a little room for people to reach inside.

She reached over and held Su Mansheng's hand, using the warmth on her flesh to console the woman, and said, "Why don't you talk it out and we can both try to find a solution together."

Su Mansheng closed her eyes out of exhaustion. Moments later, she asked, "Doctor Song, is multiple personality disorder a real illness that exists?"

This question was strange; as an experienced forensic scientist who had worked in public security for years, Su Mansheng would know that dissociative identity disorder was an actual condition in psychology. Song Qilian nodded and said, "It's typically a mental health condition that bores from extreme psychological trauma and stimulation. The patient would develop a second or even more personalities who act as their 'guardian' to protect their main personality. These different 'persons' coexist independently within the same body. Sometimes these personalities eventually vanish or sleep as time passes and the main personality heals, but further stimulation and untreated conditions can trigger the sub-personalities to reappear or sometimes even overtake the main personality."

Su Mansheng seemed to have expected this answer and asked, trembling, "Can you promise me that you will not reveal what I have to say next to anyone, no matter what happens?"

Song Qilian recognized the severity of the issue and nodded her head solemnly to promise.

Su Mansheng nodded, grateful, but her lips suddenly lifted strangely as she said, "I've been experiencing periods of time where I felt I'm in a trance, and sometimes not even sure where I am... There's a piece of human skin from one of the victim's bodies hidden beneath my pillow. I found over ten years' worth of letters written to me by Qiao Hui in the depths of my wardrobe, and I'm even wearing the necklace he gave to me right now, carved with the words 'mother'..."

Su Mansheng paused, in pain, and closed her eyes. She caught her breath and finally said after a while, "I think I'm a patient of dissociative identity disorder, and that I'm the mastermind who was controlling Qiao Hui."

(iv)

Recalling how the last time they tried to move, Duan Licheng interrupted, and now that the serial murder case was boiling up, the plans to move in with Shen Liufei had ground to a halt. While the case was nearing its end and Xie Lanshan was busy chasing down Qiao Hui, Shen Liufei took the opportunity to return to his residential building. He planned on cleaning up a bit more and officially move in with his lover.

The night of early winter was silent and hollow. Black clouds covered the sky, and no starlight shone through, leaving only a sharp crescent moon lingering in the darkness. The house was also dimly lit. Shen Liufei sat before his desk and fell into deep thought, facing the laptop screen before him.

Old case files filled the screen. He wanted to clean them all up but still couldn't bring himself to click delete on the files. Amidst his hesitation, cold sweat already covered the palm of his hand.

Shen Liufei opened up the folder named 0001 and looked carefully at the photo of the suspect.

The Xie Lanshan now and Ye Shen in the past, their faces and expressions looked identical but also slightly different. Despite sharing the same body, the soul inside was completely different. He carried his hatred from the massacre and an unsolved mystery on his shoulders, planned for his revenge, attempted to poke into the life of his target, only for it all to become a sappy love story that started with a beautiful meeting that could last for a lifetime. How awfully ironic.

He had never expected any of this to happen before the curtains of this carefully written show were lifted.

Xie Lanshan had once said before his car accident: *I feel like I've seen you somewhere.*

Shen Liufei responded now to the dimly lit screen: *I do too.*

The doorbell rang. The door opened to a breeze of chilly wind, and along with it came Song Qilian.

Shen Liufei didn't expect Song Qilian to pay him a visit and invited her in, patiently waiting for her to explain her sudden visit.

Shen Liufei took out a can of soda from the fridge, opened it up, and offered it to Song Qilian. He said, "My apologies, I've been busy moving, so this is all I can offer."

"No need for the trouble, I'm here to ask for your help," Song Qilian said without touching the soda on the coffee table. "Someone came to me for help regarding her mental health condition, it's extremely severe, and has something to do with the current serial murder case. I want to help the person and also help A'Lan solve the case."

She took a sip of the soda and continued a little timidly, "I am the one who had caused him trouble by writing that mental health assessment."

Realizing that the patient mentioned was Su Mansheng,

Shen Liufei pressed his eyebrows together slightly and asked, "Why didn't you go ask Xie Lanshan yourself?"

Song Qilian said, "He already paid me a visit, Tao Longyue also came as well. But I promised the patient that I will not reveal her secret, and as a professional, I cannot give you details about the patient's condition."

Shen Liufei asked, "Then what brings you here today?"

Song Qilian's eyes lit up, her tone grew more anxious as she said, "I know you majored in forensic sketching when you studied in the States, but you were also involved in criminal profiling, right?"

Shen Liufei nodded. "Correct."

Song Qilian let out a sigh of relief and said, "Since you're an expert in criminal psychology, can I ask you about a difficult case as a psychologist for my patient?"

This was quite a smart move; it not only was within the ethical grounds of a professional, but this consultation could also potentially help the police solve the case. Shen Liufei gave his silent approval and said, "You may go on."

She briefly summarized the condition by using "the patient" instead of the person's actual name, then said, "The greatest crime in the world is the violation of young girls, like Fang Siqi's experience." This was a reference to a novel that delved into the lives of little girls such as Fang Siqi, who had been sexually assaulted, who had gone mad because of all the malicious shaming by outsiders. Outside the novel, these similar harmless rumors on the internet were just as vicious as the fangs of a beast, ripping through the shells of a certain woman until every last bit of her senses and pride were torn apart.

Song Qilian said that the patient refused to discuss the case further and chose to close herself in a heavy cocoon away from the world. The doctor was worried that the patient was reaching her limit and feared that the patient would soon do something even more awful and regrettable. She finally said that rather than forcefully invading the patient's personal space to offer a helping hand, she sincerely hoped that this strong and brilliant woman she once knew could take a courageous step and ask for help first.

That crescent moon still lingered in the sky. Su Mansheng once again woke up from her trance-like state. She couldn't remember what she did and only stared down to look at herself; her palm was cold, half of her body wet.

The room was still dark. She had grown to despise the light and voices of people ever since the storm on the internet went viral. She wasn't afraid; the rumors simply annoyed her. In the darkness, Su Mansheng heard sounds of water running from the bathroom and carefully made her way over.

Su Mansheng opened the door to a dim light and was immediately stunned; her eyes widened as if her soul had left her body.

Beside the bathtub were three lit candles, and an old and dirty doll had been placed on the ground. The doll was covered in blood and stared at her as if it was sentient with an eerie smile.

The scene before her eyes triggered the most horrifying nightmare deep in her memories; Su Mansheng shook violently and almost fell to the ground. She managed to regain her balance. Within a split second, she saw her own eyes through the mirror in the bathroom—those eyes were foreign, evil, and mad.

The strange noise summoned Xiao Qun, and she followed the sounds through the darkness. Yet her little gestures alarmed the woman in the bathroom. Su Mansheng suddenly rushed toward the little girl and grabbed onto her shoulders uncontrollably, shaking as she called, "You did this, right? You were the one that did this, right?!"

Xiao Qun was stunned by this act and struggled to run. But Su Mansheng rushed forth and knocked the girl to the ground; a warm liquid rolled down her face after her forehead hit the hard flooring.

The girl reached a hand past her straight fringes over her forehead and stained her hands with fresh blood.

"Who did this? Just who in the world did this?" Su Mansheng was on the brink of madness. She shook the girl's shoulder as she kneeled on the ground, ignoring the fact that the girl was already injured.

"It..." Xiao Qun was already suffering from a headache earlier. This violent shaking only worsened her pain as she struggled to speak up. She stared at the woman with hazy eyes and pointed a shaking finger at her, then called out, "You... you did it!"

Su Mansheng was taken aback and loosened her grip. Xiao Qun quickly took this opportunity to run back in fear.

Su Mansheng stood up in a daze and turned to stare at the bathtub that was already overfilled with water. Words such as whore and criminal rang beside her ears. The entire world thought she was a criminal, and the laughable fact was that she now also believed those rumors. Guilt, fear, regret, and other negative emotions poured at her like a tsunami; she suddenly let out a chuckle.

She wanted to return to her mother's womb, that safe haven before she was born. She wanted to be wrapped in its warmth and stay away from all the pain and conflicts.

At that moment, the bathtub filled with warm water before her eyes looked just like a mother's womb. Su Mansheng noticed that there was a surgical knife placed on the bathtub.

The blade was sharp and cold—just one slice on her wrist and she could go home.

Su Mansheng carefully picked up the surgical knife. Just as she was about to cut her wrist, a beaming red light suddenly shone from outside the window; police sirens screamed as groups of police cars rushed over.

Moments later, someone called outside and knocked on her door—it was Tao Longyue's voice.

Su Mansheng awoke from her state of trance and quickly opened the door.

Before Su Mansheng could speak, Tao Longyue grabbed onto her arm and dragged her out of the house, then shouted, "Someone just called the cops! Qiao Hui acted again right by your house. We might need a forensic scientist at the scene!"

Su Mansheng was physically dragged to the crime scene by her boyfriend, only to hear from Ding Li, who had been waiting, that someone called the cops as they passed by. It was just in time, so the victim was only injured and was now on their way to the hospital.

Tao Longyue howled, "Where's Qiao Hui?"

Ding Li felt her eardrums throb at this loud call and took a step back before she said, "He... he ran away... we were so close too..."

Tao Longyue cursed, "Damnit! Again! If we don't capture this madman as soon as we can, he could start murdering indiscriminately. Who knows how many innocent young women will die by his hand by then!"

Xie Lanshan was also called out. His expression grew grave once again seeing how close they were to arrest the culprit and suggested, "We don't know where he's hiding within the city. Now that we know Qiao Hui has an obsession with long hair and red dresses, let's put out a bait with the help of a female officer to send him back to where he belongs."

He eyed Ding Li as he spoke.

Ding Li felt her soul leave her body as she heard about potentially facing a serial murderer head-on and shook her head to say, "N-no, no, no, I can't... I-I'm just a back end worker..."

Captain Tao said, "You're the only woman in the entire violent crimes unit. Who else is going to do this if you can't?!"

Ding Li refused to back down and said, almost sobbing, "But he's a real creep. I don't even know self-defense. You guys never even let me go in to infiltrate Miss T's club last time."

"That was last time," Tao Longyue said as he glanced towards Su Mansheng. "This is an order. You can't possibly ask us to put a random civilian's life in danger."

"I... can't I just... I just quit my job..."

"Oh, come on, you're—"

Su Mansheng suddenly spoke up, "I'll do it."

Xie Lanshan and Tao Longyue both turned to her and asked, "You?"

She was ready to do something inconceivable a second ago, but now the spirit of a public security official reignited within her. Perhaps it was a work habit, or perhaps she always had this kind of powerful energy within her. Like a freshly blooming flower that could withstand storms and harsh weather, she would always stand up at every opportunity. All the regret and guilt she felt for the victims and the fear and hatred for the criminal fueled into a torch of shining fire, giving her strength to fight with her life. Su Mansheng said with confidence, "Please trust me. If there's anyone that could lure out that madman in this world, the person is me."

Xie Lanshan asked, "What do you plan on doing?"

Su Mansheng pondered a little and said, "It's too ineffective to just walk on the streets. I need to go on television. I will accept the Eastern Eye Witness's interview."

(v)

Su Mansheng knew before she went on television that this was a setup by Song Qilian. There was no assault by Qiao Hui that night she almost committed suicide.

Song Qilian didn't break her promise with her patient. Aside from Shen Liufei, nobody knew that Su Mansheng suspected she had a second personality. She simply passed on Shen Liufei's idea to Tao Longyue and Xie Lanshan, gambling on the courage and sense of justice in Su Mansheng's heart.

Su Mansheng was thankful to Song Qilian; this charade came at the right time and knocked her awake from this nightmarish life. She planned on exposing her mental health history after she completed the interview and they captured Qiao Hui.

Xie Lanshan was also thankful to Song Qilian. He said to her that if it wasn't for her help, young Tao might still be crying his heart out at home right now.

Of course, this wasn't completely her idea. Two petals of pink blush surfaced on her face as she said, embarrassed, "I'm just doing what I must. Besides, I owe you an apology. It's my honor to be able to help you out."

The conflict between them that seemed like a deep trench felt like it was never meant to be there in the first place. All the questions she had that seemed to have no answers to suddenly became trivial as soon as she learned how to let them go. Song Qilian looked at Xie Lanshan, mustered up some courage, and grabbed his hand.

The faint and sweet scent from her soft skin floated up. It took Xie Lanshan aback at first, but didn't pull his hand away. He thought she was still feeling guilty about the assessment and held her hand. He smiled and said softly to her, "You've contributed a lot to this case, so once it's all settled, we'll make ol'Tao treat us to dinner. You can bring Changchang over too."

At the potential of another date, Song Qilian felt her heart jump. She wanted to smile, but was also scared. Her lips opened up slightly on her face that looked like a flower bulb ready to bloom.

Shen Liufei never planned on fighting over someone with a lady and was a man of his word. He stood on the side and watched them for a bit, strangely feeling that it was quite nice to see this woman become close to Xie Lanshan again. His throat became dry as he backed off and asked Xiao Liang for a cigarette.

"Wait, I thought Mr. Shen didn't smoke?" Xiao Liang was a little shocked but quickly pulled out a pack for the man. The Hanhai City Municipal Bureau wasn't lacking in handsome men, but Mr. Shen was particularly more cold and handsome than others. Anyone that stood next to him would immediately feel inferior, as if they were no better looking than a pile of mud on the ground.

Shen Liufei bit down on the cigarette without lighting it up. He only smelled the tobacco inside and watched Xie Lanshan and Song Qilian from a distance, wondering how he should go about quitting this bad habit of smoking.

Su Mansheng had heard of the Eastern Eye Witness even before she went on screen. The program was known for covering the most controversial news within the country, insisting on always filming live even after seven to eight years of operation. The host, Xing Ming, was known for his sharp tongue and blunt words. Yet he still maintained a level of moral integrity and humanity to not offend the guests. On top of that, his handsome face and good reputation earned him many fans; it always ensured his programs would become a hot topic of discussion across cities.

In other words, viewership was guaranteed. This was also the first time Su Mansheng appeared in public as well, so this was bound to become the next trending topic on the internet; she was certain that Qiao Hui would see her.

Su Mansheng wore a red dress and did her hair on the day of the filming. She rarely presented herself like this; her long black hair trailed down like a smooth waterfall behind her back, her elegance unparalleled. The program agreed to allow her some time for a confession before the show ended.

In front of the camera and the audience, Su Mansheng didn't express anger or frustration, despite knowing that any sort of uncontrollable rant after days of malicious rumors could justify her poor attitude.

She looked at the audience with a calm face, the first words out of her mouth being, "I didn't do anything wrong."

As the head journalist of the case, Hao Sijing sat in the audience and stared at her.

"I'm not wrong for being violated because I'm beautiful. The ones that are wrong are the people here who put the blame for the assault on the narrative of 'skirts are too short'. I'm not wrong for not fighting back against slander that I cannot win against. The ones that are wrong are the same people who call me ugly names like 'prostitute' and 'whore' because I survived." Su Mansheng said as she met Hao Sijing's gaze. She spoke with confidence, "You all are even worse than those rapists who violate people physically. Every single one of you is an emotional abuser."

These words were too blunt and harsh; the director feared that Su Mansheng would become too worked up and held up a sign from backstage to remind host Xing Ming to control the situation or cut right to commercial.

Su Mansheng stood on the stage, Hao Sijing was down below. Xing Ming could read the scene of the two women exchanging blades through their gazes. The host furrowed his brows slightly and held up his hand, gesturing to the director to let the woman continue.

"However, I choose to forgive." Su Mansheng suddenly removed her gaze from Hao Sijing and turned toward the audience, "I'm not forgiving you all who don't deserve my forgiveness. I'm forgiving myself because I don't believe I should be punished again for being hurt in the past."

Just before the program ended, Su Mansheng found Tao Longyue in the audience and gave him a smile before calmly giving her last line:

"I deserve to love and be loved; I deserve to stand with my head upright and walk under the sunlight."

A roar of applause filled the studio. Tao Longyue's eyes reddened. He quickly rubbed his eyes in fear people were going to see him and joined in with the clapping.

Su Mansheng felt a new sense of relief when she walked down the stage, as if she had just let go of a burden. She turned to find Xing Ming and thanked the man for letting her speak her mind. The host left an impression on her; in terms of style, his words certainly were sharp like a blade. He was the same type of cool and handsome man as Shen Liufei, but while the latter was too aloof and distant, the former was sharper and more ambitious beneath his cold surface.

"To be quite honest, I'm very surprised that you accepted the Eastern Eye Witness's interview. I admire your courage; it's not easy to rip through your old wounds and expose yourself in front of the entire country." Xing Ming had recently become the vice-editor of the editorial section of the company within the last two years, managing over a hundred employees beneath him. His only television program was just a particular section in the Eastern Eye Witness. He now rarely engaged in scouting for first-hand reports as a journalist.

He turned slightly to shoot a glance at Hao Sijing before

turning back to Su Mansheng and said, "I've seen those awful comments on the internet. I will look into it, and if I discover that the mastermind behind those rumors was someone from our program, I promise I will give you a proper apology."

Su Mansheng gave him a smile and said, "Sure." She then turned to find Tao Longyue.

This episode quickly became the next trending topic on social media websites. In fear of what might happen, Su Mansheng asked Tao Longyue to send Xiao Qun over to stay with Song Qilian temporarily, waiting patiently for the fish to take the bait.

Gentle Teeth

Judging by the timing between Luo Xin's death and the following two victims, Qiao Hui would act within two to three days after he locked in on a target. After the episode about sexual assault on the Eastern Eye Witness, the violent crimes unit had been keeping an eye around Su Mansheng's residence around the clock, waiting for Qiao Hui to take the bait.

Qiao Hui may have taken a more conservative route this time. The police had been waiting for a full week and didn't see even a sign of the man.

The sky darkened earlier during winter and streetlights glowed in a warm yellow. Xiao Liang's old car parked on the street side looked no different from a car parked overnight in a residential area. He was on duty with Ding Li tonight.

"Why are we the only two tonight?" This was the first time Ding Li participated in a frontline mission like this, reluctance and dread written all over her face as she complained, "Where's Cap'n Tao?"

"He's been waiting for days already with an injury, he's gonna end up back in the hospital again if he stays here any longer." Xiao Liang sipped his boba coffee slowly. A special blend coffee with boba was certainly a unique taste, but he was most afraid of falling asleep. He said, "Besides, Old Tao is checking out of the hospital today. Cap's got his hands tied up."

"What about senior Xie?"

"Big bro's also been on standby the last few days. We can't let him die from overwork." Xiao Liang's sharp and clear eyes stared outside the window—his vision was top-notch even among his colleagues. He split his attention between keeping an eye out the window and listening to the situation inside Su Mansheng's house.

"What about Mr. Shen?" Ding Li pestered.

"Mr. Shen's just a specialist in the bureau, not a cop. Dang, why do you have so many questions?!" Xiao Liang turned and flicked her forehead with his free hand and said, "Stay alert, remember that we have to serve the people! I know Cap'n Tao said to contact him immediately if anything happens, but listen, I can handle Qiao Hui on my own, don't worry."

Ding Li couldn't stand being bullied and flicked her colleague back. While the two were engaged in a childish fight, a delivery person arrived on his bike. Deliveries often came in and out of the residential area during the day. It was already 7 P.M., close to the end of the rush hour for food deliveries.

Xiao Liang allowed Ding Li to continue hitting his arm as he turned and said, defeated, "Alright, alright, that's enough. We have work to do still."

"But it's not even that late? He can't possibly commit a murder this early."

"That's not true," Xiao Liang said. He was still more experienced in these types of situations than her and explained, "Gotta strike when people least expect, you know?"

"Is he really going to show up?" Ding Li rubbed her head

and pouted. "We have eyes everywhere. If I was Qiao Hui, I wouldn't show up."

"What kind of young woman would dare walk out in a time like this in a red dress? This guy's like an obsessive drug addict, he'll take the bait as soon as he sniffs something out." Xiao Liang took another large gulp of his coffee and said as he chewed on the boba, "Besides, doesn't Doctor Su know him? He has to show up."

The two stopped their conversation, but nothing came out of the other side of the listening device.

"Say, what do you think Dr. Su's role is in the Cangnan case?" Ding Li broke the silence after a few minutes. She was a typical internet addict who loved reading gossip, believing every word on the web. She asked, "Didn't the internet say that she was that Kong Xiangping person's accomplice?"

"You still believe that? That female journalist from the Eastern Eye Witness already got fired—" Xiao Liang stopped abruptly, his eyes widened, and he shouted, "How long has that delivery boy been inside?"

There were still no sounds from the other side of the listening device. Xiao Liang recognized something was off and carefully adjusted his headset to listen in closer. Stray dogs barked around this residential area every night. There was no reason for the headset to be completely silent.

Xiao Liang quickly got out of the car and called out to Ding Li, "Give Captain Tao a call, quick!"

In the eyes of the violent crimes unit, Su Mansheng's appearance on the news program was the lure that struck Qiao Hui's obsession. However, Su Mansheng herself believed that her performance on screen was the real bait for the man. Judging from her strange relationship with Qiao Hui, the words she had said were a blatant betrayal as a "mother" to him—and an angered child certainly had the right to question his mother.

Convinced that she had a split personality and to avoid her other self from contacting Qiao Hui, Su Mansheng voluntarily turned off all of her communication devices and requested the violent crimes unit to place listening devices throughout her house.

Su Mansheng stood up from the darkness as she heard someone sneak into her house and turned off the listening devices. She still wore the vibrant red dress but cut off the excess long fabric on the skirt to maximize mobility. Her strong and slender legs were exposed beneath the dress like a proud goddess of war.

She was a woman, a victim, a hidden criminal, and a cop.

As a woman, she had already stood up and spoken up for all women who were victims of sexual abuse. As a victim, she needed to fight for her justice. As a hidden criminal, she planned on offering her own blood to atone for her sins. As a cop, she was ready to give to life to accomplish her goals at any moment.

The lights inside the living room were off, leaving only the moonlight piercing through the windows. Su Mansheng purposely left on the lights in her bedroom and played relaxing music to fool Qiao Hui, luring him into the trap. She hid herself in a corner of the bedroom.

By the time the police outside noticed something was off, she thought, there would only be two different ends inside this house. Either Qiao Hui died or Qiao Hui was injured and she died; either way, she did not plan on letting this evil murderer leave tonight.

The house was spacious and large—she could clearly hear every little creak on the flooring—that invader certainly walked toward the light in the bedroom.

Su Mansheng tightly gripped the knife in her hand. She often trained in boxing clubs during her free time and gained some muscles that made her body stiffer than the average woman. At this moment, every muscle in her body tensed up, ready to strike.

The air grew colder, her opponent drew closer. Sweat rolled down her tall nose as she reminded herself to control her breathing, then wait for the right moment to strike down her enemy.

A silhouette first peeked in across the flooring and grew larger as the person stepped closer. Su Mansheng found the right time and struck out.

Qiao Hui instinctively dodged past the flash of a blade. The knife stabbed right into his shoulder and he growled in pain. He quickly turned with a bloodied human skin mask on his face, disgusting and horrifying. Su Mansheng was caught off guard for a moment, then immediately took a blow to her head by the metal rod in Qiao Hui's hands.

The delivery disguise and bike helmet were all tossed outside the house. This metal rod was something he took out from the delivery box. It was also the tool he had been using to violate his victims.

Su Mansheng's head spun as she took two steps back, then after regaining her balance, quickly struck forward again.

The two soon engaged in a fistfight—more accurately, they were ripping, cutting, and scratching each other.

The knife and metal rod dropped to the ground, the mask and skirt both ripped. Qiao Hui fought like a madman, but Su Mansheng was also fighting for her life. Even though she was much smaller than him, she still held up a good fight; she was more dexterous and professional; she did not fear pain nor death.

The two fell onto the ground once again, and Su Mansheng used the opportunity to choke the man's neck with her thighs.

Qiao Hui was out of breath but dared not to cry out; both in fear of attracting the police and accelerating his suffocation by this powerful force. After another brawl on the ground, Su Mansheng found an opportunity to jump back up. She sat on the man's chest, spread her legs out to pin down his arms with her body. She picked up the knife she had dropped earlier and prepared to give him a fatal blow.

The man began begging for his life and repeated, "Sorry, I won't do it again." He wanted to find a moment of hesitation to strike back at Su Mansheng using the surgical knife he hid in his sleeves.

"I'm sorry, I'm a bastard... I promise I won't do it again..." Qiao Hui said as he reached for his knife.

"That's right, you're a bastard." Su Mansheng stabbed down without hesitation just before the man was able to strike, cutting through his throat.

Fresh blood spilled out and stained the walls along with her face. The dying man twitched in an ugly manner beneath her.

Su Mansheng lowered her head and exposed the face beneath that ugly mask, her eyes on his features. Qiao Hui was rather decent-looking in appearance and tall, but his death was ugly and pitiful, his face twisted in tears. The fearsome serial murderer was merely another coward who could only hide behind a mask. Su Mansheng stood up and spat in disdain on his body.

The red police lights shone outside the window. Su Mansheng opened the window and lifted her head amidst the gentle breeze that blew inside her house, greeting the brightest moonlight with a face stained in blood.

The music that played from the bedroom continued with a serene melody. She could hear the dogs barking, the sirens, and cries of pedestrians, and footsteps outside. She also heard that powerful heartbeat within her chest.

Hundreds and thousands of years ago, almost as long as the start of creation, there lived a group of people on this land. They were helpless wives and enduring mothers. They were benevolent and kind, who still offered love and kindness to the world that only opened their fangs to them.

But gentleness must come with sharp teeth.

By the time Tao Longyue arrived, the battle had already ended.

Su Mansheng wiped off Qiao Hui's blood that splashed onto her face but couldn't stop her own blood from rolling down her nose and mouth. She trudged with injuries toward her lover and smiled. "Do I look like a mess right now?"

Her forehead and chin were bruised, teeth covered in blood inside her mouth.

Tao Longyue embraced this woman tightly. He buried his face in her neck and wept. "You still look great, you're always beautiful."

The next day, Su Mansheng turned herself into the bureau with Tao Longyue by her side. She gave the necklace, the letters spanning over ten years, and that piece of human skin to the police. She confessed she was a patient of dissociative identity disorder, and judging from the contents of the letters, also the mastermind that incited Qiao Hui to murder innocent girls.

Su Mansheng was very cooperative and confessed that she would shoulder all legal consequences that came with this.

Yet the tech team reported a surprising discovery. Among the letters that spanned over ten years of exchange, some paper was purposely made to artificially look old and the writing was tampered with to look a little different between letters. It was as if they were made to look like the writer matured over the years, but in actuality, they were all written very recently. In other words, while it was indeed Qiao Hui's writing, these were all written around the same time not that long ago.

Even more shocking was that after an investigation of Su Mansheng's residence, the team discovered that there were traces of drugs in her water cups. All the strange migraines, trance-like states of mind, and depression originated from a drug called Mefloquine, which could even trigger thoughts of suicide.

(ii)

The investigation team assumed that the serial murder case would finally end with Qiao Hui's death, but the confirmation that Su Mansheng did not have a dissociative personality disorder and was unacquainted with Qiao Hui proved that the "mother" who was behind the murder cases was someone else.

The violent crimes unit summoned an emergency meeting in response. Xie Lanshan rubbed his chin and analyzed, "Su Mansheng is a doctor, so the only way to drug her without letting her find out is to do small doses over a long period of time—there's only one person who could possibly do this."

Shen Liufei nodded at the revelation and said, "We missed the most important person."

Despite the mysteries of the case clearing up and all evidence pointing at Xiao Qun, Xie Lanshan still couldn't believe it and said, "But she only looks to be about 14 or 15. She wasn't even born when the Cangnan incident occurred.

There was no way she could have been able to obtain all this information that not even the police knew."

Shen Liufei pondered briefly with his eyebrows together, then gave a bold hypothesis. "Appearance isn't an accurate determinant of age. Do you remember? She had once cried and yelled about not wanting to go through a physical examination in the Puren Hospital. Now that we pieced everything together, it seems likely that she feared the doctor would discover she had once borne a child."

Tao Longyue was in a state of disbelief as he asked, "A child? You mean that child is Qiao Hui?"

Shen Liufei said, "In the Cangnan murder case, the police had found feminine products and infant supplies in the culprit Kong Xiangping's home. We had thus been assuming that Su Mansheng was that spiritual 'mother' Qiao Hui referred to, judging based on their ages that they have known each other since childhood and kept in contact with Su Mansheng's assumed secondary personality. Yet Kong Xiangping never married, so it's possible that the child was stolen or picked up. It could also possibly be a child he had with one of the girls he kidnapped in his basement. And that person is the second survivor of the Cangnan case beside Su Mansheng, who is also the mastermind behind the current serial murder case."

Tao Longyue gasped. "And you're saying that person is Xiao Qun?" Not that he didn't want to believe it, but this sounded like an impossible fantasy novel. This young girl looked innocent and young, sheepish around everyone except for the Captain himself; who could have imagined she would be an evil middle-aged woman?

Xie Lanshan continued, "This also explains why the culprit waited twenty years later to replicate the murder in the past. Qiao Hui was a first-year graduate medical student when he first came to Hanhai City. It's possible that Xiao Qun, who came to Hanhai City with her son, had seen Su Mansheng on the streets one day."

Tao Longyue still wasn't following and asked, "Then why does she have such a twisted hatred towards Mansheng, to where she is willing to plan out such a meticulous and evil plot to force her into committing suicide? Wasn't Xiao Man also a victim like herself back then?"

Xie Lanshan responded, "It must be either her evil heart to wish ill on others or to fulfill her own selfish desires. I have a theory: Xiao Qun may have Stockholm syndrome and truly fell in love with Kong Xiangping, so she developed a hatred toward Su Mansheng, the last victim, who caused Kong Xiangping's death."

Tao Longyue responded after considering the possibility, "These are all just assumptions right now. Either way, we need to bring Xiao Qun back to the bureau and ask her to find out the truth." He added after a little more thought, "She must still be at Qilian's house. Because we were busy chasing down Qiao Hui, we told the girl that we'll have her stay temporarily with Qilian for therapy and sent her over."

Shen Liufei checked the time and asked with a frown, "What time is News China airing?"

Mr. Shen came back from the U.S. and didn't have a habit of watching the news every day in China, but he knew that the country's biggest news channel would announce the death of murderer Qiao Hui today—and Song Qilian was the person credited for the plan to capture him.

This would mean that they were letting a dangerous killer live under the same roof as her sworn enemy. Xie Lanshan recognized the danger of the situation and ran out the door with a stern expression.

It was rush hour in the evening; the streets were filled with traffic. It would almost be impossible to pass through, even with a police car. Rescuing a person was as urgent as putting out a fire; Shen Liufei called out to him, "Xie Lanshan, I'll take you over."

Night fell, the sky darkened like the abyss. The television was tuned to the News China channel while Song Qilian was cooking for the two children in the kitchen. She carefully prepared the ingredients. Through the sizzling sounds of hot oil and cooking, she heard the news report that Qiao Hui seemed to have been captured.

A refreshing stir-fried vegetable, steamed fish, and chicken soup with red dates were set on the table. Xiao Qun had always preferred light dishes, and Song Qilian's son had a small ulcer in his mouth, so dinner was simple and healthy.

"Xiao Qun, Changchang, time to eat." Song Qilian called out to the children's room after she placed the utensils down, but received no response.

She turned to look into the living room when she suddenly heard a loud banging sound from the bathroom and rushed over.

As soon as she opened the door, she saw her son's mouth taped up, limbs tied, and tossed into the large tub—that loud noise must have been the boy's desperate cry for help from kicking the walls.

Song Qilian gasped. As she was about to run to save her son, a dark shadow crept up from behind and knocked her down with a glass bottle.

She struggled to get up but received another heavy blow on her head. The force this time was even greater than before and caused bleeding.

The glass bottle shattered on the ground. Song Qilian was

unable to stand up from the pain. She desperately crawled toward her son while turning her head back.

She was surprised to find that the attacker was Xiao Qun.

The "little girl" had already turned off her cellphone and tossed it on the ground. She looked at the woman from above and sneered, "How did you all think the person who was controlling Qiao Hui to kill people was Su Mansheng?"

Song Qilian immediately understood that she was facing an extremely dangerous situation right now. She quickly came to a reasonable conclusion and attempted to talk to the hateful girl in front of her, "You weren't wrong for being sexually assaulted. It's natural for you to develop Stockholm syndrome under those circumstances, so there's no need to feel burdened by guilt. You should not worry about submitting and bowing down to such a horrible person who harmed you; please, believe me, a professional doctor can help you..."

"A professional? Like you? You couldn't even tell I was putting on an act." The "little girl" laughed sharply, then bent down and patted Song Qilian's face, "You're too young, little girl."

That's when Song Qilian noticed that Xiao Qun's voice didn't fit her supposed age; it was too dry and rough.

"It's tiring to put on an act for long periods of time, but if I don't pretend I'm still in a state of trauma, you guys will certainly question me and expose my identity." Xiao Qun—or perhaps the middle-aged woman whose real name wasn't Xiao Qun—seemed to look much different just with a change of her expression. Her appearance also seemed to transform along with the tone of her voice, becoming evil and mature, filled with hatred. She kicked Song Qilian's stomach heavily and cursed, "You bitch with all these stupid ideas, that man you indirectly killed was my son!"

(iii)

Song Qilian curled up from the pain and asked, "Who... who's your son...?"

"You fool, you still don't understand? I've never had what you call 'victim complex,' I love my son like I love my husband!" The "little girl" once again kicked Song Qilian violently a few times before squatting down and taping the woman up. She explained as she wrapped the tape, "I've been engaged in everything willingly since the beginning. I was fourteen that year. I lived with my grandmother and aunt in the small village. My parents took my two little brothers to the big cities and worked restlessly for them. They poured out everything they could to make sure those two idiots could live a good life, but never even gave me a look in the eye. My aunt didn't think girls should spend their time in school and wanted me to quit to get a job or find a single man in the village to get married to. That way, at least her son could also live a relatively good life by proxy and use the dowry to buy him some nice shoes.

"And then I met him. He was a volunteer doctor at the village; he was tall, not particularly handsome, but very classy. He's like Leon from The Professional—oh, by the way, I watched that film with him in his house. We were laying on the bed together, the screen was above us; I'd never seen such a good movie in my life before and ended up crying for a whole night in my bed afterward. He bought me dolls and red dresses, then told me about those intimate things between a man and woman. I'd asked my aunt about it before too, because I kept seeing her sneak out of the house in the middle of the night. Our neighbors were also always talking about how she was sleeping with the managers of the village while my uncle was working out of town. But my aunt freaked out when she heard me ask; she took out a scissor and cut my hair, saying that I'm learning all bad things... Ah, and the doctor would be moving to another place soon to help out. Realizing that I couldn't find anyone else who would make me laugh like him, I eloped with him.

"I was deathly afraid of the police when I first ran off with him, worried that I would be captured and brought back to that shabby place. But I quickly discovered that they didn't call the cops and instead were probably pleased a burden was dragged off their shoulders. I became pregnant soon after, and of course, I discovered his slightly abnormal little kinks. So, I helped him lure those little girls into the house so that he can play around with the toys. I hid very well, so nobody knew of my existence. He was also very well-respected in the village, so nobody suspected him. Life was great up until then. He later betrayed me and fell in love with that little slut! He became less interested in me, so I had no choice but to kill him. I drugged his drinks and sliced his throat while he was bathing intoxicated."

The little girl walked toward the bathtub and turned on the faucet. Cold water ran down on the little boy inside; he tried to struggle but slipped inside the tub.

"You killed my son so I'm going to kill yours." The girl lifted her face and put on an innocent smile as she purposely spoke in a higher range. "I want you to watch him drown slowly before your eyes, and you foolish so-called psychologist will have no way of saving him."

Song Qilian's tears rolled down as she began begging, "Xiao... whatever your name is, I've never harmed you before. I understand the feeling of loneliness and being unwanted since you were young; I've always wanted to help you. If you are here to get your revenge on me, please, don't hurt my son, take it out on me!"

The little girl shook her head in disdain and clicked her tongue. She had lived with this family for almost a week now and seemed to have grown quite interested in professional psychoanalysis. Her eyes locked on Song Qilian and studied the woman as she asked, "Are you a saint or something? Do you really like helping people that much? Why don't you psychoanalyze yourself instead? You're like a bitch in heat waiting for that Officer Xie to ride back on you, only to discover that he no longer loves you anymore. You feel insulted, betrayed, and you're extremely jealous of his new interest, also extremely angered. That's why you finally wrote that mental health report to ruin his life...Love is always blind and selfish, you're no better than me."

Song Qilian refused to be put down by these words and denied it out loud, "I am not! I've never wanted to ruin him!"

"The sudden lift in your tone proves that you're getting defensive, you're lying." The little girl stared into Song Qilian's eyes, then suddenly twisted her lips up in an eerie manner and said, "Look, I can analyze you just like the way you do with me."

The water level in the tub was getting higher, the boy's nose was still barely outside but was getting close to being devoured by water. Song Qilian was already scared to death, but amidst her fear she had a strange feeling: *Xie Lanshan will come.*

Song Qilian realized that this twisted woman before her enjoyed sending out orders, so she used that grotesque obsession with control to buy herself some time. To keep the other's attention away while she attempted to pull her hands out of the tape, she looked at the woman before her and said as if speaking to a mentor, "That's right, he doesn't love me anymore! I'm restless everyday thinking about how to get my revenge on him. Maybe I should have met you sooner. I'm sure you could have given me a better idea than writing a psychological assessment."

This satisfied little girl's twisted heart as she laughed, dancing around like a madwoman.

"I spent a lot of effort to raise him into adulthood; he shared a lot of similarities with his father. Yet he even dared to be like his father and wanted to ignore and run away from me. He wrote a love letter to a girl in his class during high school, so I kidnapped the girl and put her in a red dress, showing him his father's favorite image. Then, I forced him to murder her right in front of me. Luckily nobody found that girl's dead body, and my son also developed the same strange interest as his father... He feared me, hated me, and of course, I had thought he loved me."

Song Qilian broke out of the tape in time and heard a bike rushing toward her house outside the window. Suddenly, she called out to the twisted woman, "Listen, he's here!"

While Xiao Qun turned to look outside the window, Song Qilian pulled herself off the ground and shoved the former down onto the ground. She then quickly picked up her son drowning in the cold water and rushed out the door.

The little girl crawled up and chased after her with a knife in hand. Danger was steps away, Song Qilian used all of her strength to carry her son downstairs, running right into Xie Lanshan who was making his way up the stairs.

After she saw this handsome and anxious face, Song Qilian's tears rolled down her face. She no longer felt exhausted or in pain. She knew she was finally safe.

Xiao Qun came down with a knife, then quickly turned to run back upstairs as soon as she saw Xie Lanshan.

"A'Lan, please save Changchang! He, he isn't breathing..."

Xie Lanshan was already making his way up when he heard Song Qilian's cries, then paused and hesitated to turn back. Shen Liufei arrived at the moment and called out to him, "Go deal with the culprit. I'll take care of the boy."

. . .

Xie Lanshan swiftly made his way up, forcing the mastermind to go up to the rooftop with nowhere else to hide.

The little girl stood at the edge of the roof and called out in the chilly night with a knife in her hand, "Don't come any closer or I'll jump!"

Xie Lanshan didn't pull his gun, nor did he pursue the woman. He stood still and tried to convince her to turn herself in.

The woman certainly looked much younger than her actual age, but when she wasn't purposely trying to disguise herself as a young woman, her expression grotesquely exposed her age. In addition to her doll-like long hair, it made the woman look even more disturbing and twisted.

She was still looking around hoping to find a route of escape, then cried out as she swung her knife around, "The real culprit is Su Mansheng! If she didn't seduce my lover, our family would have been living in peace and happiness! How dare she be able to restart her life after causing this tragedy? I hate her, I despise her!"

"Your hatred is directed toward the wrong person." Xie Lanshan took a step forward and said calmly, "You should hate Kong Xiangping and your parents who neglected you. Because of their negligence, this evil man easily stole your virginity and love with one red dress. Unfortunately, he had never loved you, nor had he ever loved Xiao Man. I'm assuming the reason why you two didn't get killed was because he wasn't just an extremely awful sexual assaulter. He was also a disgusting and ugly pedophile."

"You're lying!" She screamed in a frenzy, "He loved me! Before that whore came, he had always loved me!"

"This was never a love story to begin with." Xie Lanshan

shrugged coldly to indicate his disinterest in her own delusions and love. He said, "This is just a story of a poor and lonely girl with an inferiority complex who found the wrong teacher for sexual education."

Xiao Qun felt her whole life's belief in love shattered at that moment. She charged toward Xie Lanshan like a madwoman. The latter dodged the attack with ease. Soon after, he threw a kick from the side and knocked the knife from the perpetrator's hand away.

Xiao Qun rushed to pick up the knife, then lost her balance for a moment and fell off the roof. Xie Lanshan ran up just in time and caught the woman's wrist before she dropped to the ground.

The winds blew harshly as her legs hung twenty stories above the ground; the looming shadow of death could easily consume her at any moment. Xiao Qun grew fearful as she lifted her head, then pleaded to the cop above her, "Save me... I don't want to die... save me...."

She was certainly small and light. If she didn't struggle, Xie Lanshan could easily pull her up—and he was ready to do so.

In order to fight for her survival, the little girl continued to cry to him. "I'm a mental health patient. I've been sexually harassed by Kong Xiangping when I was little and suffered huge trauma. Please save me and give me a chance to repent."

"No, you're not a mental health patient." Xie Lanshan's gaze darkened at that moment, shocking even the girl he held. The man had rushed over to save her on instinct, but his gaze right now didn't seem like the same cop from moments earlier.

"I really am mentally ill. You can check with professionals." The little girl seemed to be confident that she could once again fool professional psychologists after she had succeeded once. Besides, she had a true and horrific backstory to support her claims.

And mental health patients did not need to serve sentences under the laws of the country.

"The judicial department has a database. Among the most severe violent crimes, over 70% of all criminals who have served their full sentences will repeat the crime upon release." Xie Lanshan's hand still grabbed onto the woman, his gaze locked in with her eyes as he continued, "As for demons without a heart like you, the reoffense rate is near 100%."

The man's fringes had grown long. Because of the angle he was holding this little girl, his hair fell across his forehead and blew gently against the breeze. His eyes flashed through the hair strands like flickering lights in the dark.

"So what if that's the case, what can you even do? You're a cop. Your job is to arrest me. As for what the court finally decides in the end, that's none of your business." The little girl gave an arrogant grin as she looked at him provocatively.

She would never stop killing.

Yet, as soon as she met the man's eyes, she was stunned.

This handsome face was surrounded by the mist of the night. Even though the moonlight tonight was bright, the little girl almost thought she had a delusion and saw the cop smile.

It was a very faint but beautiful smile, both carrying the light of purity like a saint and the darkness of a bloodthirsty demon.

Tao Longyue and his team finally arrived after passing through the traffic. Captain Tao had just gotten out of his car and heard an enormous thump on the ground behind him before he could rush up the stairs.

He turned his head to look and the hand holding his gun loosened. Extreme shock and biological discomfort appeared on his face; he felt like puking out of disgust. His breath stopped briefly.

Xiao Qun was dead on the ground less than two meters away from him. Her eyes bulged out of her sockets, brain splattered everywhere on the ground as her body twisted like her spine had been removed.

Tao Longyue stood frozen as he coldly watched this woman. Who said that fallen petals resembled the lovesick who leapt to their deaths? It was clear that poet Du Mu was lying. It may be an instinctive reaction, but the woman's face and body began to spasm. Tao Longyue noticed this woman's reddened eyes, as if she would never rest in peace, but there was no sign of fear on her face—instead, there was only a peaceful smile.

(iv)

Tao Longyue rushed up the stairs and met up with Xie Lanshan, who was walking down. The latter explained with a calm expression that the suspect refused the arrest and jumped from the building.

This reaction was too calm. Tao Longyue wanted to pursue the question further only to see Xie Lanshan walk past him with no intention of elaborating. He walked beside Song Qilian and asked about her son's situation.

Little Liu Chang had just woken from Shen Liufei's CPR and immediately puffed up proudly as he saw Xie Lanshan to say, "Uncle Xie, listen! I didn't learn to hold my breath from you for nothing. I held my breath for three minutes underwater earlier!"

Song Qilian rushed to give Xie Lanshan a tight embrace with tears all over her face, ready to consume him with the passion burning inside her chest.

"At least you and Changchang are both okay, don't worry—"

Before Xie Lanshan could finish, Song Qilian had already cupped his face, stood on her toes, and pressed her lips against his.

The woman's lips were sweet and soft, but her kiss was passionate and uncontrolled. Xie Lanshan was a little shocked and widened his eyes; even though he didn't respond to her passion, he also couldn't bring himself to push her aside.

This scene also stunned Tao Longyue, and he subconsciously glanced at Shen Liufei. The latter didn't show any reaction on his usual blank face; he simply lowered his gaze and walked away.

It was 10 P.M. and the city lights glowed. Animals returned to their huts while night predators waited for their time to hunt. Shen Liufei didn't want to return home and kept turning the handle on his bike until he reached the maximum acceleration on his engine.

The gas pedal pushed toward the bottom, speed accelerated to race against even the winds that blew past him as he darted through the ambient lights of the city.

Moonlight illuminated from above, while the scenery ahead was a dreamlike cityscape. Yet that scene from earlier could not be erased from his mind; Shen Liufei pressed his eyebrows together and his bike speed went up another notch.

He hadn't visited the boxing bar in a while, but for some reason, he felt the need to vent tonight.

The owner of the bar was happy at his arrival and greeted him enthusiastically, "Ah, Mr. Shen, haven't seen you in a while."

Shen Liufei gave a small sound of acknowledgment and

glanced half-heartedly at the people sitting inside the bar; the noisy little tavern suddenly became quiet for a few seconds.

The newcomer was almost eye-catchingly handsome. His sophisticated outfit made him look a step above most people around him. This certainly attracted looks from both men and women alike. The owner of the bar was quite acquainted with Shen Liufei and knew his customer better than others. He had always thought the artist gave off a more docile and melancholic air around him, but upon closer inspection, his expression and eyes contrasted the calm appearance. What was even more interesting was that the man's face looked awfully young, perhaps as young as seventeen or eighteen, but the maturity in those sharp eyes made him look much older than his physical appearance. The bar owner didn't shy away like others and called out to his regular, "Someone's heard of your name and came by a few times to request a spar with you. He happens to be here today, too. Should I arrange for a round?"

Shen Liufei nodded, then said, "I don't have my equipment."

It was a spur of the moment so he didn't come prepared, but he didn't mind too much since it was just a method of venting. The owner quickly brought a big man over and introduced him as A'Xun. The man was apparently a professional boxer who came for a quick buck and had been waiting for the rumored Mr. Shen for days at the bar.

A'Xun had unique features and tanned skin, sharing some physical characteristics of Southeastern Asian men. He was a tad bit taller than Shen Liufei, muscles on his whole body shined like metal. His large eyes were sharp like an unsheathed blade, making him look very intimidating.

Unfortunately, the man only looked tough in appearance. Shen Liufei didn't even change his clothes and swiftly moved across the ring, knocking his opponent down within a few strikes.

A'Xun was still on the ground in a kneeling position as he held his stomach and grumbled. Shen Liufei felt a little apologetic; he didn't hold back this time in order to release his pent-up anger and accidentally threw some heavy punches, only to harm the other more than he felt he was warranted. He let out a small breath of air, calmed himself down, and walked toward his opponent. Courteously, he waved a hand at the man and offered to pull him back up.

Yet that A'Xun person jumped like a sneaky predator waiting for an opportunity. He reached a hand out as if he were to grab onto Shen Liufei's hand, only to pull out a knife he had hidden well before the match. Then, he looked up suddenly and stabbed the knife right toward Shen Liufei's abdomen.

The latter was already distracted by his own thoughts and was completely caught off guard by this sneak attack. Thankfully, he reacted just in time to dodge a heavy impact—he held up his hand to shield his body as he took a step back. The knife didn't strike his body, but it certainly pierced through his left hand.

Fresh blood began dripping down; the audience gasped in shock. A'Xun quickly crawled up and ran out of the bar.

The bar owner called the cops amidst the chaos. Xie Lanshan received the message about a violent attack in the bar before he even made it back home.

Luckily, this stab didn't harm important nerves on his hand. Shen Liufei looked at it and recognized that the muscle would heal fully in about three weeks.

Xie Lanshan dashed back home to see Shen Liufei sitting by the bedside, his arms pressed onto his knee and his back arched forward slightly. He stared quietly ahead of him as if in deep thought.

Xie Lanshan walked over with a stern and concerned expression and got down on one knee in front of Shen Liufei. He began unwrapping the bandages on the artist's left hand as he pulled out a small bottle from his pocket, hoping to put extra medicine on the injury.

Xie Lanshan said that it was a special type of medicine the police used to deal with these kinds of injuries.

He carefully unwrapped the bandages to see a horrific and bloodied wound with blood still seeping out. Xie Lanshan's heart ached as he eyed the injury, feeling his eyes burning up. He lowered his head and poured the opened bottle onto Shen Liufei's palm, right onto the injury.

It was already shocking for him to go boxing at a time like this, even more so that it injured the man. Xie Lanshan pondered a little and immediately realized it was the kiss earlier that made the artist act up.

Xie Lanshan complained to the man for not taking care of himself and scolded as he treated the wound, "Please, you're an artist that still needs these hands to draw. Can't you just leave the beating people up part to me in the future?"

The liquid medicine stung, more painful than driving a knife into an open wound. Shen Liufei couldn't withstand the pain and asked with a frown, "Just what is this medication?"

"Cops special spice water." Xie Lanshan lifted his head and gave Shen Liufei an innocent, pure smile. "Pure healing with no side-effects, especially good for treating dishonesty."

"What?" Another sharp pain stung from his injury, mixing in with a strange tingling sensation as if countless bugs were biting into his flesh. Shen Liufei's expression remained calm, but his tone was raised, clearly upset.

"No pain, no gain, cuz. Your life isn't just your own now. I won't let you be so careless anymore." Xie Lanshan pressed Shen Liufei's injured hand beneath his palm and re-wrapped the injury with the bandages. He looked up again with a smile and said sternly, "I will always care for Qilian, like a sister and family. I am willing to protect her health and safety at all costs, but you're different from her."

The young cop kneeled before Shen Liufei and took the bullet shell necklace off his neck. He then wrapped it around the artist's injured hand and pressed rains of kisses on those palms as if holding a precious treasure.

Remember that I love you.

Remember to always remember this.

(v)

It wasn't disgusting or strange to be so intimate with someone you loved, and instead rather comfortable. Xie Lanshan felt he did well and leaned down by Shen Liufei's knee in satisfaction. He closed his eyes and rubbed his face on Shen Liufei's leg like a cat, completely ignoring the annoyed expression on the latter's face.

Moonlight leaked into the room through the windows and cast a layer of thin silver on the floor. The two kept this position for a while until Shen Liufei suddenly said, "Didn't you used to pester me about wanting to know about my family?"

Xie Lanshan looked up silently. A spark of surprise flashed across his eyes.

Shen Liufei lowered his head and met his gaze, then said firmly, "I can tell you right now."

The horrifying massacre was nothing but old news from the mouth of the survivor. Judging by the way he spoke, Shen

Liufei seemed to have a closer relationship with his mother than with his father; he would soften his voice whenever he spoke of her and called his father "that man".

He told Xie Lanshan that the police had been following the wrong clues and let the culprit escape for a whole seventeen years; he was finally caught after repeating the same crime many years later.

The brief explanation still shook Xie Lanshan. He had wanted to make a place for himself in Shen Liufei's life, but now he could feel nothing but heartache and asked, "You must hate that culprit with your whole life, don't you?"

"Not really." Shen Liufei truly never considered this question in the past and after giving some thought now, he really didn't hold such a deep grudge. He simply said, "Because it may have been rather freeing to my mom."

Xie Lanshan, surprised by that, asked, "How so?"

Shen Liufei felt a little drowsy and laid on the bed, then said with his eyes closed, "In all of my childhood memories of her, she was being beaten up by that man. There was almost no instance where she wasn't without an injury or bruise somewhere. That man would also hit me and my brother. There were a few times where my mom tried to run, but that man would say that he would kill himself along with me and my brother, so she had no choice but to endure everything. She had lived her life enduring everything around her; I tried to talk to her and even scolded her for it, but her heart was too soft. She quickly fell into the traps of that man's lies and believed she could live life if she just bit her teeth down. But that's not how you live a life."

Xie Lanshan didn't intend on pestering further and climbed up onto the bed after he listened to the story. He laid on his side and faced Shen Liufei's back, pressing their bodies against each other. He wrapped his arm around the artist's waist, buried his face into the exposed neck, then cradled the injured hand as the two fell into deep slumber.

Xie Lanshan paid another visit to the boxing bar the first few days of Shen Liufei's recovery. He was an experienced drug enforcement officer and naturally had some reliable spies that worked with him. He asked his informants to search for A'Xun's location.

A'Xun knew he screwed up and had been in hiding for a couple of days, seeing no signs of a cop showing up. He was growing bored with this life and invited a few friends over for hotpot.

He had grown used to eating the local cuisine and the spicy lamb meat hotpot. He quickly prepared a pot, fresh vegetables, lamb meat, seafood, and other common hot pot foods to pack. The location he picked was beneath a large tent outside a deserted shopping district, ready to dig into the food after his friends arrived.

The six people had just sat down around the small wooden table. While the red pot was boiling, a person suddenly walked into the tent before they could even take two bites of their food.

Xie Lanshan flashed his police badge and gave a courteous smile towards the room full of baffled men. "The party is over."

A'Xun knew the cop was after him. After confirming that it was only Xie Lanshan himself, he gave his buddies a look—the five men that sat around him all stood up. They turned and glared at Xie Lanshan, ready to surround him and take down the cop.

Unafraid to fight against these people, Xie Lanshan's gaze glossed over these boxers. Noticing that over half of them looked foreign, he said with a smile, "We Chinese people have a saying: every injustice has a perpetrator and every debt a debtor. I'm here for A'Xun, so please make way."

These boxers had all done some shady things in the past, but despite their hostile looks, most people were still afraid of cops. They circled around Xie Lanshan to intimidate the lone cop but didn't dare to throw the first punch.

Of course, Xie Lanshan paid no attention to these boxers; he wouldn't bat an eye even if there were more. Xie Lanshan didn't like beating around the bush and locked his gaze on A'Xun, then walked straight toward his target without hesitation.

This was a blatant provocation. A'Xun called out, "Get him!" A smaller, tanned man pulled up a stool and slammed it toward Xie Lanshan's head.

Xie Lanshan only dodged when the shadow of the stool fell onto his shoulders, then turned and gave a roundhouse kick right into the rib of the attacker. The man dropped to the ground instantly and cried out in pain.

Xie Lanshan eyed the man on the ground and asked the rest of the party with a grin, "Still gonna stick around?"

This one demonstration proved the cop didn't come unprepared. The crowd immediately dispersed, leaving A'Xun alone in the tent to face Xie Lanshan.

"Sorry... I didn't mean it..." The internal injury he suffered from Shen Liufei's punches was still not fully healed. A'Xun knew he couldn't fight against the cop and could only apologize with his accented Chinese, pleading as he backed away, "I'm really sorry..."

"Cops would be out of work if an apology can settle everything." Xie Lanshan lifted an eyebrow and took a step forward. He kicked over the wooden table, the boiling hot pot soup spilled across the floor. A'Xun couldn't dodge in time and fell to the ground.

Xie Lanshan clenched his fist, his knuckles cracked as he stepped over a floor of oily vegetables. He smiled again. "You can return punches."

"Can't I just turn myself in? Here, cuff me up and just take me back to the station."

"That's what a good cop does, but I'm a bad cop." Xie Lanshan's gaze darkened suddenly as he said, "He's an artist, how dare you hurt his hand."

The man looked like an elegant and beautiful pretty boy, but every punch he threw was deadly, making him look like an evil demonic god. A'Xun felt wronged and helpless. Just what kind of cop won't even accept a suspect turning himself in? With the cop drawing closer to him, he had no choice but to run desperately outside the tent.

Xie Lanshan chased after and noticed a luxurious cab drive toward him. The car flashed its headlights like sharp fangs inside the mouth of a beast, forcing Xie Lanshan to close his eyes momentarily.

The car stopped, and a man stepped out of the car. A'Xun rushed toward the man and kneeled down, grabbing onto the man's legs and called, "Boss."

The man didn't speak and only gave A'Xun a kick; the latter then ran off like a coward.

"A'Lan." The man who stood against the light called out with his deep voice, a hint of satisfaction laced through the words, "Long time no see."

The headlights turned off. The man walked forward in the dark while Xie Lanshan instinctively took steps back. With every step closer, the shadow that chased behind him for many years finally engulfed Xie Lanshan and devoured his soul. Extreme fear overtook Xie Lanshan. His heart tightened.

He knew from the moment the man spoke.

Mu Kun is here.

He should run forward to capture this drug lord right now, but Mu Kun pulled out a gun and pointed it at him with a smile. "Chinese cops aren't allowed to carry guns around on regular duty. What a shame."

Xie Lanshan held up both of his hands as if to surrender wordlessly, his breathing heavy and rough.

"The cowherd and weaver girl could at least still see one another once a year after being separated by the river of heaven in Chinese myth, but we haven't seen each other in three years." Mu Kun now finally made his way under the dim light. He raised the gun and lifted the corner of his lips, exposing a terrifying face before Xie Lanshan.

The man suffered a grave injury due to the helicopter explosion; despite going through successful plastic surgery, there were still abnormal muscle lines on his face. He lost an eye, which was replaced by a fake red pupil.

This handsome face now had a touch of horror. Mu Kun seemed to have read what Xie Lanshan was thinking and pointed at his fake eye, then said, grinning, "I needed to keep it. It reminds me that I became like this because of you, that I must come back for you."

Xie Lanshan let out a heavy breath and said, "Alright, and you found me now."

"Every day, I've been thinking of ways to kill you when I see you again." Mu Kun held the gun and walked a circle around Xie Lanshan, studying his prey. He then stopped behind Xie Lanshan and pressed the gunpoint at the back of the cop's waist, then leaned in beside his ear to blow a flirtatious air and said, "But I can't bring myself to do it anymore now that I've seen you, what should I do?"

Xie Lanshan felt goosebumps from this warm air by his

neck. He knew the man was hoping to see him beg for his life, so he responded calmly instead, "You better kill me now, or I swear the next time we meet is when I arrest you."

"Killing you is too easy." Mu Kun nudged Xie Lanshan's waist with the tip of his gun, then slid it down and pressed it up between the man's buttocks. He said, "I might as well kill that Shen artist by your side."

Xie Lanshan could feel his veins pop and shouted, "If you dare touch him, I swear I will skin you alive! Even if you try to escape to the end of the world, I will chase you down and kill you!"

Xie Lanshan's reaction was within his expectation, but Mu Kun felt disinterested in it. He felt pained by this threat and changed the topic. "I've already discovered who the Apostle is, don't you want to know?"

Almost out of raw instinct, Xie Lanshan clenched his teeth but gave in at the end. One word finally made its way out of his mouth, "Who?"

Mu Kun chuckled by Xie Lanshan's ear. "Who could have known that the famous 'flaming triangle' in the drug enforcement team had one of my men?"

These words clearly meant that it must be either Liu Yanbo or Tao Jun. Xie Lanshan grew more anxious and asked, "So who is it?"

Mu Kun didn't respond. He lifted a hand and struck the back of Xie Lanshan's head.

Before losing consciousness, the last words Xie Lanshan heard were, "A'Lan, I've missed you. Did you miss me?"

Blue Fox

Since he first went undercover, Xie Lanshan knew that not only was the area of their activity a large market of illegal drugs, human trafficking was also a major societal problem.

It was one of the poorest and most underdeveloped areas within the Golden Triangle. Mu Kun was still at odds with Guan Nuoqin, fighting over territories and wealth, so the former had brought a dozen or so men to pay a personal visit around the area. The representative of the area greeted the drug lord with fresh flower crowns and bouquets. Mu Kun laughed and tossed over half of the flowers away, but saved the most beautiful red rose to give to Xie Lanshan.

The drug lord later walked in to negotiate business, leaving his subordinates outside the building to hang around. Beggars were everywhere. Some drug dealers would use packs of cigarettes, candies, or new drugs to trade for a night of pleasure with local women. Only Xie Lanshan handed the freshly budding rose to a girl and said with his accented Burmese:

You're freer than you think you are.

These young women, who dressed shabbily were hungry,

or perhaps already addicted to drugs, laughed at the young man's gesture. Another drug dealer pulled out a pack of candy-like new drugs that grabbed the attention of the women, and the girls quickly stomped over the rose without hesitation.

"You're crazy. Why would you give a flower to a prostitute?" This mid-level boss under Mu Kun couldn't understand the gesture. He had just come back from sniffing meth with a local to see everyone else had already run out to party. Only Xie Lanshan was left sitting by the window. The small boss even tried to talk some sense into him and said, "These people who live in poverty don't know shit about self-love or dignity. They don't even know what the word 'beautiful' means. They'll sleep with you if you give them a cigarette. You might as well cast pearls at a swine and it'd be less wasteful than giving a flower to a prostitute. I swear I don't know what you're even thinking!"

Flowers were obviously worthless in a place like this that poverty and drugs had plagued. Nobody had the energy to pay attention to the finer things in life, let alone know that they existed.

The weather was humid and hot, sweat felt like wet glue on the skin. Xie Lanshan stared at this tribal-like village outside the window silently.

"You really think you're Buddha or someone, here to spread love or some shit?" Perhaps due to the effects of meth, the little boss's eyes reddened as if on fire as he glared at Xie Lanshan's profile. Then, as if enchanted by the looks of the young man, the boss suddenly jumped onto him like a madman.

"A'Lan... A'Lan, you really are beautiful..."

Before Xie Lanshan could push the man off, Mu Kun walked inside the room.

The scene in the room upset the drug lord who had just

walked out of a business meeting. He quickly pulled out his gun and fired a bullet right through the head of that little boss.

Mu Kun held out a hand toward Xie Lanshan to pull the young man up, his face covered in fresh blood and flesh.

The crew took a truck back to their base the next day. Neither Xie Lanshan nor Mu Kun sat near the middle of the car and instead stood at the tail of the truck, gazing at the village slowly vanishing into the horizon.

"I've already been suspecting he was a spy from Guan Nuoqin." Mu Kun gritted his teeth as he mentioned that little boss he shot yesterday and cursed about Guan Nuoqin. "That piece of shit doesn't deserve to be called a drug lord. He's at most just a trafficker."

Xie Lanshan's expression remained blank, and he didn't speak a word. Despair was a common emotion shared by people who spent long periods of time in hell, but his expression was clear and only faintly wistful.

"Isn't it hard to imagine how much poverty can ruin a person? Guan Nuoqin used substances to control these people. Men were sent off to become fishermen while women were sold off to do sex work. The most pitiful part is that these people don't have physical chains and shackles, but willingly let themselves be treated like cattle hopelessly."

The truck trudged forward, but Xie Lanshan's gaze suddenly lit up. He almost threw himself to the back of the truck and grabbed onto the handrail.

He saw two young women, one tall and one short, standing beside each other from afar. The younger one held a red rose in her hand with care, as if she was holding a treasure. They watched him leave and waved at him with bright grins on their faces.

A stream of warmth reached his heart; Xie Lanshan could feel his eyes burning. All doubts he had of his faith vanished with the wind. This was the only red rose in this forlorn and foreign land. Like a single spark of flame within the darkness, it filled this brutal mortal world with a touch of kindness.

The rough days in the Golden Triangle, his father who gave his life on the battlefield, his mother who went mad, the proud and successful Liu Yanbo, the old and withered Tao Jun... Xie Lanshan woke from his nightmare and found himself in a hospital.

Tao Longyue sat beside his bed, surprise and joy written all over his sun-tanned face. Even that scar by his eyebrows glowed like a spark of lightning.

Xie Lanshan finally let out a sigh of relief after realizing he wasn't dead. It was already a miracle for him to survive from Mu Kun's hands. He lifted the thin sheet covering his body and checked all over, surprised to find all his limbs still attached.

Xie Lanshan sat up from the bed with a hand behind his head, turning his stiffened neck as he asked Tao Longyue, "What happened to me?"

"You're asking me?" Captain Tao rushed to the hospital early in the morning before eating breakfast and was downing a large baozi in his hand. He said with food still in his mouth, "A rando saw you knocked out on the side of the street and called the ambulance. Just what exactly happened? Did you get assaulted or did that headache act up again?"

Xie Lanshan leaned his head back and fell into deep thought, frowning. He had been too busy investigating the serial murder a while back and didn't have time to report the clues he had been collecting about Mu Kun to the higher ups. Recalling it now, it seemed this man had been keeping an eye on him ever since they discovered Lang Li's corpse with the letters MK carved into her body.

Tao Longyue couldn't tell what his buddy was thinking, but remembered that food was always a good way to make people open their mouths. He offered, "Ya hungry? Should I buy some congee for you from the hospital's cafeteria?"

Xie Lanshan turned to him and glanced at Tao Longyue suspiciously.

He couldn't get Mu Kun's words out of his head. There's a traitor in the "flaming triangle of the drug enforcement team", that must be either Tao Jun or Liu Yanbo. Out of personal bias, of course he suspected Liu Yanbo more; but what if it was Tao Jun? The man went through many ups and downs over the last decade. He broke his leg just before he was about to receive a promotion in the bureau, virtually ending his career in public security overnight. The culprit still hadn't been caught, but the traffic police who were at the scene said the case was fishy because it was a preventable incident. After piecing together all the old puzzle pieces, including what old Zhu Mingwu said before, Xie Lanshan grew even more unsure of everything. He couldn't tell whether this mentor and father-like relationship he had with Tao Jun over the last ten years was real or fake.

Tao Longyue noticed Xie Lanshan was staring at him in a cold and distant manner, then felt as if that gaze went past him to somewhere else further away. He couldn't help but call out, "A'Lan? Is your head okay?"

Perhaps the seeds of suspicion sprouted, but everyone looked like the Apostle to him right now. He suppressed the suspicion lingering in his heart and told himself: *This could be part of Mu Kun's plot to create friction between us. He didn't actually find out who the Apostle is, and is only saying this to mess with us.*

With that thought, Xie Lanshan felt the pressure on his shoulder lighten up. He softened his gaze and teased Tao Longyue, "I see you're back to your smooth brain dumb self. I'm guessing you finally made up with Doctor Su?"

As expected, Tao Longyue scratched his head. Two red

blushes appeared on his tanned cheeks as he said in slight embarrassment, "We're planning on signing the papers this month. We won't do anything too fancy, maybe just invite some close friends and family for dinner."

"I'm claiming best man's—" Xie Lanshan stopped abruptly as he joked back, realizing that he needed to report to Sui Hong immediately now that Mu Kun was back. It was important, urgent news that couldn't be covered in just a quick phone call. He needed to pay a visit to the provincial branch.

"Huh? Where are you going?" Captain Tao was still floating in his little world of happiness, a silly expression on his face when he noticed his best man was ready to leave the hospital with a stern face.

"I need to go see Captain—take care of my hospital bills."

He quickly left the room as soon as he finished. Tao Longyue still didn't quite follow as he chased behind Xie Lanshan and called, "Hey, I thought I was your captain?"

It only took about 20 minutes to drive from Hanhai City to the provincial branch. Chi Jin had already been assigned to work with the Hanhai branch on drug cases, so there wasn't any reason for Xie Lanshan to personally pay the provincial office a visit, but he suddenly had the urge to do so.

It was around early afternoon; the sun was still bright. The golden public security logo shined under the light on the front gate of the office like a torch. There were two fierce-looking stone lions that rested by the front gate of the provincial office, flashing their fangs like two guardians that protected the justice of the land.

The scale of resources and capital in the provincial branch was clear from a glance outside; the investigation and technology unit building and command building stood proudly as twin towers that reached the heavens. The offices inside were equipped with high-end computers, satellite connections, and other well-rounded cybersecurity systems that protected the entire branch. Tall buildings were covered with clean and sharp glass walls that shone a rainbow under the sunlight.

Xie Lanshan stood outside the gate, feeling a little anxious as he approached his old workplace. He stared at the large logo above the gate. Who would have imagined that such a small logo would represent countless heroic souls who fought for the safety of their people?

It was strange; he had only stepped into the provincial branch a handful of times with Sui Hong before he went undercover, but he felt a sense of belonging and familiarity with every part of the building. From every single brick down to the grass, he felt as if the provincial branch was his second home. This place honed his skills and shaped his soul.

The glare on the logo suddenly flashed strongly through the reflecting sunlight. Xie Lanshan closed his eyes instinctively. He briefly recalled bits and pieces of his past while his eyes were closed. He had left the place determined and without hesitation, but he realized how many things had changed after he returned—including himself.

Just before Xie Lanshan arrived, Chi Jin was reporting the latest findings of the Hanhai red ice case to Sui Hong. There were still no significant breakthroughs in this major case that involved the municipal and provincial branches. Despite successfully retrieving a massive amount of red ice from the Starex Group, they still couldn't narrow in on the mastermind behind it. The special task unit in charge of the case had thoroughly investigated multiple times through intel delivered by their informants, only to lead to a dead end.

Chi Jin believed that Mu Kun had installed a man in the Hanhai City bureau, who had been leaking information out to the drug lord before the public security forces could act.

Sui Hong was about to speak when Xie Lanshan knocked on the door and walked inside the meeting room.

Aside from Chi Jin and Ling Yun, there were at least seven to eight young men sitting inside the room. The Blue Fox was a team made of young men. All of them looked capable despite their age, uniquely handsome in their own ways, even when dressed casually. With the sleek and fitted police uniforms, the entire group of young men looked as if they could be a top boyband.

Xie Lanshan cut the small talk and told Sui Hong that Mu Kun came for him. He quickly picked out all the suspicious points in the last few major cases in Hanhai City; from the initials found on Lang Li's corpse to the sudden appearance of red ice among high school girls, he concluded they were likely all connected to Mu Kun.

Sui Hong coughed a few times, and instead of commenting on Xie Lanshan's analysis, asked, "A'Lan, do you want to come back?"

It stunned Xie Lanshan for a good while before he realized that Sui Hong was asking if he wanted to return to the Blue Fox Commando.

Sui Hong let out another small cough as he noticed that Xie Lanshan didn't respond, his face troubled. He smiled at the latter and said, "What, is being an internet-famous cop too good that you don't want to come back to the drug enforcement unit now?"

Sui Hong had the intention to provoke the young man, certainly hoping that Xie Lanshan would rejoin them. Yet before Xie Lanshan could respond, Chi Jin stepped out and said, "I object to this proposal."

(ii)

"I object to this proposal."

Sui Hong glanced at Chi Jin, eyebrows furrowed as he said, "Chi Jin, please think before you speak."

Chi Jin didn't respond to his boss. Instead, he walked up to Xie Lanshan, then suddenly grabbed onto the latter's wrist. His eyes were sharp as he sneered, "He came to find you, but you returned unharmed, right?"

Xie Lanshan knew what Chi Jin wanted to ask and paused slightly before confessing, "He left after knocking me out."

Chi Jin pursued further and asked, "So Mu Kun came looking for you just so he could chat about the old days with you?"

Xie Lanshan didn't respond.

"Hah!" Chi Jin laughed. "Mu Kun sure is kind to you! Do you know how many of our comrades sacrificed their lives for us to capture him, the biggest drug lord in East Asia? And why is he so kind only to you?"

Xie Lanshan still didn't speak, hoping to pull his hand from Chi Jin's grip, but the latter only grabbed on tighter.

"Such clean and sophisticated hands!" Chi Jin called out, pulling the attention of everyone in the room onto Xie Lanshan's hand. They were clean and scarless, skin white and smooth, looking a little more fragile than an average man's hand and even less like a drug enforcement officer's.

Chi Jin asked, "Forget about your hands. Is there even a single scar on your body? I sure want to hear your reasoning behind how a drug enforcement officer like you could survive six years of undercover without a single injury on your body."

Xie Lanshan felt as if someone was choking his throat; he let out a breath of air before finally saying, "I don't need to explain myself to you."

Sui Hong knew where this clean body came from but couldn't tell his teammate, especially not with Xie Lanshan here right now. He was both regretful and pained. After two violent coughs, he interrupted coldly, "Chi Jin, that's enough."

Chi Jin still didn't give up and turned toward Ling Yun beside him. "Ling Yun, roll up your pants!"

Ling Yun hesitated a little after looking around, then rolled up one side of his pants to expose a horrible scar on his lower leg.

"Once, for an ambush, we stayed beneath a flood of water under the storm for an entire night, just to capture a drug dealer under Mu Kun! Ling Yun's leg had already been injured earlier during the operation; the open wound was left to rot under the water, so he had to cut off some muscles around that area. Every single one of us here is gambling our lives on the line every day, but how could you, someone who was under-cover for six years, leave without even a scratch on your body?"

Ling Yun quickly fixed his pants and saw the difficult expression on their captain's face. He turned to call out to Vice-Captain Chi, "Chi Jin... that's enough..."

But Chi Jin's anger boiled. Ling Yun couldn't convince him to stop, and Sui Hong's words would not even get through to him. Before a whole room of Blue Fox members, he glared at Xie Lanshan and scolded, "If Mu Kun came for you, you should have run up to him like a wolf catching a prey, capturing him even if it meant risking your life! But why didn't you do so? That's because you're the traitor of our team!"

Sui Hong's expression darkened as he strolled in front of Chi Jin.

Chi Jin lifted his head and said to Sui Hong, "Captain, I will be first to reject letting him back--"

Before he could finish, Sui Hong lifted a hand and gave Chi Jin a heavy slap in the face.

Chi Jin wasn't the only one who was speechless; even Xie Lanshan was taken aback for a moment. The bitterness inside him began spreading like moss; he opened his lips and gave Sui Hong a forced smile, saying, "Public security doesn't mean we all have to carry the burden of an entire nation on our shoulders every day. I'm proud to protect a city, its people, or even just one person."

Unwilling to see his beloved team get into more conflict because of him, Xie Lanshan turned and walked toward the door. His footsteps stopped just before he was a step away from leaving. Xie Lanshan turned around and stood straight, giving a salute to Sui Hong. His eyes began burning up as he said with a slightly hoarse voice, "But the Blue Fox will forever be my home, and you are forever my captain."

Xie Lanshan left without another word. He rubbed his eyes and took a deep breath to calm himself down.

He had first stepped into this building with Sui Hong and dreamed about working here proudly one day when he was young. This sudden feeling of nostalgia prompted him to spend a little more time touring the provincial branch. The building had just been constructed a little before he was sent off undercover, but many places remained the same even years later.

He aimlessly wandered until he found himself in front of the old file room. The door was secured with a fingerprint lock. There weren't any top-secret files kept here—Xie Lanshan had once pulled out information from the file room in the past. The old officer in charge of the database didn't know the young man was about to go undercover and assumed he was here to stay, recording the young man's fingerprint into the lock. Sui Hong may not even know about this either, and that old officer may have already retired.

Xie Lanshan pondered a little before placing his thumb on the lock in front of the room.

As expected, but also strangely surprising, the door didn't open.

While he was trying to find an excuse about how the locks must have been upgraded over the last few years, he suddenly heard a harsh call from behind, "Xie Lanshan, what are you doing here?"

He turned around and cursed his luck; it was Chi Jin.

The Vice-Captain had just suffered a slap from his own boss earlier and was still boiling with rage. Seeing Xie Lanshan, he immediately vented his anger on the man and asked, "Why are you loitering so suspiciously around here, huh?"

Xie Lanshan didn't want to get into another fight with him and was ready to leave, only to discover Chi Jin blocked his way.

Xie Lanshan didn't speak, attempting to force his way through. Chi Jin quickly gave up on words as well and threw a punch.

Chi Jin certainly acted on the spur of the moment, but he was confident in how to control his punches, hoping he could at least teach Xie Lanshan a lesson. It surprised him that Xie Lanshan also returned an even more aggressive attack. Before his punch landed, Chi Jin felt his opponent grab onto his arm, twist it behind him, and then push him against the wall.

Chi Jin clenched his teeth in pain, attempting to struggle out, only to discover that Xie Lanshan didn't hold back at all and pinned him down like a heavy rock.

Xie Lanshan pressed his whole body against the young man, then twisted the arm a little more as if interrogating a suspect. He leaned forward and said in his ear, "I've had enough of you."

"Ugh..." Vice-Captain Chi refused to admit defeat. His body tensed; his teeth clenched as he tried to fight back in silence.

Xie Lanshan freed one of his own arms and grabbed onto the back of Chi Jin's neck, then said in a small voice, "Don't get on my nerves again, do you hear me?"

Chi Jin tried to lift his head despite the discomfort, but the moment he met Xie Lanshan's eyes left him stunned. He was taken aback by the look in those eyes.

The two men had only worked alongside each other for a brief period. He had met Xie Lanshan two or three times while Xie Lanshan was undercover, and another two or three times after the man returned to the team. The Xie Lanshan he heard about from Sui Hong was kind, persevering, tolerating, and benevolent. Of course, Chi Jin couldn't fathom it, nor did he plan on experiencing it; but from the brief exchanges they had in the past, he knew that Xie Lanshan really had perseverance and could fight.

However, the Xie Lanshan before him now had cold eyes like a madman. He could even feel something dangerous and terrifying about to awaken beneath that gaze.

"I said don't get on my nerves again, got it?" Xie Lanshan didn't loosen his grip as he repeated his question like he was waiting for a satisfying answer. His powerful grip pressed on Chi Jin's neck, forcing the latter to nod back.

Before other officers arrived to check on the commotion, Xie Lanshan let go of a shocked Chi Jin, fixed his jacket, and left the building.

(iii)

The serial murder ended with the death of Qiao Hui and his mother, but Shen Liufei still believed there were suspicious points about the case. He couldn't find the connection between Xia Hong and Qiao Hui. The first victim, Luo Xin, was Qiao Hui's neighbor, while the other two victims had medical records in Puren Hospital. Xia Hong and Qiao Hui's social circles did not overlap, and their usual areas of activity were completely different. Xia Hong was killed the night Qiao Hui encountered Tao Longyue, and it was unusual for Qiao Hui to assault a victim without a period of stalking within such a short timeframe.

While Xie Lanshan was in the provincial branch, Shen Liufei requested Duan Licheng to pull up the surveillance footage in the Puren Hospital and confirmed Xia Hong had never stepped foot in the facility. The artist sat in front of the window in deep thought. The sunlight cast a shadow on half of his face.

Duan Licheng wasn't interested in the case and rather had his attention on Shen Liufei's injury, asking, "Do you think it's a coincidence that someone attacked you?"

Shen Liufei glanced at his injury and then recalled the night at the bar. He shook his head and answered, "I think someone is after my life."

Duan Licheng kneeled slightly before Shen Liufei and asked, "Do you still want to find out the truth of what happened that year?"

Shen Liufei didn't respond, but his answer was clear: he had already given up.

Duan Licheng's expression grew grave as he said, "I risked everything to let you become involved with this experiment because of our long-time relationship. You told me you couldn't stand the fact that the culprit was living freely under a different identity, that you wanted to bring him to face justice."

All related parties involved with that experiment had kept their mouths shut. No mass media had caught on to the truth, only a few unreliable sources barely scratched the surface in the vast space of the internet, making it sound more like a baseless rumor. The ethical debate about human brain transplant surgery was still an ongoing discourse, but the experiment had indeed been halted with the leading organizer imprisoned for illegally conducting live human experimentations.

As the second direct surgeon involved in the experiment, Duan Licheng knew just how complicated the internal business and political struggle was; he wouldn't have run back to China in such a haste after cutting off all connections overseas if that wasn't the case.

"I didn't tell you the truth for you to put your life in danger." Duan Licheng pressed a hand on Shen Liufei's shoulder and persuaded sincerely, "Since you've given up on finding the truth and refuse to reveal Xie Lanshan's true identity, you should just go back to the States with me."

Shen Liufei lifted an eye to glance at the doctor, then shook his head.

Duan Licheng was first shocked by the blunt refusal, then quickly gave a sneer and said, "You've been blinded by this foolish love of yours. He isn't a cop, he's the culprit that murdered your whole family, a heinous criminal."

"You're right about part of it, but not all." Shen Liufei frowned slightly and finally said after a moment of silence, "Perhaps it's the strange trust between a mother and son, but I always had a feeling that my mother isn't dead."

"The only person who knows the truth behind that case now is Ye Shen, but you won't even tell him who he really is. How do you expect to investigate further?" Duan Licheng stared right into Shen Liufei's eyes and said in a cold and chiding voice, "Or are you telling me the little bit of excitement in bed is more important than avenging your dead family?"

"Duan Licheng!" Shen Liufei grabbed onto the man's collar as a harsh warning.

When Duan Licheng first met Shen Liufei, the latter had just arrived in the States with his mentor. Shared heritage on foreign land and Duan Licheng's mere six to seven years age difference with the young boy quickly made the two close friends. In Duan Licheng's eyes, Shen Liufei was a cold and stubborn man. Coldness allowed Shen Liufei to remain still in his own corner even when the world was in chaos, observing it through a neutral and distant lens. Yet, when he was stubborn, the artist could easily fight back like an immovable warrior.

The two men confronted each other wordlessly until a phone call interrupted the stalemate. Shen Liufei picked up the call from Xie Lanshan; the latter was back from his trip to the provincial bureau.

Shen Liufei let out a heavy breath of air as soon as he hung up, then stood up and walked off.

Duan Licheng knew he couldn't stop the man and didn't bother calling Shen Liufei back. He only stared at the latter's figure from behind and said in determination, "I promise I will bring you back."

The place they met at was a small park within the city. There was an artificial lake with clear water and plenty of fishes, a popular location for the elderly to spend their time and fish for the whole day.

It was a cloudy day with a chilling breeze that brushed on the surface of the water. Sharp coldness kept people away from the lakeside for warmth.

Xie Lanshan sat on a large rock beside the lake and stared at the reflection of a man's face on the water, oblivious to the person walking toward him from behind.

The face on the reflection was both familiar and foreign; he squinted his eyes and studied it carefully with every detail. He pulled the corner of his lips numbly and saw the man in the reflection give him a smile, but his gaze was still cold and chilling.

Xie Lanshan turned to look at his own hands. His face was

fiercely handsome, but his hands were a contrasting elegance. His fingers were slender and long, skin white like lotus—just as Chi Jin said, they certainly didn't look like the hands of a drug enforcement officer. Remembering the data room he couldn't open with his fingerprint, he suddenly recalled some things from the past.

It was difficult to earn the trust of the drug dealers in the early days of his undercover mission. He would sometimes be forced to take drugs to prove himself and had no choice but to tamper with the aluminum sheets to pretend he had really done so. Then, he would fake being stoned and engaged in brawls, cut his arm with a knife, and would even pull on his own legs just to earn their trust.

Xie Lanshan finally realized the horrible changes happening to his body. Not that he hadn't thought about this possibility in the past, but it sounded like a fantasy. Perhaps out of some internal self-defense mechanism, he had subconsciously convinced himself that it was impossible for something like this to happen.

Yet connecting many of the incidents lately where he felt at a loss of control, the strange victims that kept flashing in his memories, and that "Ye Shen" person who Zhuo Tian was begging, he had no choice but to consider the possibility that perhaps this body no longer belonged to himself.

By the time Shen Liufei approached him, Xie Lanshan was holding himself up against the rock, leaning his upper body toward the surface of the lake, eyebrows furrowed. He stared in great attention at the reflection, the chilly winds around him ready to pierce him and push him down into the lake.

It wasn't until Xie Lanshan felt a pair of hands almost reach his shoulders that he realized someone was behind him. He turned his head abruptly—

Those hands grabbed onto his shoulders tightly and pulled him back to safety on land.

Xie Lanshan noticed the person who pulled him back was Shen Liufei. Joy surfaced on his face as he quietly embraced the man beneath the gentle sunset. Both men had been mentally exhausted and only found some peace and energy through the warmth of each other's body.

Shen Liufei finally let go after a long while, then cupped Xie Lanshan's face with his hands. He pressed his forehead against Xie Lanshan's and said through their close distance, "What were you thinking about?"

Xie Lanshan couldn't talk about the secret of his body. It was too ridiculous. He bopped the tip of his nose with Shen Liufei's playfully and squeezed out a smile, asking, "What about you? Where were you at earlier?"

The setting sun glowed on the gentle and weary man's face. Shen Liufei tried to cover the fatigue in his mind in front of Xie Lanshan and said, "I discovered some additional points of suspicion about Xia Hong's case. I just came back from Puren Hospital and am planning on visiting her house."

"Take the car, I'll go with you." Xie Lanshan lifted an eyebrow lazily, then suddenly widened his eyes. That same terrible feeling of being watched by predatory eyes once again engulfed him. He turned to Shen Liufei and said, "Do you feel as if someone's following us?"

"So you've noticed too." Shen Liufei also scanned their surroundings; there were still people walking in the park, though very few, and the scenery was still clear and visible under the light. They looked around to search for the source of that predatory feeling, then noticed a shadow flash from behind the little hill near the back of the park. Yet upon closer inspection, it also seemed like just the shadows of the swaying tree branches.

Xie Lanshan froze on the spot, his expression still cautious, as if an enemy would show up at any moment. Shen Liufei tapped him on the shoulder and said, "Let's go."

There was a conversation left on Xia Hong's cellphone between the woman and a seller on Taobao. The seller had sent the wrong color product; the purple sheet cover she requested became red in the mail. She threw a fit over this incident and refused any apologies or compensation.

The two men first paid a visit to Xia Hong's own residence; while Xie Lanshan wasn't as sensitive to color as Shen Liufei, he noticed something was off around the house at first glance. His first impression of the house was that it looked cold and dark, but he couldn't place his finger on where exactly this strange feeling came from.

Shen Liufei reminded him, "There's no red."

After a closer look, there really was no trace of red in the house.

Then, following the schedule recorded on Xia Hong's cell phone, they drove off to another place.

It was a traditional Chinese Chiropractor clinic. A large "Fortune" sign hung above the building. An old blind man wearing sunglasses was doing fortune telling for people on the side of the street. His business wasn't doing well, but the man seemed to enjoy his time; the old man would mumble to himself and sometimes even sing by the street side.

The blind man certainly wasn't blind to business. He hired a few students to do chiropractic medicine on one side and a few more to sell Feng-Shui artifacts. Of course, the old man also had some crazier fans with enough money to buy out the whole city, often paying hundreds and thousands to hire the old man to perform sacred Feng-Shui rituals.

Xie Lanshan walked up to the old blind man, spread his arms out, and pressed intimidatingly on the old man's little table. He opened his mouth and called out in half-jest, "Master."

The blind man didn't answer and instead reached out his old and withered hand, then tapped on his table. He quickly pulled all the copper coins, bamboo sticks, and other fortune-telling tools on the table back into his arms.

Xie Lanshan's gaze fell cold and asked, "What are you doing?"

"Closing up, nothing good happens when the police arrive." The old man waved him off in a haste, as if he didn't even want to consider giving the man before him a reading. He reached down and attempted to search for his cane as he said, "Bad omens, almost as bad as the evil spirits and reapers behind your back."

Xie Lanshan didn't even pull out his police badge, but the old man knew who he was with just one line. He wasn't sure if the old man really had some skills or if it was just a lucky guess.

"I'm not here for you personally, and I know you're not actually blind. No need to fake it." Xie Lanshan kicked out a stool from beneath the table, stood to the side, and let Shen Liufei sit down.

"I'm not a cop, I certainly won't be cursed by those evil spirits of yours," Shen Liufei said calmly, "There's a female customer who frequents your place. Her name is Xia Hong, do you happen to remember her?"

The old man slammed on the table and nodded, saying he remembered her. The young woman was very generous with money and had been hoping to marry that rich boss of hers who had just divorced.

That boss of hers—Liu Mingfang? Shen Liufei pressed his eyebrows slightly and asked, "What did you tell her?"

"Her Chinese zodiac's a tiger, bound within a cage. Her name 'Hong' is also a homophone for red. On top of that, this year is the year of fire—doubling the fire upsets the balance of the five elements, which is a bad omen..." The old blind man continued on, but the gist was that red was the color Xia Hong needed to avoid this year.

Xie Lanshan didn't believe in these weird fortune-telling businesses but understood an important fact from these words: Someone as superstitious as Xia Hong would never walk out on the streets in a red dress and become a target of Qiao Hui's crimes.

Shen Liufei thanked the man and was about to leave when he heard the old man suddenly said, "We often say that like how people don't have a place of belonging with a home, fate has no meaning without a guide. Most people only have one astrological house and fate path, but you have two; life is unpredictable and ever-changing, are you sure you don't want a reading?"

It was quite true that these self-proclaimed psychics and mystics masters had their own way of tampering with the hearts of people. Xie Lanshan felt these words aimed right at the troubles in his heart, then quickly responded harshly, "You even dare to lie to a cop, huh? Be careful or I'll take you back to the station."

"I said I don't do readings for cops, I wasn't talking to you." The old man lifted those old eyes behind the sunglasses and turned to Shen Liufei. "Your double-path fate is very unusual. Look, even the birds on the trees don't dare to chirp with you around."

A vibrant and beautiful bird was resting on the tree branch. The bird had built its nest right under the roof of the chiropractic clinic, watching over the students day and night, practicing their trade and the occult. Over the years, the animal seemed to have earned itself some spiritual powers and believed itself to be a phoenix, often singing and posing proudly under the sun. The old man complained that the bird was too noisy and had his students attempt to shoo it away multiple times to no avail, but this bird suddenly quieted down the moment the cop and his friend arrived.

The old man lifted a hand and twirled his finger. The bird sang another short line before flying off.

The two men paid little attention to the old man's last words before they left and focused their attention on Xia Hong's case.

Xie Lanshan said, "Can it be possible that someone jumped in on the news while the whole serial murder case was still trending? They used the opportunity to kill Xia Hong, rip off her skin and sew her mouth shut to pretend that it was part of the serial murder?"

Shen Liufei nodded slightly and said, "Even though Xia Hong's body was dealt with very professionally and almost believably, the key clue of 'red dress' was only exposed after Xia Hong's death. The culprit certainly didn't expect this despite having a very thorough plan."

Xie Lanshan followed up immediately, "Liu Mingfang had once left a witness account at the bureau right after Xia Hong's death, but he didn't mention anything about the relationship he had with that woman."

Shen Liufei turned to him and asked, "Are you sure your suspicion isn't tainted by your own bias?"

The two men's rough relationship lasted two whole generations. Many differences often set them apart. Xie Lanshan pondered this question seriously before confidently responding, "I have no bias. I won't dare say he's the culprit, but he is for sure hiding something."

(iv)

It wasn't until long after Xie Lanshan had left and the sun had set below the horizon that Chi Jin finally dared to step into Sui Hong's office. Ling Yun and the rest of the team had already left; his captain sat alone in front of the desk, expression gloomy and silent.

The two men's first meeting was a dramatic tale. Chi Jin was around twelve to thirteen that year when he was home alone. The unit below his house suddenly caught on fire and quickly spread up to his house. His grandmother had locked the doors and windows when she left, leaving the poor child trapped inside the house. At that moment, a young cop broke into his house and picked him up, rushing out the door. The newspaper that night gave a tiny section on this incident, titled: Drug Enforcement Officer Passed By Fire, Transforming into Firefighting Hero Overnight.

That young officer from the story was the newly enlisted Sui Hong.

The hero came and went silently, like the wind. Chi Jin didn't have time to thank Sui Hong from the fire, almost coughing out a lung after he was saved. Yet he decided at that moment that he, too, would become a cop when he grew up.

Sui Hong had fought against drug dealers on the frontlines for over ten years, yet despite not smoking or drinking, the man had a chronic coughing condition. It wasn't anything serious, but it had no cure. That was why Chi Jin always kept a bottle of Nin Jiom Cough Syrup ever since he joined the Blue Fox. It was a special type of cough syrup he spent a long time tracking down that was said to be great for treating the throat.

His Captain often lost track of time when busy. Chi Jin assumed it was about time that his captain finished the last bottle and offered a new one to his boss.

He walked towards Sui Hong and called out gently, "Captain."

"You're here?" Sui Hong turned to look at him and smiled, then coughed a bit before saying, "I thought you were still mad at me. Did it hurt?"

Chi Jin shook his head, then met his captain's gaze. The light and look behind those eyes looked much more familiar now. The glow of the sunset danced like droplets of water on his face. His eyes were wistful—they would only look so melancholic whenever there was a mention of Xie Lanshan. Like a stream of fresh water that flowed into the depths of the mountain, it was both curious and majestic, but also pitiful to look at.

This thought soured his heart; he wasn't upset at the slap in the face earlier today. He simply couldn't fathom why his captain would always sing praises for Xie Lanshan while those eyes of his looked so wistful.

Chi Jin clenched the Nin Jiom Cough Syrup bottle in his hands and gave Sui Hong another glance, then said after suppressing the sourness inside him, "Mu Kun let Xie Lanshan free more than once already, I doubt it's as simple as what he had claimed."

The temperature inside the room dropped. Chi Jin noticed his captain's expression darkened, as if "Xie Lanshan" was a taboo to the older man.

Sui Hong shook his head and said sternly, "I know what you're trying to say, but Xie Lanshan would never be a traitor. How do you want me to prove to you that he's a good cop?"

Chi Jin still believed he had reasonable suspicion against the man and fought back, "You punish Ling Yun and I harshly for every little mistake, but why are you so lenient towards Xie Lanshan? You think he isn't a troublemaker?"

Sui Hong closed his eyes, his eyelashes flickered slightly as he said, "You don't understand."

"I really don't... so can you please explain to me so that I do? You know that... you..." Chi Jin didn't dare to finish the sentence. He clenched his fist and gripped onto the bottle in his hand tightly, feeling his eyes burn up.

Sui Hong let out a small cough and waved a hand, interrupting the young man coldly, "You can put the bottle on my desk and leave."

"Captain..."

"I'm asking you to leave."

Chi Jin gave a hurtful expression, eyes wide as if he was an injured dog. He waited for a few minutes in silence without receiving another word from his captain. He carefully placed that warmed cough syrup bottle before Sui Hong and walked out the door without another word.

Even the most cunning drug dealer could not escape the sharp eyes of Sui Hong. He knew very well what his Vice-Captain was thinking.

Ever since the day he saved Chi Jin from the fire and found out that the child's parents had passed and he was living with his grandmother, Sui Hong kept in contact with the child out of concern. He would pay the young boy a visit during holidays, buy some groceries, and chat with him.

He wasn't exactly sure when he first noticed the way the young boy looked at him had changed. The gaze was burning with passion; Sui Hong knew what was behind that look, but he didn't respond. He watched coldly as that yearning grew stronger over the years, the suppression of that love with nowhere to vent until it clouded the young man's eyes.

Sui Hong dared not to walk too close to his subordinates. He was and will forever owe a lifetime's worth of guilt to Xie Lanshan, whether it was to the one who gave his life in a foreign land or to the one who now lived in a different body.

The sky blackened after sunset, a few grey clouds still decorated the sky like imprints on a backdrop. Sui Hong was still wallowing in guilt when his phone rang.

"Haven't contacted you in a long time, Captain Sui."

The voice on the other line was a deep and unique man's voice that immediately reminded Sui Hong of his identity. Because of the secret surgery, he was acquainted with Duan Licheng.

Two weeks had passed since the serial murder case. Qiao Hui and his mother had both passed away. The bureau had also publicly announced that the case was closed. It certainly was a headache for Vice Chief Liu when he heard the violent crimes unit was now requesting the reopening of the case.

The media and public all had their eyes on them; any wrong move could mean risking his career as the Vice Chief.

Liu Yanbo didn't respond to whether he would reopen the case and returned home with a grave expression. He turned to his son and asked immediately upon his return, "Do you have anything to do with your secretary's death?"

Liu Mingfang could feel cold sweat rolling down his back as soon as his father questioned him, and he quickly responded, "You mean Xia Hong? We're just colleagues with no other strings attached. Didn't her case close already?"

Liu Yanbo still trusted his son. The young man might not be particularly intelligent, but he wasn't someone who would cause such great harm to others. After some thought, the old Chief said, "Xie Lanshan wanted to reopen Xia Hong's case. He said that the culprit of her murder may be someone else that was copying the serial murderer to hide their identity. This could possibly mean that the person behind her death is someone close to her."

Liu Mingfang nodded in agreement to hide the guilt inside him and said, "I don't understand much about this investigation stuff, so what're your thoughts on it?"

Liu Yanbo sighed at this difficult situation and said, "Xie Lanshan does have a point. I have no choice but to approve the reopening."

After the old man returned to his study after dinner, Liu Mingfang quickly gave Tang Qinglan a call and explained the situation, then asked what he should do.

"You're asking me? I'm not the one that killed her. I don't even know your secretary." Tang Qinglan laughed playfully on the other side of the line as if she had nothing to do with the case and asked, "I thought your dad's the Chief of the bureau, can he not even handle something like this?"

Liu Mingfang was on the edge of breakdown when he realized how he could no longer escape this situation and said, "But I didn't kill her either. Look, I know I joined hands with you guys because I was stupid earlier, but you can't just leave me on my own with this now."

Miss T showed no sympathy and said, "What are you scared of? Even if they find out it wasn't done by the actual serial murderer, there's no guarantee that they'll suspect you."

Liu Mingfang felt he was dancing in fire and didn't feel comforted at all, then said, "Xie Lanshan's the one that requested to reopen the case. You know he's got beef with me, and even aside from that, he's good at this whole catching criminals thing; there aren't any cases he can't solve!"

"Ah, him." Miss T's voice audibly rose as her interest was piqued. "If Xie Lanshan's after you, might as well shoot him in the foot first then, right?"

Liu Mingfang was puzzled. "What do you mean?"

Tang Qinglan pondered for a bit before saying, "Didn't you say your ex-wife suddenly got into a fight with Xie Lanshan and even wrote that mental health assessment about him having violent tendencies and needing to be removed from his current post?"

Liu Mingfang had temporarily let go of his plans to recover their marriage when he saw Song Qilian return to the embrace of her first love, but now remembered how unusual the woman's behavior was after these words. He asked, "So what should I do now?"

"You fool, shouldn't you know already?" Tang Qinglan was already annoyed with him and said, "Go dig up some dirt on him and then shove it in your dad's face. You'll be safe if he really gets transferred to a different unit."

Liu Mingfang finally understood and nodded in agreement. He was determined that even if he couldn't find any real dirt, he would fabricate a story if he had to.

"I can help you in this case." Tang Qinglan chuckled once again. "But you will need to do something for me too."

"I've helped you enough. I even installed that fake app for you to listen in to my dad's conversations on his phone." Unsure what the woman wanted, Liu Mingfang grew even more anxious and said, "You guys have managed to escape a few times from the Blue Foxes, but remember they're all elites; you guys can't run from them forever."

"That's why I need you to help me," Tang Qinglan said. After a few seconds of pause, she lifted a cold sneer and said, "I need you to find a way to get a Blue Fox member on our side."

(v)

After getting inspiration from Tang Qinglan, Liu Mingfang decided he was going to dig up the truth behind Xie Lanshan's report. There must be something serious if it had such an effect on Song Qilian. Of course, Song Qilian would never respond if he were to ask her directly. He decided his son was a good way to get his foot in the door.

Liu Chang had quite a good relationship with his dad, even

after his parents' divorce. The man and child sat together in a small park. Liu Chang sat quietly, a burger in one hand and a toy airplane in the other.

The little boy had similar features to his dad, earning some kind glances from pedestrians that passed by the father and son duo. Liu Mingfang felt proud and refreshed, offering to buy new toys for his son to play with him. Liu Chang munched on the burger while playing with the airplane, occasionally making little gleeful engine sounds from his mouth.

After satisfying his job as a kind father, Liu Mingfang quietly asked his son, "So why was your mom having a fight with your uncle Xie earlier?"

Liu Chang might be small, but he certainly had a sharp mind. He quickly shook his head and said he had no idea.

Liu Mingfang noticed his son wasn't telling the truth and gently knocked the boy on the head. "What happened? Got so used to hanging out with that uncle that now you won't even talk to your own dad?"

Liu Chang lifted his round little face and stared at his own dad with judgement and distrust.

If it was any other day, Liu Mingfang would have given this little rascal a smack already. However, he had a request to make and had to keep his cool; the older man smiled back and said, "Don't you want daddy to get back with mom? When we get back together, I'll buy you burgers every day and your favorite toys!"

Liu Chang weighed the value of his airplane toy, lowered his head, and thought about it briefly before concluding he still wanted to stay on his mother's side. He said, "If you promise to not hit her again then I'll tell you."

Liu Mingfang promised the boy, "How could I? I didn't do it on purpose before, either. Sometimes I got a little tipsy from work in the past and couldn't control my temper. How about this? You can hit me if there's a next time."

The child still couldn't betray his own father for Uncle Xie. Liu Chang dug through his memories and said, "There was a time my mom wouldn't let me go out with uncle Xie and told me that I have to stay away from him. When I asked her why, she would only cry and not respond."

"And?" Liu Mingfang pestered.

"And," the little boy said as he reached out a hand slyly, "you give me 50 yuan, then I'll tell you everything."

"You money-loving little rascal, at least this proves you still take something from me." Liu Mingfang pulled out his wallet and handed his son a 100-yuan bill then said, "Here's 100, don't try and bargain with me again."

"Yay!" Liu Chang exclaimed in joy as he held the bill up in front of the sun to check if it was real. After confirming the authenticity of the bill, he gestured for his old man to lean closer.

Liu Mingfang leaned in toward his son.

Liu Chang whispered, "Mom cried for a long time that night, super loud. I saw she was writing something and heard it was supposed to go to uncle Xie's boss in the provincial branch."

Provincial branch? Liu Mingfang was puzzled; Xie Lanshan was no longer a member of the Blue Foxes, but a cop in Hanhai City's violent crimes unit. Just what could he have possibly done to warrant such a serious condemnation that must be brought to the Provincial Branch's attention?

Liu Chang continued, "She wrapped the stuff up to mail out the next day and brought it to her office. I don't know if she ended up mailing it out in the end though."

"What kind of paperwork was it?"

"A yellow envelope, about this big, and it was very thick." Liu Chang gestured.

Liu Mingfang never heard anything about Xie Lanshan being investigated by the Provincial Branch from his dad and assumed that this package was never sent out, then lifted a knowing smile. He gave his son a pat on the head and said, "You might be onto something big this time. Quick, finish your burger and dad will send you home. I need to go pay your mom a visit later."

He drove straight to Song Qilian's office after dropping his son off, put on his customer service smile, and greeted the nurses courteously. The people in the hospital all recognized him as Doctor Song's ex-husband, easily letting him pass through without trouble. Liu Mingfang knew that Song Qilian would be out today to report to the Municipal Bureau and wouldn't return so soon, so he locked the door to her office as soon as he walked in. With his limited understanding of his ex-wife, he began searching through all possible places where that package might have been kept.

Song Qilian kept the keys to the locked drawer inside her pen holder. Liu Mingfang had no luck looking elsewhere and opened the drawer to continue his search.

As expected, he found that yellow envelope beneath heavy files at the bottom of the drawer.

He took it out and noticed the recipient's name: Peng Huaili, the director of the Public Security's Provincial Branch. He was the mentor of the famous flaming triangle of the drug enforcement team when he was younger, also an old acquaintance and boss of Liu Yanbo.

Liu Mingfang opened the envelope and saw Xie Lanshan's name on the file. After confirming he found the right item, he heard someone walk toward the office, quickly closed the drawer, and relocked it.

Before Song Qilian returned, he held this envelope carefully in his arms and quietly left her office.

After Mu Kun's reappearance, Chi Jin and his team returned briefly back to the Provincial Branch before returning to Hanhai after receiving a new mission.

The young man requested a day off the same day he returned to the city. He left Ling Yun and carried a chest full of frustration into a bar where many drug dealers often met, hoping to catch some clues, only to find himself drinking glass after glass.

People say that alcohol is the solution to depression, and Chi Jin only now realized that ancient wisdom never lied. Literature often described wine as a poison that pierced the stomach while also being a magical potion to forget all despair. Chi Jin didn't feel the latter, but he did feel a bit relieved from the burning sensation of the alcohol.

Only his heart remained in pain.

Alcohol also exposed all of those hidden emotions he never dared to express normally. He had survived deadly battles through raging tides, hoping to protect his homeland even if it meant giving his life on foreign land. He had prepared himself for the worst, only to discover that the worst was the one he loved had never even looked at him.

A pretty young woman partied hard after being intoxicated and gave kisses to everyone she could lay hands on. As her gaze shifted to see a young and handsome man sitting in the bar alone, she rushed over like a butterfly finding a sweet flower.

She pressed herself against him and said, "Hey handsome, wanna spend some time together?"

Chi Jin was taken aback slightly before an expression of disgust surfaced on his face. He growled, "Leave."

Before the first young woman could leave, another one slid over and said, "Don't be so mean, handsome, let's all have a good time."

The intimate contact and heavy scent of perfume gave him a headache. Chi Jin couldn't withstand it and slammed the glass in his hand on the table. The glass shattered immediately, the golden liquor splashed everywhere while glass shards cut through the palm of his hand.

"Why are you so mean!? Your wine got all over me. Do you know how expensive this outfit is?"

"Alright, alright, how expensive could it be? Just wipe it off." Liu Mingfang appeared and quickly held back the girl, who was about to throw a fit. He pulled out a handful of cash from his wallet and shoved it in her hands, then said with a grin, "How about wiping it with some cash?"

Liu Mingfang was a busy bee today; almost as soon as he left Song Qilian's office, he had to make his way to the bar to meet with a client. The bar was crowded with dimmed lighting, yet even amidst this chaotic scene, he recognized Chi Jin out of everyone. He recalled Miss T's words, quickly bid his client farewell, and walked toward Chi Jin, finding an opportunity to help the young man out of a difficult situation.

Liu Yanbo had often invited members of the Blue Fox out for dinner with his influence in the bureau, so Chi Jin had seen Liu Mingfang before and knew the young man was Vice Chief Liu's son. He yielded slightly and gave a glance of approval for Liu Mingfang to sit down.

Liu Mingfang poured a new glass of wine for him and said, "I heard Xie Lanshan returned to the Provincial Branch a few days ago."

"Don't mention him to me." Chi Jin felt tipsy already and downed the liquor in the glass.

Ever since receiving the request from Miss T, Liu Mingfang had been actively asking his father about the members of the Blue Fox, hoping to figure out who could possibly work with him. So he knew that Chi Jin had always been at odds with Xie Lanshan.

He smiled and didn't mention the name again, offering more liquor to the young man after letting go of all doubts he had earlier about this job. Desire is a weakness; these elite members of the Blue Fox were human like everyone else—they had their weak spots. He then thought about how cunning Miss T was and her skills in manipulating people; it wouldn't be hard to lure this cop to their side if she could handle him.

A quiet but calculating drinking session ended with quite some satisfaction. Liu Mingfang escorted Chi Jin back to his house and let his roommate Ling Yun take care of the drunk cop, then took a cab back to his own house. Reality and fantasy seemed to blend before his eyes. Liu Mingfang wanted to knock out right on his bed when he suddenly remembered that yellow envelope, then stood up and took a peek at it.

This little peek woke him up completely. His mouth hung wide open, eyeballs ready to pop out of their sockets.

It was too unreal, too ridiculous, but connecting it to Xie Lanshan's changes, everything seemed to make too much sense. After extreme shock and disbelief, he laughed out loud. He had the cat by its tail. What else could he be afraid of now?

Liu Mingfang stayed up the whole night studying this file. He resealed it after a careful reading, called up a courier service, and delivered this to Sui Hong's boss, Director Peng, smiling as he waited for a violent storm to strike.

Gone Missing

Two more events occurred in the Handong province during the days right before New Year's Day.

First, one of the country's most popular members of a new boy idol group, Wen Jue, went missing. The news exploded on social media. Wen Jue was a fortunate man who made himself a name in the entertainment industry despite not having talent in singing or dancing; he was quite childish in personality as well. Yet, because of his good looks, he gained popularity overnight through a talent scouting show at age 22 and became the next hot celebrity of his generation. Wen Jue's manager was Han Guangming, a smooth-talking and dramatic man who had a knack for doing business. He clung hard to Wen Jue as a source of income and worked day and night to keep his talent the trending topic on social media every day. The difference between a celebrity and the average citizen is their attitude—most celebrities nowadays don't take things too seriously. For example, while most people would worry about rushing into the hospital if they got injured during work, celebrities would prioritize making a post on their social media account for fear that they would miss the opportunity to be the first to announce it. So, when Han Guangming first learned that Wen Jue had gone missing, the first thing he did wasn't to call the cops. Instead, he was busy writing up articles and posts on his social media account to spread rumors.

It wasn't until three days later, with no signs of Wen Jue, that Han Guangming realized it wasn't a joke this time and contacted the police.

Wen Jue went missing while he was filming a reality show in a small town near the border of Myanmar. After contacting the local police to pull up the surveillance from the hotel, the police concluded he was kidnapped. Further investigation revealed that the person who kidnapped Wen Jue was a subordinate of drug lord Guan Nuoxin from Thailand. Judging by the lack of a threatening call from the kidnapper, they likely didn't know who Wen Jue was and simply wanted to traffic the young man into the black market. The Provincial Bureau immediately proposed a mission to rescue the kidnapping of their citizen in foreign land, ready to carry out the rescue with the help of the Thai police department.

The second incident might be a little less exciting than the disappearance of the dream boyfriend of many young women— Captain Sui Hong from the Blue Fox took a long vacation.

Some said that Sui Hong's long-time battle on the frontlines against drug dealers had taken a toll on his body, that the man was already at his limit and needed to take a long and well rest.

Others said Director Peng excused Captain Sui after a fiery argument; the argument was kept a secret and the rumor about Sui Hong's health on the decline was merely an excuse.

This piece of news didn't come out of nowhere, and even Xie Lanshan felt something was fishy. The province was now plagued with red ice becoming the newest drug in the market. Xie Lanshan knew his boss, and as the sharpest knife in the drug enforcement team, Captain Sui was a man who would fight until his last breath. How could a man like him possibly take a vacation during such turbulent times?

It was the weekend, but Xie Lanshan had to attend a community event, jointly sponsored by the public security department and the city. The serial murder case left some in the city worried. In order to actively prevent more young women from becoming victims of sexual assault, the city proposed a collaboration event with the municipal bureau to host a special class on self-defense at local universities and high schools.

Many young men in the bureau would not turn down an opportunity to be surrounded by college girls, so Liu Yanbo purposely appointed the least enthusiastic Xie Lanshan to take on the job. Of course, Xie Lanshan couldn't help but guess that Chief Liu was using this as an excuse to distract him from investigating Xia Hong's case.

Xia Hong's case wasn't given to Tao Longyue's team, and the other teams weren't particularly interested in reopening the case either. Xie Lanshan watched as it was quickly becoming another cold case in the bureau, feeling more strongly that Liu Yanbo was the one who was holding everything up on purpose. This further deepened his suspicion that the old man was the real Apostle. The weight in his chest grew heavier by the day, ready to be exposed at any moment.

Right before heading off to the school, Xie Lanshan and Shen Liufei returned to the latter's old mansion. The unit was still empty, so the two checked their mailbox first.

In an age where the world wide web connected the globe, reaching places faster than an airplane and wider than a train track, it was certainly rare to see traditional mail being sent. As expected, the mailbox was filled with nothing but advertisements.

Xie Lanshan watched as Shen Liufei stared dumbly at a pile of junk mail and asked, "Are you waiting for someone's letter?"

Shen Liufei nodded, expression a little dark, and said, "Tang Xiaomo."

Xie Lanshan remembered this strange little girl and knew that she went out to travel because of her grandfather's case. She would always send a postcard to Shen Liufei whenever she stopped by a new place during her trip.

The three had developed quite a good relationship even before the case of her grandfather was settled. Xie Lanshan responded sourly, "How come this lil' shit only ever contacts you and not me? I don't even get a text, let alone a whole postcard."

Shen Liufei's eyebrows pressed together more as he said, "Perhaps it's just my worrisome nature, but I have a feeling that something happened to her."

Xie Lanshan was shocked and asked, "How come?"

"She had once mentioned to me that she thinks a man has been following her in the shadows." Shen Liufei explained that the last postcard he received from Tang Xiaomo was a month ago from Bangkok, Thailand. The postcard explained how she was going to kiss a drag queen and then head over to Dubai to check out gold, but that was the last the man had heard from her.

Of course, the young girl could have possibly forgotten to send a postcard when she partied hard, but her Weibo account that she updated daily also stopped having posts for a few days.

The last message she posted was a selfie. The young girl grinned brilliantly and posed with a V sign in front of a background that seemed to be from Bangkok.

A few days of sun added heat to the already moist weather, making the stickiness on the skin even more prominent.

Shen Liufei drove Xie Lanshan to the school after checking the mail.

A warm breeze blew past the men after they stepped out of the car. Xie Lanshan looked up at the sky; his temples would throb painfully whenever the weather was about to change, making him feel quite unsettled.

"Drive safe, cuz." This nickname had transformed into a pet name among lovers over time, short and simple even in bed. After giving another glance at the annoying thick clouds in the sky, Xie Lanshan said, "Look at this weather, it's growing heavy like the sky's ready to collapse."

Xie Lanshan stepped into the multimedia conference room of Normal University five minutes before the time of their scheduled session, only to discover the door was locked shut.

He waited patiently for about twenty minutes until a teacher walked over and told him that the event was canceled. They had thought the bureau would have notified Xie Lanshan already and didn't expect to see the man still come.

But nobody had notified him.

The teacher apologized sincerely and bowed. Xie Lanshan gave an understanding smile and soon called the bureau. Xiao Liang picked up the phone and said that this was a sudden order from the Provincial Branch that requested Xie Lanshan suspend all public security work immediately.

Xie Lanshan was puzzled, but Xiao Liang couldn't explain very well over the phone, then quickly hung up after giving vague responses.

Xie Lanshan walked out of the university's building, slightly in a daze, and sat alone in a quiet corner of the campus on a stone bench. There was a small little hill behind him known as the lover's hill of the university. There weren't many people on campus at this time, but by the time the sky darkened, the hill would be filled with young students exchanging audible kisses of beautiful love.

Tao Jun had reminded Xie Lanshan to watch his image as a cop of a new generation, so the latter purposely cleaned himself up and put on a freshly ironed police uniform before coming on campus. A navy blue jacket matched a light blue collared shirt. The belt circled his thin but built waist while the fabric of the clothes was fitted to the rest of his body. Xie Lanshan was already quite a handsome man, and the uniform only made his looks stand out more amongst the crowd.

Normal University had a much larger female student population than men. At least nine out of ten who walked by were pretty young women. Naturally, all eyes fell on Xie Lanshan like a horde of hungry wolves.

If this was any normal occasion when he was in a good mood, Xie Lanshan would enjoy these admiring gazes from the opposite gender and even return with a pretty smile or gaze.

But something felt off today. It was as if he had been working in public security for too long that he had developed a sort of premonition right before something bad was about to occur.

A strong feeling of unease swirled inside him until it became a raging whirlpool that churned his body from inside out. Xie Lanshan felt his throat dry and body heating him, then took off his uniform jacket under the winter breeze.

It was certainly strange; he had never thought this uniform looked good and instead would complain that its design was too fitting, difficult to move around during investigations.

But it looked beautiful in his eyes right now. He still remembered the day when he first received his uniform while he was in the police academy. He zealously put the uniform on and heard two older women call him Mr. Policeman; his face reddened almost instantly.

Recalling it now, he wasn't sure what he was so flustered for back then. He only knew that the honor and pride that he received from this uniform itself was enough to engrave a powerful impression in his heart.

Xie Lanshan suddenly lifted a hand and touched his face as if he could touch that boiling passion inside him many years ago through the chilling winds today.

His fingers retained this memory, every part of his body retained this memory. He remembered the hard material of this uniform pressing onto his skin, the heavy weight of the epaulets, and the shining badge pinned on his chest.

He gently and reverently brushed his fingers against his uniform, his fingers passing through the embroidered flower on the collar, the rank badge, and pin, his heart pounding thunderously with every touch like he was caressing the skin of his lover.

Another chilling breeze blew by, but Xie Lanshan didn't feel cold even with only one thin layer of a shirt on. He only lifted his head to see a piece of white exposing from the grey sky like a cloth covering a corpse.

The weather really is about to change, he thought.

(ii)

An express package was delivered to the Handong Provincial Branch of Public Security, quickly yielding the results the sender had wickedly hoped for. Director Peng finished reading the contents and was furious after his initial shock.

Just before being invited to the Director's office, Sui Hong received a call from Song Qilian. The woman anxiously called him and almost cried a few times during the call, explaining that the files she kept of Ye Shen that she threatened to send off had been taken by her ex-husband.

Director Peng's call arrived almost as soon as he hung up with Song Qilian.

There were no winners in a never-ending gamble and the worst was always bound to happen sooner or later. Sui Hong let out a long breath of air; that burden weighing on his heart was finally lifted after all these years. He felt only a strange sense of relief. He sat quietly at his desk for a little while, held up the bottle of Nin Jiom Cough Syrup, and took a sip. Sui Hong then stood up and left his office, preparing himself for an upcoming storm.

Director Peng slapped those files on Sui Hong's face in his office and harshly questioned him, "Are you aware of this?"

Of course, he knew. Song Qilian had already written a report that explained the entire situation within those files.

Sui Hong didn't give excuses or try to explain himself. He simply responded with the fact, "I know, I was the one who arranged this."

"This is outrageous!" Director Peng shook in anger and scolded Sui Hong, "You gave this horrible murderer the physical abilities and training of our best cop; have you ever thought about what kind of disastrous outcome this can bring about if he were to go out of control when you first made this decision? With just his skills in hiding under the radar, you'll never catch him if he ever goes mad!"

Sui Hong gave a cough and didn't speak a word. He had certainly considered this possibility, which was the exact reason he asked Liu Yanbo to not promote Xie Lanshan and even asked Song Qilian to be his therapist.

"You got that criminal out of jail just before his execution, then changed all of his profile information," Director Peng said sharply. He was determined to get to the bottom of this and continued to question Sui Hong, "Who else is aware of this? Liu Yanbo? Tao Jun?"

"I acted upon my own judgment. Nobody else was involved or was made aware of it. They simply treated it as a special mission that I was in charge of and didn't question me."

"You sure are an honorable man!" Director Peng's rage finally extinguished. The only emotions left now were ridicule and disbelief. He shook his head and let out a long sigh.

The Director's concern was that this was the very first operation in human history and nobody could say what will happen in the future. However, with his understanding, the developing technology nowadays meant that a brain implant was no different than a heart implant. From a medical perspective, the Xie Lanshan right now was, of course, not a cop and a criminal on death row. No matter how many people this criminal had saved, how many cases he had solved with a cop's name, there was no reason to excuse his previous crimes.

Therefore, Director Peng made it clear that Ye Shen must be taken back and executed as he was scheduled to be.

Sui Hong had expected to receive this response, but he still wished to turn the tables. He lowered his head and slowly kneeled down before his old boss.

Peng Huaili was shocked. Men rarely yielded to this extent, but Sui Hong was also a cop Director Peng had personally mentored since he was young. He knew this captain was made of steel, unfazed even in front of gunpoint facing criminals, and would not yield easily to anyone else.

"Director, I've never asked you for anything in all these years I've worked for you. This is the only thing I beg of you; I will shoulder all consequences if necessary. I can be suspended from my post, I can go to jail, but I am begging you to please give A'Lan one more chance." Sui Hong lifted his head. A single tear rolled down his cheek as he continued with trembling lips, "He's a good cop, perhaps even the best that I've ever seen in my life. Please, can you give him just one more chance?"

Sui Hong bought an opportunity under one condition from Director Peng. He needed to prove that Xie Lanshan was still the same cop they knew, the dignified and respected public security personnel, and not that rumored Ye Shen, who left a dirty history of sleeping around with people of all genders like in those files.

The ultimatum that the boss gave was still one last ray of hope to cling onto, so Sui Hong planned on visiting Hanhai. He summoned Ling Yun and said that he would be on a long vacation with no expected return date, so the team's operation will temporarily fall into the hands of these young officers.

Chi Jin was the Vice-Captain of the Blue Fox; Ling Yun wasn't sure why Sui Hong suddenly requested time off, nor why he was the one that was being notified first instead of their Vice-Captain. He asked with hesitation, "Should I bring Chi Jin over?"

Sui Hong thought about it before shaking his head. "Tell him after I leave. This child is too rash. He may do something out of line again. I want you to keep an eye on him and make sure to stop him when he goes overboard."

Ling Yun nodded. Sui Hong then delegated some tasks regarding the investigations on Mu Kun and the red ice case, then sent the young man out of his office.

There was only one figure left inside. The sun began to fall west; rays of warm light shone through the window and onto the bottle of Nin Jiom Cough Syrup.

It wasn't that Captain Sui was a cold-hearted man with no interest in human desires, but even at the age of 36, he had yet to find a person who he could truly trust to be on his side, which certainly was a bit odd.

He had a very short-lived close relationship with someone about seven to eight years ago. His family had asked a friend to introduce him to a young woman around his age; she was fine and pretty. Sui Hong was never very enthusiastic about these sorts of mixers and setups, but he still ended up seeing the young woman twice out of courtesy. The young woman seemed to have a good impression of him, but they didn't hit it off well and eventually stopped keeping in contact.

To Sui Hong, it was a heavy burden on his shoulders. On one hand, he certainly never gave much thought to marriage, but on the other, he also knew how dangerous his job was and didn't want to drag a young woman down into potential trouble.

His family had argued with him a few times over this discussion of marriage, and Sui Hong had always given a half-joking response that he would rather give his life to work for public security than to consider more trivial matters. After a while, his family also gave up on trying to hook him up with someone.

There was an interesting little story, however, that Sui Hong had once mentioned having an arranged marriage to Chi Jin. It was during casual conversation and spoken with a joking tone, but the then high-school boy's expression changed as he told Sui Hong sternly: You can't.

"I can't what? That girl's got quite a good personality and is pretty, she also has those cute big eyes that I like." Sui Hong teased him, then said, "People need to be with one another and have a home to survive in this world."

Chi Jin's face froze up immediately and felt his heart crushed as he heard those words. He scrunched up his eyebrows and pondered for a bit, then placed a hand on his heart and said as if he was making an oath, "Then I'll be with you."

"Can you wait a few more years? Five, just five more years should be enough." The teenage boy spoke as if he was reciting some cheesy lines from a television drama with a hand still on his heart, and another held out with his pinky toward the older man. His gaze was passionate and fiery, voice gentle but confident, "When I grow a bit older, when I learn more about love and relationships; wait until I can fight for you and for my country."

Sui Hong let his mind run free just before he left the Provincial Branch office. He gently turned the bottle of Nin Jiom Cough Syrup on his desk, remembering the sweet and bitter taste of the syrup left on his tongue.

Regarding Xie Lanshan's ex-Captain, Shen Liufei had only ever heard of a name and never met the person in question. He had heard many stories of this officer's feats, but would never have expected to see the man actually pay him a personal visit.

The man in front of the door said, "My name is Sui Hong. You may have heard from Xie Lanshan already, but I was his captain when he was still in the Blue Fox."

"A pleasure to meet you." Shen Liufei gave a nod and invited the man in.

Shen Liufei had a great first impression of the man, feeling a sense of familiarity despite their first meeting. The man was, as Xie Lanshan had described, a dignified and unique individual who stood out amongst the crowd. Sui Hong was also surprised to find that the famous artist and professional was such a young and handsome man.

"We have a mutual friend between us," Sui Hong spoke up, bypassing the small talk, "Doctor Duan."

Shen Liufei's eyebrows pressed slightly, knowing that the guest had come prepared and that Duan Licheng exposed his secret.

Sui Hong explained that the Province Branch was aware of Xie Lanshan's situation now.

This was certainly the blade of a guillotine hanging above Xie Lanshan's head. Shen Liufei said after a long silence, "And this is the reason for your suspension?"

Sui Hong nodded and said, "I've already done my best to convince our director to give him a chance."

He mentioned Song Qilian and the guilt she felt for her mistakes, that she wanted to do something to repent for the trouble she had caused. She bravely gave a suggestion to Xie Lanshan's former Captain; if Xie Lanshan can prove he never had a change of heart for his first love and married the woman he kept in his heart to form a family, Director Peng would have no more reason to suspect that he was Ye Shen.

After giving it a long and thorough thought, Sui Hong also agreed to this idea.

"He's Xie Lanshan, not Ye Shen. To ensure that he can live on, he can only ever be Xie Lanshan from now on."

There was no need to make things any clearer. Shen Liufei already knew what Sui Hong wanted to say. The Captain wished this young man could make a hard decision for the sake of everyone and Xie Lanshan himself, even if this meant it would bring about immense pain to someone involved.

"Please return him to Qilian," Sui Hong said to him. "Please, give Xie Lanshan back to Song Qilian."

(iii)

"I refuse."

Sui Hong was taken aback; Shen Liufei looked quite like an easy-going artist, so he was certainly shocked to find that the man would be so stern and straightforward in rejection.

"I refuse," Shen Liufei repeated. He poured out half a glass of the fine red wine he owned for Sui Hong and then another half glass for himself. His expression was calm, with no signs of anger, and he said, "You guys have used him enough. You've pulled out that last bit of life in his body, then took it apart to forcefully install it into a body he would never accept—but have you asked for his agreement on any of this?"

Sui Hong took the wineglass from him and downed the alcohol despite never touching liquor in public spaces. He was certainly using it to vent out all the guilt he had kept inside him over the years.

The wine was fine; sweet and smooth down the throat. Sui Hong knew he was lying to himself but still said after a sigh, "He had once sworn to give everything he had for the drug enforcement team; he voluntarily signed the form to donate his body upon death. I know A'Lan too well, his kindness and benevolence, his loyalty and courage. If I had the chance to ask him for his opinions back then, he would certainly agree to my offer."

"What about this time?"

Sui Hong placed the glass down and let out another sigh. He was only finding desperate solutions to a problem both now and back then.

Shen Liufei took a sip of his own wine and then turned to Sui Hong. His expression was still blank, but there was something else glowing in his eyes.

"If you truly think he is your best subordinate, then give him a chance to decide for himself," Shen Liufei responded. "As for me, I will stay by his side until the day he no longer needs me."

"I'm sorry, this was indeed too sudden of a request." Sui Hong recognized his wrongdoing and stood up, ready to take his leave. He then turned his head just before he stepped out of the door and asked Shen Liufei, "Can you really accept that he is Ye Shen? Can you truly say you can love the man who murdered your family with all of your heart?"

Shen Liufei blanked out for a second, but by the time he came back to his senses, Sui Hong had already left.

He walked toward the window, opened it, and let the breeze blow on his face. He lifted his head to gaze at the tall sky and birds flying through the night. *Perhaps that was a little too much wine,* he thought. He was getting a little tipsy and couldn't bring himself to answer Sui Hong's last question.

Xie Lanshan returned home at 9 P.M.

"What's all this? My last supper?" The dishes on the table were already cold, but the variety still made the food worth digging into. Xie Lanshan rushed straight to the dinner table as soon as he stepped in the door, gleefully shoving his head toward the table. He lifted his head and grinned. "Hey cuz, I could give you the whole rest of my life just for these salt and vinegar pork ribs."

Shen Liufei preferred Western cuisine but knew Xie Lanshan liked Chinese cuisine, so he stepped in the kitchen to cook some homey dishes before Xie Lanshan returned from work.

"Take off your jacket and eat," Shen Liufei said. He glanced at Xie Lanshan, the latter was still wearing his full uniform, the cap on head, and joked, "Mister Policeman, there's no need to dress yourself up like that at home."

That "Mister Policeman" once again brought back those sweet, young memories. Xie Lanshan was ready to take his jacket off, but suddenly decided against it as he brushed his fingertips by the buttons. He only took off his hat, rubbed his slightly long hair, and leaned in toward Shen Liufei, begging, "Can't I just eat like this?"

Shen Liufei knew it was a joke and didn't respond, instead

asking, "How was the event today? It certainly took you a while."

Xie Lanshan was on his way to reheat the dishes when he heard this. His hand paused right before the microwave door and he lowered his head.

After a long silence, he finally said, "I... got suspended from work today."

Shen Liufei's heart tightened; perhaps the situation really was bad enough that Sui Hong needed to pay him a visit. He asked, despite already knowing the answer, "Did they explain why you were suspended?"

"It's not that big of a deal. I can think about whether or not I want to get a new job." Xie Lanshan could feel his stomach aching from hunger. He placed the dishes into the microwave and pressed start after setting it to the precise temperature and time.

The microwave hummed a muffled buzz while the smell of food once again filled the room. Xie Lanshan turned around and said nonchalantly, "C'mon, who'd wanna be a cop anyway? You give your blood and sweat for just this handful of salary, and if you do well, you're told it's what you're supposed to do, if you screw up even just a little bit, it becomes a massive tumor that can come back to bite you. You heard of that phrase online? What a peaceful and happy world we live in, y'all can only live so safely because people like us do the damn work!"

Xie Lanshan had never complained about his job, and even if he had given literal sweat and blood, he would only ever swallow up all complaints and keep it inside his heart.

Shen Liufei watched him in silence. The man seemed to be quite riled up today and continued on in excitement after licking his lips, "There was one time while I was undercover, just right after I passed on the intel to the person from the team, Mu Kun's men trailed us back. It was too late for me to run by the time I escorted the guy to leave and could only hide. The factory our agent was hiding in had been abandoned for years, all of the tunnels and pipes were rusted, the thermal layer outside had already fallen apart—Ling Yun said he was hiding in muddy water once to capture a drug dealer, that ain't nothing compared to what I had to do! Try leaning on these broken pipes, it's the fucking same as being tortured, I tell you!" Xie Lanshan could still remember hiding from Gold Tooth that time. He hid in the dark, back stuck to the wall that had exposed steam air pipes. He bit down on his teeth and kept as quiet as he could.

As curses continued to spew out of his mouth, it became more difficult to tell whether the man was happy or upset. Xie Lanshan instead found the story more laughable the more he talked about it and laughed as he turned to Shen Liufei. "Hey cuz, have you ever smelled your own flesh being grilled in real-time? It's damn nasty. It was so bad that I couldn't even stand smelling meat for the next month after."

No wonder why he couldn't remember where his injuries were; only someone who had never been hurt would freak out over a cut and pay attention to where it was. He suffered too much, but like the salt that had melted into the seawater, he grew used to it and couldn't even tell how much pain he had been through.

"There was another time we were chasing down a thief on the streets. That kid wasn't watching where he was going and stepped right into a pool of animal waste. It was a three-meter deep well filled with poisonous gas. Any average man who fell down it would die. Tao Longyue pinched his nose and said he couldn't do it, so I tied a rope on myself and went down. When I brought that kid up, someone even asked me, 'Why are you risking your life to save a thief like him?' Tell me, it's just one damn human life. Why should I risk my own safety to save him?" Xie Lanshan's throat tickled as if he was disgusted by this particular memory. He then laughed as he coughed. The laugh and cough grew louder and more violent, until his entire mouth was filled with the bloodied taste he coughed up from his lung.

One couldn't laugh away years of bitterness and hatred, but at the very least, he felt a sense of relief at this moment.

Shen Liufei listened to him with his eyebrows pressed together, not interrupting the storm. He waited until Xie Lanshan's vent was over and finally called out his name softly, "A'Lan."

"Alright, that's enough." Xie Lanshan stopped laughing after realizing he was losing control of himself. His expression became stern, then turned to Shen Liufei with glowing eyes as he pressed his palms together and requested, "Let's get in bed."

(iv)

Regarding Xie Lanshan's suspension, the higher-ups only said it was managerial adjustments with no follow-ups. Rumors spread within the Municipal Bureau as people theorized its relationship with Sui Hong's leave, that perhaps something went wrong during the undercover mission in the Golden Triangle.

But that was a trivial matter to most people right now. Compared to the growing market of new illegal substances and drug abuse cases on the rise, a policeman's personal issues were nothing to be concerned about.

Besides, young Captain Tao of the violent crimes unit was about to get married.

As his childhood friend and best buddy of the groom, Xie Lanshan was naturally the best man, while the bridesmaid was the only female member on the team, Ding Li.

In the face of an important life event, Tao Longyue wanted to host a grand wedding, but Su Mansheng preferred not having a big to-do and wanted to just sign papers. The two finally took a step back and agreed on a simple but efficient wedding ceremony, inviting only friends and family over for dinner.

So Xie Lanshan was still quite surprised to see Peng Huaili on the list of guests invited to the wedding that day.

"It's for your sake." The dressing room in the hotel was a little cramped. Tao Longyue was still handsome and stylish in the groom's suit, but the silly man couldn't get his tie tied properly.

"For me?" Xie Lanshan was helping his buddy with the tie when he heard that, then gave a playful tease under Tao Longyue's chin and smiled. "You can love me a little less now that you're getting married."

The two men were already facing each other, but their distance was extremely close in their current position. Tao Longyue noticed that Xie Lanshan's eyes were more beautiful than he had thought; the latter had long lashes, his features sharp and well-sculpted. This playful little gesture and deep look from him would look like a beautiful encounter or sweet lie to anyone.

Tao Longyue felt his heart skip a beat and blurted out, "Don't you try and flirt with me or give me that look, stop trying to turn your bestie gay on the day of his wedding!"

Xie Lanshan lowered his head with a smile, then carefully helped tie the groom's tie. He wasn't satisfied the first time and redid it.

"Director Peng used to mentor our dads. He's pretty close to us. I thought he wasn't going to come because of his busy schedule, so I didn't expect him to say yes to the invitation." Tao Longyue certainly was trying to help Xie Lanshan out and said, "I just wanted to help find a chance for you to talk to Director Peng."

Xie Lanshan wasn't too enthusiastic about this idea and asked, "Talk about what?"

"Are you stupid? Let the things in the past stay there and prove yourself today. Talk about how you saved that whole ship of little barbies on that cruise, or that other one, the *Ode to the Goddess Luo* case. Just talk about how you snitched out the culprit nobody could have thought of and shot those illegal artifact merchants in the foot—"

"Alright, don't forget that you're the main act today." Xie Lanshan understood Tao Longyue's concern but also knew how it was something that couldn't possibly be solved through just a few good cases in his file. Despite not having confirmation, many clues pointed toward the possibility that he may not be the same person he thought he was. If he was still Xie Lanshan, just how could he explain those jumbled memories, clean body, and the loss of control he'd been displaying lately? If he wasn't Xie Lanshan, then what would all the deeds "Xie Lanshan" had done in the past do for him?

He didn't want to kill the mood at his best buddy's wedding. Xie Lanshan swallowed up that bitterness inside him and fixed the tie, then gave Tao Longyue one last look from top to bottom. After feeling the man was at his most handsome, he grinned and gave the groom a hug. Xie Lanshan whispered gently into Tao Longyue's ear, "You just take care of your own responsibilities and support your family. Su Mansheng is an incredible woman. It's your fortune to have her in your life."

Tao Longyue returned a tight embrace back to Xie Lanshan. Words were no longer needed between the two.

The door to the dressing room opened suddenly. Song Qilian donned a brilliant white dress and stood like a fine lily flower by the door. She said to Tao Longyue, "The guests are starting to arrive."

Ding Li wore a cute but fancy bridesmaid outfit, poking her little head out from behind Song Qilian. She had her attention on the best man, then gasped in delight toward a well-suited Xie Lanshan, "Xie bro, you're killin' it with that outfit! Hey, can you maybe consider me as your bride if you ever decide to get married one day?"

Tao Longyue was way more delighted than the man in question. The scar on his forehead raised as he gave a thumbs-up back to her. "That's right, our A'Lan here is the most handsome cop in all of Hanhai—no, all of China!"

Song Qilian stood with a difficult expression on her face as she once again reminded Tao Longyue, "Director Peng is here, your dad's asking you to hurry up."

Xie Lanshan was also ready to step out to help greet the guests as his best man.

Yet just before he stepped out, Song Qilian stood before him and said, "I'd like to speak with you privately."

Song Qilian seemed to be a little hesitant when she stepped gently into the room. Her expression was also a little cloudy as she walked toward Xie Lanshan like a gust of smoke and said, "You've once told me that you will give your life to protect me any time. Is this still true even now?"

Xie Lanshan was taken aback for a moment before he nodded. "Of course."

"As long as you're okay with it, but I don't want you to give your life to me," Song Qilian paused, then mustered up some courage and said, "I want you to use me."

"Qilian..." Xie Lanshan grew more puzzled, unsure what she was trying to say.

"What you're about to hear from me now may sound

completely incomprehensible to you, but please trust me. Every word I speak is the truth, and I promise I will never harm you."

Beautiful white lilies decorated the location where the wedding ceremony would be held; these were flowers Song Qilian had picked out for Su Mansheng. A faint scent of the flower filled the space, both sweet and bitter. Song Qilian opened, then closed her mouth a few times, still contemplating how she should speak up. Finally, she confessed it all to Xie Lanshan.

"As a person, Xie Lanshan is—you are already dead."

There was nothing more satirical than having someone else tell you in front of your face that you are already dead. Xie Lanshan took a step back in a daze, his gaze exposed helpless and fearful emotions, like a lost child. Song Qilian quickly noticed that he didn't go straight into breakdown or lose control of himself as she had expected him to. The despair in his eyes appeared and vanished within moments; the only thing that had ever stood before him and the truth was merely a thin piece of paper, not a tall fortress. He had always been wandering in the winds behind that paper window, knowing behind that window would be a world at the brink of destruction and forever farewell.

With tears about to roll down her cheeks, Song Qilian continued, "Just a month before you would have finished your job undercover, you gave your life on the line. Or I should say, your physical body died behind a dark and cold alleyway."

He recalled the time when Gold Tooth used his men to lure him into that small alleyway and the last strike on his head by a heavy metal pole.

"Captain Sui cooperated with the U.S. military and helped transplant your memories into the body of a death row criminal named Ye Shen through a secretive and highly dangerous brain implant surgery. Ye Shen had once killed a family of six when he was fourteen, and then later a young woman named Zhuo Tian when he reached adulthood."

When the words "criminal on death row" came out, an explanation for all the bloodied dreams he had of violence and murder became crystal clear. Xie Lanshan's lips twitched a little; this was even more disturbing news to him than learning about his own death.

"Duan Licheng joined in on your operation as a specialist from the U.S. forces, and he was the one who gave this information to Shen Liufei." Song Qilian took a step forward and placed a hand gently on Xie Lanshan's face. "Shen Liufei came for Ye Shen, he was the only survivor of that family Ye Shen had murdered."

It felt like something heavy pounded on his heart, but instead of feeling the bleeding and ripping pain, he only felt heavy.

Like he was standing alone in the center of the world, all cold eyes landed on him from everyone around. Xie Lanshan frowned. He stared at the woman before him with guilt and confusion.

Song Qilian brushed her fingers gently by those slightly moist eyes and caressed his face as if she was touching the most precious treasure in the world. Her hands were like the warm sun that kindly shone on his face. She was in awe and disbelief; this certainly was a miracle of creation, as the two men shared almost an identical face. Yet, upon closer inspection, the two were also different. Xie Lanshan was more proper and clean, but this face was a little more apathetic and lethargic. The man she loved left quietly for six whole years, enough time to let everyone overlook the little bit of difference.

The Xie Lanshan before her right now didn't reject her touch as she had expected, just like the night where he didn't reject her kiss.

Nobody had experience handling a situation like this, so Song Qilian could only rely on her professional knowledge and treat him as a case of dissociative identity disorder. She needed to carefully interact with him, guide him to recall his memories, then finally lead his main personality back to his place.

"Director Peng is here today to see if there are traces of Ye Shen on you, so I have asked Mansheng to toss her bouquet at me today, to let him know that you haven't changed. He will then see that you will soon build a family for yourself as you had said in the past."

The man before her stood frozen. His eyes also stopped blinking for a while. Finally, Song Qilian took out a small wooden sculpture from her handbag and carefully placed it in Xie Lanshan's hand.

She had played with this figure too many times over the years. The face on the sculpture was already smoothed out. The sculpture looked as if it was rusted, but it was simply dyed with the blood of the sculptor and could no longer be wiped off.

The same wedding scenery triggered another piece of memory that was close to fading away. Xie Lanshan finally pulled his senses back as if he had woken from a stiff daze. As he looked down at the sculpture, his heart sank in an indescribable manner.

Song Qilian believed firmly that even if this man only kept a portion of Xie Lanshan's memories, that portion was powerful and still a part of the man's soul. She also believed that this man she had loved since she was twelve would return her love.

"Use me," she said as she cupped Xie Lanshan's face. She lifted her gaze and pleaded in desperation, "Just let it be my way of compensating for you; we were never supposed to have walked away from each other back then."

(v)

Su Mansheng donned a fitted and simple wedding dress designed with the motif of a fish. There were no fancy laces or decorations around the dress. Even her makeup was quite simplistic. But the model was already beautiful, her figure tall and slender, capturing all attention as she walked toward the crowd. Tao Longyue felt more like a bodyguard than the groom as he watched, but his heart was full of warmth. He lifted his head to see Xie Lanshan step out of the dressing room, then asked cheerily without noticing the strange expression on the latter's face, "Hey, where's your boyfriend?"

Song Qilian took her son to pay grandpa Liu Yanbo a visit. Xie Lanshan walked past Tao Longyue as if he didn't even notice he was being called out, walking with a hollowed gaze down the hall.

Tao Longyue rushed forward and tapped on his shoulder, then said, "Director Peng wants to meet Shen Liufei. He's holding a bit of a grudge against us because the Hanhai Bureau kept the professional the provincial branch sponsored to fly in."

He was 'trapped' here in Hanhai because of vengeance, Xie Lanshan thought as he turned around in a daze to stare at Liu Mingfang. His eyes were filled with anger and pain, like a stray dog that was kicked on the side of the road by a pedestrian.

Tao Longyue was shocked by this look on his best friend and noticed something was off, then asked, "What's up, do you feel sick?"

"No... it's nothing." Xie Lanshan attempted to recall where Shen Liufei went today but didn't have a clue, almost as if any memories connected to this name became a blur. Everything sweet and bitter swarmed in and gave him a headache. He stuttered a little and said, "Duan Licheng is going back to the

States today... Maybe, maybe he sent the doctor off and will be here a little later."

"Alright, that's fine. We all know each other here, no need for the best man to stand around and greet every guest, go take a seat." Tao Longyue gave a pat on Xie Lanshan's shoulders and whispered to the latter's ears, "You're seated with Director Peng, don't forget what I said and act your best!"

Shen Liufei indeed took the doctor to the airport. Duan Licheng had bought two tickets, hoping to bring the artist along with him, but failed in the end.

He shook his head and gave a defeated smile to Shen Liufei as he was about to board, then said, "I miss the time when we first met. You were young and weak back then, but you trusted and relied on me without any questions."

Shen Liufei lowered his gaze and listened to the man speak, remembering what he owed the doctor.

"I'm very thankful to you for caring for me when I was severely ill, and for giving me a second chance in life." Shen Liufei's expression remained blank, but gratitude could be heard from those words. He asked, "But you can no longer work as a surgeon in the States, what do you plan on doing in the future?"

"I have plans already." Duan Licheng smiled and gave the young man an embrace.

Like dazzling stars in the sky, thousands of lights filled the cityscape at this hour. Shen Liufei walked out of the airport and checked the time. It was 30 minutes before Captain Tao's wedding, and traffic would take a little while even if he drove back right now.

A young Thai couple walked past him with all sorts of luggage, rushing to board their airplane. This suddenly reminded him of Tang Xiaomo once again. Shen Liufei didn't normally check social media, he only saved the few photos she had posted on her Weibo after she went missing. He pulled up the photo on his phone and noticed a minor detail that he had missed out on before.

In the last selfie Tang Xiaomo posted, there was a figure of a man with blurred features in the background. The man stood far away in the back and dangerously stared at the young girl.

Tao Longyue's wedding had just started. Captain Tao was an expressive and emotional man despite his looks; he cried once while saying the vows to his bride, then cried once more while thanking his father. When Xiao Liang and the crew egged him on to sing, the man also sang with a loud and off-tune voice that sounded like he was whimpering more than singing.

Tao Jun took this opportunity to report his work to his boss on this wonderful day, only to have Director Peng interrupt with a laugh. "We're not talking about work today, just family affairs. A good man who protects his people deserves a good home to rest too."

Xie Lanshan sat diagonally across from the man.

Director Peng acted as if he hadn't heard about Xie Lanshan being suspended from work and asked, "Oh, young Xie, I heard that you've been doing well in the investigation unit. You've even helped solve many big cases, huh?"

Xie Lanshan didn't seem to have heard the question. He lifted his head to look at Director Peng and gave a small sound of acknowledgment.

Director Peng looked at him and said, "I've told you before you went undercover that you can only shoulder what you can protect. If you succeed, you'll return as a hero, but if you fail, you'll be like Ma Su, who failed to protect his town. No matter how reluctant you are, you need to uphold the rule of law and understand punishment. Am I right?"

The story of Ma Su was a famous tale in the history of the Three Kingdoms; what happened to General Ma Su in the end? He was executed by Zhuge Liang's orders, falling to the ground to atone for his mistakes.

Song Qilian sat beside Xie Lanshan and understood the unspoken words behind this line. Her face grew pale, unable to speak.

Two dishes were served on the table; one was a cleanly prepared shellfish dish, another raw oyster with dipping sauce. The placement of the utensils and plates on the table were of elegant taste. The bureau might be full of a lot of big eaters, but nobody was particularly obsessed with seafood or shellfish. Tao Longyue was quite shocked at the raw seafood. He turned to say to his bride, "I don't think we had these two dishes on the menu."

Su Mansheng shook her head, saying she was unaware of the changes on the menu.

That was when Liu Mingfang and his father walked over to offer a glass to their boss. The young Liu first nodded toward Tao Longyue and then said with a smile, "Sorry bro, I didn't prepare enough red envelopes for this event. Thankfully, I've frequented this hotel in the past for work, so I went ahead and told the chefs to add two extra dishes for us. I hope everyone enjoys it."

Liu Mingfang was seated at a different table with his father. Of course, Tao Longyue didn't even want to invite the man over, but Tao Jun said that it was courtesy to Chief Liu. The three boys also grew up together, so even if some hiccups occurred during their young days, it was all in the past.

Liu Yanbo greeted the old director and introduced his son, offering more wine and tobacco.

Liu Mingfang finally noticed Xie Lanshan on the side after greeting Director Peng. He went up and tapped on the latter's shoulder, asking, "I added these two dishes for you, why aren't you even moving those chopsticks?"

Before Xie Lanshan could answer, he eyed Director Peng and then called out to Tao Longyue, "Remember when we all went to Qingdao that time during college? We went fishing for our own shellfish and seafood in the waters and beaches, then killed whole buckets of them with just the three of us with some beer. Hey, do you remember that, ol'Tao?"

Tao Longyue dug through his memories to recall this event and gave a nod. "I think... I remember that..."

Liu Mingfang turned back to Xie Lanshan and placed two raw oysters on Xie Lanshan's plate with the common chopsticks. He then said with a smile, "I remember these were your favorite. I swear if you don't eat up at least ten of them we ain't bros anymore!"

It may not be his favorite, but with dozens of eyes on him now, he had no way to refuse. This was obviously a ploy by Liu Mingfang; if he refused it would show he couldn't take a joke, but what if he accepted? Xie Lanshan knew he couldn't touch shellfish, a tiny bit could trigger his allergic reaction. A severe reaction could cause his heartbeat to stop, and both Song Qilian and Peng Huaili knew this.

Director Peng pressed his eyebrows slightly and looked at Xie Lanshan like a hawk.

"I... today..." Xie Lanshan wanted to find an excuse for not feeling too well today. That was when Song Qilian suddenly held his hand and shook her head, giving him a smile.

"Let me say it." Song Qilian found Su Mansheng on the

other side and gave a small grin. "I'm waiting to catch your bouquet later."

Shen Liufei had arrived at the venue five minutes ago, but he sat in the back and wasn't anywhere near the main table. He wasn't fond of chatting with strangers, but also he and Xie Lanshan agreed to keep away from each other in public after they'd officially been together. Especially in a place filled with men like the police department, they were extra careful about exposing their relationship.

He saw Song Qilian hold Xie Lanshan's hand and how she caught Su Mansheng's bouquet. She announced in front of everyone that she was about to be engaged to Xie Lanshan.

"Huh?"

Now everyone's attention had been shifted away from the oysters on the plate. The groom was shocked and old Tao was speechless; Liu Mingfang was ready to curse out when his old man stopped him with a threatening glance. It was improper to act out of line before his seniors.

"I mean that's great news, congrats... but..." Tao Longyue stared dumbly at Xie Lanshan, unable to process everything at once. *Hold on, this wasn't what we had written in the script!*

"We've been together since before he went undercover, but he left for six years and didn't speak a word about this secretive mission to me. I am also to be blamed for being young and foolish. I couldn't keep him, nor did I wait for him. Now he's safe and back home. He's solved many cases and served the community, many injuries were carved on his body to prove it. He had even saved me a few times from danger. We trust that we still have feelings for each other, so we wanted to make up for all the times we've lost together." Song Qilian shed a tear as she held the beautiful bouquet in her hands and reminded Director Peng of everything Xie Lanshan had done as a cop. She then turned and said to him,

"Director Peng, can we ask you to officiate the wedding for us?"

Director Peng gave Song Qilian a smile, his expression softened, and turned to Tao Jun, "Is this true?"

"Of course. If A'Lan never went to the Golden Triangle back then, I'm afraid their kids would be calling me 'god-grandpa' by now," Tao Jun admitted truthfully and sincerely. He had hoped for Xie Lanshan to step back into the peaceful world and live a fulfilling life that could keep his father's soul at peace.

"Young Xie certainly sacrificed too much." The coldness on Director Peng's face melted a little more. He finally remembered the blood and sweat the young man had shed, the sacrifices he made, and felt both pained and relieved. He turned and gave Song Qilian a grin and promised, "A hero and the beauty's wedding is as beautiful as a love story. I promise I will be there for the wedding!"

Events occurred one after another as if there was no end. Xie Lanshan seemed to have tacitly acknowledged this relationship and gave little response from start to end. His eyes were still clouded in shock and sternness. All sorts of awful emotions overfilled his body. He really needed someone to hold him.

His fingers brushed against the wooden sculpture beneath the table, his gaze fell onto Shen Liufei seated afar. He saw Shen Liufei lower his gaze and turned around.

"I want to bring mom back to stay with us after marriage. Her situation is stable now and she can't live in the psych ward forever." Song Qilian held Xie Lanshan's hand again and gave him a smile. "How about it, A'Lan?"

Xie Lanshan could only force out a smile under Peng Huaili's gaze and nod in agreement.

Tao Jun hadn't had a good drink since he got sick and downed another glass of wine. He turned to Xie Lanshan and said, "I'm relieved now to see that both of you are going to have families of your own. Don't bother too much with fancy setups. Do it like Longyue, find a good date, and set up a simple wedding."

Song Qilian responded with a flustered face, but Xie Lanshan didn't catch what she said.

He was still playing with that wooden sculpture beneath that table. Once, he had yearned for the kind of clean and straightforward love as his sculpting; sculpting was also his way of proving his existence in this world. He had once loved carving small animals for her. He would feel happy when she laughed at receiving those little gifts. The two didn't need any passionate love or romance between them. He had always wanted to bring this young woman to the gravesite and feel the breeze, for her to call "Dad" with him by old Xie's tombstone.

Xie Lanshan traced the face of the woman on the sculpture with his fingers, only to discover that he could no longer trace out a shape of her face in his head.

Memories carved into his soul, but even without this unexpected encounter many years later, that which had passed was left in the past.

"Qilian, winter is a downtime for weddings. It's easy to book hotels and chapels now, but I'm sure it will become difficult if we drag it out too long."

"I understand." Song Qilian smiled towards Tao Longyue, happy that everything was progressing as she had expected. She then turned back to Xie Lanshan and said, "But we still have to listen to A'Lan's opinions. He's not in a rush and neither am I—A'Lan, what do you say?"

Xie Lanshan didn't respond.

"A'Lan?" Tao Longyue called out.

"I'm sorry." Xie Lanshan suddenly stood up and bowed toward Director Peng, the Taos, and Song Qilian apologetically. He said with a hoarse voice, "There won't be a wedding anymore; there was not supposed to be one in the first place."

Xie Lanshan gave everyone a smile; this grin spread across his face and whole body, and his heart lifted. He turned around and chased after Shen Liufei without hesitation.

(vi)

Xie Lanshan rushed out of the hotel but was a step too late. The figure of the man had already disappeared, and a phone call showed that the man had already turned off his phone.

He kept running under the heat of alcohol. He ran and ran until he was completely exhausted. Lights from houses shone while the moon peeked out from the layers of clouds; as if the sky had opened its eyes, the silver glow illuminated the ground.

Xie Lanshan panted heavily after a sprint, hands on his knees while he called out desperately:

Shen Liufei!

Xie Lanshan returned home to see no sign of the man, then rushed to his old residential unit, only to see that a new tenant had already occupied the place. Xie Lanshan searched for a whole night like a blind cat, returning to his house only near dawn and crashed on his bed.

Solitude and fatigue crawled up his body when he finally laid in darkness, but he couldn't stop calling Shen Liufei's name. Before the chaos dispersed, the truth revealed, he had always felt a dark and bloodied hole in his heart. And Shen Liufei had always been the one strand of hope that he clung onto to escape his loneliness and tiredness.

That's why he kept crying that name soundlessly and endlessly. Again and again, until a single sound managed to come out of his dried throat. The broken sounds of the word fell into the night, then melted into the boundless darkness until nothing else could escape.

Two days passed without a trace of the man and no calls. Xie Lanshan finally panicked. Thinking that Shen Liufei was determined to leave him for good, he quickly used the last bit of his professional connections to search for the whereabouts of the artist.

He discovered that the man had left on a plane the night after Tao Longyue's wedding, but instead of going back to the States, he flew to Thailand.

Xie Lanshan immediately thought of Tang Xiaomo and figured Shen Liufei must have found some new clues, which may be why he was in such a rush to fly out.

Yet regardless if that was the truth or not, it was relieving to know that the man didn't go back to America. Xie Lanshan's heart lightened up a little, and he decided to also make a trip to Thailand.

Requesting a vacation would require the stamp of his boss, but Tao Jun had just recovered from his illness and wasn't back on his post. Tao Longyue had just gotten married and it wouldn't be a good time to disturb him right now, but if he tried to send the request to Chief Liu, the process of approving the leave would take forever. Xie Lanshan figured that since he was already suspended from work, he could just leave a note and take off.

While Xie Lanshan was preparing for his own trip, the provincial branch was also preparing to dispatch a rescue team to the same place. The missing person may not be an official, but he was still a celebrity that needed to be found. The Blue Fox was a team that often worked across borders for their anti-drug operations, so they were familiar dealing with the local situations in Thailand and Myanmar. With their knowledge and experience in cross-national investigation efforts, they were the most ideal candidates to take on this mission compared to the other teams in the Chinese public security system.

After Sui Hong was suspended from work, Chi Jin became the temporary commander of the Blue Fox. Director Peng called Chi Jin into his office to hand off the order of rescuing Chinese national Wen Jue.

To his surprise, Chi Jin refused to carry out the order and sternly said no.

"If Captain Sui doesn't return to his post, then I refuse to work as well. You can ask Ling Yun, Pei Dongqing, or even Melon Cai—I don't care, they can be the new Captain of the Blue Foxes if they want to!" He called both full names and nicknames. The frustration of his captain's suspension clouded his mind. Desperation made him give up on even the most basic courtesy before his senior.

"Is that what you really want?" Chi Jin's attitude angered Director Peng. The older man asked twice if the young man was serious before exploding in rage, "If you're serious with this attitude, then take off that uniform on you right now. No coward and child like you deserves to wear this uniform!"

Director Peng was both authoritative and ruthless. A howl like this already left Chi Jin with a back covered in cold sweat. The young man realized he had gone overboard with his words but refused to yield, then shot back, "You can call me childish, but I'm no coward!"

Director Peng answered, "You still haven't settled the case of Hanhai's red ice and now you want to quit because you can't solve it. Is this not cowardly of you?"

Chi Jin's face flustered as he explained, "It's not that I'm quitting because we aren't making progress, but the red ice market in Hanhai suddenly vanished and all clues disappeared overnight—"

Director Peng scolded, "Don't give me excuses. If you guys

weren't able to find new clues over the last few months, that's a failure on your Captain Sui's leadership! I can suspend him for this reason alone right now, don't even mention the mistake he made in the past!"

"They say drug enforcement is a war of attrition during times of peace, and of course, we, as the soldiers on the front-lines, need to protect our bases. But not all cases can be settled that quickly overnight; don't forget what our ancestors have taught us about the importance of resilience and preservation." Chi Jin could not withstand anyone criticizing Sui Hong, not even if it was from the Director himself. He frowned and gave an almost naïve look of displeasure. "Either way, there's nothing wrong with our captain's leadership. Director Peng doesn't understand the struggles of us frontline fighters, so you can say such things, but I refuse to step down!"

"Watch your mouth! You little rascal, did you forget your position?" Director Peng held in the urge to laugh and kept a steel face. He kept the anger in his expression but asked numbly, "I just have one question for you right now: can you settle this case?"

Chi Jin clenched his teeth and said, "I can."

Seeing that this provocation worked, Director Peng followed up with another question, "So, are you able to settle this cross-national rescue mission as well?"

Chi Jin held a hand to his chest and felt an adrenaline rush as he responded, "Yes, I can."

"Okay, don't forget what you've said today." Director Peng gave a small smile of satisfaction and said, "You may take your leave now."

"But... I also have a request." Chi Jin eyed for silent approval to continue from Director Peng and mustered up his courage, saying, "I fight for my country and for my captain. If I can settle both cases, can I request to have my captain back on his post?"

"Are you trying to bargain with me here?" Peng Huaili was also quite puzzled; what made this 20-something-year-old child think he had the right to bargain with him? But he noticed that there was no hint of jest on this child's face. The light in his eyes burned like a torch of fire that could heat up anyone around him. Peng Huaili stared at Chi Jin for a while before finally nodding. "I'll give you one month."

"Yes, sir!" Chi Jin gave a grin and rushed out of the office in excitement.

He returned to the apartment he rented out with Ling Yun. The latter had already gotten the notice and was packing up his luggage for the trip.

"What did the director say? Can our Cap come back?" He asked hastily the moment he saw Chi Jin return. Ling Yun may not be as strong-headed and rash as Chi Jin, but also had Sui Hong's case weighing in his mind every day.

"We'll need to work harder; drag out the source of the red ice and bring back that celebrity from Thailand in a month, and Cap'n will be back." Of course, neither of the cases were easy. Chi Jin was out of ideas at the moment and tossed his jacket on the sofa, looking sternly as he pondered his options.

His cell phone suddenly rang; he took a peek and saw it was a message from Liu Mingfang.

Chi Jin didn't want to become too close with Liu Mingfang; he couldn't explain it exactly, but he simply found it uncomfortable to hang out around this man. But Liu Mingfang seemed to have a sincere interest in befriending him. He could often talk about how he admired the legendary Blue Fox and had some friends in the business world that would like to become acquainted with Chi Jin, or sometimes offer to say he wanted to talk about Xie Lanshan—and it was indeed Xie Lanshan's case that caused the suspension of Sui Hong's job.

Chi Jin wasn't interested in those business elites, but he would run toward anything that had to do with his captain and lost sight of everything else. He responded to the message and stood up. Chi Jin put his jacket back on and left after telling Ling Yun, "Don't wait for me to come back tonight."

It was still the same bar Liu Mingfang often hung around in. He stood up and made space for Chi Jin as soon as he saw the young man walk into the bar.

"I'm going to be leaving the country for a mission soon, so spill your beans now," Chi Jin said coldly, reminding the other that time was golden and to get straight to the point.

Liu Mingfang still had a smile on his face as he pointed at a larger man beside him, saying that this was a friend of his who wanted to open up a business in warehousing services. He explained the friend might run into some trouble with import and export merchandise like the Starex group and wanted to have a public security friend to help keep an eye out in case anyone tried to use their trade channels for illegal activities.

This was quite a huge stretch of a request. Despite being frontline fighters in law and crime, public security personnel were still not as well-read in the realms of law as actual lawyers. It would make more sense to consult a criminal lawyer to prevent illegal activities in business.

Chi Jin suppressed his frustration and answered a few questions for the friend. Yet he was growing tired after not hearing Liu Mingfang mention even Xie Lanshan's name and was ready to leave.

The businessman knew how to talk business and called two ladies over, saying that they should have a little fun before taking off.

Two young and beautiful women stepped out from the

crowd of hostesses; Chi Jin first shot them an annoyed glance before suddenly feeling chills go down his spine. He saw a young lady among the women wearing a crop top that exposed a black tattoo on her belly.

Two letters were tattooed like poison ivy on her stomach: MK.

He recalled that Xie Lanshan had once mentioned Mu Kun had a particular interest: the drug lord liked to tattoo his name on his lovers. The design of these letters on her body was identical to the ones found on Lang Li. The information on this tattoo was not made public; he had only told Liu Yanbo during a meeting and hoped that Hanhai City's violent crimes unit could find a new direction to investigate after all clues disappeared.

The surprise came so suddenly. Chi Jin quickly changed his attitude, reached a hand over to the businessman, and began acting friendlier than before.

"Can I get a different girl?" He squinted his eyes as if he wasn't interested, then pointed at the young woman in crop top. "This one looks better."

For the next two days, Chi Jin spent his free time with Liu Mingfang and the newly acquainted young women at the bar— all for the sake of tracing the one clue he could find to settle this case. He knew Sui Hong too well; a career was not just a burden in life for his captain, it was love and passion.

Chi Jin grew anxious as he considered this and already picked out some intel from this young woman, hoping to meet her boss as well.

The young woman's expression became difficult as she nudged closer to Chi Jin and laughed. "Don't try and make me talk! I know you're a cop, you're trying to frame me."

"There are different types of cops out there. All those stringent and traditional ones are happy living in poverty, but I'm not stupid." Chi Jin withstood the strong scent of perfume and wrapped an arm around the young woman's soft shoulders. He lowered his head and whispered into the woman's ears seductively, "Besides, we're already so close. Are you saying you still can't trust me?"

After another heated and intimate embrace, the young woman grew more flustered. As if she couldn't help but give in to the request of the young and handsome man before her, she finally said, "I can introduce you guys, but only people who are one of us can join our little circle. So, do you dare to prove that you're one of us?"

Chi Jin held up her hand and gave a playful bite on her finger as he asked, "How do I do that?"

The young woman giggled as if she was ticklish, calling out, "That's enough." Then, she suddenly pulled out a small bag of what looked like amethyst from her purse. The object inside glowed alluringly and dangerously under the dimmed lights of the bar.

She leaned her face towards Chi Jin, a breath of sweet air came through her red lips as she said, "Want to try some of this?"

Stowaway

Tang Xiaomo's photo also captured the face of a man behind her, but because of the distance and the glass door of the cafe obscuring him, his features were difficult to trace out. Shen Liufei asked a flight attendant for a cup of coffee and a pencil. He slowly gathered his focus and began drawing on paper. Before the coffee cooled and the plane landed, he successfully traced out a figure of the man.

It was a man with straight eyebrows, large eyes, and slim face; handsome and reserved. This kind of man could easily draw in the opposite sex even if he was dangerous, like a carnivore that reeked of sweetness to lure in its prey.

Shen Liufei knew where his next stop was as soon as he left the airport and rushed right to the coffee shop where Tang Xiaomo took her selfie.

He had already assumed that Tang Xiaomo was involved in a kidnapping case. Because of his mother's case, he had once kept a very close eye on female kidnappings. Among the files he had investigated, almost every single one of them noted Thailand was a highly dangerous place for women to travel alone.

This paradise land of beautiful scenery was also the biggest market for human trafficking in Southeast Asia. Many of those trafficked were tourists who were kidnapped during their trip to the country or stowaways who stopped in the country. A young and beautiful lone traveler like Tang Xiaomo was a popular target for human traffickers.

Geographically, the coffee shop was located right near a popular tourist hotspot. If the man in the photo was a known offender of human trafficking, it would also be likely for him to hang around the same area to prey on others.

There were many Chinese immigrants near the tourist district, so Shen Liufei took the portrait he had drawn and asked the owner of the coffee shop, "Have you seen this man before?"

As he handed the artwork over, Xie Lanshan's bullet necklace that was still wrapped around his wrist dropped out from his sleeves. Shen Liufei's hand froze for a moment while a gentle breeze blew by, jabbing right into his heart.

He stared at the necklace and suddenly recalled a poem:

Even if tomorrow's dawn spun
gun fire and a bloodied sun
I swear to not give up this night;
I swear to not give you up.

Poems from the north were notoriously pleasant, but it was too romanticized. Nobody can remain completely calm in the face of a bloodied death. Shen Liufei had thought about being a little selfish and keeping the man beside him—even if it might be a betrayal to his mother—but he couldn't bring himself to do it. Love bore out of the void, inexplicable and deep, yet he couldn't trust his own selfishness even at a time like this.

The owner responded with something, but he didn't catch it.

"Sir? Sir?" The owner called out.

"I'm sorry." Shen Liufei gave a slight apologetic bow for his sudden daze.

The owner gave him a smile and told him the man's name was Anuchit, a very kind local chemistry teacher who often visited the area.

Now that he knew the man's name and occupation, it wouldn't be hard to find his address. Shen Liufei recalled he had never been to Thailand, but felt a strange familiarity in this city.

The place Anuchit lived in wasn't very safe to walk around, and by the time he made his way to the residence, night had already fallen. Shen Liufei strolled casually on the streets and saw a person run toward him.

It was a man dressed in a grey trench coat; his sharp, triangular physique was quite noticeable even at a distance. He seemed to be about the same height as Shen Liufei, but much more muscular. The man buried his head in his trench coat, collar popped up high as if he was intentionally hiding his face. He even leaned to the side a little and lifted his left hand up to cover his face as he passed by Shen Liufei. His right hand pressed onto his hip.

This instinctive motion caught Shen Liufei's brief attention; he noticed the man was wearing a pair of clean black leather boots, the same type that the Thai police often wore.

The strange motion earlier suddenly had an explanation. Thai police officers often wore tight uniforms and had their belts hanging below their waist. All of their guns, communication devices, and tools hung on their belt, so the police would often subconsciously keep a hand on them at all times.

The police siren suddenly blared, and the man rushed

forward. He avoided the direction where the police cars arrived and disappeared into a small alleyway.

Shen Liufei arrived at Anuchit's residence only to discover that the police had already surrounded the building. According to the crowd of pedestrians, a chemistry teacher was just discovered to be stabbed to death in his own home.

As a foreigner who was also investigating Anuchit, Shen Liufei recognized that he might become a suspect if he tried to enter now. He turned and left while the police discussed the case, settling in at a small hotel in the nearby Chinatown.

Now that he knew the man in the trench coat earlier was a policeman, he could pay a visit to the police department tomorrow and find some new clues.

The hotel room was hot and humid, with very thin walls. Shen Liufei laid on the bed and stared at the cracks and uneven paint on the walls, pondering about Tang Xiaomo's whereabouts and then inevitably reminded himself of Xie Lanshan.

The two's relationship was both insipid and passionate. When they were separate, they knew each other had work to take care of, but once everything was settled and they were back together, they could spend a whole day in bed together without tiring of each other. Shen Liufei was used to keeping a distance from everyone and everything as if mortal matters were of no interest to him. Yet when he finally found time to let his mind run free, he would discover that every piece of his memories was filled with painful suffering.

The room's lights were off, only shades of red ambiance passed through the windows and colored the room a seductive crimson. Korean and Hakkanese dialogue passed through the thin walls, yet despite not understanding a word of the conversation, the sounds were strangely familiar.

The desire to find an old friend in a foreign land weighed heavily on his heart and made him feel exhausted. He turned and played with the bullet necklace on his wrist in the dark and closed his eyes.

Xie Lanshan followed to Bangkok two days after Shen Liufei arrived. He figured that if Tang Xiaomo disappeared in Bangkok, Shen Liufei would certainly follow to investigate her disappearance. The two may have temporarily lost contact with each other, but their goal was the same.

Xie Lanshan had befriended a Thai policeman during his years undercover in the Golden Triangle. The old cop's name was Somsak, and he knew that Xie Lanshan was an undercover officer from China. He was very cooperative and kept Xie Lanshan's identity a secret, as well as helped him on some onerous tasks during the undercover times. The two men formed a lasting friendship over their careers and shared goals. Xie Lanshan heard Somsak was transferred to Bangkok and immediately thought that this old friend could help him find the missing Tang Xiaomo.

The two exchanged a passionate hug as soon as the door opened and they skipped all the small talk to chat like old friends.

Old man Somsak was a typical and pure-blooded Thai man. He wasn't particularly pretty, but very amiable. His skin was a shade darker than Xie Lanshan, his full lips grinned into a friendly smile. The man wasn't tall but was very fit. White hair was growing from the sideburns, but his strong spirits as a cop remained lively. His Chinese was quite good, and he called Xie Lanshan "A'Lan" as well.

The old cop was ready to retire, not expecting to run into another murder case right as he was able to leave his post. He half-joked around with Xie Lanshan about having a condition to helping with searching for the missing little girl—that Xie Lanshan needed to help him solve this murder case first.

Xie Lanshan thought about it briefly and decided that it

was a fair trade-off. However, a foreign cop had no authority in Thailand, and he was still on suspension at home. He lifted an eyebrow and gave a playful grin at Somsak. "I'm cool with that, but I don't want to drag an old cop who's about to retire to break the rules at the last minute."

"Don't worry about it." Somsak laughed. "We've already gotten news from the higher-ups that we're set to work with the police from your place in a cross-border operation for a case to bring back a big celebrity too."

A cross-border operation might sound like a piece of cake, but it certainly wasn't easy to execute. Everything from the exact jurisdiction and authority each side had was something that needed to be settled. However, the initial negotiation had confirmed that the Handong Provincial Public Security Branch would send in two special agents from the Blue Fox Commando to help negotiate the case of Chinese celebrity Wen Jue in Thailand.

Now that he was reminded of it, Somsak was surprised and asked Xie Lanshan, "Aren't you part of the Blue Fox too? How come you arrived earlier than expected?"

"I'm no longer part of it." It had been almost three years since he left the Blue Foxes, and the entire story behind it all was quite complicated to explain. Xie Lanshan's expression darkened slightly before he sighed and said, "It's a long story, but I'm also not here for that celebrity. I'm here to find a friend."

Somsak didn't understand the sourness and bitterness in that small sigh and only nodded in response. "Staying out of drug enforcement is good too. Those days in the past... were too hard for you."

Xie Lanshan didn't want to talk about the past and then gave another sweet smile to the old man. "So, tell me about this murder case of yours."

"The victim is an adult man called Anuchit, a 38-year-old

single man. He was a chemistry teacher at an international school here. The school's quite prestigious, you can say it's the best school in Bangkok." Somsak walked back toward his desk as he explained and pulled out some photos from the file folder for Xie Lanshan. He had been pondering over this case right before Xie Lanshan came knocking on his door.

Xie Lanshan looked at the photo; Anuchit was a clean and handsome man. His face was on the long side, eyes large and complemented by strong eyebrows. It was almost difficult to tell he was nearing his 40s, and he rather looked quite like a celebrity.

"The neighborhood he lived in wasn't the safest area, and there were no surveillance cameras around. The time of his death was around 9 P.M. two days ago and the crime was reported within 20 minutes of his death. A neighbor noticed that the man's door wasn't closed and wanted to remind the man, but as they walked in the door, they discovered the victim was already dead."

"Isn't this neighbor a little too friendly?" Xie Lanshan was suspicious out of instinct.

"Anuchit mentioned he wanted to move because he felt his life was threatened," the old cop said, "and he was right."

"Anything else?" Xie Lanshan questioned.

"We don't have any more information. The neighbor said the victim was quite vague."

Xie Lanshan looked at the photos of the crime scene. The victim died from a heavy blow on the back of his head from an ashtray that shattered his skull; the culprit had hit him twice with the ashtray that belonged to the victim.

"The neighbor also said that they heard the victim open the doors to greet a guest at around 8:30 P.M. that night. They couldn't make out the features of the guest but can confirm it was a man."

That meant the victim and culprit were acquainted. Xie Lanshan nodded and continued to flip through the photos. He noticed that one of the photos was of a wall in the victim's home that was normally covered by a piece of white cloth. Behind the cloth was a wall covered in various photos of young women. The photos looked to be candid shots taken in secret.

The demon hid beneath human skin. Xie Lanshan frowned and pulled out this photo, commenting, "You said the victim was a well-respected chemistry teacher, but it sure looks like he's got a hidden side that nobody was aware of."

"This is also one of the reasons why I thought about pulling you into this case when I heard you were looking for a missing female friend." Somsak let out a sigh as he took the photo and said, "Based on my years of experience as a cop, I'm almost certain this guy's a human trafficker."

Gambling was banned in Thailand, but pornography was a robust business. Young women who fell into the hands of human traffickers were unlikely to be saved. Xie Lanshan turned toward Somsak, his gaze cold as he pressed his eyebrows together even more and waited for the old cop to continue.

"We've been very hard on fighting drugs lately. Many of those old opium farms have now been transformed to grow tea leaves. The business is actually doing quite well, too. Drugs like heroin no longer have a market here as big as before, so most of the mafia and criminals shifted their focus to human trafficking. You can only sell drugs once, but you can trade people more than once." The old cop lowered his head and let out another sigh.

"Mafia?" Xie Lanshan pondered a little before asking with a heavy expression, "Do you mean Guan Nuoqin?"

"That's the man." Somsak nodded and said, "And after some investigation with the bank, this Anuchit person has been making massive transactions lately."

Xie Lanshan fell silent and continued flipping through the photos. One photo quickly caught his attention.

Anuchit's house didn't have an entryway inside, like how traditional Chinese houses were built, and the layout of the interior was visibly different from most traditional families; it was difficult to tell if it was intentional. Regardless, the first item one would see upon entering the house was a large antique carved cabinet. The detailed sculptures on the cabinet complemented an elegant old clock that also hung right above it. Yet on top of the cabinet was a wooden toy that looked like a children's abacus that contrasted the decoration of the rest of the house.

There were six wooden sticks on the toy abacus, each stick hung ten beads that ranged in color from red, black, yellow, green, blue, and purple.

Xie Lanshan noticed that there were two even holes on the top of the toy, which meant that someone must have taken off a stick from the toy that was supposed to be composed of seven wooden sticks.

The beads had been moved to form a series of numbers: 679234.

(ii)

With the patience of Job, Shen Liufei waited for about two days near the police station before he finally saw the man that he ran into the night of the murder. Even if the man now wore a uniform, his physique and mannerism gave his identity away to the perceptive artist.

The man was tall and built, had tanned skin and black hair, and he donned a messy hairstyle that shined like horsehair. Faint stubbles above his lips gave him a wild look that covered his rather good-looking face. The man had a wide face which highlighted his big eyes that were clear as water.

Shen Liufei purchased a knife at a local shop for self-defense and found out from the shop owner in English that the cop's name was Kang Xin, of Chinese descent.

Kang Xin didn't go back home after leaving the station and instead stopped at a bar all by himself. Shen Liufei tailed the man and entered the bar.

The man ordered a drink but didn't take a sip, looking anxiously at his watch like he was waiting for someone. Shen Liufei assumed that the man had an important appointment today and didn't startle the snake, sitting quietly in the corner as he watched.

About half an hour later, Kang Xin received a call. He seemed very nervous and murmured into the phone with his hand over his mouth. Then he stood up abruptly and left the bar in haste.

Shen Liufei stood up and followed the man, snaking through the city streets carefully but swiftly.

The man was indeed an experienced cop with a sharp eye and anti-investigation abilities. Shen Liufei stood out too much with his pale skin and handsome appearance. The cop noticed someone was trailing him and walked faster, then turned into a small alleyway.

Shen Liufei also made his way into the alleyway, but the man had already disappeared in the dark and narrow street. There was only junk placed on both sides of the street, with a foul smell looming in the air.

Above his head was a crescent moon, which was the only source of light on this seemingly never-ending narrow road. There were places to hide in every corner.

Shen Liufei walked slowly into the alleyway. His eyebrows pressed slightly together, lips closed as his gaze remained fixed on the road ahead. His ink-black eyes scanned from left to right with every step forward.

His eyesight and hearing were both very sensitive, but the person hiding in the dark right now was holding his breath. It was deathly silent around the alley; even the sound of a needle dropping on the ground could be heard.

Shen Liufei walked about 2/3 of the way into the alleyway. He didn't notice that a little crossbow peeked out from behind a broken shelf and was aimed at him.

Kang Xin recognized that his prey was under the light and squinted his eyes as he locked on his target, waiting until the man walked past to shoot an arrow right into his head.

A spark of light seemed to appear in the air as the arrow shot out of the bow. To Kang Xin's surprise, Shen Liufei noticed something was up right at that time and swiftly dodged the attack. Just before the arrow hit the ground, Shen Liufei kicked to the side and knocked down the shelf.

The items on the shelf rained down on Kang Xin, who quickly jumped out to avoid impact. He utilized his height and thrust the mini crossbow in his hand toward Shen Liufei.

The artist didn't waste time and greeted the man with a fist. He moved swiftly like lightning, dexterously blocking all attacks while making aggressive advances against the cop. To his surprise, the tall man didn't dodge and took a heavy blow right to his chest. This impact sent the tall man back half a meter, proving that Shen Liufei was an experienced fighter.

Kang Xin was also quite skilled in martial arts and pushed Shen Liufei back with aggressive counterattacks. The two men engaged in a violent brawl for a while, until Shen Liufei took the upper hand and pinned the man down beneath him. He said, "I'm not here for you, I'm looking for Anuchit. I know he's a human trafficker—he kidnapped one of our friends."

Kang Xin pretended to surrender and responded in

Chinese that he wouldn't be fighting back, then suddenly pulled himself up and fought back more aggressively.

Shen Liufei was knocked onto the ground as if he had just been run over by a bull. The two men fought on the ground until Shen Liufei once again dominated him. This time, he held out the knife in his pocket and pressed the blade against the man's neck, saying in a hoarse voice, "I could be a colleague of yours in China, I can tell the police that I've witnessed you at the scene of the crime that night and get you in trouble. But I can also only ask you one simple question—I'm here for my friend. I could care less if you were the one that killed that scum or not! Do you understand?"

The blade pressed toward the man's throat and cut a crimson mark. Shen Liufei called back sternly, "Answer me, do you understand?"

"I... I understand..." Kang Xin no longer struggled and gave in.

Shen Liufei noticed a photo-frame necklace draped around the man's neck. He pulled the silver necklace off with the tip of the knife and looked inside to see that it was a photo of a little girl. She had similar features as the man, bright eyes and a wide face, a very pretty little girl.

This was likely his daughter.

Kang Xin grew anxious and rushed forward to grab the necklace, ignoring the blade, and called out, "Give it back!"

"Sorry." Shen Liufei didn't jest and returned the necklace with care and sincerity. He knew very well how people could be trapped and bonded by a specific kind of emotion for the rest of their lives—just like what the bracelet around his wrist was to him.

"She's very beautiful." The man was aggressive, like an experienced predator during a fight, but beneath that armor was a courteous gentleman who remained calm in the face of an enemy. Shen Liufei wiped the blood from the corner of his lips and asked, "Is this your daughter?"

Kang Xin suffered quite a blow; his face was purple and blue while his cheekbone bruised with a little bump on his face. He sat on the ground, fatigued, head hanging as he stared down at his necklace and gently caressed the photo of the girl. He said, "Her name's Poonaya, I call her Yaya. She's my little princess that just turned 10 this year."

Shen Liufei noticed the bitterness and pain in the man's eyes as he looked at his daughter's photo. He paused slightly before asking, almost reluctantly, "Is your daughter..."

"Oh, no." Kang Xin shook his head after realizing what the other was about to ask and said, "She wasn't kidnapped, she lives with her mother right now. She... is sick."

"A severe illness?"

"Very." Kang Xin frowned in pain, his lips pressed together tightly. He then explained, "Dilated cardiomyopathy. The only cure is a heart transplant, but we couldn't find any donors that match. The doctor said that if we don't do the transplant soon, she'll... I wish I could just give my heart to her."

A moment of silence fell between the two. The dark alleyway was long and narrow, the entrance like a tiny dot of light. A pedestrian passed by the entrance and saw two men sitting alone in the dark alleyway, immediately relating it to some inappropriate business; they spat on the ground in disgust.

After a long while, Kang Xin shook his head and said, "Whether you believe me or not, I didn't kill the man."

"So, what were you doing at the place at a time like that?" Shen Liufei didn't suspect the man. He noticed that the man had gotten enough rest and held out a hand to pull the man back on his feet.

"I did intend to kill him." Kang Xin was impressed by the

young man's class and admitted, "But he was dead by the time I arrived at his place."

"Why do you want to kill him?"

"I can't tell you." Kang Xin lowered his head again to give one last look at his daughter's photo before putting the necklace back into his pocket, then turned around to leave.

Shen Liufei didn't stop him and only said airily, "Officer Kang Xin."

The man refused to turn his head, but stopped walking.

"My friend is also a young girl, also a daughter of a father. Her father will be worried for her safety like you are concerned for your daughter's health." Tang Xiaomo lived with her grandfather since she was young and never brought up her parents; he recalled she glossed over briefly and said she was abandoned. But Shen Liufei knew this was the only way to open up the kind heart in this man.

He could tell that the man was a cop, and that his sense of justice had not wavered because of his earlier confession.

After a brief pause, Shen Liufei continued, "I can't and won't exercise any official authority in your country. I simply wish to know my friend's whereabouts so that I can bring her back to her father."

The man's shoulder shivered a little, as if that last bit of stubbornness finally deflated and vanished. He turned his head slightly and said, "I don't know where your friend is, but I know that the local stowaway organization here is planning on doing a big human trafficking trade lately. Among them are some other stowaways along with tourists who were kidnapped or sold off; if you can withstand hardships, I can help open a door for you to go inside."

(iii)

Looking at photos was not enough to solve a crime. Somsak was confident in Xie Lanshan's abilities and used his connections to open a door for him to check the locked crime scene in person.

Xie Lanshan searched the house carefully without skipping over any details, ensuring that nothing escaped his eyes.

He soon noticed that the cabinet from the photo was supposed to be against the wall inside a room and not facing the front door. The old collected dust gave away the original location of the cabinet. Judging from the slight marks left from dragging the furniture over, the layout was not the homeowner's personal preference and was changed recently on purpose.

"If the victim doesn't die immediately in a murder case, they will usually leave a dying message that points directly to the identity of the culprit. But this message may not have been left on the day of the murder." Xie Lanshan squatted down beside the cabinet to investigate as he explained to Somsak behind him, "Judging by the witness account from the neighbor, Anuchit may have changed the layout of the furniture in his house after realizing his life was in danger to ensure that he could leave an obvious dying message if he was killed."

Almost as soon as he finished the last line, he discovered something. There was a small object beneath the cabinet; Xie Lanshan leaned forward and reached for the item, pulling out a wooden bead with his vinyl gloves. The bead was painted white and was a little larger than his thumb, with two even holes on both sides.

After checking there was nothing else beneath the cabinet, Xie Lanshan stood up and handed the white bead to Somsak.

The crime scene was left untouched and the toy abacus was still resting on the top of the cabinet. Somsak compared the white bead in his hand with the beads on the abacus and confirmed that it was the missing seventh bead from the toy.

He asked Xie Lanshan, "But what does this mean?"

Of course, Xie Lanshan didn't have an answer yet and licked the corner of his lips like a leopard with a half-empty stomach without a word.

"Six digits... could it be some sort of pass code for a safe?" Somsak shook his head almost as soon as he asked and said with a sigh, "We've searched Anuchit's room thoroughly and couldn't find anything that needed a passcode. They tried his phone and computer to no avail, nor did they find any safe kept in his bank, all clues leading to a dead end."

Xie Lanshan pondered slightly before saying, "The police can access computers, phones, and safes even without a passcode. There's no need for him to leave this kind of message."

It certainly didn't make sense to leave this kind of a dying message from an analytical point of view. Somsak nodded and asked, "True, but what do these six numbers mean then?"

"679234... 679234..." Xie Lanshan circled around the room as he mumbled the numbers. Suddenly, he lifted his head and looked at the antique clock hanging above the wooden cabinet.

He frowned and asked Somsak, "What time is it right now?"

Somsak responded, "2:40 P.M., what's wrong?"

Xie Lanshan lifted his chin and shot a glance towards the clock and said, "Look."

The time on the clock froze at 1:47 A.M., which meant that it was possible that someone purposely stopped the clock.

"1:47 A.M... 147... 147..." Xie Lanshan placed a hand on his chin as he mumbled. Then, his eyebrows relaxed, as if the mist before his eyes suddenly cleared up. His eyes lit up brighter and brighter.

"A toy abacus with only seven wooden sticks isn't enough to display a nine-digit number but also too much to display a six-digit. That's why Anuchit took one stick off at the last minute. The beads that dropped to the ground are proof." Xie Lanshan lifted a confident smile and grew more certain of his analysis. He turned and said to Somsak, "This isn't a six-digit passcode, it's a nine-digit dying message."

Somsak couldn't catch up to the logic and asked, "But it's 147679234, what do the extra three digits mean?"

Xie Lanshan didn't respond and instead walked up toward the cabinet in excitement. He leaned down to use it as a table and reached a hand back to ask, "Do you have a pen and paper?"

Somsak pulled out the items from his pocket and handed them to him.

"You said Anuchit was a chemistry teacher, so let's try looking at this using the periodic table of elements." Xie Lanshan wrote nine numbers on the paper and was quickly able to separate the digits into logical number sets. He drew lines between the digits and explained, "14 is Silicon, the symbol is Si. 7 is Nitrogen, which is N, 67 is... 67..."

Xie Lanshan didn't even think about searching the internet and instead pressed his fingers on his forehead a few times, attempting to recall from his memories. After a moment, he remembered—or perhaps it was more accurate to say that the other piece of memory that existed in his head remembered.

"67 is Holmium, HO. 92 is Uranium, U, and 34 is Selenium, which is Se... if we combine the letters it becomes..." Xie Lanshan wrote something on the paper and then held it up to Somsak behind him.

SIN HOUSE.

"This, this is..." Somsak recognized the fancy words written on the paper and called out, "It's the name of a pole-dancing club on the bar street around here!"

Another person walked into Anuchit's house just as they deciphered the dying message. The footsteps were heavy, like a muffled drum on the ground.

A tall and fit man that donned a police uniform stepped in. His eyes stood out the most, big and bright, which contrasted his physical age.

Somsak introduced the newcomer to Xie Lanshan. He pointed at the tall man and said with a smile, "This is my buddy, Officer Kang Xin. He's a Chinese immigrant that taught me most of my Mandarin. I guess you can call him my teacher." He then turned and introduced Xie Lanshan to Kang Xin, saying that the former was a cop from China that he became acquainted with through a drug enforcement operation. He then praised Xie Lanshan's abilities as an investigator, also mentioning that Xie Lanshan was the kindest and most benevolent cop he'd ever met. Sometimes the young man didn't even seem like a cop and was instead like Buddha with immense compassion.

This was the highest praise a man could receive from a Buddhist follower. Somsak already spoke very good Chinese eight to nine years ago when Xie Lanshan was still undercover, so his introduction on both sides was very humble while exaggerating on some extra feats. Xie Lanshan turned toward the cop and lifted an eyebrow, then asked nonchalantly, "Officer Kang, what's with the injury on your face?"

A hint of unease flashed across Kang Xin's face as he reached a hand up to touch the bruise on his cheeks. He explained, "I was catching a thief on the street and ended up letting them go because I underestimated them and screwed up."

"That's one powerful fighter!" Somsak was surprised and said, "You're one of the best fighters we have in the bureau."

"Not a chance, we just exchanged a few fists." Kang Xin waved his hand and then quickly removed his gaze as soon as he met Xie Lanshan's.

With that sharp sixth sense as a cop, Xie Lanshan suspected that the man was hiding something but couldn't place his finger on it. He simply studied the unease on the man's face and asked with a small smile, "Does Officer Kang have anything to add to the case since you arrived late?"

"Kang Xin's daughter is very sick, at terminal last stage, so he would sometimes request time off for his daughter. The higher-ups have all been very understanding of this," Somsak explained. "He wasn't involved very much in this case, but Kang here is a good cop, just like you. I don't know if you've seen this news before about a man who barged into the police department with a knife. The man was extremely agitated, but a cop didn't choose to shoot him down lawfully and instead walked up to the invader and gave him an embrace."

"I've heard of it." Xie Lanshan certainly had heard of this case due to its unique circumstances. It even sparked a debate among the violent crimes unit once. Regardless of if this was the most appropriate action to take, the police ended up moving the agitated man and saved a life that could have been in danger.

Kang Xin lowered his head in embarrassment before the old cop could continue. He wasn't being humble out of courtesy and believed this incident wasn't worth mentioning, then said, "That's too long ago, no need to bring it up again."

Even without Somsak's explanation, Xie Lanshan also realized that his reaction had been a little too rash. It was as if he was now walking on wire without Shen Liufei around and carried suspicion around anyone that walked near him. He suppressed the suspicious attitude welling up within him and held out a hand to Kang Xin, once again introducing himself properly this time, "Xie Lanshan, officer from Hanhai, China."

Kang Xin smiled and held out his hand to respond, "Kang Xin, officer from Bangkok, Thailand."

Bangkok had a much hotter climate with longer daylight; even at 4 P.M., the sky was still crystal clear and blue across the horizon. Cars drove by one by one in this place that looked like paradise on earth while pedestrians on the street swarmed the city like a flood. Xie Lanshan got in Somsak's car and followed the officers back to the bureau. During the traffic-filled trip back, his eyes were fixed on the people outside, hoping to find the person he had been searching for.

A figure briefly swept by from afar like a fleeting image. That figure was solitary and tall and looked very much like Shen Liufei.

Yet, after a blink of an eye, the figure vanished into the crowd of strange faces. Xie Lanshan almost hit his head on the car's roof earlier from surprise, but quickly sat back down in silence.

It must have been someone else.

Considering the possibility of never searching for that person again, he turned his gaze back onto the people outside. Men, women, young and old; the more people there were outside, the more he feared loneliness. The surrounding air suddenly felt chilly. This coldness seeped into his skin and through his bones until it froze his blood and numbed his limbs. Xie Lanshan leaned by the window and held his shoulders. He gave himself warmth with his own hands, but it wasn't enough.

Cuz, I miss you so much, he mumbled silently.

As soon as he walked into the bureau, Xie Lanshan was shocked to be greeted by another man who shared an identical face with Kang Xin.

From Somsak's introduction, this was the branch chief of their bureau and Kang Xin's twin brother, Kang Tai.

The brothers looked almost identical at first glance, but after careful assessment, it wasn't difficult to tell the twins apart by their expressions and body language. Kang Xin was fit and tall, his expression strangely down and out and even a little disheveled. But Kang Tai was different.

He was thinner in physique and donned a clean all-back hairstyle that looked as if his entire head was covered in a layer of oil and face in a layer of foundation. A strong, fragrant scent attacked the nose even meters apart.

The brothers didn't seem to be close, judging by their interaction. The branch chief seemed to not care for his younger brother and simply glanced at Xie Lanshan before standing up and asking Somsak, "Who's this man?"

Somsak told his branch chief that this was Officer Xie Lanshan from China, a former Blue Fox team member. Since the two countries were now cooperating in an operation, he decided he could have Xie Lanshan assist in investigating Anuchit's case.

"Why send two teams at different times? You think these Chinese cops can help investigate our case?" Kang Tai pulled out a silk handkerchief from his pocket and wiped the sweat on his nose. He said, snarling, in frustration to the side, "The Blue Fox should be arriving soon. Prepare yourselves and don't embarrass me in front of these foreigners."

(iv)

That night, Xie Lanshan followed Somsak to Sin House.

This famous pole-dancing club belonged to a rich businessman by the name of Zhong Zhuohai. The man was a Chinese immigrant in Thailand and an honorable representative of the Chinese diaspora around the region. His corporation and group were among the top ten businesses in Thailand, with companies spread out all over the continent of Asia. Zhong Zhuohai was already at the old age of 70 with a long-time heart condition, according to the media.

Outside Sin House stood six large and wide-shouldered security guards, three men on each side of the door. Their sharp eyes studied every guest that walked in and out of the door in case of any unwanted trouble. Xie Lanshan walked past the guards and felt that those gazes on him were nowhere close to friendly. Just as he pondered, an upbeat and catchy rhythm rang out through the crowd of people. He looked past the wave of people and saw a fancy stage at the center.

Beautiful women dressed in seductive outfits on the stage were blowing kisses to the audience. They scanned the club and gestured coquettishly toward the men in the audience, who took all sorts of hints from those gazes.

One woman had a sharp eye and locked her gaze on the most handsome man in the club. She gave Xie Lanshan a smile and began moving her body in a passionately seductive and bold dance move. Xie Lanshan lifted the corner of his lips and pulled open his button-up shirt to expose that silk-like smooth chest, ready to throw himself into the dance pool.

Somsak grabbed onto Xie Lanshan's arms and reminded the latter with a stern face, "You're here for work."

Xie Lanshan pulled his arm out of Somsak's grip smoothly like a snake and said with a grin, "Let me have some fun first."

Xie Lanshan originally wanted to let himself free and join in the spirit of this culture. Anuchit left a dying message that pointed at this bar, which meant that the culprit must not be an ordinary customer. The club was big with many people. It would be difficult to pick out one person from this massive crowd. He wanted to get close to one of the dancers at the club so that he could use their connections to search for their target.

Yet as soon as he stepped into the dance pool, Xie Lanshan felt a sudden sense of familiarity and ease. He certainly was just a man who had no hobbies outside of his job as a drug enforcement officer in the past; the most he would do was carve little wooden animals for the girl he liked. But now he wanted to make himself happy—and he knew how to do that.

The man was beautiful and had sharp dance moves that easily made him the center of attention. All the dancers on stage moved around him as if they could glue themselves onto him the next moment. The men down below also had their eyes on him. Some looked visibly envious, while others showed a hint of interest toward him.

The Xie Lanshan on stage stood out amongst everyone in the club, both the handsome men and beautiful women. His hair was long and draped down his neck, giving his clean features an even more attractive layer that looked a bit androgynous. He didn't shy away from dancing with the pretty ladies on stage; the women also welcomed him with open hands—literally. Their hands slid inside his open shirt, hoping to get a feel of those fit abs.

Then, he stood on the stage and turned his back to the crowd and fell backward—

The audience quickly rushed forth with arms out and caught the man.

Old Somsak finally couldn't withstand this scene and made his way into the crowd of people. He walked beside Xie Lanshan and asked him in a low voice, "Just what are you doing?"

"Can't you see?" Xie Lanshan said with that same attractive smile and called with his arms out, "I'm a party queen!"

The entire club cheered him on, high-tension filled the whole establishment.

Somsak pulled Xie Lanshan's arm angrily against the crowd's booing around him and dragged Xie Lanshan over to the side.

"I'm helping you solve the case, and that's how you treat me?" Xie Lanshan gave an almost smug response, "You've had 'I'm a cop' written all over your face since you walked into the bar. Trust me, if you carry a sign like that, you'll never be able to get to the bottom of this case."

While there was truth in those words, Somsak couldn't understand the craziness Xie Lanshan showed earlier and said numbly, "Well, I am a cop. What about you—are you still one?"

Those words from the old cop were killjoys that would expose their identities if anyone were to hear them. Xie Lanshan took a glass of wine from a waiter passing by and walked out of the bar to calm himself down and get a fresh breath of air.

Something else caught his attention as soon as he walked out the door. At the front door of a neighboring bar to Sin House, a portly middle-aged man got kicked out of the door by the security guards. He was wearing only his underwear, the rest of his clothes gone, exposing the thick white skin on his body.

The middle-aged man cried loudly while holding a sign in his hands. Xie Lanshan paid him a little more attention because the man spoke in Chinese. This time, he finally noticed this funny-looking middle-aged man was that celebrity manager who often appeared on television back home.

What was his name again? Xie Lanshan thought briefly. *Oh, Han Guangming.*

He then glanced at the sign Han Guangming held and

almost laughed; the sign had two English sentences written that read "Kidnap me" and "Give my boy back".

Recalling it now, human traffickers also kidnapped that young celebrity called Wen Jue in Thailand. The main reason the Blue Foxes were dispatched this time was to bring back that lost child. Xie Lanshan had seen photos of Wen Jue on the internet before. This child was only in his early 20s but had a very delicate model-like face. Unfortunately, it was almost too average even among models and wasn't too memorable.

"Take me away!" Han Guangming seemed to be putting on a comedic skit. Like a fat white goose who didn't know when to stop, he held up the sign and called out in front of all bars around the area, "Give my Wen Jue back to me, take me instead!"

A crowd of young and old women surrounded him and snapped photos on their phones, giggling as they passed. Perhaps a few Chinese tourists recognized him and decided that this was even more interesting than to simply walk around a red-light district.

Xie Lanshan quickly analyzed the situation at hand. Bangkok was filled with all sorts of clubs and bars and bountiful red-light district streets. Among them were hubs of human trafficking businesses that were hard to detect by tourists. But if Han Guangming was able to find his way here, it meant that he at least had some ideas about where to search for the underground trade routes.

However, there was one thing Xie Lanshan couldn't fathom: Only females would usually be sold to red-light districts while men were more often sold to become slaves or engage in organ trades. Han Guangming may have been looking in the wrong places for Wen Jue.

"What are you all snapping at? Huh? I'm suing anyone that posts on Weibo for invading my privacy!" Han Guangming shooed the crowd away with his signboard and called out once again, perhaps on purpose to garner more attention, "Take me away! Take me—"

This area was a hotspot for Chinese tourists, so most waiters and guards in the bars spoke Chinese as well. A tall white man who dressed as a bodyguard walked out of a bar in fury. He seemed to be frustrated at Han Guangming's ruckus that affected their business and lifted a fist, ready to punch the middle-aged man.

One punch knocked the middle-aged man down, but the white bodyguard didn't stop. His veins popped in anger, fist clenched hard, looking determined to punch the old man dead.

"He's gonna kill me! Murderer!" Han Guangming called out to the crowd while covering his bloodied nose, "Are you fellow Chinese people just going to watch me like this?"

That bodyguard kicked and stepped on Han Guangming continuously. Just then, Xie Lanshan darted forward and grabbed onto the guard's wrist.

Sometimes words weren't needed between two fighters. As their eyes met, the white man immediately realized that this newcomer was not someone he could mess with. The white man's lips clicked in displeasure and he purposely bumped a shoulder to Xie Lanshan, then walked away with irritation.

"Go back home," Xie Lanshan said coolly as he helped Han Guangming up from the ground. "It's our job as cops to search for missing persons. There's no need for you to risk your life even if it's to bring back your source of income."

Yet Han Guangming did not listen and instead beamed in excitement as soon as he heard fluent Mandarin. He leaned in toward Xie Lanshan and asked, "Oh, mister policeman, are you part of the Blue Fox Commando? I heard our government sent the Blue Fox over to save our little Jue here, so please take me along with you to find him!"

"You're in the wrong place to search," Xie Lanshan said. The chubby man looked quite silly upon a closer glance. The flesh on his face scrunched up like he was both crying and laughing, the bruises also colored his face purple and green like a child's doodle. Xie Lanshan couldn't laugh hearing a man much older than him call him "mister policeman" and said sternly, "You should go back. Since nobody had contacted you so far for money, that means they really didn't know the person they kidnapped is a celebrity. Usually in a case like this, young men would be sold into slavery."

"This isn't a normal case! You think our lil' Jue is just a small case?" The chubby man jumped instantly as if he heard a grave insult from Xie Lanshan's mouth and said, "I've checked a report on Thailand's human trafficking market online before, some pretty young men would be forced into prostitution too... What if...."

Han Guangming made a scissor-hand gesture with a frightened face and then cried, "What if I'm too late and he got forced to cut off his little buddy! Oh, my poor ol' Jue!"

"You are... not wrong..." Xie Lanshan felt a vein on his forehead pop. He rubbed on his temples to ease that growing headache and thought, *no wonder even that bodyguard couldn't help but beat this guy up. If I could, I would do the same right now.*

"Let's just settle for tonight, don't forget that your teammates will be arriving soon." Even a Thai policeman like Somsak knew the name of the Blue Fox Commando and said to Xie Lanshan, "Go organize all the clues we have so far so you can report to your teammates."

"They're not my teammates." Colorful lights in this busy street shone on Xie Lanshan's face, turning red one second and white another. The light in his eyes strangely glistened in the colors. He told Somsak coldly, "They've abandoned me."

"You..." Somsak didn't know what happened to Xie Lanshan, but noticed the hint of cruelty hidden beneath the young man's gaze. Of course, the word "cruelness" was far removed from the young undercover he knew many years ago. The old cop took a step back and asked, "Are you still Xie Lanshan?"

"I'm here to look for my friend, not to cooperate with the Thai police." Xie Lanshan didn't want to answer the old cop's question and gave a smile, "Here's an old Chinese saying to learn: those who trudge down different paths will never meet. You can go solve your case with the Blue Foxes you admire, and I..."

He lowered his gaze to look at the still naked Han Guangming, then picked the man up by the nape of his neck like picking up a chick. Xie Lanshan grinned and said, "I'll go find my friend with this old Han here. You're paying for our entire trip, old Han, you hear me?"

(v)

The new group of slaves needed to be separated into two groups to work on an island or for fishermen, but there were not enough people to manage them. Shen Liufei found his way onto the managing team through Kang Xin and became the left-hand to a supervisor.

Kang Xin only said two words before the young man left: Take care.

Those words weighed heavily on his shoulders while Shen Liufei made his way over to an unknown destination. He was aware of the dangers and troubles that awaited and gave this newly acquainted Thai cop a small smile. He was soon blind-folded by someone and then led on a truck that drove off to somewhere out in this foreign land. Shen Liufei couldn't see anything through the black cloth along the way and could only rely on his nose and ears to remember this mysterious route. He knew he would end up in a place completely cut off from the rest of the world and witness firsthand what hell on earth was like.

The slaves were temporarily locked in an abandoned factory in the rural mountain area. Outside the factory building were a few rusted metal cages that imprisoned those captured young slaves; the youngest ones seemed to be only thirteen or fourteen, while the eldest ones looked to still be in puberty. Bruises and whip scars covered their bodies, all of them thin like paper and on their last breath. These poor souls would helplessly reach their hands out of the cage to beg as soon as they saw someone walk by.

That was the first impression Shen Liufei had of this place: eyes filled with despair and the crimson blood-like color of the setting sun.

There were already about a hundred or so slaves kept here, with only three guards holding submachine guns in their hands. All of them worked under Guan Nuoqin. Shen Liufei didn't expect to find Tang Xiaomo at a place like this, but he could obtain intel from Guan Nuoqin's men discreetly and decided to go with the flow for now. He was led to view his room, which was only a little better than the rooms of the slaves. Flies filled the air and there was only some cotton laid on the floor that seemed to be his bed. After he tossed his small bag of belongings, Shen Liufei was taken to the place where the slaves were locked.

The traffickers had one more task to complete and needed to wait inside this factory. Some slaves were scammed over, others kidnapped, while the rest were stowaways who were unfortunately sold to the traffickers by their leaders. Their inevitable end here was a nightmarish 20-hour workday every day with violent beatings if they were caught resting. One of Guan Nuoqin's subordinates who worked here was called A'Liang, who proudly showed Shen Liufei the unique 'weapon' they had created. They would dry up the stingrays they caught and use the sharp and poisonous edges on the back of the rays to beat anyone who tried to escape. The poison would bring a severe allergic reaction and stinging sensation that hurt more than a simple whip.

Sometimes, out of their twisted hearts, the guards would also whip the slaves for entertainment. Just like the Stanford jail, these people who had even the slightest authority in their hands turned into monsters overnight.

"The luckier ones would be sent to work in the factories, and the less fortunate were on the island or boat. If they die there, you won't even find their corpses." A'Liang said with a grotesque expression and laughed. "Who could have imagined that this beautiful blue sea is actually filled with human bones down beneath?"

Shen Liufei didn't ask for more information but already seemed to have pieced together some puzzle pieces. Kang Xin engaged in criminal activities with Guan Nuoqin because the drug lord could find a matching heart donation for his daughter.

From the bodies of these slaves.

The other man who followed A'Liang hadn't stopped cursing the whole time and kept rambling until night fell and the large constellations became visible above the cityscape. This man and another lackey were Burmese. Because they captured a portion of these slaves from Myanmar, the drug lord had dispatched a few people who spoke Burmese to watch over the slaves in case anyone attempted to riot.

"Curse my damn luck for taking this job! Food's all stinky fishes and shrimp, even the water tastes muddy, and I have to watch over these smelly bastards! Job at Sin House was much better than this. At least there are pretty girls to look at and we could even 'test the product' before we sell them off."

All sorts of complaints and curses shot out of his mouth. The two Burmese men always spoke in their mother tongue in private. They assumed that Shen Liufei couldn't understand as a Chinese man and didn't particularly hide their conversations before him.

Yet Shen Liufei suddenly discovered something. He understood Burmese, but he had never studied the language.

Shen Liufei couldn't let the workers discover that he actually understood Burmese and purposely distanced himself from those two men. He sat near the slave cage and lowered his head to polish his dagger, removing himself from all commotion around him.

Suddenly, someone behind him banged on the cage and made a sound loud enough to alert him, but not the rest of the guards.

"Bai Shuo! Bai Shou, it's me!" Someone called out in Chinese as they rattled the cage bar.

Most Chinese people who lived near the borders of Thailand and Myanmar spoke Mandarin with a heavy Yunnan accent. It was certainly rare to hear such clean and crisp Mandarin at a place like this. Shen Liufei turned his head and immediately saw the person who called him.

The cage was filled with people like a pack of sardines. These slaves have been starving for days and had faces covered in dust, but this person had a clean and handsome face that not even the ripped clothing could hide.

Shen Liufei narrowed his eyes and studied the man carefully; this young man had eyes that vaguely resembled Xie Lanshan, filled with emotion and light engraved on his soul. Yet the slight difference still set the two apart. And, at least in his eyes, this young man was nowhere near as attractive as Xie Lanshan.

Yet soon, Shen Liufei recognized that face—this was the Chinese celebrity who had gone missing in Thailand, Wen Jue.

Wen Jue kept calling Shen Liufei "Bai Shuo" because the latter looked too uncannily similar to an old friend of his. The young celebrity kept calling out like a broken record, "You... really... really look like him..."

With the unexpected news about Sin House, Shen Liufei had originally thought about finding a way to leave this place as soon as possible. Yet now that he saw Wen Jue, he had no reason to leave this kid behind. He leaned a little closer and whispered quietly to Wen Jue, "I work at Hanhai City's Public Security Department. I'm here to rescue you, stay calm."

Just as soon as the word "calm" was spoken, Wen Jue jumped and called out, "You're a c—"

He quickly caught himself and covered his mouth just in time, only revealing those large and bright eyes behind the bars.

Thankfully, there was no other Chinese man inside the cage, but this commotion still caught A'Liang's attention. The guard called out to Shen Liufei, but the latter didn't break a sweat and raised the knife in his hand to greet the man back.

A'Liang turned his head back after realizing nothing occurred. The two Burmese men then poked their heads out to look at Wen Jue, then turned to laugh with each other in Burmese.

Even though he couldn't understand a word being said, Wen Jue knew it wasn't something good, judging by their nasty expressions. He felt like he was prey under the eyes of two predators and felt uneasy, then quietly asked Shen Liufei, "Bro, do you know what they're saying?"

Shen Liufei translated for him, "They said you're too pretty to be sold to the fishermen, you should be sold to the red-light district instead."

Wen Jue cried in fear at that moment. Tears rolled down his face like he was a real damsel in distress. His parents were not around, and his manager, Han Guangming, had always spoiled him, not letting the young man even lift a bag when traveling. He couldn't have imagined he would be captured while filming a reality show in a foreign country and sold into slavery.

After this tall and pretty young man cried for a while, he lowered his shoulders and told Shen Liufei, "B-bro, I want to ask you for something."

Assuming the young man wanted to get out of here, Shen Liufei responded, "Sure."

"I want to ask you..." Wen Jue wiped the tears on his cheeks and said without hesitation, "I want to ask if you can get me some sunscreen, please?"

Shen Liufei turned his head to look at him, those eyes questioning the young man: *Are you serious?*

"The sun's too deadly here." Of course, Wen Jue was being serious. His face was more important than his life. Just how could he explain to all of his fans if he were to come out with sunburns on his face? He tugged on the collar of his shirt and exposed a small piece of white skin to Shen Liufei. "Look, I even tanned over the last few days I've been locked up in here."

Shen Liufei didn't agree to this celebrity's unreasonable request and simply said, "I'm here to rescue you, so you have to listen to everything I say now. Do as I request without any questions, understood?"

Wen Jue finally stopped sobbing and tilted his head. Through the dim moonlight shining above their heads, he began studying this undercover cop that was here to rescue him. The more he looked, the more he felt this man looked just like his friend and said, "You really look a lot like my friend. His name is Bai Shuo—"

Shen Liufei interrupted him, "My last name is Shen."

"I know you're not him. You're much more sophisticated than that guy. He's a real dumbass, the kind who's just all muscles and no brains..." Wen Jue's nervousness manifested into ramblings. He saw Shen Liufei as the one ray of hope in this situation and instinctively wanted to cling onto him, so the only method he could think of to get closer to the cop was to talk about that friend of his. Continuing to ramble aimlessly, Wen Jue said, "Before my manager found me, I used to hang out with Bai Shuo all the time. He's a hopeless guy that spends all his time hanging around the Golden Triangle, he even almost got killed by some of those local drug dealers... He said someone saved him during that time and changed his life, so then he moved to the U.S. after to become a professional boxer."

"I'm not interested in your friend's story." Shen Liufei once again interrupted him.

Yet his gaze was still glued onto this cage behind him. Wen Jue was only 22, but there were many more boys who were younger than him enslaved here. They were to be sold to fishermen or isolated islands, working until they finally became corpses that rested forever beneath the ocean.

There was an old Chinese saying: Blood must be seen at every kill, and all lives must be saved at every rescue. Shen Liufei didn't plan on befriending this celebrity; his thought was to rescue all of the slaves in this factory.

(vi)

It was still difficult to narrow in on the culprit and human traffickers with just the clue of Sin House. This wasn't Hanhai, so Xie Lanshan couldn't simply flash his police badge. Of course, it would be no use in a foreign land, so he had no choice but to secretly investigate.

Han Guangming complained that Xie Lanshan was too slow and nagged him every day to hurry with the search.

His ears buzzed with the relentless nagging. Annoyed, Xie Lanshan shifted his gaze and saw a bell hanging beneath the ambient lights, then immediately decided on a way to pay back the man.

"Alright, alright, I'll just call the server over and ask where they hid the culprit." The two men were seated on the second level of the bar. Xie Lanshan walked over to the bell on the side and reached a hand toward it.

"No, no, no! This isn't... this isn't a bell to call the server over!" A person only rang the bell in question if they intended to pay for all checks ordered by this round of customers in the bar. Han Guangming saw Xie Lanshan's hand on the bell and popped his eyes in horror, attempting to stop the latter.

But it was too late.

One ring of a bell earned cheering from the entire bar.

"Huh? Sorry." Xie Lanshan pretended he was oblivious to the rules in this bar and turned his head, then apologized to Han Guangming with a lifted eyebrow, "Apologies to your wallet."

They'd agreed that the older man was going to pay for all expenses, and this easily took over ten thousand RMB out of his pocket. As one of the most famous celebrity managers in the country, this was nothing but a small sum to Han Guangming. But the man had always been a selfish businessman who would never engage in a trade that did not benefit himself; if he didn't care so much about profit, he wouldn't have risked his life to rescue his source of income in a foreign land.

Losing his celebrity certainly hit him hard to the point where he was willing to risk anything to bring the boy back.

"You, you... you..." He wobbled his way toward Xie Lanshan and pointed at the latter, ready to scold loudly.

Xie Lanshan gave a snarky grin and reached a hand toward the bell once again.

Han Guangming rushed forward and grabbed onto Xie Lanshan's arm, then cried out, "Oh mister policeman... no, buddy, wait, my lord mister policeman, my lord! I don't think we'll be able to find anything today. How about we call it a day?"

And that was how Han Guangming and Officer Xie returned to their hotel, the former still enraged. In order to save money, the manager insisted on sharing a twin room with Xie Lanshan. He removed his smelly socks and shoes, then knocked out on the bed inside the room without showering.

Xie Lanshan was also at a loss; he didn't find any clues in or out of the bar. Even as the owner of Sin House, old Zhong Zhuohai was clearly just an owner in name who didn't involve himself in the bar's management. There was nothing they could find from his house or company.

After cleaning himself up from a day's worth of fatigue and dust, Xie Lanshan laid on the bed and closed his eyes.

He had a dream and knew he was in a dream. In the dream, his face was reddened with affection while he embraced Shen Liufei tightly. He allowed his raw desires to run free in the dream; Xie Lanshan glued his limbs onto the other man's body until no space was left between them.

They exchanged kisses again and again, from the nose, lips, neck, and down to each other's collarbone, carefully without missing a spot. Shen Liufei caressed his face and kissed his eyes; Xie Lanshan knew he was in a dream, but could still feel himself tearing up.

Before he could get closer to the man, Xie Lanshan noticed his lover freeze. He opened his eyes and saw a gunshot pierce through Shen Liufei's chest, blood dripping out from the black hole.

"Cuz! Shen Liufei!"

He cried out and woke up from the dream, covered in a cold sweat. On the other bed, Han Guangming turned and continued his thunderous snoring.

It was certainly a strange dream. He was first tossed into a hot pot of temptation before suddenly thrown out into a blazing snowstorm to freeze to death. Xie Lanshan opened his eyes, got up from his bed, and sat still in the dark. Worry consumed him. He hadn't heard any news of Shen Liufei since he arrived in Thailand and grew concerned that his lover was now in a dangerous situation, like in his dream.

Xie Lanshan wasn't sure how long he sat alone when he heard a sudden rustling sound outside the door. He peeked at the door and discovered something was shoved through the crack.

He quickly jumped out of bed and opened the door, but the person had already left, and he could see no traces of a figure in the dark hallway.

Xie Lanshan returned to his room, suspicious, and picked up the item that was sent to him. It was a photo of two men together.

He recognized both men in the photo. One was the victim of this case, Anuchit, and the other was his old friend, Gold Tooth.

There was an address left on the back of the photograph that pointed at a quiet rural area.

Xie Lanshan went out the next morning and confirmed that Gold Tooth was one of the managers of Sin House through some investigation. The man currently went by Kay Ponpai and, judging by the situation, it was likely that he now worked for Guan Nuoqin. After the multi-national drug enforcement effort that forced Mu Kun to go missing years ago, many of the drug lord's former subordinates who escaped ended up working for Guan Nuoqin.

It was difficult to tell whether the person secretly relaying to him was a friend or foe, but with Shen Liufei and Tang Xiaomo weighing on his heart, Xie Lanshan would still cling to this clue even if the address was a trap.

While Han Guangming slept that night, Xie Lanshan secretly left the room on his own and arrived at the address. It was a small house with no immediate threat upon careful investigation. Judging from what he could tell from peeking in the window, Gold Tooth was the only one inside the house.

Xie Lanshan was pondering how to sneak in when he realized that Gold Tooth had called for food delivery. The delivery boy arrived just in time and was knocked out immediately from behind by Xie Lanshan.

Xie Lanshan changed into the delivery boy's outfit and pressed the hat down to cover his face while he knocked on the door.

"Why so late?" Gold Tooth didn't notice the commotion outside and opened the door.

Xie Lanshan looked up and lifted a smile at the man inside, then quickly knocked the latter down before Gold Tooth could react.

By the time Gold Tooth woke up, he was already tied to a chair. He turned his head to check his surroundings and noticed he was inside a messy room that looked like an old storage unit. A dim light that hung from the ceiling swayed soundlessly, flashing uneven glows in the room while large flies circled around the lamp.

Xie Lanshan pulled up an old wooden chair and sat in front

of Gold Tooth, then gave the latter a smile as soon as he woke. "Long time no see, do you still remember me?"

The storage unit was well-ventilated, but because of the hot climate, only moist and hot air managed to flow in. In front of his old friend, Gold Tooth began sweating nervously. He had recognized Xie Lanshan the first day the young cop appeared in Sin House and thought he could get away with hiding for a few days, but reality proved him wrong.

Gold Tooth knew that the Thai police were investigating Anuchit's death and assumed Xie Lanshan was here for the same reason, so he quickly explained, "I didn't kill Anuchit. I wanted to kill him that day, but I already found him dead by the time I got to his house..."

Xie Lanshan was not interested in Anuchit's death and simply took out a photo of Tang Xiaomo to ask if the man had seen this girl, as she was likely taken by one of their men.

Gold Tooth moved his dried lips and denied, "I don't know her... Never seen her before."

"Wrong answer." The flash of shock across his eyes the moment he saw the photo gave away the truth. Xie Lanshan stood up beside Gold Tooth and dislocated the man's right shoulder without hesitation.

Gold Tooth was caught off guard by this violent attack and cried out in pain.

"Have you seen this girl before? Where did you take her?" Xie Lanshan leaned down and whispered into his hostage's ear, "This is the second time I'm asking, I hope your memory doesn't fail you this time."

Gold Tooth knew Xie Lanshan's docile nature and could never forget this man, even if he hated him. This young cop was a man of few words and always had an air of justice around him. It was this strange aura that always made him suspect Xie Lanshan's true identity, but it was also the same reason he wasn't too afraid of falling into Xie Lanshan's hands.

Yet now, he felt like he was facing the devil himself.

"You... let me go this once. I can tell you anything you want to know. I'm only just working for Guan Nuoqin." Out of self-defense instinct, Gold Tooth confessed that all the pretty young ladies that were kidnapped were sent to a secret club called "The Morphia Show" where the rich would pay huge sums of money to satiate their twisted interests.

By the time Gold Tooth had given out the exact address of the club, he was already drenched in a cold sweat. He once again begged, "Alright, that's all I know, so please let me go."

Xie Lanshan smiled and sat back down on the wooden chair, then said, "What's the rush? We haven't even had the chance to catch up yet."

The source of his suffering could be traced back to that day. He had fallen into Gold Tooth's trap and lost his life, where the gangs stole his body.

That was how he now ended up in this horrible predicament, trapped in another person's body, betrayed by his comrades, and almost even lost his loved one.

Xie Lanshan gave a dark smile before his prey; the grin became colored with hatred—a beautiful yet horrifying image. He said, "I remember that you were the one that ordered the gangs to trail me... you let me lay dead inside a dark alleyway."

Afraid that Mu Kun would discover it was his doing, Gold Tooth had paid extra to gangs who didn't work for him. He ordered the gangs to run as fast as they could after they killed Xie Lanshan and never return or contact him again. As soon as he discovered that Xie Lanshan was still alive, Gold Tooth had always assumed that the hitman he hired didn't do their job right and was quite upset with the result.

"But aren't you still alive?" Gold Tooth was admittedly a

little relieved right now and attempted to find an excuse to get out. He began struggling and moved around the chair as he said, "You're fine now... I heard someone who passed by took you to the hospital later."

The commotion on the chair was too loud, so Xie Lanshan shushed Gold Tooth quietly. Then he pulled out a pair of vinyl gloves from his pocket and slowly put them on. The vinyl gloves fit well onto his long fingers. The white color made them look like sharp blades in the night.

He stood up and pushed the light hanging above his head gently. Beneath the swaying light, he slowly strode toward his horrified, despairing prey.

(vii)

"I spent too much money on you already, don't you dare try and leave me behind!"

Han Guangming had followed Xie Lanshan out but was too scared to go in closer, fearing being found out. Yet within a blink of an eye, the young cop disappeared before his eyes. By the time he discovered the man by an abandoned storage unit, he barged in the door.

Han Guangming was stunned by the scene before him; the man tied to the wooden chair had his face covered in blood, barely breathing, and was already unrecognizable. The man struggled to lift his head as soon as he heard someone walk in and opened his eyes. His trembling lips looked as if they were ready to cry out for help, but he couldn't even close his mouth properly as fresh blood rolled out along with a tooth.

His jaw was dislocated; the pain was unimaginable, but it wasn't a difficult injury to fix with proper equipment.

"What... what happened here..." Han Guangming saw Xie Lanshan stand beneath the swaying lamp, staring at his bloodied gloves under the dim light. Han Guangming could feel himself stuttering in shock.

As if he wasn't the one that had just interrogated Gold Tooth earlier, Xie Lanshan turned his expressionless face to glance at Han Guangming and asked nonchalantly, "Did you rent a car?"

Han Guangming was still shaking when he answered, "I... did. The car's still waiting outside."

"Alright." Xie Lanshan smiled and stepped out of the storage unit. He then told Han Guangming, "Clean up this place for me and we'll be off."

Clean up what? Han Guangming lowered his head to see splashes of blood on the ground and felt a chill. He picked up a photo of a young girl that dropped to the ground and then checked his surroundings to make sure nothing else was left behind.

Xie Lanshan called out from outside, annoyed, "Hurry up!"

The young cop had already removed the bloodied gloves and perhaps disposed of them as well. He got in the car that Han Guangming rented out and stared forward without blinking, his whole body frozen like a statue. His expression was calm, almost as if he was dissociating, but also maintained all madness in the world within him. It made him look as if he was a demon in the mortal world.

Han Guangming had been eyeing Xie Lanshan for the last few days. He realized that this young cop was prettier than Wen Jue, a rare gem in the wild who could give up being a cop and find a new career in the entertainment industry. But now, he no longer dared to ask.

This man was mad, insanely mad.

Night was like a turbulent black river in the sky. The place was warm like an oven during the day, but the cold breeze at night sent chills into the car. The two men didn't converse during the road trip. Han Guangming was fearful of the expression on the cop's face. He shivered once, then a second time.

Xie Lanshan turned to him and gave a mocking grin, "Why are you still following me if you're so scared of me?"

Han Guangming didn't dare to let his guard down and denied, "H-how am I scared of you? Besides, who's going to find my little Jue if I don't follow you?"

Xie Lanshan only responded mildly, "You don't have to follow anymore, the Blue Foxes are here already. They're not like me, a bad cop who was suspended and abandoned. They're the elites of the elites. I'm sure you'll be able to find your celebrity soon if you follow them."

Han Guangming pondered a little before he suddenly came to a conclusion and said, shaking his head, "I don't know them, and I'm sure they won't take me along with their investigations. Either way, I'm following you; you go find your friend and I'll go find my little Jue, that's all."

"Whatever." Xie Lanshan gave a small chuckle and then turned his gaze forward. His black eyes blended in with the darkness of the night in this foreign land. Han Guangming almost couldn't tell if the darkness was from the sky or this man.

The driver that Han Guangming had hired was a cautious man who was quite proficient in Chinese as well. After the two suspicious men left, he immediately called the cops.

By the time the police department received the report, Chi Jin and Ling Yun had already arrived and were discussing Wen Jue's kidnapping case overnight with the Bangkok police. Realizing that one of the men the driver met was Xie Lanshan by the description, old cop Somsak immediately rushed to the abandoned storage unit.

But he was a step too late. The tied-up Gold Tooth was already dead.

There were many injuries on the victim's body, but the actual cause of death was asphyxiation by suffocation.

Chi Jin checked the corpse with Somsak and said with a frown, "The victim's dislocated joints are clearly done by professional wrestling techniques; it's impossible for an average person to do this. The culprit must be Xie Lanshan."

Xie Lanshan's secret was exposed as soon as he left the bureau on his own. Chi Jing already heard the truth from Director Peng and knew that it was Xie Lanshan's fault that Sui Hong was suspended.

Of course, Ling Yun knew about the changes in Xie Lanshan, but he wasn't convinced the latter was the culprit. The soul of the Blue Fox was engraved onto every member, whether they were new or veteran, that was what he believed in. After giving it some thought, he gave a different perspective to the team, "There's about an hour between the time Xie Lanshan left and we arrived at this place, so even if Xie Lanshan did interrogate this man, the true culprit could have been someone else—"

"Why are you always speaking up for an outsider?" Chi Jin interrupted Ling Yun harshly and pulled on his collar in annoyance, or perhaps heat. He grew anxious and said, "I'll report everything to Director Peng here and let him decide what to do with Xie Lanshan!"

Ling Yun felt that Chi Jin was becoming more irritable as of late. Sweat covered the latter's forehead, his fist clenched so tight that a few veins popped up unnaturally around his hand. Seeing more sweat roll down Chi Jin's face and the young Vice Captain's breathing grow rough, Ling Yun sensed something was off. He didn't feel that the night in Thailand was particularly hot and asked, "A'Chi, are you alright?"

Chi Jin's expression was still filled with rage when he shot back, "You should call me Captain right now."

Before Ling Yun could respond, Chi Jin turned to Somsak and said, "Xie Lanshan was long kicked out of the Blue Foxes and was suspended from the violent crimes unit back home, too. He's not one of us nor a cop anymore. You guys don't need to go easy on him!"

The team returned to the bureau. Somsak reported the incident along with the details of all the internal conflicts among the Blue Fox to Chief Kang Tai.

Kang Tai was nothing like his twin brother Kang Xin; the latter was honest and humble, not very good with social situations. Yet he always spoke with confidence in Chinese and ordered the entire bureau to cooperate with the Blue Foxes to bring the suspect back.

Just as soon as the old cop left the Chief's office, Kang Tai called Guan Nuoqin and said, "Those Chinese have their men over now. I arranged for Gold Tooth to take care of Anuchit, but I didn't expect that guy to die too. The situation's complicated right now. I'm not sure if we can safely send out those people we caught."

After the Chinese, American, and Burmese forces hunted Mu Kun down, Guan Nuoqin quickly overtook Mu Kun's territory and regrouped his men. In order to avoid the same fate, the man stepped away from the dying old drug trade and had been staying under the radar for a while. Thailand was his home base; not only did he manage to get some police on his side, but he also had a close relationship with the local rich businessmen.

Guan Nuoqin stated the situation was tough right now, so he needed to find the culprit that killed Gold Tooth as soon as possible, regardless if the person was dead or not. He would rather not risk letting the killer run free and ruin his human trafficking business.

Of course, his worry wasn't baseless. Most of the men and women they sold were from Myanmar or Cambodia, but sometimes they would also kidnap celebrities like Wen Jue from Thailand. These people tended to be tourists who got lost, and the local police on the borders would never imagine this would involve human trafficking. Kang Tai pondered a little before lifting a smile; it wouldn't be hard to keep evidence away from the Blue Foxes, and he could just let them fight amongst themselves.

He told his drug lord partner that he would report this to his boss and twist it so that Chinese police murdered a man here in Thailand.

As soon as Kang Tai hung up, Kang Xin walked into the office. The latter closed the door at his brother's gesture, a difficult look on his face.

They were a strange pair of twins; despite having the same face, their demeanors were completely different. The younger brother was tough but ruffled while the older brother was always a little too well-dressed for any occasion. His hair was always smooth and shiny, cheekbones visible, and had a sharp jaw that made him look sly. That was why, despite working in the same police department, nobody ever had problems telling the twins apart.

Kang Tai was quite annoyed at his brother. He always wanted his brother to work for Guan Nuoqin. With Kang Xin's abilities, it wouldn't be hard for the man to earn some profits from the mafia. If the brothers could get benefits from both the mafia and the police department, their social status would naturally inflate in value. Yet Kang Xin refused to give away his job as a cop, stubbornly working this low-paying job to support his dying daughter.

On the other hand, Kang Xin knew his brother was tied up with the biggest drug lord of the Golden Triangle right now, knowing well the tragic ends of those missing persons. Kang Xin stared angrily at his brother and said coldly, "Stop what you're doing. You've already pocketed more money than you can ever spend in your life, so why are you still harming so many others?"

Kang Tai refused to look at his brother and carefully fixed his sleeves, then said, "And what makes you think you're better than me? You're doing it for your daughter, I'm doing it for money. We share the same genes, neither of us are good men."

Kang Xin was speechless. He certainly decided to step in for his daughter, allowing the promise he made to her blind his sight and heart. He allowed A'Liang to order him around and do all those things he never wanted to do. Even if he was constantly being burned at the stake by his kind heart in between these two morally difficult choices, he still chose to step in.

Kang Tai took this opportunity and rolled up his left sleeves, exposing a menacing burn scar on his arm.

That was an injury he got when they were little. Their house suddenly caught on fire, and he burned himself to save his younger brother.

Kang Tai hinted that his brother owed him a favor, then patted the younger one's face before tossing him out of the office with arrogance and disgust.

Still stuck on the murder cases and annoyed by the confrontation, Kang Xin dragged his tired body out of the bureau to buy some hot street food back home. He opened the door and called his daughter's name gently. There was no response. Perhaps she had already fallen asleep.

The house this father and daughter lived in was quite small, but it was bright and homey. Kang Xin put down the food in the kitchen and tiptoed into the girl's room. The bedroom walls were repainted into a light pink color. A wind chime hung by the window that trilled a beautiful sound when the wind blew.

His ten-year-old daughter was sleeping with a dirty teddy bear in her arms. Kang Xin gently touched Yaya's hair and watched her quiet, sleeping face with affection. The girl's face was pale and lips purple; the only way she could live was with lots of medication every day.

According to the doctor, her small liver was also at its limit.

Suddenly, the little girl on the bed frowned in pain, either due to a nightmare or illness, and her whole body shivered.

"Yaya? Yaya!" Kang Xin almost forgot to breathe out of anxiety; he called his daughter's name while rushing to find her medication.

Thankfully, the girl wasn't in pain and simply hugged her teddy bear tighter before falling back asleep.

DCM meant that her heart was already swollen inside her small body. Yaya couldn't even walk normally and knelt down in pain after a few steps, panting heavily by her feet.

With her condition now, she completely dropped out of school to rest at home. Her heart was still swelling, and she couldn't even perform everyday tasks. Her father carried his daughter around all the major hospitals in Thailand for help, and yet despite the inevitable death looming above her, he still refused to give up.

But all doctors agreed that a heart transplant was the only way to save her.

Kang Xin left his daughter's room after the scare and closed the door.

He gave A'Liang a call to ask if they found an appropriate donor yet.

"You guys keep dragging day after day. Just when will you find a donor?"

"Your daughter is so small and thin, we can't even be sure if an adult's heart can be placed in her chest." Knowing that the man was the brother of the police department's branch Chief, A'Liang didn't curse out loud and only said, "Even our big boss can't just get a heart surgery as he pleases, so let your daughter wait."

"She can't!" As soon as she gets a heart transplant, he would be able to leave this disgusting trade and use his blood and life to repent for his sins. The man was on the verge of a breakdown and growled like a trapped beast, "Even if I have to kill someone right now, I will do it so that Yaya can get her heart trans—"

He wasn't sure when Yaya appeared behind him with the dirty stuffed animal in her hands. Kang Xin had thought about buying a new one for his daughter multiple times, but Yaya was a sentimental girl that would never give up an old toy even after it was dirtied.

Kang Xin turned around to see his daughter, froze on the spot, and quietly hung up the phone.

He looked down at her while she looked up to meet his gaze. Yaya was smarter and more mature than most girls her age and heard every word that her father had said earlier.

When she wasn't bedridden, she would praise her father and show off all sorts of heroic stories she had of the man. She would walk proudly at school and say that her dad was a hero.

To this sickly young girl, the rare happiness and hope in her life came only from her father, who was like the dawning sun that shone brightly in the world.

Yet the man before her right now that shouted about murder made her fearful.

"Daddy, are you still a hero?" After a long silence, the girl finally spoke up.

Kang Xin was taken aback; he wanted to respond with confidence that he was, but also didn't want to lie to his daughter. He finally kneeled before her, embraced her gently, and buried his face in her small shoulders. Tears welled up in his eyes. He refused to let them fall and sniffed heavily, before finally saying, "Yaya, go back to sleep. We still need to go to the hospital tomorrow."

The girl was deeply disappointed by her father's avoidance of the question, pulled her body out of his embrace, and walked away. She was exhausted and couldn't even hold the teddy bear in her hands. She could only grab one of its legs and drag it forward with her.

She stopped before her bedroom door and turned to look at her father again. A heavy shadow cast on her bright and large eyes like a solar eclipse. It was heartbreaking to see such a vibrant life hold such a deathly silent gaze.

Kang Xin also felt his heart bleeding at this gaze. He finally dropped to the ground after sending his daughter back into her room. His head hung down, and he cried as he bit on his fist, letting his teeth sink into his flesh. He really didn't know how to find a way out of this situation.

Hello, My Dear

Before Wen Jue was kidnapped, the celebrity's life was fully taken care of by manager Han Guangming—a real life of a prince. He refused to live in anything that wasn't a well-rated five-star hotel, traveled in a Ferrari, and bathed in fresh mineral water. Even during mealtimes, all fishbones were hand-taken out of the dish by Han Guangming before he ate. Despite everything, complaints from Wen Jue were still common for the purpose of causing more trouble.

Wen Jue was also a crybaby. He often cried more than a girl on screen, but his fans praised him for being sensitive and having a delicate heart. He had always thought that even if his life was now being dictated by flowers, cheers, and countless admiring gazes from young women, it was worth living. Before he became famous, he had lived a tough life: taking up part-time jobs everywhere, and during the toughest times he had also cut down his own meals to save money. Recalling those experiences, he would often cry about his horrible past.

Of course, he never would have imagined living a day even worse than when he was working five jobs a day. He also never realized that the world also had such a cruel, raw, and monstrous side.

The hundred or so men froze on the ground as if they were waiting for a serious order. Afraid that a well-satiated slave would cause trouble, the slaveholders never fed them fully during meals. The meal itself was also rice mixed with fish and shrimp served inside a rusted tin can. The people would fight for the food without mercy. Some unlucky ones who didn't get to eat had nobody else to blame but themselves.

Wen Jue obviously wasn't fit enough to grab even a bite against everyone else, and if he managed to get something, he couldn't swallow down the stinky fish smell. This left him still hungry, and he stared at Shen Liufei like a lost puppy as he called, "Big bro."

Shen Liufei tossed a cookie to him.

"Bro..." Wen Jue wasn't satisfied and begged for more, "Can I get something to drink too? I prefer milk."

Just as he was about to gripe about the cookie in his hand, he met Shen Liufei's cold gaze and swallowed up all his complaints.

He quickly opened the package of the cookie; the smell of wheat almost made tears roll down his face. As Wen Jue was about to take a bite, he noticed a little boy beside him staring right at his food.

The boy was deathly thin from head to toe. He was only thirteen or fourteen but looked like he was a dried-up tree trunk. The boy stared at the cookie in Wen Jue's hand; his eyes glistened until drool rolled down his mouth.

"I'm starving." Wen Jue didn't feel comfortable with this gaze and turned around to eat his cookie. But he still had a feeling that the boy was looking at him from behind.

"Alright, you can have one bite... Just one bite." He turned around and broke the cookie in half. After checking the size of the cookie, he kept the larger piece for himself and handed the smaller one out.

Just as they munched on the food, another car drove by from afar. A team of medics dressed in white lab coats got out of the car and said they were here to do physical checkups for all the slaves.

Everyone was marked with a number before blood tests were taken. A slave took this opportunity to escape but was quickly caught by A'Liang, who whipped the runaway with the stingray whip on the face.

The sting on the back of the whip struck violently into the neck of the runaway.

Fresh blood poured out; the man's eyes widened in shock and he dropped to the ground with his hand on his neck.

A'Liang remained unfazed at this scene. To him, these people were like the moles growing in the Golden Triangle that could easily be replaced. Shen Liufei darted up and helped stop the man's bleeding and treated the wound.

The injury was quite small and didn't hurt the vital points, but a neck injury was still a serious wound that needed immediate attention. Shen Liufei ripped a piece of cloth from the man's clothes, lifted the arm near the injury above his head, and pressed down to stop the bleeding.

As soon as he reached for the man's arm, the man on the ground reached out a bloodied hand toward Shen Liufei as if grabbing onto the last ray of hope and begged in Burmese, "Save me... save me..."

Bro... I'm also Chinese... save me...

A familiar scene flashed in Shen Liufei's mind under the bloodied situation and strong stimulation before his eyes. The artist was taken aback by this sudden scene, and his memories rolled back like an old silent film—

Drug dealers were scattered like flocks of pigeons, police

cars and ambulances rushed over to carry a dying young man with a neck injury into the car. One second too late and he would have died at the scene.

Because he received immediate treatment at the time, the young boy's life was saved.

After saving the injured man, Shen Liufei stepped back and sat down, staring down at the bullet necklace around his wrist.

Night once again fell on this deserted land like a flood of black water while the moon stood out bright and round. Wen Jue was done with his blood test and was being sent back into his cage. He turned and leaned toward Shen Liufei, asking curiously, "Why are you always staring at this bracelet? Is it from your girlfriend?"

Shen Liufei didn't respond and kept his gaze fixed on his wrist. The blood on his fingers had already dried out; the dark crimson complimented the pale white skin and long fingers.

"Hey bro? Bro?"

Shen Liufei didn't respond.

After a long while, Wen Jue saw the man's lips move slightly. Like a melted layer of snow, a beautiful grin arose on that stony face.

The hidden bit of mark left in his life was suddenly revitalized in this quiet night; no coincidences in the world occurred without reason, and the most delightful part of this karmic cycle was their reunion.

Shen Liufei lowered his gaze and smiled, then whispered, "So it was you."

Xie Lanshan wasn't sure if anyone else aside from Gold Tooth would recognize him and had no choice but to disguise himself to sneak his way into that secret club. As a man with a career in the entertainment industry, Han Guangming was skilled in theatrical makeup. He prepared everything from a fake beard to makeup supplies for Xie Lanshan, and even offered to help put it on the man's face with special effect makeup.

He curled his hair and tied it up in the back. He wore a pair of fake glasses on his face and changed into an expensive suit, quickly transforming himself into a luring delinquent rich master.

Xie Lanshan examined himself in front of the mirror and scratched on his fake beard with his thumb in satisfaction. He turned around to see Han Guangming also putting on makeup and asked in shock, "Why are you dressing up too?"

"I'm coming with you! I don't feel comfortable letting you go on your own." Han Guangming was leaning down toward the mirror and putting on false lashes. His careful actions were obviously from an experienced hand. He said as he dressed himself up, "Besides, you won't be able to get in without my money."

He finished putting the fake lashes on as soon as the last word dropped. Han Guangming turned abruptly after putting down his arm and winked at Xie Lanshan, then said in a high-pitched voice, "How do I look, darling?"

A colorful large face appeared right before Xie Lanshan's eyes, almost making the cop choke on air. He immediately thought of *Strange Tales from a Chinese Studio*—everything from the horrifying monsters and demons described in the text —and compared it to the ugly face before him.

Han Guangming was short and bulky, though the makeup wasn't particularly strange on his face. Their clothes were purchased locally. In order to properly disguise himself as a woman, Han Guangming changed into a wine-red silk dress. The dress skillfully hid his thick and hairy legs and squeezed tight around his hefty body, making him look like a sausage stuffed in its casing.

Han Guangming's plan was for them to disguise themselves as a couple with unique kinks. This secret club also offered sex services and allowed the customers to do anything they wanted to the workers they purchased. People who were willing to drop the money to use this service were clearly rich individuals with nasty interests.

Thankfully, Han Guangming had plenty of money, the most versatile form of power that could also buy off the security guards. The two successfully found their way inside the club. This disguised "couple" pretended to exchange passionate kisses on the cheeks before everyone else in the club. They certainly looked like a rich madame who brought her young, handsome, and vulgar husband down for some fun in the club.

After one kiss on each cheek, Han Guangming perked up his lips suddenly and reached for Xie Lanshan's lips. The latter couldn't reject the gesture and had to muster up the courage for this lip-to-lip kiss.

The waiter received a hefty tip and led the two into a private room with a smile.

Xie Lanshan couldn't afford to let them suspect their fake identities and kept a smile on his face, then whispered very lightly into Han Guangming's ear, "I will kill you if you kiss me again."

Perhaps something awoke inside of Han Guangming, but he was rather pleased with this response and held Xie Lanshan's arm as they walked inside. He swayed his large body as he walked and said into Xie Lanshan's ear, "Look how beautiful I am, don't you want to kiss me?"

Xie Lanshan responded with a smile on his face, "I want to die."

Unlike the crowded bars outside, the club's lights were

dimmed and had only a few strange red lights shining from the corners, like they were slicing through the silence in this room.

A strange scent of weed mixed with other curious herbs lingered in the air. Xie Lanshan could hear small weeping sounds the moment he stepped into the club; those voices were like wordless cries for help.

Even Han Guangming, who had been in high spirits, was shocked. He passed through these alarming red lights still clinging onto Xie Lanshan. He would turn his head to glance at the young man beside him occasionally, noticing the red glow cast on his face like a stream of blood.

There were around twenty people who offered special services, including both men and women, with the majority being women. They all had good looks and youthful bodies, using them to satisfy the most twisted and dark desires of the world in fear and despair every day. Xie Lanshan saw a young woman tied up in metal chains. She was topless; some sort of strong acid already destroyed the skin on her back and turned it into snake-like scales.

The woman noticed someone staring at her and turned her head, then hissed angrily at the man.

Xie Lanshan noticed that her tongue had been artificially cut at the tip; her role here was a snake woman.

There were security guards and bodyguards inside and outside the club, who were all perhaps Guan Nuoqin's subordinates. Xie Lanshan was on his own and could only act when an opportunity opened.

He didn't see Tang Xiaomo among these service men and women. Xie Lanshan pretended to have high standards and complained that he wasn't interested in the existing cast, then asked the waiter if there were any newcomers lately.

The waiter gave a difficult look and refused to tell the truth until Han Guangming took off a ring from his fingers and quietly shoved it in his hands. It was a two-karat diamond ring.

The waiter could immediately tell the value of the ring and purposely ignored the rough man's hand that exposed his identity. He happily introduced the new products they received but mentioned that they had been sent to Zhong Zhuohai's mansion.

"Some Thai people are very superstitious. The man's about to take on a very important surgery, so he requested people to perform for him before he goes in—in other words," the waiter said with a smile, "offering sacrifices."

(ii)

On a foggy night in Bangkok, old Somsak was attacked on his way home. The perpetrator was an expert with swift and deadly moves.

Somsak didn't have a chance to fight back and quickly gave in. He was quite a fighter himself when he was younger, but old age had gotten to him in recent years. He could sense that the perpetrator didn't have any ill intent when his hands were freed. The perpetrator ripped off the fake 'stache on his face and gave a small smile to the older cop, "You're getting old."

"Xie Lanshan?" After confirming this familiar face before him, Somsak was stunned. The news had just revealed that this man was a murder suspect, yet Xie Lanshan still dared to show up in front of a cop.

Clinging onto their old friendship, Somsak told him that their branch Chief Kang Tai was the one who insisted he killed Gold Tooth and had already reported it to the branch's bosses.

It seemed as if bad luck followed him everywhere; Xie Lanshan almost wanted to laugh, but instead, said with confidence, "I didn't kill anyone. If your Chief insists that I'm the killer, he's either dumb or has a hidden agenda."

Xie Lanshan risked getting in touch with Somsak originally to let the old cop report to their branch about the hostages in Zhong Zhuohai's mansion, hoping the Blue Foxes and Thai police could save those people. Yet that complaint earlier also felt strange after some thought.

There may be a mole in the Bangkok police department.

Somsak stood frozen and didn't respond to Xie Lanshan's guess. Xie Lanshan could tell the old man didn't trust him and spoke up to break the silence, "Do you really think I'm the culprit?"

"If the suspect was you a few years ago, I certainly would never believe that." Somsak looked right into Xie Lanshan's eyes to study the subtle changes on the face's face, then finally let out a long sigh after a while, "But if it's you now... I can't say."

This old cop may not know the complications behind this situation, but he was still an experienced investigator with a keen eye. He instinctively felt that this Xie Lanshan before him was not the same person as the young undercover he met many years ago.

"I beat him up for something he did that I couldn't forgive, or more precisely, I interrogated him." Xie Lanshan's eyes looked to be a tide that was ready to overturn dangerously. The coldness within that gaze stared at the old cop as he said firmly, "But I didn't kill him."

After a long silent stare between the two, Somsak finally removed his suspicion and said, "Alright, I believe you. So, what are you here for tonight?"

Assuming that a millionaire like Zhong Zhuohai would have more than just one estate in the area, Xie Lanshan asked, "Do you know where Zhong Zhuohai is at lately?"

Despite knowing that Zhong Zhuohai was one of the investors of Sin House, the police couldn't find anything else about him. He was a clean businessman with a history of donating to civil services and no hints of criminal acts. Somsak couldn't understand the question and responded after giving it some thought, "Zhong Zhuohai attended an Asia business conference earlier. He's on his way back in his private jet tonight."

Xie Lanshan's expression darkened as he said, "I have two requests from you. First, please find out where Zhong Zhuohai is staying after he lands today and tell both me and the Blue Foxes, but don't tell any police officers in your branch, no matter who they are. This includes your partner, officer Kang Xin."

Xie Lanshan didn't know how well Chi Jin and Ling Yun could trust Somsak, so he left a handwritten note for them instead. He borrowed a pen from Somsak and wrote down the situation on a piece of paper.

Considering that the two young men might not recognize his handwriting, he drew a little Blue Fox symbol at the bottom of the note. Drawing required skills, and Xie Lanshan clearly lacked that sort of talent with his barely distinguishable fox doodle. This made him remember Shen Liufei once again, which left his heart feeling heavy.

He wasn't sure where the man was right now but optimistically thought that if Shen Liufei was also tracking Tang Xiaomo down, perhaps they will meet again very soon.

He then remembered that nightmare; the scene where a bullet passed through Shen Liufei's chest was engraved in his mind. He was fearful and wouldn't risk any chances where he might lose this man.

Therefore, he told the old cop his second request, "Second, find me a gun."

. . .

Less than two days later, A'Liang received a new mission to send hostage number 49 to a designated location.

Shen Liufei hinted at Wen Jue to change numbers with number 49 while he volunteered to complete the job.

Coincidentally, this number 49 was the young boy that he shared a cookie with once.

Human trafficking still ran rampant in Southeast Asia, and while some people were sold into slavery, others became unwilling organ donors in the black market. Being sent off wasn't something to celebrate. Every slave here knew that this was a trip of no return and that there would only be tragedy awaiting them. The boy was in debt to Wen Jue and secretly pulled on the young man's sleeve, then shook his head.

If this was any normal circumstance, Wen Jue would have been crying and begging to not risk his life right now. Yet, because he saw his former best friend in Shen Liufei, he blindly trusted the latter and did as he was told.

Or perhaps he was moved by the torment of this mortal world. Wen Jue didn't expect the little boy to even know about repaying others for their kindness. He held the little hand that grabbed onto his sleeve and gave the boy a smile.

A'Liang and his crew had just gotten high and gambled with playing cards; nobody was in the mood to take on the job, so they were more than happy to let Shen Liufei handle it. A'Liang didn't move from his seat and asked Shen Liufei to bring some good booze back after he finished.

Shen Liufei knew what these people were like and gave a quiet nod, then dragged Wen Jue off.

The original plan was for him to send off the hostage personally, and once they left this dangerous zone, he could escape with Wen Jue halfway on the road. Of course, things didn't go as planned. As soon as he left the factory, a car drove by from afar. Perhaps the receiver was being cautious and decided to send in someone to watch over them.

Shen Liufei had gotten a good grasp of the area over the last few days. The factory was located in a deserted mountain area with no sign of people around; it was difficult to even find a hiding spot if one managed to escape. Of course, being caught was another horrifying story to tell. That's why he immediately came up with the idea of changing identities with Wen Jue.

Before the cars could drive closer, Shen Liufei quickly took off his clean shirt to change into Wen Jue's smelly and old clothes.

There was no time to hesitate and ponder the risks, so Wen Jue also took off his clothes. He suddenly looked up to see Shen Liufei's topless body; the man's body was like an artfully sculpted marble statue, the phoenix tattoo on his back breathing, alive on the flesh. Wen Jue gasped out loud.

He recognized that tattoo. It was Bai Shuo's.

Shen Liufei explained quickly as he changed, "If Guan Nuoqin can roam around so freely, that means he has one of his men in the police department—perhaps a high-ranking official. If you escape, don't call the cops. Go to one of the Chinese embassies around the area or find a Blue Fox member."

His advice didn't receive a response even after he finished changing. Shen Liufei turned to see Wen Jue stare wide-eyed and dumbly at him and had a good guess on what the young celebrity was thinking. Yet he still responded calmly, "If you don't want to die, listen to every word I say."

After pulling himself out of shock, Wen Jue nodded his head, afraid to think too deeply about the true identity of this man before him.

Shen Liufei hid the dagger in his clothes and wiped a

handful of dirt on his face. The next moment, a large black Jeep stopped in front of them almost menacingly.

There were two other people in the car aside from the driver. Every one of them held a gun in their hands; Shen Liufei scanned the surroundings and didn't plan on alarming the predators.

The destination they were told earlier now changed, which was why they sent in another escort. The mastermind was clearly very cautious.

Shen Liufei was pushed to the back seat and sandwiched between two men while Wen Jue sat nervously on the passenger side.

"Why so dirty?" One man in the backseat gave Shen Liufei a disgusted look at first, then suddenly studied him from top to bottom. His eyes glowed the more he looked, before he finally clicked his tongue and complained, "This kid's got quite the looks. Should have been sold to please those rich bitches. It's almost a waste to just take his heart out."

"Guy's a millionaire. He could easily buy off the best host in the red-light district if he wanted to. Too bad the results came out, and it was a match." The other man gave a snarky laugh and said, "Who cares if you're a millionaire or some philanthropist? Everyone wants to live longer when they're in the face of death!"

Shen Liufei understood the conversation in Burmese, but he soon had a question. As one of the Golden Triangle's drug lords, Guan Nuoqin's forces had always been in Thailand. Why were his subordinates from Myanmar? He had heard about Mu Kun from Xie Lanshan before. Mu Kun disappeared for a while and perhaps left a few underlings around the region, which likely meant that Guan Nuoqin took these lackeys in.

The car drove further out of the mountain region, and the

fog within the woods finally cleared up as the road became smoother and wider.

The driver glanced toward Wen Jue a little and joined in this pointless conversation, "This kid's not bad either, hah!"

He said something vulgar in Thai, and the three men in the car who understood it laughed.

The laughter was too sharp and vulgar, almost like they were spitting right on Wen Jue's face. Wen Jue's English was bad, and he couldn't understand a word of Thai; he could only feel fear, to the point where his lips trembled while strange sounds came out of his mouth.

But he didn't even need to turn his head to know that Shen Liufei was still as calm as usual behind him.

That's why he decided to use all of his skills as an actor to maintain his cool. He refused to speak, move, or tremble, but most importantly—he could not expose their identities.

(iii)

The black Jeep rushed on the road like a raging tornado until it finally arrived at a secret mansion hidden within the mountains. From afar, it looked like an ethereal castle resting in the midst of nature.

A few people dressed in black were already waiting by the front gate, all standing with their hands crossed in front of them, expressionless like puppets ready to fight. They noticed the Jeep and hurried over to the car. Shen Liufei finally noticed that all of these people dressed in black had a gun around their waist.

As soon as everyone got out of the car, Shen Liufei was dragged toward the mansion by these black-suited people, one on each side.

The rope was on his wrists, but he had already secretly

untied himself in the car—he was only pretending to still be tied up. In terms of just close combat, Shen Liufei was confident he could take on anyone in this place. He knew well that the former owner of this body was an MMA Champion. But he needed to be patient and act only after Wen Jue left. He didn't want to worry about the young man's safety, it would only end up distracting him during a fight. Keeping him around would greatly reduce the chances of them escaping, even possibly putting Wen Jue's life in more danger.

One escort tossed a bag at Wen Jue, said something in English to him, which sounded like they wanted him to bring something back to A'Liang.

The person opened his suit jacket and exposed the gun at his waist; Wen Jue noticed the gun and was immediately covered in cold sweat. He took in a breath of cold air and choked into a coughing fit. He could only pretend he was in a dangerous action movie—that the cameras were filming in secret—to calm himself down or he would have stood frozen on the spot.

He already guessed the purpose of this trip; the people here were planning on taking out Shen Liufei's heart for a rich man's surgery.

He also confirmed Shen Liufei's identity. Bai Shuo lost contact after his car accident. The last piece of news he had received about his best friend was that Bai Shuo suffered brain damage and became vegetative.

Wen Jue and another man in a suit walked behind Shen Liufei, staring at the latter with a complicated expression on his face. The man's figure from the back was especially elegant and tall, like a majestic mountain range.

The group of people entered the Zhong mansion. Before entering the residence, Shen Liufei turned and glanced at the young man. This gaze was calm and reassuring, filled with kindness and power. Wen Jue saw his old friend at this moment, the forgotten story of the young man he lost contact with once again retold itself silently. Wen Jue felt warmth in his heart; his nose also grew itchy.

The guards sent Shen Liufei off to the main surgery room, leaving only Shen Liufei and that man in black. The man was at least half a head taller than Wen Jue, built and tanned; his rough features also made him look menacing. He spoke a little Chinese and gave some orders to Wen Jue about the slaves. The two spoke in a mix of English and Chinese that confused both parties; the man noticed Wen Jue's slowness and quickly lost his patience. He complained about A'Liang being too lazy, and that he must be gambling while high again, sending off a useless pawn to do the job instead.

As the man complained while taking out a cigarette from his pocket, Wen Jue heard a voice not too far away. After careful listening, he recognized it was a young girl's voice crying for help in Chinese.

Help me.

Wen Jue was stunned to hear a fellow Mandarin speaker under these circumstances. He quickly turned to take the lighter from the man's hand, then pretended to show admiration as he respectfully helped light the man's cigarette. He called the man in the suit boss and asked in English, "Is there anyone else being locked up here?"

This praise certainly worked on the man in black, he responded as he blew out a cloud of smoke that they pulled out two virgin girls from the Morphia Club. However, Mr. Zhong was still waiting to have his heart transplant, and no longer had the energy to play around with the girls.

Withstanding that awful smell from the man's mouth, Wen Jue leaned in and mustered up his courage to ask if he could be taken to go see the girls as well.

"See them for what?" The man was a bit irritated and gave a cruel response, "Don't forget to deliver the message I asked. There's nothing else for you here. Now get lost."

"Huh, hey..." Wen Jue took a few steps back and suddenly noticed something from the corner of his eyes. He saw a dragon-shaped ceramic decoration on a display; the item was well-polished, the carvings of its hair so realistic it was almost ghoulish.

He remembered the last gaze Shen Liufei gave him before they parted. This cowardly celebrity suddenly gathered courage and pulled the ceramic sculpture up, then slammed it hard right on the man's head.

The latter dropped to the ground the next moment and was knocked out; even Wen Jue was surprised it worked.

He checked the man's breathing and confirmed he was still alive, just unconscious, and quickly searched the man's clothing. He went through all his pockets and took out a cellphone and some keys.

The cry for help rang out again. If it was the past Wen Jue, he would certainly run away as far as he could right now, pretending he heard nothing. But now he felt a rush of adrenaline inside him like the main character in a wuxia novel who was filled with power, wanting to save the person crying for help.

He followed the sound and found a room that housed a large cage. Inside the cage were two young women who looked to be only teenagers.

The girls were all tied up and dressed in fancy saris, one in red and one in green. Shiny gold accessories also covered the girls from head to toe like they were performers. Wen Jue quickly pulled out the key as soon as he saw them and attempted to open the cage.

One of the girls dressed in red leaned in forward behind

the cage bars and stared at the young man in front of her. The face outside was an ethereal image that looked like something that could only exist in a comic; his features were delicate and refined, those big eyes and slightly grayish-green pupils gave him an even more dreamy image.

She finally recognized him. While still being tied up, the girl banged on the cage bars and called out, "Oh my god I can't believe I saw you live. You're Wen Jue, right? You must be Wen Jue!"

This girl was the first person who recognized him after being sold off in a foreign land. Wen Jue was deeply moved by this familiar call and almost broke out in tears on the spot.

Am I really not that famous? He thought. He has thought countless times after being whipped, tortured, and starved: *I must give Han Guangming a good scolding after I return. This old man better watch out and pay more attention to my likes and follows. I didn't even know that I was so unknown that my fanbase hasn't even made it across the continent of Asia yet. I can't believe nobody here recognized me!*

The girl in red must have gone through a tough time as well after being traded and sold off in a foreign land; her cheeks sank visibly but her spirits were still quite high. Seeing the young man outside the cage tacitly admit he was indeed Wen Jue, the girl quickly introduced herself gleefully and said, "My name's Tang Xiaomo, I'm your fan. I know the lyrics to all of your songs. I'm a really, really big fan—"

"Alright, alright, I love you too." Wen Jue lowered his head to open the lock as he half-heartedly responded. When the lock finally opened, he let out a small sigh of relief and then suddenly recalled, "Your name sounds kind of familiar."

Unsure if there would be other guards chasing after them, the three quickly analyzed their situation and stopped wasting time on celebrity worship. They knew there were a handful of guards waiting outside, so after sneaking up and knocking out the one closest to the door, they escaped the room.

The fog in the night descended silently into the forest, the runaways unsure where to run. Wen Jue recalled what Shen Liufei told him and pulled the cellphone he had stolen from the man in black earlier and dialed a number.

Tang Xiaomo stared at him and asked, "Who are you calling?"

"China's country call-code is 86, right...?" Wen Jue didn't answer the question directly and continued dialing the number, acting confident in what he was doing.

The call finally connected after three different number attempts. A "hello" answered from the other end, and the celebrity said courteously, "Hello, I'm Wen Jue. I was kidnapped while filming for a reality show in Thailand and I'm stuck in the mountains with another Chinese girl—"

An irritated voice suddenly interrupted from the other line, cursing, "Bullshit! If you think you're Wen Jue, I must be veteran actor Hugh Hu!"

The call hung up.

The police had always been active in educating the masses on how to deal with scam calls, so obviously, nobody would believe a word from a call like this. Tang Xiaomo grew more puzzled and finally asked, "Why are you making yourself sound like a scammer?"

"The guy that saved me, Shen bro, told me that we can't call the local cops here because there might be moles in the bureau. So I thought maybe we can do a roundabout way and ask someone back home to call the cops for us first, then let the police in China contact the embassy here and send someone out to save us." Wen Jue stared back at Tang Xiaomo, confusion written all over his face. He didn't think he did anything wrong.

Tang Xiaomo was shocked by this naïve thinking from this

sheltered young man; she rolled her eyes dramatically and said, "Can't you just call 110!?"

Before they could dial in another number, a car appeared within the fog. Its strong headlights were like massive eyes in the dark that locked in on them.

The three screamed and ran, knowing that they had already been found.

Of course, human legs couldn't outrun a car, and it quickly caught up to them. The other girl, who had been locked in the cage with Tang Xiaomo, disappeared. Perhaps she had tripped and fallen, but she was left behind in the run.

The car stopped in front of them, and two figures came out. Judging from the silhouette in the mist, they both seemed to carry guns.

Wen Jue and Tang Xiaomo dropped to the ground in fear, with no more energy left to fight back.

The individual walked toward them. Afraid that they would be silenced, Wen Jue covered Tang Xiaomo's eyes with one hand and held up another before his face to cry out loud.

He didn't care about his image right now and cried desperately with the girl beside him, "Don't kill me, please don't kill me... I can tell my manager to give you however much money you want. I'm a celebrity in China, I'm famous there!"

Tang Xiaomo also cried, "He's really famous and has money!"

The young man who walked up to the two crying hostages gave a cheerful laugh at how scared the two were. He then said in clear Mandarin to them that sounded like a blessing from heaven,

"I'm Ling Yun from the Blue Fox. You guys are safe now."

(iv)

Zhong Zhuohai was laying on the surgical bed, and Shen Liufei was scheduled for a blood test to ensure he was safe for the transplant right before being sent in.

It wasn't difficult for a man like him to move an entire surgical room into his mansion, and Shen Liufei was also quite familiar with this scene—he had also once been through surgery by Duan Licheng in his own mansion in the past.

The guards couldn't follow into the sterilized surgical room. Shen Liufei only saw a doctor in a white lab coat and face mask walk up to him, reaching out a hand to roll up his sleeves for the blood test.

At that moment, the hostage quickly broke out of the already loose rope tying his hands together and jumped up. Before the doctor could react, he quickly grabbed onto the doctor's arm with one hand and choked his neck with another.

Noticing a commotion inside, the guard barged into the room and fired rounds of bullets toward Shen Liufei. Yet the latter had already hidden behind the doctor, using the poor man as a human shield to block the bullets.

After tossing the dead doctor onto the floor, Shen Liufei dropped to the ground and dodged a second round of firing, then rushed right into the main surgery room.

There were three surgeons surrounding the surgical bed, all covered in medical wear and face masks. Judging by the exposed features on their faces above the mask, it was one white man and two Asian surgeons. Their eyes were wide with shock as soon as they saw Shen Liufei run in. One of them called out in English, "Get out!"

Shen Liufei kicked two men down without a word. The last one standing rushed out the door in a panic, right into the guard that was chasing after the runaway.

An old man laid drowsy on the surgical bed; his clothes were already changed, as he was ready to accept a life-changing heart surgery. Shen Liufei walked toward the old man and took out the knife he had hidden in his sleeves. As if still insisting on paying respects in this dangerous situation, he gave a small bow to the frightened old man and said courteously, "My apologies."

The next instant, he pulled the old man up from the surgical bed, one hand on the old man's neck, and dragged the patient before him like a shield. Shen Liufei held up the old man before the guards, who were attempting to attack.

With their boss being held hostage, the guards had no choice but to hold their hands and guns up as they slowly backed away.

Shen Liufei pressed his knife to Zhong Zhuohai's neck and took careful steps forward until he left the surgery room and disappeared into the empty end of the hallway.

He was still a single prey in a den of lions and couldn't afford to let his guard down. Shen Liufei could only keep his eyes on the guards around him and didn't notice another killer in the dark was closing in from behind.

The killer had a gun in his hand, ready to shoot down Shen Liufei as soon as the young man passed the dead-end corner of the wall.

One more step, just one more step back, and his head would be exposed to his shooting range.

Bang—!

Shen Liufei turned his head in time and saw Xie Lanshan standing behind him with a gun in hand. The killer that was hiding in the shadows took a direct hit to his head and dropped to the ground, his skull cracked open like a fresh watermelon.

Xie Lanshan smiled after a brief exchange of glances and said, "It's not time to be sentimental, cuz."

He leaned down to pick up the gun the killer left and

handed it to Shen Liufei. The two men stood back to back in the hallway.

"When did you sneak in?" Now that he gave his back to a trusted comrade, Shen Liufei focused all of his attention on dealing with the enemies before him.

"Just now," Xie Lanshan said with a hint of pride in his tone. "This place only looks well-guarded to outsiders, it's nothing but a piece of cake to me."

"Let's get out of here," Shen Liufei said calmly.

"I don't wanna." Xie Lanshan somehow found the energy to bargain during a life and death situation and said, "I just saved your life earlier. Tell me how you're gonna thank me first, hm?"

"What are you expecting?"

"Let's go with the good ol' method. How about you offer your body to me?"

Shen Liufei was about to answer when Zhong Zhuohai, who was still being held hostage by him, suddenly shook as he held a hand to his chest. The old man's heart attack acted up during such a high-intensity situation. If he were to die right at this point without immediate medical attention, the two men would immediately be shot dead on the spot by the chasing guards.

The guards in suits took another step forward. Before Shen Liufei could answer, Xie Lanshan grabbed onto Zhong Zhuohai's throat violently and whispered into the old man's ear, "Get us a car ready and tell your men to stand down."

The old man panted heavily as he held a hand up. The suited men all took a few steps back.

Despite having a hostage in hand, the health situation of the hostage was too difficult to handle. Neither man wanted to take on the entire crowd right now and murder their way out; they simply wanted to escape as soon as possible. Shen

Liufei and Xie Lanshan remained in the same position with their backs against each other, their muscles tense and twitching in high alert. They carefully and slowly stepped toward the door. A sniper hiding on a higher level was ready to hold up a gun to shoot, but Xie Lanshan noticed first and shot the sniper down.

With another man dead, the air in the mansion grew even more grave. Just as the guards were about to make a move, a police siren blared from outside and a group of police officers armed with weapons barged into the establishment.

Leading the team were Chi Jin, Ling Yun, and Somsak. They contacted the Thai police after they successfully rescued Wen Jue and Tang Xiaomo. Somsak kept his promise with Xie Lanshan and didn't notify anyone before the operation, in fear of alerting the enemy. However, the old cop insisted on joining the infiltration. This was still Thailand, and even as members of the Blue Fox, neither Chi Jin nor Ling Yun had the authority to act independently here.

In the end, the snipers and killers inside the mansion were all cleaned up, and Zhong Zhuohai died of a spontaneous heart attack while he was in the ambulance.

Xie Lanshan was not supposed to have the right to hold and fire a gun, so it was quite difficult to explain the two lives under him. Thanks to Somsak, he was let off the hook in the name of self-defense during an intense situation.

"What about the two murder cases?" Back in the bureau, branch chief Kang Tai asked in his office. He lost some weight and looked much different from his brother Kang Xin now. The pressure from Guan Nuoqin clearly took a toll on him.

"The initial report showed that it was part of an internal conflict within the trafficking organizations. Gold Tooth killed Anuchit, and then someone else killed Gold Tooth."

"Who killed him then?"

"That... we're still investigating." Somsak knew what his boss meant and didn't dare to explain it further.

Kang Tai knew he was being kept in the dark. There were certainly people who followed him loyally in the bureau, but not everyone was on the branch chief's side. He didn't think someone like Somsak would refuse to tell the truth and join forces with someone else. Yet with an eye above him and excited subordinates below, he couldn't make a move right now and simply listened to the report half-heartedly. In his mind, he was already planning on using Gold Tooth's death to ruin the career of Chinese cop Xie Lanshan.

After recording all witness accounts and completing final clean-up, the crew had already spent an entire night in the bureau. They were finally let out of the police department by dawn.

Wen Jue and Tang Xiaomo were the first to get out of the police car. The two young people of similar age had been through life and death together and naturally felt a sense of kinship. They held each other's hand as if to encourage one another when they got in the car. Bangkok's weather was still humid and hot during this time, so their palms were already covered in sweat. Yet they refused to let go of each other's hand, even after getting out of the car.

Han Guangming already received the news from the police and waited in front of the hotel lobby. He first noticed Tang Xiaomo and then saw who she held in her hand, Wen Jue. The manager already had a round appearance, and after crying a whole night until his eyes puffed into a walnut, it almost looked as if two balls of meat grew on his face.

Han Guangming rushed forward as soon as he saw the two; Tang Xiaomo thought the man was going to hug her and dodged in shock. But Han Guangming grabbed onto Wen Jue and started crying out loud again. He cried without restraint out of his heart. The same lines came out of his trembling lips, "I won't leave you anymore, I'll repay you for everything I've done..."

Of course, there was no repaying or this kind of relationship between a celebrity and his manager, but even if it wasn't true, these heartfelt words certainly moved the eyes of everyone watching. Wen Jue was warmed at first until he began feeling disgusted by those tears and snot.

"O-okay, that's enough... look I'm back safe now..." He gave a reassuring pat on the man's large back, but Han Guangming still didn't let him go. Wen Jue felt like he was suffocating and got irritated. He shoved Han Guangming aside and lightly slapped the man's face, "Stop crying, that's enough!"

Of course, it wasn't a truly hard slap, and just a joking gesture. This celebrity boy learned to be more reserved and forgiving over the last few days. These frightening times made him realize that life under the sun was heaven compared to other places, that he should be grateful for what he has.

Han Guangming closed his mouth, but a whimpering voice still rolled out from his throat. He trembled and panted to hold himself back, like an ox catching its breath.

The surrounding people watched and gave a little laughter at this comedic scene.

As an artist, Shen Liufei had a keen eye for detail and an exceptional memory. He turned to look at Han Guangming and frowned slightly at the man.

The man looked awfully familiar. He was almost certain he'd seen him before.

Xie Lanshan sat in another corner of the hotel with a translucent red cloth in hand. He waited until the sun was about to set before seeing Shen Liufei once again.

The two couldn't spare a moment to think about anything else yesterday in the face of death. Now that they were both safe, the atmosphere finally grew a little awkward. Xie Lanshan hung his head a little and watched Shen Liufei walk over against a backdrop of deep crimson. He squinted slightly but didn't get up to greet the man.

Shen Liufei noticed the red satin cloth in Xie Lanshan's hand and asked, "Whose is that?"

The cloth was covered with a unique scent that smelled a little like some sort of Rosemary mix. Xie Lanshan smiled and said, "Tang Xiaomo's. They forced her to wear a dancer's outfit while in the Morphia Club and she somehow kept the clothes."

Shen Liufei asked, "Where is she at?"

Xie Lanshan put on a disappointed expression and said, "You know how women are, she's off with that pretty boy Wen."

Xie Lanshan was in the mood to chat after finally meeting up with his old friend in this foreign land, but Tang Xiaomo clearly wasn't interested. She took off the sari that she wore when the two ran into each other in the hotel and shoved the clothes at Xie Lanshan. Then, she kept saying, "Talk to ya later," while she ran off to go play with Wen Jue and Han Guangming.

Shen Liufei sat beside Xie Lanshan without a word. He seemed to have only kept a little peace in his mind, hoping to spend some time admiring the romantic and beautiful scenery of this country.

Xie Lanshan didn't speak and looked out into the distance; the setting sun was like a blazing ball of fire on desert land, slowly disappearing after it had burnt proudly.

They sat for a while until Xie Lanshan finally confessed, "Song Qilian told me the truth, and I think I remember everything now."

This wasn't a traditional fairytale story, so of course it wouldn't have a typical ending. The relationship they had built over solving the cases in the past now sounded like a joke; every scene that ran in his mind was like a blade that slashed deeply into his flesh.

It was almost laughable the more he thought about it. Xie Lanshan shook his head and asked, "You hate me, right?"

Shen Liufei didn't explain further and only nodded. "Yes."

The last ray of sunlight was too bright to look at. Xie Lanshan lowered his head and added, in one last desperate plea, "But you also love me, right?"

Shen Liufei didn't give an answer and simply turned around to look at Xie Lanshan. Suddenly, he reached out a hand and popped the red satin out of Xie Lanshan's hand into the air. The satin exploded like a cloud of red smoke in his palm as it floated down, then he grabbed onto the ends and covered Xie Lanshan's face behind it.

The red satin was more translucent than the setting sun right now. Xie Lanshan's face was still visible behind this thin layer of cloth. The latter's eyes were wide open, his expression both shocked and puzzled.

Shen Liufei stood up and bent down before Xie Lanshan until their eyes were level. Xie Lanshan also stared back at the man. Behind the cold expression, those eyes were like a burning furnace; flames of love and hatred danced within them as they smelted all other emotions.

Finally, he saw a faint smile on Shen Liufei's face. It wasn't a heart-throbbing smile, but it was like a small beam of light within the darkness.

"You said you will take my body, and I accept your offer now." Shen Liufei held up another hand and pulled up the red satin covering Xie Lanshan's face, then said softly, "I affirm my love, my bride."

(v)

The night was long, and the two men weren't in a rush for round two in their room. Sounds of chatter rang outside the door; the walls weren't that thick in the hotel, and Xie Lanshan could make out it was Tang Xiaomo's voice speaking. He glanced at the clock and noticed it was already 1:30 in the morning. *This girl sure has a big heart*, he thought. For someone who had just escaped the reaper's scythe, she was already back in vacation mode with someone she just met.

Still worried, Xie Lanshan got off the bed, wrapped a towel around his waist and walked toward the door.

He opened the door and looked in the direction of the noise.

Shen Liufei also got off the bed in the hotel's sleeping gown, then made his way next to Xie Lanshan.

Tang Xiaomo stayed on the same floor as them. She had just gotten back from touring town today with Wen Jue, and Han Guangming followed behind the two with luggage in hand. The old manager was nodding his head and bowing slightly as he handed some souvenirs and gifts to Tang Xiaomo.

Shen Liufei's eyes lit up at this gesture, then he quickly frowned and said, "I remember now, I have seen this man before."

He was referring to Han Guangming. It had been only a few months since Shen Liufei returned to China, and he paid little attention to local celebrity gossip. Even as well-known as Han Guangming was, he was still only a manager and never really showed his own face in public.

Shen Liufei recognized him because he was the same old man that dressed shaggy to buy fake paintings from Tang Xiaomo from the antique market once.

With this reminder, Xie Lanshan also remembered. That

painting was a copy of Wu Changshuo's red plums which ended up in the house of branch chief Liu Yanbo.

"You said Han Guangming was with you the day Gold Tooth died?" Shen Liufei had already gotten all the details about the night Xie Lanshan left the storage unit. The victim inside died soon after Xie Lanshan left, and if they couldn't find the true culprit, this young cop would once again be accused as the murderer.

"Now that you mention it, I do remember something." His heart had been on searching for Shen Liufei ever since he came to Thailand and he didn't pay much attention to his own surroundings. Now that he achieved his initial goal, something felt suspicious about this whole event. After pondering for a moment, Xie Lanshan said, "Han Guangming had been following me everywhere these last few days, mostly into hostess bars in the red-light district. It's almost like finding Wen Jue wasn't his priority."

"His reaction when he saw Wen Jue was also quite abnormal." A normal manager wouldn't have such a strong bond with their celebrities to offer personal repayments or anything beyond a business relationship. Shen Liufei recalled and said, "Tang Xiaomo told me before that she felt like she was being followed. I had once assumed that she was being followed by Anuchit after arriving in Thailand, but now that I think about it, perhaps it was someone else that was following her."

"But why would he want to kill Gold Tooth?" Xie Lanshan didn't quite understand. Gold Tooth now followed Guan Nuoqin of the Golden Triangle, which had nothing to do with a celebrity manager like Han Guangming.

There was no answer, so he stopped thinking. Now that Shen Liufei was back by his side, Xie Lanshan was finally at peace and joyful. Even if he was still a murder suspect right now, he didn't feel threatened by the situation.

"We've tied the knot today. Every second of our first night is golden. Hey cuz— wait no—" Xie Lanshan spoke in a high-pitched voice similar to a Chinese opera singer and lifted an eyebrow playfully, then pulled the blanket on the bed up and covered both men inside. He sat with his legs clipped around Shen Liufei's waist as he chuckled, "My husband."

It was a joyful reunion and new marriage, so even without the traditional auspicious dates and fancy ceremonial procedures, the two embraced each other tirelessly and passionately for the entire night. Xie Lanshan slept until the sun was over his head and noticed Shen Liufei had already left the bed. He stretched his back in satisfaction; his waist and back ached as if his whole body was taken apart and put back together. Yet despite the pain, this was the first time he'd felt such comfort and security inside him.

He got up to take a cold shower to wake himself up, then left the hotel room after cleaning up.

The self-serve cafeteria in the hotel ended at 10 A.M. Xie Lanshan figured he could snatch some food and look for Shen Liufei at the cafeteria.

As expected, the artist was indeed at the cafeteria to find someone.

Wen Jue also woke up late this morning after staying out last night. The young celebrity was dumbly staring at his plate full of food. He had eaten too much last night without thought, and now that he'd finally come back to his senses, he remembered he needed to count his calorie intake.

The buffet at the hotel was mostly western-style breakfast. The young celebrity came too late and saw only some bread, salad, bacon, and eggs left. Chinese-style cold stir-fry dishes were also almost gone, with only bamboo shoots, radish, and broccoli left. Not very appetizing upon first glance.

Wen Jue looked up to see Shen Liufei and instinctively

called him "Bai Shuo", but quickly realized he called the wrong name and corrected himself, "Shen bro."

Shen Liufei didn't mind that the young celebrity stood awkwardly before him and scanned his surroundings before asking, "Where's manager Han?"

"Oh him," Wen Jue said as he served himself a plateful of fresh salad. Unwilling to only eat leaves, he placed a Spanish omelet on his plate as well. "Xiaomo said she wanted to have Hong Kong-style breakfast, so he went off to buy food for her from a restaurant in Chinatown."

Chinatown wasn't too far from the hotel, but it was a tourist hotspot with a lot of traffic. Realizing this was a rare chance to speak with the young man individually, Shen Liufei also grabbed a plate and served himself some breakfast food as he asked, "So you must know your manager quite well, right?"

Wen Jue said as the two sat down in the cafeteria, "I've known him since I was 19, so I guess you can say that."

After some small talk, Shen Liufei jumped right to the point after realizing he wasn't in the mood to eat. "Do you know if he has any family?"

"I think he mentioned once that he has a daughter. What's her name again?" Wen Jue thought as he munched on his food. He could feel the name at the tip of his tongue but couldn't recall exactly. After a while, he finally said, "Either way, she was abandoned when he was very young, and I don't think he ever had the intention of finding her later."

Shen Liufei frowned slightly and pondered before asking, "How much more do you know about Han Guangming? For example, do you know what his job was before he became your manager?"

"That I'm not sure." One omelet wasn't enough to fill Wen Jue's stomach as he glanced back at the food, debating if he wanted to give up his reputation and grab another serving. He then said, "But I do know that he was a chemistry major in university. It was an accident that he ended up getting a job in a completely unrelated field."

Speaking of the devil, Han Guangming returned with Tang Xiaomo's order and called Wen Jue's name from afar.

Shen Liufei also looked up to search for the manager, only to see Xie Lanshan walking toward him.

"Our schedule is also full today, I'm gonna head out first." Wen Jue stood up and got ready to leave, then stopped after a few steps and stared back at Shen Liufei. "Bai... Shen bro, I'm very happy to see you again."

Xie Lanshan walked past Wen Jue and took the seat the young celebrity sat in earlier. He noticed the subtle change of Wen Jue's expression; the young man's gaze towards Shen Liufei was filled with adoration. Xie Lanshan taunted, "This pretty boy seems to admire you a lot."

"You sure are serving yourself some vinegar on an empty stomach right now." Shen Liufei didn't touch any of the food on his plate, and after realizing that Xie Lanshan hadn't eaten, he placed an omelet onto a plate of beef salad and slid it toward Xie Lanshan.

"You spoil me." Xie Lanshan gave a pretty and flirtatious smile before quickly downing the food on his plate. "What did you find out?"

Shen Liufei said, "Han Guangming graduated with a degree in Chemistry and has a daughter he abandoned when she was little."

This simple line gave Xie Lanshan an epiphany and bold guess. He asked, "Are you saying Tang Xiaomo is his daughter?"

This theory cleared the fog in his mind. Xie Lanshan continued, "This explains why he didn't follow the Blue Fox to find Wen Jue and instead kept clinging onto me to find Tang Xiaomo."

Shen Liufei nodded in agreement, "The plum painting Tang Zhaozhong replicated purposely left a visible mistake. Anyone who is familiar with calligraphy art knows this replica isn't worth the price. Yet Han Guangming chose to offer a huge sum of money at that time without hesitation. Perhaps the father wasn't in a position to expose himself and could only use this method to help support his daughter financially."

Xie Lanshan attempted to trace back the cases to find Han Guangming's criminal motive. He twirled the fork in his hand instinctively as he mumbled in thought, "Tang Xiaomo's kidnapper was Anuchit, and Gold Tooth is only just a proxy in the trade, so if he committed murder out of revenge for his daughter..."

Shen Liufei gave his perspective, "Perhaps Gold Tooth wasn't the only one he killed."

"You're saying that he also killed Anuchit?" The two understood each other well enough that no further explanation was needed to come to the same conclusion. Xie Lanshan recalled the night he met with Gold Tooth that the latter never admitted he killed Anuchit. This directed him to consider all the missed details of the case; Xie Lanshan tapped on his temples as he recited some numbers, "19... 84... 7... 91... 53..."

Shen Liufei asked, puzzled, "What does that mean?"

"Kay Ponpai, K. Ponpai." Xie Lanshan found an answer and said with a confident smile on his face, "Gold Tooth's new name can also be left in code with chemical elements in a dying message. If Gold Tooth really killed Anuchit, the victim wouldn't need to leave a cryptic message that expands the pool of suspects. He could have just left the culprit's name instead of writing the name of the bar the culprit worked at."

Shen Liufei followed, "Anuchit certainly left a dying

message at the crime scene, but the culprit wanted to lead the police to Sin House to save his daughter, so he decided last minute to change the numbers on the abacus."

"It would require seven sets of numbers to spell out Gold Tooth's name, but you only need six to spell out the word house." Xie Lanshan nodded and said, "That's why the culprit took apart a piece of the abacus, which explains why an extra abacus bead was left in Anuchit's room."

"When you have eliminated the impossible, all that's left is the truth." With this deduction, the answer surfaced. The key to solving the puzzle fit comfortably in the lock of mystery. Shen Liufei said, "From the time Anuchit was killed at 9 P.M. until his neighbor called the cops at 9:15 P.M., three men entered the house within those fifteen minutes. Time was limited. It would be impossible to connect those numbers Anuchit left on the abacus to chemical element symbols. However, that would be a different story if the culprit had a background in chemistry."

Alas, strong evidence was still necessary to settle the case.

While the two pondered silently as breakfast time was over, a handful of men in police uniform suddenly appeared in the closing cafeteria. In front stood two familiar faces: Somsak and Kang Xin. They were here under branch chief Kang Tai's order to arrest criminal suspect Xie Lanshan.

Knowing that the cops were here for him, Xie Lanshan took another bite of egg in revel. He squinted slightly as he chewed and gave Shen Liufei another smile. "Egg's not as good as your cooking, cuz."

Shen Liufei sat calmly and took a sip of his coffee, then said, "I can cook for you every day when we return."

Watching the two still nonchalantly eating breakfast, Somsak and Kang Tai's expressions grew grave as they clenched tightly onto the gun in hand. They both knew that this cop from China wasn't easy to capture.

After finishing the last bit of the egg, Xie Lanshan stood up. In the face of the nervous and hostile Thai police, he carefully fixed his shirt collar and cuffs. Xie Lanshan squinted his eyes in satisfaction like a satiated cat.

"I know who the true culprit is," he said with a grin, as if he wasn't ready to be arrested. "But I'll need you all to help put on an act with me in order to arrest the guy."

(vii)

The Thai police asked Anuchit's neighbor to help identify the man's voice they heard during the night of the crime. The neighbor had peeked outside the door that night, and while they couldn't see the person inside because of the curtains, the voices of two men were clear.

Xie Lanshan was tall. The curtains hanging by the window weren't high enough to cover his face. After checking with the neighbor to confirm Xie Lanshan wasn't the man who paid Anuchit a visit that night, they finally removed him from the suspect list.

But that wasn't enough. He was still a suspect of Gold Tooth's murder. After Somsak left the man, Xie Lanshan stayed with Han Guangming for a few days during the dangerous times, creating a strange bond between the two. He didn't go back to find Shen Liufei in the hotel and instead detoured to check out Han Guangming's room.

The manager came to find Wen Jue with loads of cash on hand. Thailand was hot, and the man changed out of clothing quickly like tissue. Only one black and yellow Hermes brand waist bag was carried everywhere he went. Xie Lanshan reached over to play around with it.

"Hey you, hands off, don't touch my stuff." Han Guangming turned around and took the bag away to carry around his waist. He said, "I'm going back tomorrow with my lil'Jue and Xiaomo. Southeast Asia sure can be dangerous. I won't let them come next time."

The way he said "Xiaomo" was filled with affection. Xie Lanshan gave a faint smile and said to the man, "Anuchit and Gold Tooth belong to the same criminal organization, and because of how close their time of deaths are, the Thai police suspect the same person committed their murders. You'll need to follow me to the bureau as a witness."

Surprised that he was now a suspect, Han Guangming asked in shock, "Me too? Why do I have to go?"

Xie Lanshan responded confidently, "Of course you have to go. You and I both were at the crime scene when Gold Tooth was killed; not to mention you left later than I did."

"I did not!" Han Guangming took in a deep breath of air in shock and explained as he attempted to calm himself down, "You were the one that dropped all those photos and stuff on the ground. I was just helping you clean up!"

"I know, I know." Xie Lanshan wrapped an arm around the man's shoulders and led the man out the door. Then, just like how they were roleplaying a couple at the club last time, he joked, "My wife sure needs to be a bit more alert. These dumb Thai police are too busy trying to settle the case that they're trying to drag us poor souls down."

Han Guangming was concerned about his own safety now and instead shoved Xie Lanshan's hand away in disgust, then scolded, "Who's your wife? That's disgusting!"

Xie Lanshan continued to jest and squeezed Han Guangming's cheeks, playfully calling the latter "fat lady" even in the face of opposition.

Xie Lanshan wasted no time and took Han Guangming to

the police station in the warm heat and through the blooming streets of Bangkok. The popular tourist city was peaceful and tranquil beneath the sun.

Stepping into a foreign country's police department for the first time, and as a criminal suspect, Han Guangming could feel himself losing some touch with reality. He dragged himself to follow Xie Lanshan, occasionally scanning his surroundings sheepishly. All the cops working hard around him would lift their heads and glare at him harshly whenever they walked near. He had grown used to seeing Wen Jue's pretty face every day, so he was naturally put off by unfamiliar strangers' faces around him right now. He only felt like these Southeast Asians all seemed to carry a cloud of suspicion on their faces like ferocious statues in a temple, sending chills down his spine.

Of course, it could also be that Han Guangming felt guilty.

There were two policemen in the bureau conversing loudly, pulling everyone's attention toward them. Han Guangming remembered the taller and more handsome one was called Kang Xin, but he didn't recognize the shorter man. Both men had a stern face as they discussed something in Thai. Han Guangming didn't understand Thai, but he could make out that they were talking about Anuchit's case from the fact that they were gesturing toward a photo of the victim's body. He also noticed that one man was holding a wooden stick in hand.

Nobody would have recognized this item, but Han Guangming knew immediately upon first glance—this was a piece taken off from the toy abacus.

In contrast to that eerie Morphia Show clubhouse filled with ambient red lights, Han Guangming felt that the bureau was much more fearsome. The cops here were like standing snakes waiting to capture prey.

At that moment, Xie Lanshan suddenly leaned by his ear and gave a cryptic message to him, "When I was here yesterday for investigation, I overheard the cops say the culprit kept the most decisive evidence on them."

Han Guangming shivered and asked, stuttering, "Wh-what evidence?"

As if afraid to let the cops hear him, Xie Lanshan pulled on Han Guangming's arm and said in a low voice, "Anuchit was afraid he would get killed, so he prepared a dying message in his house beforehand. But for some reason, the culprit ended up changing his message and took something from the item that had the message. That item was taken apart and the cops only found a portion of it in Anuchit's house. They suspect that the culprit didn't throw everything away and kept it on them, and whatever they took must still have Anuchit's fingerprint."

Han Guangming grew even more restless and asked, "What... What item?"

Just as Xie Lanshan was about to answer, he heard Somsak call him from behind, "You're next." The old cop left after dropping the message.

The anxious atmosphere clouded Han Guangming's memories. As soon as Xie Lanshan left, the manager quickly found a corner and carefully searched his bag. Thankfully, he found one white bead in the bottom of his waist bag before the police would get to him.

In order to distract the police's attention toward Sin House during the night of Anuchit's murder, he had no choice but to quickly change the dying message. He certainly took apart a piece of the abacus, but had nowhere else to place those large beads and could only put them into his pocket.

Han Guangming took in a breath of cold air as he saw this missing piece of evidence and clenched the bead in his hand. He wanted to find an excuse to flush it down the toilet but didn't realize Xie Lanshan suddenly appeared behind him. The young cop leaned in by his ear and said, "What do you have there, wife?"

He had no time to toss the bead now. To hide the piece of evidence, Han Guangming's first instinct was to toss the bead into his mouth and swallow it.

The large bead was stuck in his throat; he couldn't swallow or spit it out. Han Guangming choked until his eyes rolled, pounding on his chest to get it down his stomach.

"You sure have a big appetite." Xie Lanshan tried to hold in his laughter as he saw everything was going as planned, then gave a friendly pat on the manager's back to say, "What's the rush?"

"Uh... um..." After finally managing to swallow it down, Han Guangming panted heavily and responded, "Candy... I was just eating candy."

(vii)

After an hour-long questioning, Han Guangming quickly ran off to the restroom and sat on the toilet. It was uncomfortable knowing such a large bead was inside his stomach; he needed to release it as soon as possible.

He clenched his teeth on the toilet, face reddening and legs numb, until he heard someone knock lightly on the door.

"Wife?" A taunting voice rang from outside that asked, "Is my wife in there?"

It was obvious the person behind the door was Xie Lanshan. Han Guangming was still stuck in the stall when he answered in irritation, "What do you want?"

"I dropped something and couldn't find it anywhere, and then I remembered I think I dropped it in your bag this morning." Xie Lanshan said as he pinched his nose against the foul smell in the restroom, then asked innocently, "You didn't happen to eat it, did you?"

Han Guangming felt his heart skip a beat at this question and assumed he fell for a trick. His body stiffened as he attempted to find excuses. "Who, who would eat your stuff?!"

"If you manage to poop it out, don't forget to give it back. If you can't, then don't waste your time in there." Not enough time had passed for his stomach to digest anything since he swallowed the bead. Xie Lanshan knowingly joked back and said, "What did you even eat this morning? It sure smells like crap in here."

Xie Lanshan then left as soon as he dropped the last sentence.

Han Guangming was tired of squatting and pulled himself and his pants back up. After he cleaned himself up and walked out of the restroom, he was greeted by the policemen he had just spoken with earlier. Somsak and the other cop that was talking about the case earlier were also there. Everyone looked at him with eyebrows furrowed, frowning sternly.

Only Xie Lanshan was still smiling at him. Behind those pretty eyes were stars, glittering slyly like a fox.

"What are you all looking at?" Han Guangming was ready to fight; he was going to insist that he ate a bead even if they suspected him. Even at the cost of taking out the item from his stomach, he wasn't going to back down—what could they do if he just insisted he liked eating strange beads? Were they going to shoot him for that?

Xie Lanshan raised a hand and pointed at the walls in the hallway, chuckling, "Look, there are cameras all over."

It was obvious that his act of swallowing the bead earlier was already recorded. Han Guangming still didn't back down and asked with confidence, "So what?"

"Nothing, I just wanna ask you something, darling." Xie Lanshan continued to speak in that coquettish tone to annoy him. He raised a hand and displayed a bead with two holes on each end in between two fingers. He waved it quickly before Han Guangming's eyes and said, "Did I leave this in your bag? And what did you just swallow earlier right in front of the camera?"

"Why do you care what I ate? Even if I decide that I like eating abacus beads, that's my personal preference—"

"W-wait..." Xie Lanshan lifted a brow and then held up the item in his hand before the manager. "I only said I left something in your bag. How did you recognize that it was an abacus bead?"

Han Guangming finally took a good look at the item in the young cop's hand—it wasn't the bead left in his bag, it was a rubber bead that toddlers grind their teeth on.

The smile on Xie Lanshan's face disappeared as he stared sharply at Han Guangming and said quickly, "Because you've been to the crime scene. You were also the one that changed Anuchit's dying message and had no choice but to take away all the extra abacus beads. You're scared that Anuchit's finger-prints would be left on those beads, so you decided to swallow it at the last minute."

Han Guangming was panicking, but it wasn't decisive proof. He saw that the two cops earlier were both glaring at him, and after recalling what Xie Lanshan said about how these idiot cops wanted to settle the case by pinning the blame on someone random, he quickly came up with an idea.

"Hey wife," the words out of Xie Lanshan's mouth were still playful despite the stern tone. "I only explained that the culprit brought a key piece of evidence with them from the crime scene. I didn't even mention the part about the abacus. If you don't have a good explanation right now, I'm afraid you're going to be the primary suspect. Even your husband won't be able to save you."

"I overheard those two cops talk about the case earlier and picked up bits of their conversation, so I knew about the abacus. That's when I saw something in my bag that didn't belong to me and suspected someone was trying to put the blame on me. I ended up swallowing the bead in a panic." Han Guangming stubbornly defended himself and then grabbed onto Xie Lanshan's collar, shouting back, "You could be the true culprit trying to pin it all on me for all I care!"

"That's a good explanation. Not only did you clear yourself of suspicion, you even found a scapegoat." Xie Lanshan pretended to ponder for a little before he stared back in shock, "But I thought you didn't know Thai?"

"It's just one or two words, I can at least understand a little bit." Han Guangming had been spending quite some time in Thailand already and could pick out some easy phrases. He certainly said some very accented words and then insisted on not speaking anymore, then turned his attention back to Xie Lanshan.

The latter looked at Han Guangming, frowning, and asked, "Are you sure they were talking about this case?"

Han Guangming said confidently, "Yes, they were. I heard some words earlier but now I forgot the details."

Xie Lanshan let out a sigh and walked toward Kang Xin. He took out a recorder from the cop's jacket and turned the time back to when Han Guangming just stepped into the bureau right in front of everyone. He turned up the volume and made sure everyone could hear the conversation the two had earlier.

Kang Xin was having a stern discussion with his colleague while holding a photo of the crime scene and an abacus stick— about what they were going to eat for dinner.

Despite not knowing Thai, Han Guangming could tell from the expressions of everyone that nobody mentioned a word about this case from start to finish.

Only the culprit who had been to the crime scene would know about the abacus and was the only person who would possibly attempt to hide this fact.

"I shoved that in your bag just before we left. Anuchit's fingerprints are not on there. You've already disposed of all the evidence, but you had no time to think in a situation like this because your instincts told you to hide the truth."

Han Guangming refused to speak and glared back; he assumed that silence was better than breaking down in front of the cops.

"There were cameras installed on the streets to the storage unit Gold Tooth was found dead in. All surveillance has already been extracted. I left earlier than you, and the cameras showed that nobody else walked into the unit after you left. You're the only one that had the time to murder the victim, and you've also been to the crime scene of Anuchit's murder. The only thing we're missing is a motive." Xie Lanshan lifted his head suddenly and glanced out the window before saying, "I can arrange a DNA test for you right now."

Han Guangming followed Xie Lanshan's gaze and saw that Shen Liufei took Tang Xiaomo and Wen Jue out. Perhaps they had this planned beforehand, but he saw the three walking closer to them. The young girl and boy held hands as they walked, chatting happily amongst themselves.

Han Guangming's gaze fixed on the young girl; he noticed her smile was brilliant and joyous, shining under the sun.

"N-no..." He finally gave up, a miserable tone came out from his hoarse throat. "Don't do a DNA test. I don't want her to know about me."

The three quickly made their way into the bureau. Tang

Xiaomo looked at Xie Lanshan, puzzled. "Did you call us over as witnesses? Where do we go?"

Han Guangming stared at Xie Lanshan desperately, implying that he would confess everything if they gave him space in private.

Three men were left inside the office of the bureau.

Shen Liufei also helped plan this act; he had assumed Han Guangming would refuse to confess, even if they both participated in this performance. Tang Xiaomo and Wen Jue were taken to another office by Somsak. The artist turned to ask Han Guangming, "Is Tang Xiaomo really your daughter?"

Han Guangming looked out the window. The green bushes outside danced in rhythm under the wind, almost as if they were shivering in fear.

But perhaps fear was no longer accurate. His heart was now only filled with warm emotions that were slowly opening up after despair.

Xie Lanshan lowered his gaze a little and asked, "You went to Tang Xiaomo's little shop to buy fake artworks to secretly give support to her financially, right?"

"I'm not blind or stupid. Do you think an obvious fake painting like that is worth that much?" Han Guangming glanced at Xie Lanshan and then said, "This story is kind of long. I'll tell you everything I know if I can have some booze."

"One moment." Shen Liufei knew this was going to be a tragic story and decided to fulfill this angered and despondent father's last request. He stepped out of the office and quickly came back in with a few bottles of beer. There was only one brand in the nearest shop and there were no bottle openers. He had to turn the bottle upside down and open up one bottle using the force of another.

Shen Liufei swiftly and handsomely handed an open bottle to Han Guangming, then opened another bottle for Xie Lanshan.

"Thank you." Han Guangming downed a large mouthful before spitting a little toward Shen Liufei in a complaint. "What kind of booze is this? It's not even as good as Tsingtao."

"Huh?" Shen Liufei obviously ran to buy the beer to save time. Xie Lanshan wasn't too happy that Han Guangming was being picky and shoved the man's arm with his own beer bottle. "My good cuz here bought you a drink and even opened a bottle for you, don't get ahead of yourself."

Of course, it wasn't as bad as he said. Han Guangming took another mouthful and finally began his story.

"I never married her mother; she had always just followed me around until she gave birth to Xiaomo. Later, when my career was finally starting to look good, and I knew I was going to become a successful man, naturally those pretty girls began flocking over like pigeons. I admit that I did lose myself in that lucid dream for a little while. Xiaomo's mother got mad at me and took Xiaomo with her, but at that time I didn't even think about chasing her down. But who knew that the mother would get into an accident and never contact me, even up until she died. She only asked someone to relay a message to me, saying that she left Xiaomo with a painter." Han Guangming shook his head and let out a long sigh, "In the end, it's really just because her mother was too stubborn..."

Shen Liufei didn't leave time for him to dwell in the past and said, "Go on."

Han Guangming said, "After that, my business got better. You know, the more successful you get, the lonelier you become, and I started to recall my family almost every night until I couldn't withstand the pain. So, I started looking for Xiaomo. It took me a whole ten years, and I only managed to find some clues last year, but I wasn't ready to confirm. Fortunately, that *Ode to the Goddess Luo* case became national headlines, and after I saw Tang Zhaozhong's information on the news, I finally confirmed her mother gave Xiaomo to that painter. I was planning on revealing myself to her after I got closer, but I didn't realize her grandfather's case shocked her so much that she decided to travel on her own. She's a pretty young lady who isn't even 20 yet, and with all the money she made from selling art, it was too dangerous for her to be roaming around all on her own. That's why I followed her."

Xie Lanshan was shocked. "You've followed her to all those countries she visited? How?"

Han Guangming suddenly lifted his eyebrows proudly and smiled. "I added her on WeChat as a client and followed her Weibo. I even got to know some of her friends—the point is, as long as I'm willing to shell out some money and time, I can find out where she's going any time. Don't underestimate a dad's investigation skills; we're just as good as cops!"

Shen Liufei continued, "She did tell me that she felt someone was following her. Yet because she was already in Thailand when she said this, I mistakenly assumed the person was Anuchit—but it turned out to be you all along."

"I'm just scared that she wouldn't forgive me and accept me. If I knew this was going to happen one day, I would have told her the truth much earlier." Han Guangming's eyes dimmed down, a cloud of pain coloring his face. "I later followed her to Thailand and saw Anuchit flirting with her near the bar, then within a blink of an eye she was gone."

"So you discovered Anuchit's address, found out he kidnapped and sold your daughter, and thought to kill the man?" Xie Lanshan said, confused, "You have so much money, you could have easily bought her back instead of dirtying your hands."

"I didn't plan on killing him. I was on my knees at that time, crying and begging him to tell me where Xiaomo was. I brought a lot of money with me and told him I will pay however much he wants, that I'm willing to give everything I have to bring my daughter back. But he only told me nonchalantly that he already sold the girl to a club called Sin House. But that isn't going to be the final place where she serves customers, even he doesn't know where she'll end up being sold to." Han Guang-ming's eyes grew evil, his round face turned menacing as he spoke. He clenched his fist and said, "He even said that if I have so much money, I might as well go find another woman and have her give birth to another child. Because Xiaomo is likely already being violated and harassed by some disgusting pervert by now..."

Nobody could understand the anger this man felt when he heard these words. At that time, he took an object on the table and violently hit the trafficker's head like an uncontrollable beast.

Likewise, when he picked up the photo from that dimly lit storage unit and saw that innocent smile of the girl he was willing to love for his whole life, he was reminded of the pain and suffering she might have been going through at that exact moment.

In that instant, regret and anger consumed him. He couldn't forgive this sinful man who dared to harm his daughter and suffocated Gold Tooth until he was dead.

Outside the bureau, a colorful dusk painted the skies as the wind continued to blow on the bushes. A gust of gentle breeze blew into the office. The window frame creaked as if it was sighing or humming.

After a long silence, Han Guangming downed the last bit of the beer and said, "Alright, and that's the end of the story." He shrugged as if to laugh at himself and said, "I guess there really isn't any climax to it, huh? Aren't all those murder suspects in movies super smart? That's not like me, I'm just loopholes all over that can easily be seen through."

After a brief pause, Shen Liufei asked, "You refused to accept the DNA test and even offered to confess your crimes for it. Do you not plan on letting her know that you're her father?"

Han Guangming shook his head and laughed bitterly. "What's the point of letting her know now? She's had a tough life, all these years have been too painful for her."

He knew how hurtful the incident with the old painter was to her and didn't want the same tragedy to dawn upon the girl, making her suffer again another loss.

Xie Lanshan wasn't sure if this was the right decision and took a step forward, asking, "Are you sure you don't want to tell her? You killed the man for her, perhaps she wouldn't blame you—"

Shen Liufei pressed on his shoulders and nodded toward Han Guangming, "We promise we won't say a word."

As if the last worry in his heart finally settled, Han Guangming let out another long sigh and gave Shen Liufei a grateful smile. "Thank you."

After the questioning, Wen Jue and Tang Xiaomo ran out to the yard to escape the heat inside the bureau. They waited for Xie Lanshan to come out so that they could all return to the hotel together.

Tang Xiaomo seemed to be interested in everything in this foreign country as she dragged Wen Jue around like two little bees in a flower garden.

The girl looked like her mother, but her gleeful and cute round face certainly took after her father. In the man's eyes, the girl was virtually flawless; she was like a beauty carved from a jade sculpture, just a little thin. He recalled that she also loved going to new places when she was little. Sometimes she would cry after tripping from excitement, but unlike the little girl, his pain could only be kept silent in his heart. He swore to himself that he would protect her for the rest of her life, allowing her to fall comfortably into his powerful and dependable arms.

Perhaps there was something in spirit that connected them. Tang Xiaomo suddenly stood up and lifted her head, then turned toward Han Guangming's direction.

As their gazes met, Tang Xiaomo held up a hand and waved at him. She had a good impression of this pudgy manager, who answered all of her requests in contrast to Wen Jue's occasional complaints and coldness.

This might be the last time he could see this girl look at him with a smile in his lifetime. Han Guangming could feel his blood boil as he quickly lifted his arm to wave back. But before he could even move his arm, Tang Xiaomo's attention was distracted by another exotic plant in the yard. She turned her head over and shoved her face into it, nagging Wen Jue to take a photo for her.

The man couldn't express his disappointment. His hand froze in mid-air, his fingers slowly curled down. Yet, after a brief moment, he once again opened his palms and pressed them gently on the glass window. As if touching his beloved daughter's face light-years away, he quietly repeated to himself, "Hello, my dear."

Hello, my dear.

After all the questioning was over, Wen Jue and Tang Xiaomo were told that Han Guangming confessed his crimes.

"Your manager doesn't look like a bad guy at all." The girl looked up at the boy beside her in shock—only in shock.

"Maybe it was because of me. I told him before that greed will kill him one day." Wen Jue also felt he was in a daze, assuming his manager had also made a mistake because greed blinded him. He didn't make any other remarks and looked at his manager. Two Thai police took Han Guangming out, one on each side from the interrogation room, walking slowly toward the two young people.

The man didn't look at the two as he passed by them, afraid that he would expose some emotions. He walked past her, the girl he loved with his life.

He couldn't bring himself to look at her right now. He remembered watching old videos of the little girl again and again since she first went missing. He watched the little girl, who was like a ball of white sticky rice, call him dad. He would often find himself stuck between two extreme emotions—feeling overjoyed at the video or ready to cry on his knees in regret.

In the end, he couldn't hold it in. His hands were cuffed, his head hung toward the ground as he walked. At first, it was just tears welling in his eyes. But as soon as he realized this would be the last time they would ever see one another, tears finally streamed down his cheeks.

The man wasn't very attractive, and with tears and snot rolling down his face, he felt even more ugly. Tang Xiaomo clung onto Wen Jue's arm and stared at the crying Han Guangming for a while until the police took him away. That short and round figure disappeared before her.

"Look at boss Han, look..." Tang Xiaomo leaned in to speak quietly into Wen Jue's ear, "He's crying so ugly..."

Revenge

The cross-national operation ended on a joyous note with the true culprit arrested and hostages saved. The duties of the Blue Foxes in Thailand were finally completed. While the officers were preparing to return to their home country, Somsak paid them one last visit.

He told the two young officers that the Thai police infiltrated the abandoned factory according to the location that Wen Jue and Shen Liufei gave, but discovered it was already empty. The traffickers had already transferred all the slaves to a different location, and they only captured a few insignificant people in Sin House. In short, Guan Nuoqin and his human traffickers were still nowhere to be found. All leads were cut off. Bangkok Police Branch Chief Kang Tai was also busy reporting the news of settling the big cases to his bosses and didn't seem to care much about following up on these human trafficking cases. Of course, Somsak worried that someone in the bureau was already working with Guan Nuoqin. If the Blue Fox members were to leave right now, this case with Guan Nuoqin would likely become a cold case like all the other missing persons in Thailand.

For the sake of those children and young women that were captured, the old cop asked for their help.

Xie Lanshan was well-acquainted with Somsak and knew how stubborn the old man could be, then instead provoked the old cop, "Your leaders said this case is closed now. Why do you want to give yourself more work?"

"Saving lives even at the cost of our own is a universal moral and duty that all cops around the world should share." The old cop was short in height, but his words stood grandly above him. With a confident and courageous look on his face, he said, "This isn't going to change because we're of different nationalities."

If Shen Liufei wasn't beside him right now, Xie Lanshan would not have been able to stand under the same roof as Chi Jin. The two quickly exchanged a glance. Shen Liufei gave him a light nod. This stubborn old cop reminded Xie Lanshan of his father and captain; they all shared the desire to save all lives within their reach, even if it was just one person.

Ling Yun, also in the room, understood what the old cop was asking. The young man's blood boiled with passion as soon as he heard the request. Yet they arrived only at the special request of Director Peng and had no real jurisdiction to act on their own. While Ling Yun hesitated in silence, the temporary captain, Chi Jin, accepted the offer.

"Sure," Chi Jin said with certainty, "we'll stay."

"W-wait." Ling Yun was surprised that Chi Jin didn't oppose Xie Lanshan directly this time, but also recognized that this wasn't any trivial matter. He attempted to persuade his leader, "Uh... should we at least send a report to Director Peng first? It might not be a good idea to just act on our own..."

Annoyed, Chi Jin interrupted him. "I'm the captain now. There's no need for me to wait for approval to act in an emergency. Besides, even if we saved Wen Jue and Tang Xiaomo, this case isn't completely settled yet. Officer Somsak is right; our duty is to protect innocent lives and we should not be afraid of making sacrifices. We shouldn't make any exceptions just because we're not from the same country."

Ling Yun grew more puzzled; with Chi Jin's stringent and careful attitude, he would never have accepted Somsak's request. Law enforcement in a foreign country was one of the biggest taboos in public security due to the differences in governing laws and customs. They were police officers of China and could not conduct investigations on their own on foreign land. Even in a case of collaborative efforts, they still needed approval from their bosses on both sides in order to act.

Ever since coming to Thailand, Ling Yun had noticed the changes in Chi Jin. The young captain's mood was a roller coaster that often swung between rage and idleness. Ling Yun originally thought it was just the effects of a different climate, but he recalled the time he accidentally went into Chi Jin's room during their stay. He noticed the latter frantically hiding a half-filled bottle in the room—the bottle looked familiar, and he was almost certain it was a meth bottle.

Despite being the youngest member of the Blue Fox, Ling Yun was still a drug-enforcement officer that had sharp senses when it came to illegal substances.

Yet, out of concern for his comrade and colleague, he couldn't bring himself to accept his suspicion.

Using Wen Jue's witness account about another Chinese boy being sold into slavery, the Blue Fox members stayed a little longer in Thailand after reporting back to their home base. They were asked to collaborate with the Thai police to completely annihilate the human trafficking organizations and ensure the safety of their own citizens. Yet while planning to take down Guan Nuoqin, they also had to be careful around the spy within the bureau, causing the case to be delayed longer than they expected.

Kang Xin didn't participate too much in this case, but knew he wasn't in a position to help out because of his complicated background. He already gave up hope on A'Liang providing a heart donation and no longer had the energy to focus on anything else with his daughter's illness worsening by the day.

Yaya fell while going down the stairs one day and ended up in the emergency room. The hospital reported that once again she was in critical condition.

Her symptoms had improved after using medication, but the hospital warned that her overall condition was still worsening and only a heart transplant could save her life.

Yet where was a capable donor? The wait seemed to have no end.

Shen Liufei took a break and went to visit the sick girl at Kang Xin's house. He had heard her late stage illness forced her to leave the hospital. During a time where their only hope was to wait for a donor, the hospital had nothing else they could do to treat her.

Xie Lanshan waited on the ground level. He was still a cop and wasn't in a position to speak with Kang Xin, so he could only let Shen Liufei handle the social activity.

The house was located in the corner of a rather quiet city. Shen Liufei scanned the house as he stepped in; the small living space was clean and bright. It was difficult to imagine this was the residence of a single father and his daughter.

After rescuing Wen Jue, Shen Liufei had also passed by Kang Xin a few times in the bureau. But he kept his promise and didn't speak of how he snuck into the criminal organization. Kang Xin was grateful to Shen Liufei for not exposing his secret during a turbulent time in the bureau.

"The place is small, but please make yourself at home."

Kang Xin wasn't great at social activities. He scratched his face and head as he looked at his guest, slightly antsy, and said, "Yaya might still be awake right now. You can go visit her."

They carefully opened the door to the girl's bedroom and saw her already laying on her hard wooden bed. She wasn't asleep, just extremely weak. Most of her time was now spent in a coma-like state, as she went to bed much earlier than most people.

"Yaya?" The man called his daughter.

The girl didn't respond.

"Yaya? " Afraid that his daughter was in a coma, Kang Xin called her again. He was on edge at every interaction with her now. Any response would shock him.

The girl frowned slightly and turned. She heard him, she just didn't want to respond.

The girl was very mature and used to be close to her father. As if she was afraid she would fall asleep and never wake up again, she would cling herself onto Kang Xin day and night. She wouldn't ask him to read fairytale stories and instead listened to him talk about stories of solving cases. Her eyes would grow wide as she stared in admiration.

Yet Yaya refused to talk to him after that night. She was disappointed in this man, just like how Kang Xin felt about himself.

"She's asleep... Let's talk outside." Kang Xin felt a bit awkward and led Shen Liufei out of the bedroom as he closed the door.

"How is Yaya's situation?" Shen Liufei asked, concerned.

"Same old. The only cure is a heart transplant. Her heart is almost at its limit right now and there's nothing else we can do." The wind outside banged on the windows as the man wept.

"That may not be true." After a moment of pondering, Shen Liufei said, "There is another method we can try, aside from waiting for a donor. I have a friend who's an expert brain surgeon in the U.S., who also has many connections to other neurosurgeons. If you can accept the concept of an artificial human heart transplant, perhaps Yaya can be saved."

Kang Xin had never heard of this. Shocked, he asked, "Artificial human heart transplant? What is that? Is it possible?"

Shen Liufei nodded and continued, "There was a young man in the U.S. that had once lived an extra 500 days through an artificial heart while waiting for a donor. His life during the time was no different from any other person as well."

This was a torch of fire in the darkness. Kang Xin wanted to grab onto it, but he knew the situation right now wasn't optimistic and said with a difficult expression, "But this surgery... this must cost a lot of money."

Shen Liufei said, "A single artificial heart could cost around 250,000 dollars."

That didn't include the fees of flying over to the US and hospitalization. Kang Xin calculated an estimate in his mind and realized how hefty the cost was; perhaps the only solution was to sell the house. But if they sold the house, they would have nowhere else to stay.

Shen Liufei seemed to know what the man was thinking and offered, "I can front the cost for you."

Kang Xin was stunned. He immediately shook his head and said, "No, no, we're not family nor friends. There's no reason for me to accept your sponsorship."

"I'm not sponsoring you," Shen Liufei said. He understood the pride of the man and didn't push it further. Instead, he told the man calmly, "Just take it as a loan. You still have a while before you retire; you can pay it back eventually."

"But..." Kang Xin was still hesitating. It wasn't that he didn't trust this surgeon, he still felt guilt inside his heart. "I'm still a cop. I may have done some bad things in the past, but... helping you sneak into the organization was part of my job. There's no need for you to repay me for that."

"No, you certainly helped me a lot." Shen Liufei lifted a faint smile but said sternly, "You helped me find a vital piece of memory I'd lost; you helped me realize how important a certain someone is in my life."

Shen Liufei had wanted to sponsor the surgery in order to exchange information from Kang Xin regarding the drug lord. Yet as soon as he saw the sickly young girl, he suddenly felt it was inhumane to threaten a father like that. Relying on bargains and threats would only make him the same as those heartless criminals who worked for Guan Nuoqin.

That's why he decided to not speak a word of his plan.

"I'll give you some time to think." Right before stepping out of the door, Shen Liufei noticed some colorful clay animals placed on the cabinet in the living room. Judging from the shape, they seemed to be crafted by Yaya. He took one from the cabinet and said to Kang Xin, "Your daughter has artistic talent. I'll be waiting for her to become a professional in the future. Until then, I'll take this as interest from you."

Yaya certainly loved drawing and crafting because of her inability to do extreme exercises. Kang Xin had been a cop for almost two decades and had seen many different faces through the countless cases he was involved in. Yet even among the thousands of people he'd met, he'd never met someone as cold and caring as Shen Liufei. The two contradicting characteristics blended perfectly in this man; his empathy and kindness became visibly sincere to Kang Xin.

Before Shen Liufei could walk down the stairs, the man inside the house rushed out.

"I accept your sponsorship, but I can't accept it without anything in return." Kang Xin looked at Shen Liufei with his bright eyes and said, "I have a way to get close to Guan Nuoqin."

(ii)

Mouths had been tight lately. Despite successfully transferring the hostages and slaves to a new location, Guan Nuoqin wasn't sure how involved the Chinese and Thai cops were in this case. Kang Tai coincidentally contacted him at this time to meet up in person at one of Guan Nuoqin's personal hideouts.

Of course, a sly old man like Guan Nuoqin would have more than one hideout. He had his men scattered around the residence, each one sharp and dangerous; there were even snipers waiting on top of trees. The men were like an army, armed and tightly surrounding the mansion.

Kang Tai didn't bring many people with him. There were some cops in casual wear waiting on the outside; all of them carried guns on their waist. Kang Tai was a careful man who didn't feel safe talking to a fearsome drug lord like Guan Nuoqin if he didn't bring some of his men along. Therefore, he had specifically asked his close subordinates to bring a few reliable allies to follow him along to the drug lord's place before leaving the bureau.

It was nighttime at the mansion, and despite being the biggest drug lord of the Golden Triangle right now, Guan Nuoqin was still nowhere near as powerful as Mu Kun was in his prime. He looked like an ordinary old man, hair white and skin crusty and dry. He looked to be no different from any other old man who enjoyed a relaxing afternoon in nature.

Yet he had a pair of sharp hawk-like eyes and a tall aquiline nose that exposed the brutality and evil inside him. It was almost fleeting, making it difficult for anyone to judge his true nature.

The drug lord was now gleefully planting flowers in his garden in a cheap Hawaiian shirt, his hands dirtied by the mud in the yard. He lifted his head as he heard someone open the door and greeted Kang Tai courteously, asking, "Want to see the flowers I'm planting?"

Kang Tai dressed well even outside of the bureau, donning a suit. He seemed quite displeased at how dirty the plants and gardens were and waved his hand in disgust, then waited patiently inside the living room.

Guan Nuoqin knew that Kang Tai had a younger brother named Kang Xin, who also helped with his business a few times because of his daughter's situation. Yet he never confused the two brothers. Kang Xin had an unshakeable air of roughness in him while Kang Tai was slim, pale, and much more well-dressed. The latter had the eyes of a soldier with a hint of slyness, like a fox.

The old man was finally done fiddling with his plants and left his garden. As he wiped his hands, he said, "It's not a big deal. Why do you even need to pay me a visit?"

"Not a big deal? Those Blue Foxes are about to destroy your nest, and you think this isn't a big deal?" Kang Tai's words were harsh and condescending as he said, "The Pulitzer Prize report two years ago was on the illegal labor and sweatshops culture in Southeast Asia—the slaves and fishermen are already a world-known problem. But you're telling me you still dare to capture people near the China-Myanmar border at a time like this? Great, it's easy to lure the hunters in, but now they won't leave. Those Blue Foxes aren't going to leave this country until they completely destroy you."

His blood was boiling with rage as he scolded, "You call yourself a drug lord yet you continue to involve yourself in these kidnappings and this human trafficking business."

This didn't provoke Guan Nuoqin, who only let out a sigh.

"Almost 600,000 acres of opium plants near the Golden Triangle have now been taken over by tea, corn, and other crops. Traditional drugs like heroin are also going down in demand in the market; I've thought about upgrading the narcotics but it's not that easy."

Puzzled, Kang Tai asked, "Isn't it just ice? What's so hard about upgrading?"

Guan Nuoqin shook his head and said, "Of course it's not hard for small businesses to fight in a market, but the new drug market in Southeast Asia is now already well-established. If I want to get into this market and control it, I'll need to consider many aspects like how to obtain recipes, develop new drugs efficiently, and maximize output. The most important aspect of all of this is also the purity of the ice."

Kang Tai understood the logic behind this; the higher the purity percentage of meth, the more profitable it was. If Guan Nuoqin wanted to solidify his position as the drug lord in the Golden Triangle, he must be able to create a high-purity ice that could completely control the local market.

Guan Nuoqin didn't like the heat today. Because of his joint problems, he couldn't sit in a room with AC, so he ordered his servants to fan him. He continued, "Anuchit wasn't just a normal chemistry teacher. I had plans to promote him to lead the development of red ice. I didn't think..."

Kang Tai's eyes widened slightly at this new term and asked, "Red ice?"

"Pure crystal meth extract, the purity can go as high as 99.9%. There is already some floating around the market right now, but it's still very scarce." Recalling how the most promising source of income was now gone, Guan Nuoqin shook his head in disappointment. "How could I have known he'd be killed by that Chinese fatty?"

After a moment of regret, the old drug lord suddenly realized he had once mentioned red ice to Kang Tai, and the latter expressed great interest.

The sudden but fleeting reaction earlier was clearly abnormal.

Guan Nuoqin spent many years swimming in the dangerous Golden Triangle and had a sharp mind. A simple hint was enough to let him realize that the man standing before him wasn't Kang Tai but Kang Xin. It was almost shocking for him to slim down at least ten kilograms within such a short period of time and act as his brother so perfectly.

During the conversation, everyone else aside from the servant fanning the boss had left the room. Guan Nuoqin decided to not play with fire and continued to converse with "Kang Tai" about his business while he slowly walked around the room. The mansion was equipped with all sorts of traps; he knew exactly which vase or antique had guns hidden in them.

Guan Nuoqin wasn't sure what the man wanted and intended to capture him alive. This wasn't the real Kang Tai, but the cops that came with him were real officers. Even those cops were being played, so he couldn't just kill these people without reason.

"Kang Tai, we've been working together for all these years. I've always wanted to ask you something—you're always so well-dressed no matter where you go. Is it not hot?" Guan Nuoqin had his back to "Kang Tai" right now with a gun in hand, confident he could take the man down. The two men were left alone inside the house. Knowing that the guest always needed to be searched before entering, Kang Xin couldn't possibly have a gun in hand right now.

"I still think it's hot," the old drug lord said with a smile before the cop could respond. He slowly turned around and said, "How about you take off that jacket and roll up your sleeves. We'll talk when it's a little cooler, hm?"

He didn't let the cop find excuses and already pointed his gun at the latter. The drug lord knew that Kang Tai had a burn scar on his arm, but Kan Xin didn't. This was a fact everyone in the bureau knew.

"What's this? Are you suspecting me?" Kang Xin didn't panic and opened his arms, allowing Guan Nuoqin's servant to take off his suit jacket. He then quickly rolled up his sleeves to expose a gruesome burn scar.

"I-I'm not suspecting you..." Shocked that he was just being paranoid, Guan Nuoqin gave a relieved smile. His suspicion dwindled as he put his gun away.

To his surprise, the cop in front of him acted swiftly and jumped the moment the gun was put away. Soon after, the sound of a gunshot reverberated.

The people outside rushed into the mansion, their guns unsure where to point.

Kang Xin had already taken a bullet and was struggling to stand. There was blood rolling out from the injury on his chest. He waved his burnt arm and pointed at Guan Nuoqin, who was still holding a gun with his other gun, calling out to his subordinates, "He betrayed me! He's going to kill all of you too—"

Within a blink of an eye, Guan Nuoqin could only fire a few rounds at this man before he could say any more words. He didn't have time to think, explain, or even determine the situation, and shot the man down to the ground.

Seeing their Chief shot down right in front of their eyes, the cops who followed him pulled out their guns without hesitation, marking the start of a large and chaotic warfare.

(iii)

Guan Nuoqin died under a rain of bullets, and this

gunfight also exposed all the internal problems within the police department. Branch Chief Kang Tai was hanging onto his last breath by the time he was discovered. His brother Kang Xin had tied him up, stripped him of his clothes, and locked him in the basement of his own house. In front of him was evidence to prove his association with organized crime, and facing him was a full investigation and legal consequences for his actions.

Kang Xin burnt himself to fake an injury that his brother had. He had already determined that creating an illusion of truths and falsehood was the only way to fight against the calculating and sly drug lord.

With the death of Guan Nuoqin and the fall of Kang Tai, the subordinates that worked beneath them lost all reason to fight against the police. With the help of the Chinese Blue Fox team, the Thai police rescued over 800 slaves and hostages that were tortured under the criminal organization. Many of them were kidnapped or sold off to the criminals.

This good news shook the entire world, but a better piece of news turned up: Yaya's heart donor finally arrived. A woman who died in a car accident donated her heart. She had a smaller heart than most average people, and it fit perfectly into Yaya's little chest.

The little girl also knew about the death of her father. Crowds of police officers, journalists, and locals paid her visits. Everyone cried by her bedside, from loud cries to silent weeping. Only she didn't cry. Her small face was blank and silent, as if her soul had left her body.

Yaya saw Shen Liufei when she arrived at the surgery room. She had a good impression of this man. Shen Liufei walked toward her, and she reached out a hand to hold his. She lifted her head and asked quietly, "Is my dad a bad guy?"

Shen Liufei got onto his knees by the girl's bed and held her small hand gently and warmly. He shook his head and said in confidence, "Your father is a hero."

It stunned the girl for a few seconds. Then she lifted a little smile. This smile seemed to trigger some sort of emotion in her; the laugh quickly became a cry, and tears rolled down her cheeks like droplets.

"I knew he was a hero. I told many people about it, that my dad is a hero." She was too prideful and regretful. This young girl wasn't able to face the cruelty of separation in the adult world, so she could only grab tightly onto Shen Liufei's hand. She looked at the only man she could trust for help and said, "But there's nothing special about a hero. My dad's gone, my daddy's gone..."

"He's here," Shen Liufei said lightly. "Of course he's still here."

"But... Where is he? Where?" The little girl looked up at the man kneeling beside her bed as she cried.

"He's deep in the sun, the end of the stars. He will always protect and watch over you." Shen Liufei lifted his head and guided the little girl to look in the same direction. His gaze fell outside the window toward the reddish and gold leaves of the trees until it flew out to a freer and higher sky above them. His voice was cold and deep, almost emotionless, but there was undeniable sincerity and softness in those words that had the power of persuasion.

Finally, he gave the little girl a faint smile and said, "Like now, he's watching to see if his little girl can stay brave. He wants to see if she can handle this surgery that will give her a new life without tears."

With the encouragement of this pretty adult before her, Yaya held back her tears. She didn't want her dad to leave with concern and still worry about her in the afterlife.

· · ·

After he watched the girl be sent into the surgery room, Xie Lanshan walked up from behind. The latter noticed Shen Liufei's grave expression and wrapped an arm around the artist's waist, asking, "Are you alright?"

"I'm fine." Shen Liufei turned back to glance at Xie Lanshan. The light on his lover's face softened his expression as he nodded. "I just saw that Kang Xin left me a message in the end. He said that he must do this because his crimes can only be atoned for by blood, so that he can't disappoint his daughter. Their country has a compensation reward for sacrifices on duty for public security; this money could be used to pay for Yaya's surgery, so that he wouldn't need to owe anyone for his daughter's transplant."

"So Kang Xin had planned on giving his life since the start of this operation." Xie Lanshan felt admiration toward this quiet and almost insignificant Thai police officer and said, "He reminded me of my own father. They're very similar in certain ways... both of them were quiet but strong. They were people who would give their lives to fulfill their duties and set an example for their children. Most importantly, they left without regret when they met their inevitable ends."

It was quite strange indeed. Ever since arriving in Thailand, the two fathers he came in contact with differed vastly from old Xie, but they both reminded Xie Lanshan of his own father. Kang Xin was confident but lacked sophistication, while Han Guangming shared almost no common traits as old Xie. Xie Lanshan looked out the window; his vision blurred and eyes reddened.

He recalled the time when old Xie's body was returned to China, how his mother broke down in tears, but he didn't cry.

For a long time after old Xie passed, the boy grew quieter and more conservative. Aside from going to and from school, he would not speak a word to anyone. He would spend the daytime staring at the crabapple flower outside his front door, from its blooming until its withering. At night, he would look at the moon in the sky from full moon to new moon.

Everyone around him told him to cry it out. Liu Yanbo and Tao Jun, the two family friends closest to him would often visit him during that time and look at him with sympathy. They would persuade him to cry, saying that crying it out would make him feel better and finally settle everything.

"He's not even here anymore, what's the point of crying?" That was what Xie Lanshan told him back then, and what he told Shen Liufei right now. "I promised myself back then that I will honor him with the rest of my life's glory. As for tears, they can just blend in with the rice and tea we consume—gone when they get digested."

"We're about to return, are you sure you thought everything through?" Shen Liufei reached a hand over to Xie Lanshan's shoulders and turned the man to face him. He cupped Xie Lanshan's face in his hands and caressed his cheeks. His fingers then brushed past the frame of Xie Lanshan's eyes and eyebrows as if to wipe away the invisible tears of sorrow. The artist frowned slightly and reminded the cop, "Even if Han Guangming admitted to his crimes, you still interrogated Gold Tooth. Considering your situation right now, it's very likely that you will face severe consequences when we return—"

"Shh." Before Shen Liufei could finish, Xie Lanshan winked playfully and interrupted with a hush. Then, he grabbed onto Shen Liufei's hand that held the bullet and nudged his face against the palm. He closed his eyes as he felt his lover's cold but soft palm and murmured, "I not only have to carry on his unfinished duty, I also need to bring him justice."

The last few days had been busy in the bureau as the police worked to clean up the last of Guan Nuoqin's criminal organization and free the slaves. Now that he had some time for himself, Xie Lanshan used the last day in Thailand to do some personal investigations and find answers to a long-time question.

He paid Han Guangming a visit in jail and asked if the manager often bought off Hanhai City Vice Branch Chief Liu Yanbo.

Against Xie Lanshan's expectation, Han Guangming shook his head and denied it, saying, "I've only met Chief Liu through a friend during a social mixer and had a couple of meals with him. But from what I understand, he's not that kind of person."

"What?" Xie Lanshan refused to believe a word and said coldly, "You said he isn't that kind of person, but that plum painting you gifted him is still hanging in his living room."

"Oh c'mon, it's not even the real deal. He just likes little fancy things like that, but if I were to actually bring in something worth the original price, he'd insist on paying me back." Han Guangming shook his head and continued, trusting Liu Yanbo's character. "I founded my own company and began doing this sort of cultural business back home. Befriending a cop wasn't just for face; I was also looking for some conveniences in business. There are certainly some celebrities under me that have broken laws before, so I've asked him to help me out a bit in the past. I tried offering at least seven to eight digits to have him cover up for me back then! Even if you were a drug dealer you'd have to be in business for a while to earn this kind of money, but that man got extremely mad at me and rejected my offer. He even almost threatened to cut ties with me! It was only thanks to a mutual friend helping mediate this that we still maintained our relationship."

Xie Lanshan still refused to believe those words and squinted in suspicion. He didn't speak and waited for the man to continue.

"I'm sure you've seen that news about that one kid who's

around Wen Jue's age being caught doing drugs. That's because Chief Liu refused to work with me and insisted on arresting him. He had many friends asking him to handle these sorts of things, but he never once agreed." Han Guangming finished everything off with confidence and said sincerely, "Chief Liu is not that kind of person. I know he's got some flaws, quite a bit of them actually, but he's not someone who would make grave mistakes overall."

Xie Lanshan's expression was still stern as he stared at the manager with sharp eyes. "You're not lying to me, are you?"

"Why would I lie to you?" Han Guangming shook the handcuffs around his wrists and said, "I'm already stuck like this. What good is lying to you?"

Han Guangming's words certainly disappointed Xie Lanshan. No matter how much he tried to study the nuanced changes on the man's face to rip through a lie, he found his efforts to be in vain. Han Guangming was very open about everything—therefore, if Liu Yanbo wasn't a master of disguise, then the man must not be who he thought he was.

And even if the man was not a traitor... Xie Lanshan had always assumed that Chief Liu was the Apostle who betrayed the police and killed his father. On one hand, Liu Yanbo was always at odds with him and refused to promote or give any bonuses despite his efforts. On the other, he knew that Liu Yanbo was engaged in shady businesses behind the bureau. Now, it seemed as if the Chief was simply following Sui Hong's orders to watch over Xie Lanshan, and the man really had nothing wrong with him.

If Liu Yanbo wasn't the Apostle, then the last one remaining in the flaming triangle...

This horrifying thought pained his chest. He didn't want to think about it, but he couldn't stop himself.

Xie Lanshan suddenly recalled a detail that everyone had

missed just before he left. He stopped by the door and turned around to ask the criminal, "Do you remember what Anuchit's actual dying message was the day he was killed? The one on the clock and abacus."

Han Guangming attempted to trace back his memories and said, "I don't remember what the time was on the clock, but the beads... I think it was... 42... 42 19886..."

"4... 2... 42..." Xie Lanshan mumbled those words as quickly searched on the periodic table of elements in his head, attempting to piece together a message or phrase."42 is Mo... 19 is K..."

His face grew pale as his body shivered, then he called out in shock, "Shit!"

His worst nightmare.

Mokorn, the other alias for Mu Kun.

Caged bird expert chemist Anuchit grew a suspicious eye for the man he was working for. Afraid that he would be killed for no reason, he purposely left a message that identified the man who threatened his life. Yet, almost as if the heavens were pranking everyone, a father who came to search for his daughter disrupted the case and removed the last dying message left by the chemist. Then, the drug lord borrowed Xie Lanshan's hand to get rid of Gold Tooth as revenge for betraying his old boss. Mu Kun had the purest red ice on the market in his hands. There was no way he couldn't buy off Guan Nuoqin's subordinates if he wanted to with the profits he could offer.

Even with all this careful planning, the key to success was the involvement of the police forces in both China and Thailand. If the Blue Foxes never joined in, Guan Nuoqin would never have fallen so easily with all the connections this man had with the Thai police. Mu Kun would have never been able to wait in the shadows for his enemy to fall and quickly regain control of this ever-changing climate of the Golden Triangle.

He finally returned to his usual spot. Once again claiming the throne of the Golden Triangle, Mu Kun stood on high ground with his arms out. He lifted his head in silence, embracing his rebirth in a symbolic position.

The man was very handsome, so much that even the scar on his face only added a unique flavor to his looks rather than make him look ugly. His fake eye was still red, as if he purposely left this burning mad love and rage engraved on his body.

Tang Qinglan said to him, "That little Captain Chi is quite useful, but he seems to think he's just undercover."

Mu Kun didn't respond to this woman. The swift winds around him sounded like a hymn of the heavens. He waved his hands out as if he was a conductor of the night, joyfully leading this orchestra of nature.

"I've also heard that Xie Lanshan isn't Xie Lanshan anymore—"

"Shut up! You really believe in that nonsense?" Mu Kun stopped, his good mood ruined at that instant. He turned and interrupted Tang Qinglan venomously. He certainly didn't believe in those rumors, nor did he dare to. "Only I can kill him; he promised me he will live on until the day I return to him."

The Golden Triangle was a place of mystery in the dark. His gaze once again turned toward the direction of China in the distance.

"Has the wait been long?" He stared at the man he could only see in the void. Mu Kun lifted a wide but affectionate smile as he said, "I'm coming for you for real this time, Xie Lanshan."

Hello, My Dear

After the annihilation of Guan Nuoqin's massive stowaway organization, the Thai police discovered a mass grave while rescuing the hostages and slaves near the border between Thailand and Myanmar.

The area was rural, near the point of interaction between the forest and river, between a village and farmland. It was like a rare otherworldly emerald, tranquil and peaceful, that the outside world would normally not disturb. Yet after days and nights of digging, the police unearthed skeleton after skeleton, exposing the ugly truth.

The initial autopsy identified that most of these corpses were female. At least hundreds of them were found in this area. From the ID cards and other items left inside to identify the corpses, there were countless Chinese women that were buried as well.

The police determined that these young women were likely kidnapped and sold into prostitution, then killed if they were caught attempting to escape or found ill during transport. The evil practice continued until it left these disposed bodies to become bones in the ground.

The Blue Fox members had just left Thailand on the last flight. Somsak didn't dare to delay this discovery and immediately contacted Xie Lanshan and Shen Liufei.

This was supposed to be the last night in Thailand for them. The two were enjoying their rare time of peace together after the case was settled, only to be disturbed by a phone call from Somsak.

The two men fell silent as soon as the line hung up.

Shen Liufei was silent because he immediately thought of his mother, followed by his suspicion that perhaps she was also buried among these hundreds of female corpses. He had been very interested in female kidnapping cases over the years. His laptop contained countless solved and cold cases; Zhuo Tian's case was merely one of many.

Out of a strange and unexplainable intuition connected by familial bonds, he always stubbornly believed that his mother actually survived that massacre and was still living in this world. Or perhaps she died somewhere without anyone knowing.

Xie Lanshan's silence was also a reflexive reaction. He could understand what Shen Liufei was thinking, but because he was still using Ye Shen's body, he couldn't speak up. Rather, it was an almost cruel and awkward position for him.

Xie Lanshan finally broke this long silence and asked, "You plan on staying to investigate, right?"

Shen Liufei was used to hiding all his emotions behind his stony face, but now he found it difficult to cover himself up in front of his lover. His expression remained empty, but the worry deep in his eyes was clear. He nodded slightly and said, "But you need to go back."

Xie Lanshan certainly had to return. He knew that his interrogation this time would need to be addressed properly back home. The Municipal Bureau was calling him, the provincial branch was also summoning him. Phone calls and messages after one another were like spells sent from abroad to drag him back home. History books said Yue Fei died in a temple of thorns, a corpse shoved into the corner of a wall. He didn't think he would face the same tragic death as the famed military general, but these endless phone calls certainly weren't a good omen.

And no matter what, he was still a cop; a cop must follow orders given to him and fulfill his duty. In addition, that bit of suspicion stuck inside him was ready to explode. He needed to ask Tao Jun what the truth was.

The separation came as soon as they were reunited. Xie Lanshan was a bit upset. He lowered his head and pressed his forehead against that of Shen Liufei's, then laughed nonchalantly. "It's almost like we're always saying goodbye to each other."

"People constantly say that cops are always spending more time away from instead of with family. This may be the case from an outsider's point of view, but for us who share the same burden on our shoulders," Shen Liufei said as he lifted his head a little, pressing the tips of their noses together. He closed his eyes slightly and drowned himself in this moment of intimacy, then whispered, "Every temporary separation we face to discover the truth is proof of our bond—'til death do us apart."

"You're right, we do share the same burden." Xie Lanshan chuckled at these words; it was sincere and kind, but also filled with enough affection to brush the mist in Xie Lanshan's heart away. He said, "But you're not a cop, at most you're just a cop's wife."

As soon as this thought arose, Xie Lanshan pressed forward and closed their distance with a kiss.

Shen Liufei answered those desires. Almost as soon as their lips touched, he stuck a tongue into Xie Lanshan's mouth, invading the latter like a predator consuming his prey. The two deepened the kiss until it was engraved onto each other's soul.

Shen Liufei didn't want to part with Xie Lanshan at a time like this; aside from his own desires, he worried that Xie Lanshan would have a difficult time facing the complex situation back home. With that worry in mind, Shen Liufei pressed Xie Lanshan down onto the bed of the hotel and began unzipping the latter's pants, promising, "Give me ten days, ten days at most, I will come back for you before the end of the month."

Somsak thought that all members of the Blue Fox had ady left, but Chi Jin and Ling Yun didn't actually go to the airport. Including temporary captain Chi Jin, the Blue Fox sent in a total of four members for this operation. The other two had a different departure time and left for the airport first.

Already delayed on the way to the airport, Chi Jin received a phone call that shook him up. He lowered his voice and said something in secret to the person on the other side of the line, then quickly hung up.

Halfway to the airport, Chi Jin suddenly asked to get out of the car. He told Ling Yun to go back first because he had some personal business to take care of.

Of course, Ling Yun wouldn't believe any of this. He complained in his head, *you and I got on the same plane to Thailand for work, even taking up a subquest while we're at it, and now you're trying to say you have personal business?* The suspicion in his mind grew as odd signs piled up around him. The young officer was now determined to get down to the bottom of this abnormality. After the car had driven far enough and out of Chi Jin's sight, Ling Yun asked the driver to turn around and quietly follow the cab that Chi Jin had just called.

They were already in a rush to the airport before this episode, so now they would certainly miss their flight. Their comrades back home had been sending them messages these past few days, complaining they needed to return so they could celebrate a closed case. But they all knew it was just another excuse to party among young people. Turning halfway, Ling Yun took out the phone from his pocket and saw another message asking him to come back home soon. The young man who sent this message was Tu Lang, a renowned "sharpshooter" on the team. He was quite a handsome lad, tall with slightly tanned skin. However, due to spending all day at the shooting range for training and hugging his face to the scope when practicing ranged targets, his face slowly formed around the shape of the gun these last few years.

Tu Lang was even more at odds with Chi Jin normally, so he wouldn't personally send a message to their temporary captain and instead bombarded Ling Yun's inbox with messages —mostly about games. The last message Ling Yun received said: *What time you arriving tonight? Man, my luck's been shit lately, waiting for you to get back so we can get our revenge!*

Ling Yun clenched his phone tightly. After some hesitation, he responded: There might be a traitor in our team. I'm checking up on him right now. Don't ask questions or make a scene, wait for my message.

Tu Lang might be a young man who liked to party, but he quickly realized the importance of this response and quieted down with the messages.

The driver was quite impressive, maintaining the perfect distance with the car they were trailing without alerting Chi Jin. Though maybe Chi Jin's mind wasn't on the job—he'd often drifted off at work lately.

The sky grew dark while the car continued to drive through unfamiliar and rounding roads. They passed through the busy city streets until they headed toward a deserted and rural area. The driver spoke Chinese, quite well even, but didn't know the tall and handsome young man he was driving was a special forces officer. He kindly warned the young man that the area they were heading toward was quite dangerous, that tourists like him should be careful.

"Don't worry, thanks for your concern." Ling Yun thanked the driver and looked out the window. His gaze fell to a distance.

They were certainly going further and further away from the city. The tall mountains were visible above them, shimmering golden under the foggy weather of dusk. The shape of the mountain was almost cute. Because it was a tea leaf farm, the plants were divided up cleanly like quilts from afar.

But Ling Yun's heart was racing, his frowning eyebrows still pressed tightly together.

The car drove for another ten minutes, and night finally fell. The sky was dark. Ling Yun saw Chi Jin's car stop. The latter got out of the car and walked alone toward a solitary house at the end of the mountain road.

(ii)

Night fell like a giant anvil weighing on one's shoulder, but also provided the best disguise for the lurker. Ling Yun was slightly shorter and thinner than Chi Jin, but he was much more dexterous. He carefully hid himself outside the house, unsure if he would be found out.

It was a cleanly decorated house with minimal furnishings that looked nothing like a place a female drug dealer would live. There was a man and woman inside; the man stood while the woman sat. Above them was a warm light that cast an elegant glow on their faces.

Using the dim light inside, Ling Yun clearly saw the two e-cigarettes and bag of red ice on the coffee table and felt his heart constrict.

"You helped me a lot. I'm the only one in charge of the red ice business here now that Guan Nuoqin is dead." Tang Qinglan said with a pretty smile, her voice the sound of a siren. She took an e-cigarette and placed it in her mouth. She took in a breath, then leaned in toward Chi Jin and blew a cloud of white smoke through her red lips.

"Then why did you say those threatening words to me if I helped you over the phone? Do we not even have that bit of trust between us now?" Guan Nuoqin was an evil drug dealer and human trafficker, so staying behind to clean up the nest of demons with the Thai police was a natural act as his duty. His thoughts were justified, but the smoky red ice on his face made Chi Jin uncomfortable. He loosened his collar a little and held in the urge to look at the other cigarette on the table.

Tang Qinglan seemed to notice the man's discomfort and continued to blow out smoke, pushing the young man another step down toward the abyss.

Ling Yun recognized this woman—she seemed to be a famous business owner in Hanhai City. There were rumors about her being involved in black market antique sales, but no evidence had been found. Though now it seemed like she was involved in an even more dangerous trade than antiques.

"Give me this bag of red ice. I'm leaving if you have nothing else to say. I'll notify you ahead of time if there're any moves within the team." Chi Jin wanted to act like an addicted officer who had no choice but to bow down to the drug dealers. He was convinced he already gained the woman's trust.

"Why not have a taste now?" Tang Qinglan handed him the

other e-cigarette on the table and once again blew out a cloud of smoke. She then gave this young captain a small smile and said, "There's a bit of number 4 and ya ba mixed in this, a really unique blend that will give you an unforgettable experience."

Meth was nothing like heroin and had almost immediate addictive qualities. Meth users were often irritable and easily angered, and something as pure as 99.9% red ice was even more dangerous. Just like how, a few months ago, a high school girl who was taking "beauty pills" had bitten off a classmate's ear. Chi Jin was already doing his best to maintain his cool. Ever since being interrupted by Ling Yun by accident last time, he started forcing himself to keep his mind off the drug. Yet at a time and place like this, he was nearly on the verge of a break-down already.

The vein on his forehead popped, cold sweat rolled down his face. His body twitched, and that handsome face scrunched up in anger. This was a biological reaction of an episode. Ling Yun could tell with one glance.

"You can leave now or take a sip." Tang Qinglan didn't force the man to take drugs. She smiled at him, but beneath those pretty eyes was all the evilness in the world.

Recalling the mood swings and attitude changes he'd noticed over the past few days and the meth bottle that was hidden in the hotel room, Ling Yun's heart sank. Yet, he still forced himself to observe his colleague's actions. He tried to convince himself that this was just a special undercover mission Chi Jin was on.

But the latter's reaction was disappointing. Chi Jin walked up to the woman on his own, took the e-cigarette from the woman with a shaking hand, and was about to place it into his mouth.

Overdosing occurred when a mixture of drugs was taken in the body without prescription. This was digging one's grave for anyone who never had experienced drug intake before. After witnessing the last veil of shame stripped down, Ling Yun's heart pained as he watched in shock. Seeing Chi Jin was about to sacrifice his own well-being to take the drug, he barged inside the house without hesitation, gun in hand.

"Put that thing down!" Ling Yun's eyes and gunpoint were fixed on Tang Qinglan, but those words were for Chi Jin.

"Ling Yun, don't worry about me." Chi Jin didn't realize Ling Yun had trailed him and went into a panic as soon as the young man barged in. That pain caused by drug addiction grew stronger by the second. It felt as if hundreds and thousands of worms were crawling beneath his skin and biting into his bones. Chi Jin held the urge to explode in rage and ordered his teammate with the authority of the Captain, "Get out!"

"This isn't an undercover mission. You're willingly falling down the abyss!" Ling Yun's heart shattered as he heard the man shout, yet still clung tightly onto the e-cigarette. "If Captain were to see you like this—"

"Don't..." That one word completely broke Chi Jin. He no longer cared if he still needed to keep up the act to investigate and begged in despair, "D-don't tell Captain..."

"I'm going to tell him, I'll do that as soon as I get back." The drug dealer before him was only a woman, and he still had a gun in hand. Ling Yun was confident that he could escape safely with Chi Jin, so his attention was only focused on her in case she was ready to fight back.

Rage overtook his mind in that instant. Chi Jin pulled out his gun and hit the young man on the head from behind.

Members of the Blue Fox would never suspect their team-mates; countless times working in dangerous situations had made them grow used to leaving their backs exposed to each other. Ling Yun didn't think Chi Jin would actually attack him and fell to the ground with shock written on his face. The sharp pain in his head made him unable to stand for a moment.

The moment Ling Yun fell to the ground, Tang Qinglan quickly pulled out a gun hidden beneath the coffee table and pointed it directly toward Chi Jin.

"Toss the gun over."

Chi Jin was also shocked at his own actions. Now that he was nothing but a helpless prey in the hands of his enemy, he could only do as the other ordered.

A door that had been hidden in the shadows slowly opened. Both Chi Jin and Ling Yun did not know there was another person inside this house. His sudden appearance was like a bloodthirsty beast hidden in the dark, finally ready to step out and expose its fangs at its prey.

They both recognized the man.

It was Mu Kun, who had disappeared near the Mekong river three years ago.

Ling Yun wanted to crawl up and take the gun he dropped, but Mu Kun was a step ahead and kicked the gun toward Tang Qinglan. The woman picked the gun up swiftly and confiscated the guns of both Blue Fox members.

Mu Kun walked toward Ling Yun with a gun and shot multiple rounds at Ling Yun's limbs without hesitation. The young cop didn't even have time to cry out when four bullets pierced right through his flesh and bones. Aside from Xie Lanshan, the drug lord despised all members of the Blue Fox and found pleasure in torturing them like a cat playing with a dying rat.

Chi Jin didn't know the situation would become like this and growled in anger. But Tang Qinglan reacted swiftly and fired a round near the young man, reminding Chi Jin to stay put.

"Don't move." Tang Qinglan turned her gunpoint back at Chi Jin.

Up until the point Mu Kun appeared, Chi Jin still believed he was in an act to hide his identity as an undercover officer, that all of his actions were sacrifices that were made to earn the trust of his enemies. Yet now, he wasn't sure who was the hunter and who was the prey.

"Do you still not understand?" The woman didn't want to kill two members of the Blue Fox at a time like this, knowing that she could still use this young man in front of her. She eyed the direction of a cabinet and hinted that this room had more traps than Chi Jin thought, and then said, "Your comrade died because of you, you can never return to the Blue Foxes."

Mu Kun wasn't in a rush to take revenge from the events of three years ago and didn't plan on killing this Blue Fox boy. He squatted down by Ling Yun and searched his pockets, checking to see if there was anything he could use.

Soon, he found a cellphone.

The phone was finger-print locked. Mu Kun attempted to use Ling Yun's hand to unlock the device. Ling Yun knew what the drug lord's plan was. Afraid that the information on his phone would put his comrades' lives in danger, he clenched his fists tightly.

Of course, this kind of rebellious act was useless and almost laughable.

"You Blue Fox members sure are quite stubborn." Mu Kun laughed. He pulled out a knife with intricate carvings from his waist, forced open Ling Yun's index finger, and cut it off with one swift motion.

He unlocked the device with the bloodied finger.

He soon noticed the conversation between Ling Yun and Tu Lang; the last message worked just perfectly for him. An eerie smile bloomed on his face. The man responded in fluent Chinese with five simple words:

Xie Lanshan is the traitor.

Before a response could be received, Mu Kun turned off the bloodied phone and tossed it aside.

The violent and loud sound of the phone clashing with the wall roared like raging thunder of revenge.

Finally, everything was heading in the direction he had planned.

(iii)

Despite preparing himself for the worst, Xie Lanshan could never have imagined how dramatically the world had turned around as soon as he returned from Thailand.

Starting with one message from Kang Tai that angered Director Peng, in addition to Liu Mingfang's purposeful spread of the news, the entire Municipal Bureau was made aware of the horrifying brain surgery.

After a report from sharpshooter Tu Lang, Ling Yun completely lost contact as soon as he sent out the important message about the traitor.

They questioned Xie Lanshan for three whole nights without rest. They told him it wasn't an official questioning and simply an internal chat, but the intensity was already on a par with going into court. All leaders in the bureau, including Liu Yanbo, joined in the questioning.

They shone bright light into his eyes and questioned him like a criminal suspect, asking the same two questions over and over: Why did he torture Gold Tooth so violently? And where did Ling Yun go?

Xie Lanshan wanted to laugh; he started off by answering them truthfully until he finally decided to just keep silent.

These bosses and leaders had mindfully avoided mentioning the surgery because the provincial department had made no official statements, and nobody had experienced dealing with such a ridiculous case. The ship of Theseus was an eternal philosophical question, but who was this Xie Lanshan sitting before them right now? Nobody could give a confident answer.

Because the higher-ups were tired of the endless questioning, another round that lasted until midnight finally ended. Xie Lanshan walked out of the Municipal Bureau's questioning room.

There was still light in the violent crimes unit office. Xie Lanshan walked toward it like a firefly chasing after that sole dim light in the dark.

Ding Li was brewing coffee and playing with her phone in front of the coffee maker. Most female workers didn't normally need to stay the night for overtime, but she was watching a drama in the coffee room without paying much attention to time. She knew her bosses had been coming over lately to question Xie Lanshan and left late. Afraid they would catch her and ask why she was staying in the bureau so late into the night, she had to do everything discreetly with the lights off.

Ding Li kept the cellphone on her arm while ripping open a pack of instant coffee for herself, humming the theme song of a popular movie.

Her body moved to the beat as she sang. Ding Li didn't have musical senses but was strong in language. She had only heard the Cantonese song a few times but could already sing the lyrics fluently. Consumed in her own little world with her off-tune singing, she was completely oblivious to the man walking toward her in the darkness.

"I trudged through the roads, I live and I die..."

She poured the powdered instant coffee into the coffee cup.

Ding Li was about to pour in the hot water when she turned her head unconsciously and saw someone already right in front of her. She jolted in shock; the phone resting in her arms dropped.

Xie Lanshan reacted quickly and leaned down to catch the phone in his hands.

He stood back up and wanted to return the phone to Ding Li, yet the latter frantically took a step back as soon as she saw who it was and shrieked.

This back-end employee already knew that the person in front of her wasn't her senior in the department, but a heartless murderer. This man not only massacred an entire family, he even ripped parts of the skins off the two female victims afterward.

Xiao Liang was the one on shift today and rushed to the coffee room as soon as he heard Ding Li's cries, then turned on the lights. His footsteps also visibly stopped as soon as he saw Xie Lanshan, expression complicated.

They were all staring at him. Xie Lanshan could clearly see the distance, fear, or even hatred in their eyes. This wasn't the kind of gaze anyone should give to their comrade nor any average person.

It had been three days since he returned, but he rarely had the chance to see his colleagues. Every once in a while, he would pass by someone in the bureau, but the people would hurry away as if to avoid him at all costs.

No words were necessary. He could tell from those eyes that his secret had been exposed. Now he was just a story and laughingstock in front of everyone.

The attitudes his juniors gave him hurt Xie Lanshan deeply. His eyes reddened in anger, but they were too dry to let down a single tear. Instead, he gave out a self-mocking laugh from his similarly dried throat.

It really was funny. He laughed at how he devoted everything he had to his duty and belief, but these people shoved him into the body of a monster without his consent. After they used him to the end like a tool, they all turned and looked at him in disgust as they begged him to die—

Once again.

It was the same. Amongst the most unbearable sea of pain, Avici was the worst of them all.

Xie Lanshan once thought that his days beside Mu Kun were the epitome of all suffering, only to discover that an even more horrifying fate would later turn him into a monster just like Mu Kun.

After a stiff and awkward silence, Xiao Liang attempted to ease up the atmosphere. He tried to fix his expression and said, "Senior Xie, we all believe you. You aren't the one who betrayed his teammate."

Unfortunately, it was too fake.

These kinds of fabricated lies were even more hurtful than blatant fear and crushed the last bit of his senses. Xie Lanshan's eyes dimmed as he walked out of the office with his head down.

Yet before he could fully step out, he turned back and stood in front of the two juniors.

Ding Li and Xiao Liang both stared in shock, eyes wide. They weren't sure if the lights were too old, but the Municipal Bureau's lights would often flash as if they were unstable. This handsome face became ghastly under the flickering lights. Within seconds, the juniors noticed that this man was no longer the Senior Xie they once knew.

"Why is it that everything I do is wrong?! Why do you all never believe in me?!" The angry questions ripped out of his vocal cords until they finally became the most tragic and desperate plea. He begged in tears, "Please... Please don't look at me like I'm a monster..."

. . .

The elites of the Blue Foxes were organized and efficient. They may have the authority of a quasi-military division, but their size was only that of a small commando. Including Captain Sui Hong, their members only totaled 22 people. Now that Ling Yun was missing, Director Peng gave Sui Hong permission to return to his post.

Clouds of conspiracy haunted the provincial department. Every member of the Blue Fox walked into work with a heavy face. The only good news amongst everything was the return of their captain. Without delay, Sui Hong quickly summoned the 20 members for a general meeting. His first question was directed to Chi Jin, "Wasn't Ling Yun supposed to return with you?"

It was too late for Chi Jin to regret his actions now. Out of self-defense and fear of disappointing Sui Hong, he had no choice but to run with the mill and dump all problems onto Xie Lanshan. He collected himself and attempted to explain, "We parted before we went to the airport. He told me that there was something he needed to investigate; I asked him about the details, but he said he wasn't sure right now, and that I should keep quiet and don't ask—"

Tu Lang interrupted on the side, "A'Ling and I were chatting about games just before he went missing, and that's also what he told me."

Sui Hong frowned slightly; Ling Yun was the youngest of the team, but he would never act out of line on the clock. If there was something that could make him hesitate to speak up about, it must be something of immense weight, and the person he wanted to investigate would be someone so close to him that he didn't dare to question directly. And how could this person be Xie Lanshan, a man he wasn't even close with?

Noticing Sui Hong's suspicion, Chi Jin felt his heart thump. But he remained calm on the surface and asked, "Captain, do you still not believe Xie Lanshan is the traitor?"

Sui Hong certainly didn't believe it and only coughed. "A'Lan... isn't that kind of person."

There was no point in hiding now, and Xie Lanshan's identity was the weakest spot on the man. Chi Jin raised his voice and said, "But he's no longer Xie Lanshan! He's a wolf disguised as a sheep, a monster that was injected with the memories of a special forces agent. His mental state is extremely unstable right now and at the brink of losing control!"

Sui Hong knew that Chi Jin had always been at odds with Xie Lanshan, so he turned to ask the other two members who joined the Thailand operation for opinions, "Tell me what Xie Lanshan has done while he was in Thailand."

One member answered truthfully, "He refused to act with us and instead spent time in clubs hanging out with prostitutes. The entire street's sex workers were well-acquainted with him by the time he left."

Another member followed up, "Even though Gold Tooth's killer was later determined to be Han Guangming, the victim suffered inhumane torture prior to death. There were countless bones on his body that were broken, his organs were damaged, his face deformed, even his chin was dislocated."

These words were all true. Gold Tooth's autopsy report and photos of his body were sent to the provincial branch by Kang Tai, and Xie Lanshan himself admitted to these violent acts.

Tu Lang was a veteran of the team and was even a friend of Xie Lanshan for a brief time. He said, "Cap'n, you're always defending Xie Lanshan and saying that he's always one of us. But I still don't see that. There's no trace of the Blue Fox spirit in him."

Sui Hong fell into silence. After a long while, he finally

coughed and said, "It's not that I'm biased toward Xie Lanshan, but the situation right now is that Ling is missing, and his cellphone might have fallen into the hands of the enemy. There's no guarantee that the last message he sent to us was from him. Is there any news from Thailand?"

Another team member spoke up, "The local police have been very cooperative and sent out an arrest order and began searching for clues, but there are no updates yet."

Tu Lang added, "According to our spies, Mu Kun is back. If Mu Kun's the one behind all of this, I'm afraid Ling is..."

"There's no 'I'm afraid' here," Sui Hong said firmly.

"But what if—" Chi Jin's heart skipped another beat as he carefully started to question further.

"There's no 'what if' either." Sui Hong gave another cough, but his eyes and tone of voice were filled with determination. Like his usual charismatic leadership character, he said, "The Blue Fox will never give up on any of its comrades. We will grab onto any last bit of hope to save each and every one of our members!"

"Then Xie Lanshan..." Chi Jin's heart ached for his captain's sickly body and regretted his actions. Yet he knew that at this point, one had to die between him and Xie Lanshan. He could only hold himself in and say to Sui Hong, "Director Peng is already very upset with Xie Lanshan, and the Municipal Bureau only questioned him without any other cautionary measures. Vice Chief Liu has been asking us what they should do about Xie Lanshan."

The meeting room was dead silent. It was bright inside the room, but there was a shadow cast on everyone's face. All twenty young Blue Fox officers sat stiffly, waiting for an order from their captain.

Bam—! A massive thump came after the meeting door was slammed open.

"Captain Sui, I didn't let you back into the team for you to hesitate during a critical time like this." Director Peng walked in, eyes sharp and expression grave. "I've heard everything you all said earlier."

Clearly, he no longer believed that this man who carried Xie Lanshan's memories was still Xie Lanshan himself. He gave a loud and firm order to the entire team like a large bronze gong. "We cannot let a criminal on death row like Ye Shen continue freely under the law. We must immediately arrest him and return him to where he belongs!"

"Director Peng..." Sui Hong attempted to argue for his most trusted ex-subordinate. But he couldn't bring himself to speak those words and swallowed it all with the bitter taste of hesitation. Even he wasn't sure if that man was still Xie Lanshan or not.

"But..." Chi Jin's lips trembled as he finally spoke his concern aloud, "Ye Shen now has the body of a special forces agent, I'm afraid capturing him won't be that easy."

"Aren't you all elite forces here too? You're telling me even with all of you here you can't bring one man back?" Director Peng interrupted Chi Jin's words and turned his gaze to Sui Hong, then ordered harshly, "Ensuring the safety of our citizens is the most important part of our job. We shouldn't let personal feelings cloud our judgment. Ye Shen is a dangerous criminal who threatens the peace of our society. If he refuses to comply with police orders, shoot him down on the spot!"

(iv)

Grayscale value in digital imaging is a concept that represents different shades of an image in pixel value, with pure black being the basis of an image.

o% value is white while 100% is black; most objects in

nature had an average grayscale value of around 18%. Yet now, Xie Lanshan was aware that he was growing increasingly closer to 100% black.

He returned home from the Municipal Bureau and once again buried himself in the tub as he stared at the ceiling of his bathroom. The sensitive kittens all surrounded him and called out to the man. The little girl in the neighborhood certainly took good care of the cats. He could tell from the weight they gained while he was gone.

Xie Lanshan's gaze was hollow. He stared blankly at the ceiling above until the lights suddenly flickered. The bright ceiling transformed from a bright place to a dangerous, mired land that made the bathroom look almost otherworldly for a moment. Xie Lanshan sank into the water until his face was completely inside the tub. He held in his breath and felt the demons in the dark arise. The demon leaned closer to him with his terrifying face until it possessed him—Xie Lanshan was unable to struggle and move away.

The moment before he was about to drown himself, Xie Lanshan heard his phone ring.

He quickly escaped the deadly voice and stepped out of the bathtub, then wrapped a towel around his waist and rushed out to the living room while he was still wet.

Of course, it was Shen Liufei.

It almost seemed as if the only two reasons why he still lingered in the mortal world and hadn't fallen into hell were his father and Shen Liufei.

The latter asked through the phone, "I heard about Ling Yun going missing in Thailand today. Are you alright over there?"

The man's voice was cold and bland as usual, but Xie Lanshan could make out the concern through those words and smiled.

"I'm fine, just a lot of lecturing. You know how complicated those processes in public security are; I'm questioned almost every day. It's all the same questions. I swear my ears are going to rot." Xie Lanshan didn't want Shen Liufei to worry about him and wiped away his insecurity, then asked, "How's it going over there?"

"Nothing new as of now." There were hundreds of corpses. It would be impossible to immediately identify every one of them. Shen Liufei had found nothing related to his mother. After some thought, he asked again, "Are you sure you're alright?"

"I'm fine. I'm not wearing clothes right now. Picture that; how about a round of phone sex?" Xie Lanshan was only half-joking. He was exhausted, but he didn't want his lover to hang up so quickly.

"You sound very tired." Shen Liufei didn't respond to that response and only said, "I won't hang up the phone. I'll stay here with you until you sleep."

Xie Lanshan chuckled and didn't follow up with his shameless request. Instead, he placed the phone beside his pillow in the bedroom.

The night was silent. He could hear the sounds of Shen Liufei typing on the keyboard and that gentle breathing from the other side. There was no need for words; he knew his lover was always there for him. In a trance at the peak of fatigue, Xie Lanshan finally felt as if he struggled out of the swamp to breathe in fresh air. He closed his eyes, let his head sink into the soft cotton pillow, and fell into slumber.

The next day Xie Lanshan didn't return to the Municipal Bureau, calling Tao Jun instead. He didn't feel the need to report to the office every day since he was still on suspension; if they didn't send an arrest warrant, there was no need to clock in.

Xie Lanshan also had a strange feeling that he didn't have much time left, and if he couldn't get an answer now, he would forever be left in the dark.

It was almost old Xie's death anniversary, so he could use it as an excuse to clean up his father's items left in Tao Jun's house. Tao Longyue moved out to his own nest after marriage, so old Tao was the only one left in the house. The place was quiet and clean, perfect for a private conversation.

Tao Jun's body had been weak since the surgery and he didn't return to the bureau. Tao Longyue was afraid of shocking his old father and didn't tell him about Xie Lanshan's surgery. Therefore, Tao Jun was still oblivious to everything and smiled when he saw Xie Lanshan, assuming the young man was just being too rash in Thailand and made a minor mistake.

"Why did you suddenly remember to come take back your dad's stuff?" Tao Jun leaned down beneath the yellow light to search for items old Xie left him inside the attic. The cardboard boxes were all taped up, so Tao Jun took a knife to cut them open.

There weren't many important items kept in these boxes, and Xie Lanshan was the one who said to leave everything here in the past.

"My old man's death anniversary is coming up." Xie Lanshan placed a cigarette into his mouth after he answered and blew out a small cloud of mint-scented smoke.

"Don't talk while you're smoking like that!" Tao Jun turned around upon smelling the smoke behind him and scolded. What was ironic was that this old Captain Tao was a brute and rough man who also raised a simple-minded young Captain Tao, but he was always much stricter in mentoring Xie Lanshan. He wanted the young man to inherit old Xie's honesty and charisma, becoming a cunning but powerful man

417

who could fight against all drug dealers with just words and not violence.

Xie Lanshan listened to him and placed the cigarette into the ashtray on the side, still looking at Tao Jun with a difficult face.

The man looked much older after his illness. Beneath the dimmed light, Tao Jun's face looked as if it had been baked until every last bit of water was drained out, wrinkles visible on his skin.

The man had aged; the bleak loss of heroic light had fallen from his face. For a second, Xie Lanshan's heart stung as he thought: *this man who raised me until adulthood really is old now.*

He knew how well Tao Jun had treated him over these years.

The white smoke floated in the air like a mist of memories that became visible.

"Ah, right, it's almost old Xie's death anniversary..." Tao Jun pulled out two old police uniforms and pressed a hand on his old waist. He mumbled, "It's been so many years now..."

The uniform back then was still the plain dark green '89 style. Two strips of golden lining decorated the sleeves, complementing the gold lapel pin proudly. Xie Lanshan could imagine his father wearing this uniform; how handsome he would be if he was just a little younger, being the center of attention in town among women. He was often asked to help out with certain things and never turned anyone down, which would upset his mother all the time.

"I ran into Mu Kun again in Thailand." Xie Lanshan's heart stung with those memories. Hints of malice flashed within his eyes as he said, "He was the one who sent me a message for me to follow clues to find Gold Tooth."

Tao Jun's expression grew grave at that instant as he turned and scolded, "Why are you still hanging around Mu Kun?!"

Xie Lanshan paused for a few seconds as he met the old man's gaze and smiled darkly.

"Because Mu Kun told me that he already found out who the Apostle was a while back in Hanhai." He noticed that Tao Jun's expression changed as soon as mentioned the word Apostle and took a step forward, then said coldly, "He said that the Apostle was one of the flaming triangles of the past."

(v)

While Xie Lanshan was visiting old Captain Tao, the young Captain Tao in the Municipal Bureau received an arrest order for Xie Lanshan from the provincial branch that allowed the police to kill the criminal if he refused to comply.

This was an operation that required the cops to carry guns. The Municipal Bureau separated the management of guns and ammo, so the violent crimes unit needed to take guns from the weapons storage.

Xiao Liang and Tao Longyue rushed to get their guns together, complaining in their heads along the way. Xiao Liang was hired by the Municipal Bureau upon graduation and transferred to the violent crimes unit because of his outstanding performance. Even though the cases he had been dealing with in this department were crimes such as murder and drug dealing, they rarely ever needed to use guns. The last time he held one was many months ago when they were chasing down Qiao Hui, only because they were facing a dangerous serial murderer. So, until he finally touched a gun, he was in disbelief that the operation required all officers to carry this weapon. He was taken aback and asked Tao Longyue, "Captain Tao, what's going on? Weren't we just going to bring senior Xie back for questioning? Why do we need to carry guns?"

"You think I want to carry one?" Tao Longyue's expression was grave, as if a layer of paint was brushed on his face. "The higher-ups said we're warning him if he refuses the arrest, and if the warning doesn't work, we'll have to shoot him down."

"Huh? Sh-shoot him down? But he's not... not entirely that murderer." Xiao Liang was shocked. According to the law, if a high-profile criminal on death row refused arrest after escaping prison, officers were allowed to execute the criminal on the spot. But this was a comrade they had worked with for three years. Even though Xiao Liang still had mixed feelings facing Xie Lanshan right now, he refused to see his senior colleague die before his eyes.

As if complaining that Xiao Liang was annoying, Tao Longyue frowned without another word. Instead, he focused on filling his ammo with a stern face. The standard police guns were the QSZ-92, which looked much more aesthetic than the old 52 pistol. It had a louder sound with more powerful bullets, very fit for front-line public security officers. Tao Longyue still remembered the excitement he had when he first upgraded his gun. A hero deserved a suitable weapon that they could use well.

Yet he would never have thought he would one day be pointing this gun at his best friend, Xie Lanshan.

Inside the attic of the old Tao residence, the dim yellow light showered down like thin rain. Both men stood beneath this shower, gaze foggy and hearts heavy.

The old cop stood up straight and looked at this boy he raised. He noticed the boy was now a man, handsome and strong, those sharp features and gaze filled with strength.

Tao Jun let out a sigh and took a step forward to Xie Lanshan, then nodded, "I knew you were going to ask me one day."

Is he confessing? Xie Lanshan was shocked, prepared for the man to deny everything. His heart was stinging in pain, but because he had the suspicion already, he held himself up. Xie Lanshan asked, "So you're the Apostle?"

Tao Jun shook his head; those old eyes were filled with sincerity as he said, "No I'm not."

Xie Lanshan squinted in disbelief, then asked, "So it's Liu Yanbo?"

Tao Jun shook his head again. "It wasn't old Liu either."

"Then who else could it be?" Xie Lanshan didn't realize until a while later and said in shock, stuttering, "You... you're saying... it was my dad?"

Tao Jun gave another long sigh and admitted, "Old Xie was the Apostle, and I was the one who shot him from behind back then."

"You're lying! " Xie Lanshan couldn't believe this and trembled violently. His face twisted as he attempted to reject everything, growling from his throat. "No way... there's no way my dad could be the Apostle!"

"When old Liu and I discovered old Xie was the Apostle, old Liu picked a fight with him. The situation was dire, so I fired a gun from behind and killed old Xie." Tao Jun's expression was heartbroken. He shook his head and said, "That was a brother we'd been through life and death with, so neither of us wanted his heroic deeds to be crushed overnight and carry the name of a traitor even after death. We also didn't want to upset your mother or let you lose your faith and idol, that's why we hid the truth and said he died in the line of duty while on an operation."

Xie Lanshan didn't speak; he stood frozen without even

blinking. His soul had left his body, leaving only his empty flesh.

"Director Peng knows about this, too. We turned in proof to him when we returned. If you don't believe me, you can ask him." Tao Jun added, "I've always been regretful for shooting down your father because he was once my best friend... your mother also went mad because of his death, so I've carried this pressure for a long time. I ended up getting into a car crash during a mission later and then dropped out from the frontlines."

Was this what Zhu Mingwu meant when he said this man would do something regretful that harmed both himself and the people around him?

"You're lying... you're lying... my dad always taught me to be a good person, a good cop. He wouldn't... he couldn't possibly be the Apostle..." At that moment, his faith finally shattered. Xie Lanshan still stood before this man, but he knew that as soon as he moved, he would crumble into dust. He shook his head mechanically and mumbled, "You're insulting him because he's dead, spilling lies and putting all the blame on him."

For a moment, that horrifying headache once again acted up. He trembled violently and began seeing hallucinations; shadows blurred before his eyes and sharp noises pierced his ears. Xie Lanshan's hands pressed tightly onto his head that was about to explode. He howled violently from the depths of his lungs; the cry that came out of his throat was violent, desperate, and almost inhuman.

He then picked up the knife resting on the short cabinet, shoved Tao Jun to the wall, and pressed the knife against the old man's throat. His eyes were bloodshot, expression horrible as he desperately tried to fight back, "Tell me you're lying! Tell me that my dad's a good person!"

Tao Longyue took his men and rushed up to the attic. The scene before his eyes stunned him as he fired a warning shot. After the explosive sound, he howled, "Xie Lanshan, put the knife down!"

"You have no idea what happened... your dad's a dirty liar." Xie Lanshan turned toward Tao Longyue. The sharp knife in his hand pressed even harder into Tao Jun's neck, drawing a line of blood as he said, "He lied to me, to you, and everyone else—"

Bang—!

A gunshot echoed.

Tao Longyue never intended to harm Xie Lanshan, but he also couldn't let the man do anything to his own father. That's why he fired a shot that only brushed against his skin.

Yet at such a close distance, even a touch on the shoulder burned through Xie Lanshan's shirt. The powerful force ripped through his flesh.

The knife in hand dropped to the ground, the violent trembles made him lose his balance. Xie Lanshan coughed out blood from his mouth. Xie Lanshan pressed onto his injured shoulder, his mouth filled with the taste of blood. He stared at Tao Longyue, stunned and in disbelief that the latter would pull the trigger on him.

He still remembered how he broke all ten nails and saved this boy from the ruins of an earthquake, how the boy cried and swore to be his best friend for life.

Soon, he realized these were merely memories that existed within the brain, not memories that belonged to him.

Xie Lanshan let Tao Jun go as he faced countless guns pointing at him. He wiped his face with his bloodied hand and then stared silently at Tao Longyue, at everyone.

The silence now that contrasted his madness earlier sent chills down everyone's spine.

Ever since he knew about that damned surgery, he had been desperately holding onto that bottom line of goodness. But man was born with sin. Some religions said that man was separate from god upon birth. Darwin rallied for the survival of the fittest. A sperm could only make its way into a mother's womb after killing thousands of its own kind. That was why humanity was complicated and dark; the stairway up to heaven was difficult, but the fall down was surprisingly easy. That was why his attempt to maintain the bottom line was extremely difficult and painful.

Yet at this moment, he finally realized something.

It was too painful to be Xie Lanshan, too painful to be a good person. Once he no longer stubbornly maintained that arbitrary bottom line of morality, all pain would vanish.

After this agonizing pain of drowning, he felt himself finally escaping the mother's womb and found an opportunity to be reborn.

After a moment of exchanging glances, Tao Longyue noticed that the man didn't just change expressions, it was as if his entire existence transformed. Xie Lanshan's eyes cleared up; his gaze became enchanting. There was passion and a smile on his face, enticing like a siren and completely different from the man they once knew.

"Captain Tao, my fellow officers, are you all looking for Ye Shen?" Xie Lanshan raised his bloodied hands to surrender, but the elegance made it look as if he was doing a curtain call on a stage.

Without letting the stunned men respond, he said with a smile, "I am he."

(vi)

Shen Liufei, who was still in Thailand, was oblivious to the clouds of conspiracy plaguing Hanhai City now. He didn't find his mother among these countless corpses, but made another shocking discovery.

They identified one of the female corpses as Zhuo Tian, according to her ID. After a DNA check, it was confirmed to be the supposed murder victim herself.

In order to chase down Ye Shen, Shen Liufei had been gathering all sorts of information from various channels, so he was also well-aware of Zhuo Tian's case. According to the reports, Ye Shen was arrested the same night that Zhuo Tian called the cops. A piece of human skin ripped off from a young woman was found in his bedroom; fresh blood from the girl's body also covered the living room and bathroom. Yet the police searched everywhere within the city and Ye Shen's residence for the girl's corpse—to no avail.

Ye Shen admitted to the murder and even confessed that he was the culprit in the massacre over ten years ago, but he refused to give details about the most important parts of the case. This included the whereabouts of where Shen Liufei's mother and the two other female victims' bodies were hidden.

Now, the missing Zhuo Tian reappeared in the Golden Triangle region thousands of miles away, tossed into this mass grave dug by stowaways. Shen Liufei took a wild guess that Ye Shen didn't actually kill Zhuo Tian and instead created a fake crime scene and took the blame of murder for an unknown reason. Zhuo Tian went missing years ago under the same circumstances as Tang Xiaomo—she was kidnapped by human traffickers.

This thought grew like wildfire inside Shen Liufei's mind, followed by excitement. Even his perpetual cold face seemed to glow in shock for the first time. He realized that with this sudden twist in Zhuo Tian's case, there was likely a hidden truth behind his family's murder many years ago.

After hearing about Ling Yun, Shen Liufei also took the opportunity to investigate the missing officer while searching for his mother. However, it wasn't easy to conduct a private investigation on foreign land—he wasn't even a cop back in China. It was thanks to Officer Somsak, who updated progress on the case, that he could keep up with the investigations.

That was when the search warrant was released to the public: one cab driver called the bureau after seeing the news and said he had actually taken two young men to the airport that day. One of them got out of the cab halfway, then the other quickly asked the driver to tail the one that left.

After solving a groundbreaking human trafficking case and exposing the internal corruption within the Thai police department, the cops were suffering quite a tough time of transition. They clearly weren't putting their mind on the missing Blue Fox member and sent off the witnesses after taking brief testimonies. Only Somsak contacted Shen Liufei immediately after hearing the news.

Shen Liufei wasn't part of the Blue Fox and couldn't investigate with the Thai police, so Somsak secretly contacted that cab driver and arranged for him to meet with Shen Liufei.

The artist drew a pencil sketch of the young man that got off the cab from the cab driver's description.

As expected, it was the Blue Fox's temporary captain, Chi Jin.

One witness account wasn't enough to solve the case. The artist exchanged glances with Somsak and then asked the cab driver, "Can you take us to the place where the missing young man got out of your car?"

The driver took them up the mountains, relying on his memory for directions. Somsak also requested to follow along and even took one of his students. The old cop blamed himself for Ling Yun's disappearance. After all, if he didn't insist on keeping the Blue Fox here out of his own selfishness—though the kidnapped young men and women wouldn't have been saved—Ling Yun wouldn't have gone missing.

They arrived early in the day with good weather. The sky was blue, grass green; the mountains in Thailand were as beautiful and vibrant as a painting. From the windows of the car, old temples and huts could be seen mingled with varying exotic plants in the area.

Shen Liufei's eyebrows pressed together during the entire trip, eyes outside the window and lips closed. His attention wasn't on this beautiful scenery, rather, his mind was filled with concern.

He wanted to return home as soon as he found a lead to the old case so he could be by that man's side. Yet Ling Yun's disappearance also had complicated ties to Ye Shen. He knew that Xie Lanshan must be facing a lot of hardships back home, or even watched as a suspect right now, and he must do something to prove Xie Lanshan's innocence.

The sky began to darken. The cab driver received a hefty amount of cash as he waited in the car patiently with a cigarette in his mouth. Shen Liufei and Somsak found that wooden house and entered to investigate it carefully. Shen Liufei found a few bloodstains on the wooden flooring. Even though the place had already been cleaned up, the dark crimson had already stained the wood.

He reached out a hand toward the stain with gloves on, frowning even more. He worried that it might already be too late for Ling Yun.

Somsak was busy taking photo evidence while Shen Liufei was trying to figure out how to wash away Xie Lanshan's suspicion. That was when he heard sounds of multiple car engines from afar, almost piercing the eardrums in this quiet mountain region.

Oh no! He gasped quietly. This area was far away from the city and not part of Somsak's jurisdiction. Considering the snail-pace of the Thai police, they were afraid that Ling Yun's corpse would already be tossed into a deserted land by the time they received approval to dispatch a rescue team.

That's why Somsak brought a student who was also a cop with him. Even though they all had guns in hand, they were only two people against the enemies.

"Call for backup, quick!" Shen Liufei called at Somsak and took the old officer out of the house. They ran toward the driver waiting by the cab, and Shen Liufei said, "Get in!"

The driver didn't understand the rush and instinctively wanted to get in the driver's side when he heard the artist say coldly, "I'm driving."

Almost as soon as the four men got in the car, three other vehicles were already visible from afar. The one in the lead was a black Hummer, and Shen Liufei saw from a glance the man sitting on the passenger side of the car.

The man had sharp and handsome features, but there was a burn scar on one side of his face. An eerie but faint smile appeared on his lips. His eyes were hollow, emitting a blood-thirsty aura that could be felt meters away.

The man likely set up hidden patrols along the way and had his eyes on him since he decided to stay in the country. It was possible the man was aware of Shen Liufei even earlier than that. Shen Liufei never saw a photo of this rumored drug lord of the Golden Triangle, nor did he ever find the need to investigate, but he knew the moment their eyes met—this man was the source of Xie Lanshan's nightmares, Mu Kun.

Both men's eyes narrowed as they glared at each other like beasts ready to engage in a bloodbath. After a few seconds, Shen Liufei pressed on the gas pedal, made a U-turn, and drove out.

Mu Kun growled, "Follow them! Crush him dead!"

The two sedans behind him had a faster acceleration, shooting out like two arrows at his order. They chased Shen Liufei down, attempting to sandwich the car from the front and back and crash the car down the mountains.

Somsak already called the bureau, but he wasn't sure when backup would arrive. He had no choice but to sit on the passenger's side and wait as the winds blew outside. The speed of all three vehicles sped up faster and faster; the Toyota cab rushed down the winding mountain roads with sharp turns, the rim of the car's body sometimes scratching on the cement road.

The chase grew fiercer. The old officer could feel adrenaline rush up in his body, turning his stomach upside down. He couldn't believe this sophisticated and artistic Mr. Shen had such a rough technique of driving down the mountain roads.

Behind him was a driver who obviously wasn't as skilled as Shen Liufei, losing balance almost right after a sharp turn and flipped on the roadside.

The second car also slowed down after seeing how they already suffered a loss. Mu Kun was enraged as he quickly pulled out a rifle from the backseat and began firing at the Toyota.

Mu Kun had decent aim and shot through one of the rear tires of the Toyota after a few missed shots. After violent trembles that almost caused the car to flip, Shen Liufei managed to find balance and drove forward, refusing to decelerate.

Mu Kun fired another bullet right through the cab driver's head in the backseat. The bloodied flesh splashed onto the window in the front.

Somsak and his student twisted around, pulled their guns out and fired back. They also exploded one front tire of the other sedan. The car immediately lost balance; not only did it crash onto the side, but it also turned and blocked the road of the Hummer, keeping Mu Kun behind.

Seeing the Toyota drive further and further away, Mu Kun pulled out a small rocket launcher from the backseat after cursing out loud.

This area wasn't part of the Golden Triangle's territory, so causing a ruckus would not only call the attention of authorities, it was dangerous. In addition, the weapons in hand were all left by Guan Nuoqin's subordinates, making it even more complicated to handle. Mu Kun's subordinate wanted to stop his boss, but the drug lord quickly slapped his lackey back. Mu Kun's eyes grew red as if he was going mad—he insisted on killing Shen Liufei today.

Shen Liufei's eyes widened as he saw in the side mirror that madman holding a rocket launcher. He had no choice but to turn the car right before the man fired to avoid the impact.

After a loud explosion, the rocket launcher shook off a portion of the mountain. The Toyota cab rushed out from a sea of flames at full speed.

A Door Behind the Sun

After getting the wound on his shoulders sewn up, Xie Lanshan was sent to the detention room in the Municipal Bureau. The situation was too unbelievable to grapple with, so the higher-ups needed to have multiple meetings to decide what to do with him.

In a five-square meter single cell with cold white light, he faced another cell where his "neighbor" stayed. The neighbor was a gangster who often engaged in drug trading, who caused a bit of ruckus again, and was captured by Xiao Liang for another round of ethics education. They were the only two people in the detention room. Perhaps bored and lonely, the man directly across from Xie Lanshan grew excited as soon as he saw a newcomer sent in. As soon as the cops left, the man called out to Xie Lanshan, desperately trying to strike up a conversation.

Xie Lanshan didn't respond and sat quietly in the corner of the jail cell. His face was pale and remained still, as if his soul had already left his body. He remained in this position for a long time until he seemed to have transformed into a ceramic statue. The only indication of life on him was that bloodthirsty and dangerous gaze from the depths of his eyes.

The neighbor looked to be around 30, slightly shorter and more built than Xie Lanshan, with a clean short haircut and wide eyes. He looked quite spirited overall, aside from his slightly droopy eyes, which gave him a tired appearance. Unable to withstand the silence, he shoved his face in between the metal bars and introduced himself to Xie Lanshan. "Hey newcomer, my name's Zang Yifeng. What's yours?"

Xie Lanshan didn't respond and closed his eyes. He heard a musical chime from afar that rang every day at 6 P.M. Rumors circulated it was because the shopping center was haunted and a Fengshui master said the only way to soothe the evil air was to play this kind of music at this hour. Xie Lanshan felt a sense of familiarity with this music. If there weren't any big cases in the bureau, the chime would mark the time they got off work every day.

The man once again spoke up and shoved his face further out. "You look quite fit. What do you do? Can't possibly be like me and just live in the slums, right?"

Xie Lanshan didn't respond. He knew that in another five minutes, a route 785 bus would arrive at the bus stop. The driver was always in a rush and only ever stopped at the last minute as he drove by a stop. The bus stop would be flocked by grade school students from an international school 200 meters away. He knew every inch of soil outside the bureau and every block of pavement on the roads as well.

There was no standard outfit in the detention room of the bureau, so Xie Lanshan was still wearing his white button-up that hung on his body. His hair that grew out was slightly messy, adding to a disheveled look on him. From the perspective of Zang Yifeng, he could see the young man's strong and built muscles through the opening of his shirt. He stared at Xie

Lanshan dumbly as if he'd never seen a man so pretty in his life, mouth almost drooling instinctively.

After studying the young man for a while, he made an assumption and continued pestering, "Is your family still around? You don't look like you're married, but you must have a girlfriend at least."

The mention of "girlfriend" finally seemed to summon Xie Lanshan's soul back. He suddenly opened his eyes and turned to look at the shorter man.

Time froze for those few seconds. Zan Yifeng was shocked; the man's gaze was cold and dark, like that of a murderer.

Then, Xie Lanshan stood up, and ignoring his newly healed wound, he began banging on the metal bars and called out, "Tao Longyue! Tao Longyue!"

Captain Tao of the violent crimes unit was walking around right outside the detention rooms; naturally, this commotion summoned him. As soon as he stepped in, he noticed Xie Lanshan's attitude changed slightly and he addressed him as "Captain Tao".

Tao Longyue saw Zang Yifeng sticking his head out and found a new target to release his anger on. He turned and scolded the man harshly, "Sit back down. Who told you to move?"

"Captain Tao, I have something I'd like to ask you." Their eyes met. Xie Lanshan's attitude was distant and business-like, almost ready to bow down to the Captain in front of him.

Tao Longyue felt pained; his mouth tasted sour and bitter. He had known Xie Lanshan for over twenty years. They always had strange nicknames for each other, and he recalled that the latter often refer to him as "ol'Tao" or sometimes "Longyue" when they were closer.

But the man was addressing him as "Captain Tao" right now, clearly setting a hard boundary between the two.

Tao Longyue opened his mouth with difficulty. "What's up?"

Xie Lanshan looked as if he didn't notice the awkwardness and displeasure on his old friend's face and only asked, "What's today's date?"

Tao Longyue said, "The second."

Xie Lanshan's expression changed. He asked, "It's February already?"

Tao Longyue almost wanted to laugh and thought the man grew dumber sitting in this room. But as soon as he remembered their situation right now, he held himself in and said with an agonizing expression, "Of course it's February."

Xie Lanshan grew nervous after he thought about this and asked, "Where's Shen Liufei? Where is he?"

Tao Longyue let out a sigh and said, "He's still in Thailand, I think. Do you think he wouldn't come to see you if he was already back?"

A bad feeling sank in his heart. Xie Lanshan shook his head and said, "There's no way that he's still in Thailand!"

Shen Liufei didn't return. The man would never take back his words at a time like this, knowing that Xie Lanshan was in danger.

He had a strange feeling that something must've happened to Shen Liufei.

Tao Longyue saw Xie Lanshan's face was in shock, then remembered what he wanted to tell the latter. He said, "Good timing. I also wanted to tell you that the old cop you knew in Thailand got into some trouble."

"Trouble?" Xie Lanshan's heart skipped a beat, his eyes widened.

"He's dead. They've already found his corpse. The car he was in fell down the mountain roads; he was buried alive by half of the mountain. Including that Officer Somsak, they

434

discovered three bodies there." Tao Longyue sighed again and said, "According to the police over there, it's likely that Mu Kun had something to do with it."

Xie Lanshan fell into silence again, his body frozen behind the bars. Tao Longyue called out to him a few times, but he gave no response.

The young captain felt his phone ring; it must be Su Mansheng calling him up to visit old Tao in the hospital. Old Tao already knew about Xie Lanshan's situation. After a fit of rage, he fell ill once again.

Tao Longyue didn't dare to ignore his wife and trudged out of the detention room.

After taking a few steps, he stopped and turned back to Xie Lanshan. The latter also seemed to have come back to his senses and returned the gaze.

Xie Lanshan's hair had grown down to his shoulders, making the already handsome man look even more attractive in a way that transcended gender. There was a perpetual but faint smile on his face that looked almost cocky, the dimple by his mouth flashed as if he was an otherworldly creature of beauty. The dramatic aesthetic stunned Tao Longyue, but he was also deeply regretful that he didn't notice this change earlier.

"A'Lan, I..." A faint whimper came out of Tao Longyue's throat, but he still said, "I don't intend on harming you, you're always going to be my best friend."

Xie Lanshan studied Tao Longyue almost arrogantly until he lifted the corner of his lips and said, "Sure."

He sat back down in the corner of his cell, face still blank and unmoved. He rested his elbow on his knee and pressed his chin on his arms.

There was only one thought in his mind right now: he needed to leave this place and find Shen Liufei.

The phone rang again. Tao Longyue gave Xie Lanshan one

last glance, let out a long sigh, and rushed out of the room with his hands in his pockets.

After confirming that Captain Tao had left, Zang Yifeng turned toward Xie Lanshan once again and stuck his head out, asking in disbelief, "Are... y-you a cop?"

Xie Lanshan didn't look at him and asked, "Why are you here?"

Zang Yifeng scratched his head and said, "No big deal, just sold some drugs."

Xie Lanshan lifted an eyebrow. "Sold some drugs?"

Zang Yifeng confessed, "Red ice, about a thousand grams."

Xie Lanshan pressed his eyebrows at the sound of those two words. A thousand grams of red ice was enough to warrant a death sentence here. He asked coldly, "You think this isn't a big deal?"

Zang Yifeng laughed. "The ice I sold was fake, homemade by me. You can't even tell from the outside, but it doesn't actually harm ya."

Xie Lanshan said coolly, "Law enforcement defines the selling and possession of fake narcotics shall be treated as attempted selling and possession of actual narcotics. Even if you don't get on death row, you'd be spending your life making out with the prison cell."

He was purposely scaring the latter. It was rare to find cases of selling fake narcotics in the country, so the actual sentence for these crimes was still a topic of hot debate, even in court.

Zang Yifeng called out loudly once again but was quickly hushed up by Xie Lanshan.

"Don't be so dramatic. Stop looking around so much." Xie Lanshan saw the surveillance camera diagonally above him from the corner of his eyes as he said quietly, "If you don't want to get on death row, I can help you get out of here."

(ii)

Almost as soon as the 6 P.M. chime rang, Zang Yifeng cried out, "Mister policeman! Hey good ol' mister policeman! He's gonna die! He's gonna die!"

Xiao Liang was on shift today and rushed in at the noise. He called out while attempting to look intimidating and scolded, "Don't call me old. Do I look older than you? What's going on?"

He looked toward the direction Zang Yifeng was yelling at and saw Xie Lanshan on the ground, face pale and lips slightly trembling. The man was covered in blood, his shirt and sleeves were all stained crimson.

Xiao Liang was stunned by this bloody scene before him and asked, "What happened?"

Zang Yifeng grabbed onto the bars of his cell and stared in horror at Xie Lanshan's cell. He said dramatically, "I don't know... The blood just exploded all of a sudden and he also fell to the ground. Did an artery pop or something?"

That gunshot wound wasn't a small one, and Xiao Liang could never have imagined that Xie Lanshan was the one that reopened his injury and assumed his artery was cut. He wouldn't allow even a stranger to die in their detention room, let alone a colleague of three years.

"Senior Xie... hey, hold still, I'm calling the ambulance right now."

As soon as Xiao Liang's hand reached onto his shoulder, Xie Lanshan suddenly opened his eyes. A flash of ferociousness crossed his eyes as he attacked. Xiao Liang was no match in combat against his former colleague—even if he was equipped to take on the man in an ambush, chances were he would still be the one that ended up falling to the ground.

After a few seconds, Xiao Liang's limbs were locked and

unable to move. Xie Lanshan's eyes were slightly reddened. He grabbed onto the young cop's throat and shoved him onto the wall of the detention center harshly. After two hard knocks, Xiao Liang lost consciousness. Xie Lanshan reached into the young man's pocket and pulled out a 100-yuan bill, then tossed the latter onto the ground.

"Hey, what about me?" Zang Yifeng reached out a hand and waved wildly to get Xie Lanshan's attention. "What about me?"

"Selling fake and harmless drugs would just be considered scamming. You won't die." Xie Lanshan still refused to look at the man and was ready to leave. If it was the same old Xie Lanshan in the past who would never break a promise, he would have helped the man, but he was Ye Shen now and didn't share the same morals.

"I hang out in the Gantangzi region. I can help you out if you get me out of here." Gantangzi was a small corner in Hanhai city where the criminals and drug dealers loitered. Zang Yifeng seemed to be convinced he was going to be put on death row and kept calling out to Xie Lanshan, but the latter disappeared without turning his head.

Xie Lanshan rushed out of the Municipal Bureau, and the people on duty in the surveillance room quickly called upon the cops after realizing it was a jailbreak. For a moment, the entire bureau was loud with sirens. The bureau was rather quiet with no pressing cases lately and most people could maintain a regular 9-5 schedule. In other words, there shouldn't be anyone on duty during overtime right now. But Tao Longyue paid extra attention to this case involving his buddy and still lingered in the bureau at this hour. He stood up immediately as soon as he heard the sirens signaling Xie Lanshan's escape.

Captain Tao rushed out of the bureau. He sprinted past all of his colleagues who failed to stop Xie Lanshan, on the ground with bruises everywhere.

He saw his buddy dart out to the street across and followed behind, calling out, "A'Lan! Don't repeat your mistakes. I'll shoot if you keep running!"

At that moment, a crowd of children walked out of a primary school campus. Tao Longyue had his gun pointed at Xie Lanshan when he noticed the latter suddenly picked up a young boy. He turned around, stood still, and held the boy up in front of him.

The two men's eyes locked on each other; Xie Lanshan's gaze was filled with rage and malice, no longer resembling a righteous cop. Tao Longyue was both shocked and extremely disappointed. He could never imagine that boy who risked his life to save him from an earthquake many years ago would now dare to take a child hostage.

Xie Lanshan held the boy up with his uninjured arm and ran. Tao Longyue couldn't fire in fear of harming innocent people and could only run after the man. Then, a bus suddenly drove by and stopped right in front of him, blocking his way.

Xie Lanshan's route of escape was carefully planned out based on his knowledge of this region. By the time the bus drove off and Tao Longyue could dash out, Xie Lanshan and the little boy had already disappeared.

In a dark corner on the street, Xie Lanshan placed the stunned little boy down. He lowered his head and looked at the boy with an expressionless face.

The child never had a gun pointed at him nor kidnapped, so he was scared speechless, and forgot to even call out for help. He could only look up and stare at the man covered in blood. Yet almost as soon as he looked, a strange but childish instinct told him that this man wasn't as scary as he thought—in fact, the man's gaze was both benevolent and sorrowful.

Briefly, the kindness in Xie Lanshan's consciousness took over as he touched the boy's hair. He whispered, "I'm sorry."

The boy still hadn't fully processed the two vastly contrasting personalities, but he soon noticed the man already walked away.

Night fell on the eve of the Lunar New Year. Blackness quickly consumed the warm light of dusk and befell the city. The child noticed that the silhouette of the man looked lonely. He pressed on his injury, but fresh blood still continued to roll down between his fingers and dropped onto the ground. It was almost cinematic, like an injured swordsman who trudged through pavements with a broken blade and tired horse all by himself.

Yet Xie Lanshan knew he was even more pitiful than those fictional heroes. He had no sword to wield and no horse to lean on as he disappeared into the night.

Gantangzi was a peculiar place in Hanhai City. Bars and clubs filled the streets; some saunas and hairdressers also hid among the shadows as they all engaged in shady businesses.

These businesses will do virtually anything for money.

The largest club in Gantangzi was called the Eastern Palace, a rather high-end and large establishment. The owner had some powerful sponsors with government affiliation, which was why the business was able to control this area and stay in business without trouble from public security. Most police officers also usually turned a blind eye when they passed by the area.

Sex work and the drug trade were closely connected industries, especially with meth and other narcotics that could serve as good aphrodisiacs. That's why the drug dealers tended to be much more obnoxious and active in this area where the police didn't act.

Xie Lanshan knew he had nowhere else to go, and Zang

Yifeng's words reminded him that the best place to hide right now was in the lawless land of Gantangzi.

He ran from the Municipal Bureau and had no more money aside from the 100 yuan he took out of Xiao Liang's pocket. He had no choice but to accept his fate and found a small hostel to stay in.

The hostel was hidden in the corner of the streets; its walls were stained, and it looked rather insignificant from the outside. There was a large and fanciful advertisement board right outside the door that said the cheapest room for a night was 99 yuan. Xie Lanshan stood in front of the door, pondered a little, and decided to negotiate with the owner. He wanted to at least secure a space for one night, then find some needles, alcohol, and cotton to treat his wound.

The owner of the hostel was a woman who looked to be in her 30s but was actually nearing 50. Despite her age, she still maintained a good look and had vibrant makeup; her long hair also made her look more attractive. The hostel offered other special services and most customers weren't any normal residents. The owner didn't mind the blood on Xie Lanshan nor checked his ID, easily letting him check-in.

As soon as their eyes met under this suggestive red light, an air of seduction filled the atmosphere as passionate emotions bubbled beneath a layer of ice.

"Thank you—what brand of perfume do you use? It smells fine." Xie Lanshan leaned forward toward the owner and slowly closed his eyes, acting like a bee interested in a sweet flower. The skin on his eyelids was thin but clean, the dim light fell into his eye sockets like flower petals on his face. He lifted a faint smile and struck an easy conversation with the owner using his good looks.

The owner was already very interested in this pretty man, so she didn't hesitate to hold up a thick book for Xie

Lanshan to write his name for check-in and touched his hands.

Xie Lanshan hesitated a little when he opened up the book, but finally wrote two words: Ye Shen.

It was a foreign but familiar name that seemed to have sliced through the past and restarted a new life for him. Xie Lanshan lowered his head to sign, allowing the long fringes on from his forehead to cover his mournful eyes. His fingers trembled as he wrote, his whole body also shivered slightly. He could feel his heart beat in pain with every stroke of the pen. There used to be two souls that brawled inside him as they struggled to gain control of the body, and finally, only one survived.

Unfortunately, it wasn't the one he wanted who lived.

The sweet words between the opposite sex earned Xie Lanshan a free dinner, clean clothes, and surgical needles. This area was always filled with brawls among druggies, and in order to keep her business alive, the owner had kept first aid supplies for her customers.

Inside the room of the hostel, Xie Lanshan clenched his teeth beneath the dim light and slowly resewed the injury on his shoulder. Because he was on the run right now, he couldn't go to the hospital on his own and had no choice but to treat the injury himself.

The needle passed through his flesh like a worm; the thread passed through messily, but it stopped the bleeding.

Xie Lanshan laid on the bed and panted heavily after finishing the job.

Shen Liufei's corpse wasn't at the scene of the crash, so there were only two possibilities left: the man either escaped or fell into the hands of Mu Kun.

He didn't think Mu Kun would keep Shen Liufei around for no reason, nor would he stay in Thailand with no plans.

The drug lord must already be in Hanhai and was preparing to recapture him. Xie Lanshan needed to take the initiative and find the drug lord first.

(iii)

The news of Xie Lanshan's jailbreak quickly made its way up to the provincial branch. Director Peng was enraged. He was now convinced that dependable anti-drug officer Xie Lanshan sacrificed his life in the Golden Triangle, and that this man was death row criminal Ye Shen. He immediately asked someone to send out a grade B arrest warrant with a bonus of 50,000 yuan. Yet almost as soon as they sent the warrant out, an even more worrisome event occurred.

Red ice began to engulf the drug market and quickly overtook the entire province at the speed of an unstoppable wildfire, with Hanhai City being the biggest hot spot of the trade.

Tao Longyue panicked as soon as he learned of the provincial branch's decision. The public announcement on the warrant was rather conservative in wording, but the documents circulating within the public security departments clearly stated that Xie Lanshan was an extremely dangerous criminal. The order was still the same—guns were allowed to be used if the man refused to comply.

Captain Tao was worried. He could still give Xie Lanshan a chance if he was facing his old friend to bring him in alive. But if Xie Lanshan left Hanhai City to search for Shen Liufei, nobody would care about sparing his life. No matter how strong the man was, he had no weapons to protect himself. How would he fight against fully armed police forces? In the worst-case scenario, a bullet would pierce his skull and his corpse would be left on the streets.

Song Qilian also panicked as soon as she heard about this.

She met up with Tao Longyue and said she shared his senti-ment, then offered a possible solution. They could only hope that Xie Lanshan was still in Hanhai right now so they could lure him out using his mother.

Song Qilian said, "We can bring Mrs. Gao from her facility and ask the bureau to contact the TV station. They can do an episode on a doctor transferring all patients to a new hospital, then do a short documentary on the channel. We can ask for the video to be spread online, ensuring that A'Lan sees this..."

Tao Longyue understood her plan to lure the man out with his mother. Yet he was still unsure and said with a difficult expression, "Do you think he'll still show up like that? He's... he's no longer..."

Tao Longyue rubbed on the scar on the side of his head and sighed, unable to tell the woman "he's no longer Xie Lanshan".

Song Qilian also fell into silence. She was mournful and regretful; if she had destroyed the document that exposed Xie Lanshan's identity, if she didn't choose to expose the truth at Tao Longyue's wedding... perhaps this secret could have been kept safe and none of this would have happened.

The wisdom of the Buddha said that a heart filled with struggle is the nature of a sinful mortal, while a heart filled with clarity is the true form of a wise Buddha.

Neither she nor Tao Longyue was sure if the Xie Lanshan right now was the sinful mortal or the benevolent Buddha. But Song Qilian was certain that if this man still had even one bit of Xie Lanshan's soul in him, he would visit his mother.

Gantangzi was a hub filled with prostitutes and was nearby a famous drug trade street. With the latest arrest warrant, even the most powerful government backing wouldn't be able to protect Xie Lanshan. The police paid visits to every neighborhood in the area, the sirens loud outside the windows. Xie Lanshan knew he couldn't hide anymore.

He also knew that Mu Kun must have seen his arrest warrant, and the sudden red ice outburst in the market was also a bait the drug lord was using to lure him out. If he could track down the sources of that red ice, he could find Mu Kun.

Xie Lanshan might have arrived without a penny, but he certainly left with something else in his pocket. It was impossible to walk around today's society without money. To find Shen Liufei, he snatched a bit of money from the hostel owner and left a note promising to return it.

He left in the night after dropping off the note. Night lights in Gantangzi shimmered as clubs and stores began to open up for business. The similar reddish and pink ambiance almost looked like blushes on a fine maiden. The cops had been more diligent lately, which meant more active clubs were doomed. Thankfully, the spirit never fades; the red-light district was still a robust nightless city.

Xie Lanshan ran into a loud crowd. The grade B arrest warrant had already spread across the internet. Afraid that someone would recognize him, Xie Lanshan quickly dodged into a corner of a street, only to bump right into another person as soon as he turned.

He looked up and was surprised to find Zang Yifeng, the familiar face he met in the detention room.

The latter also recognized him and said in surprise, "Oh, it's you?"

Almost as soon as he spoke, Xie Lanshan turned and put him into a head hold, then pushed the poor man's head to the wall. Xie Lanshan asked coldly, "Were you tailing me?"

Zang Yifeng cried out and explained angrily, "How could I? Gantangzi is only so damn big, and I already told you I hang out around this place!"

Xie Lanshan loosened his grip after realizing there was some truth in those words. But his gaze was still cold when he asked, "How did you get out?"

Zang Yifeng swung his twisted arms and said, upset, "You screwed me over last time! Those drugs I sold were fake, plus I didn't even get to sell them when I was caught, so they couldn't even convict me of scamming. So of course they released me after I went through some disciplinary action."

Xie Lanshan remembered the man was a local who often engaged in the mainstream businesses in the area and softened his expression. He asked, "You know this place well. Do you know where the drug trades tend to occur around here?"

Zang Yifeng thought about it for a moment before answering, "I do know a woman who lives off selling those smokes. I think she used to hang around some club here. The club's boss is also a woman who was rumored to have gotten some connections with a big drug dealer, so now they specialize in selling red ice."

"A club?" He immediately thought of Miss T, Tang Qinglan. Xie Lanshan frowned and asked, "Club Tequila?"

"Yeah, that, tacky whatever it's called."

"Can you take me to her right now?"

"I could, but you have to promise me something first." Zang Yifeng scratched his nose and glanced over with a tough expression, ready to bargain.

He said that his fake red ice messed with the market here and upset the big drug dealers locally. The dealers threatened to kill him, so he needed some money to get himself out of this area. He could tell from the detention center that Xie Lanshan was a man who could fight, so he wanted the latter to help him get the funds to escape.

They left as soon as the deal was made. While the sky was still dark, Zang Yifeng took Xie Lanshan through the narrow alley-ways and streets like rats going through tunnels. After about thirty minutes, they finally stopped in front of a rental house. The units inside were very compact; each unit was filled with foul smells and windows that looked as if they were rusted. All the doors had chipped paint. The hallways were all dark, like the streets surrounding it—clearly a place that could only exist in the slums.

"That woman used to live in a mansion and wore expensive jewelry every day, but ever since she got addicted to drugs her life just kept going downhill until she ended up here." Zang Yifeng knocked on the door while shaking his head, then called out gently, "A'Xia? A'Xia?"

The door wasn't even closed and opened at the knock.

The scene behind the door was frightening; the woman only had underwear on and cried out as soon as she saw two men walk in. She rushed forth, barefoot on the cold concrete flooring.

She was still in her drug psychosis. Yet she had no more money in her pocket, so the woman was forced into madness. Her face was pale and almost menacing, eyes bloodshot in desperation. She kept biting her tongue. Fresh blood rolled out between her white teeth like a horrific demon.

Suicide by biting one's tongue off wasn't as easy as depicted on television shows, but it was highly possible for someone to die from massive blood loss or air pipe blockage from the tongue. Xie Lanshan noticed the woman already lost her mind as she opened her mouth wide, looking as if she was ready to bite off her own tongue. He quickly stuck his pinky finger into her mouth without hesitation.

Red ice was a drug that made a person easily irritable; the psychosis state of an addict like this also temporarily gave the woman explosive strength. She clenched her teeth quickly and a crisp cracking sound echoed. Xie Lanshan's pinky bone was broken at that moment.

Finally able to vent it out, the woman stopped attempting to harm herself and instead bit down harder on the man's finger. Xie Lanshan frowned as he withheld the immense pain, raised another hand, and knocked the woman out with an uppercut on the nape of her neck.

The event occurred within a blink of an eye. It was so fast that Zang Yifeng didn't even have time to react and watched it all happen on the side. He was very puzzled and shocked at Xie Lanshan's actions. He was a criminal on the run, wanted by the police. According to the description on the warrant, he was a monster, a demon, a bastard who wouldn't even hesitate to betray his comrades. Yet this same man willingly sacrificed a finger just to save the life of a drug addict he had never met before.

Xie Lanshan carefully let the unconscious woman down on the ground, then looked at his own finger. His skin was peeled, and the bone broken; the deep teeth mark had fresh blood mixed with the woman's saliva.

"Aren't you scared..." Zang Yifeng stuttered as he asked, stunned, "scared that she might have AIDS?"

"I didn't even think about it." The woman had gone mad; it was obvious she wouldn't be able to answer his questions. Xie Lanshan calmly washed his injury and poured a cup of warm water for the woman.

"I have meds that can help deal with her situation!" Zang Yifeng pulled out a bottle of detox drugs from his pocket and took out two white pills. He took the glass of warm water and carefully fed it into the woman's mouth.

Xie Lanshan asked, "You keep the meds around?"

After moving that unconscious woman onto the sofa, Zang

Yifeng's expression shifted and finally said, after letting out a sigh, "I used to do drugs too. These were for myself."

His gaze flickered around as he spoke, lips trembled, and breathed heavily as if there was a tragic story about to be told.

The two men returned after realizing they would go back empty-handed and didn't wait for the woman to wake up.

Zang Yifeng was still in shock at Xie Lanshan's 'heroic deed' earlier and rambled the entire way back.

"You don't look as scary as what the arrest warrant said. I believe you were a cop just from what you did earlier, so then why are your bosses and colleagues trying to arrest you?"

Xie Lanshan was getting annoyed at the questions and turned around to shoot a frigid gaze at him.

The few streetlights were dim. The moon above them shifted to a position that cast a glow beneath those bloodthirsty eyes. Zang Yifeng swallowed down the rest of his words and didn't dare to speak up again. Those eyes were inhumanly icy. Zang Yifeng began suspecting this man was filled with contradictions. He was a character that seemed to contain the soul of a hero and criminal inside him, like a saint and demon.

Xie Lanshan couldn't stay in one spot too long as a wanted criminal and was in a rush to find a place to stay overnight. That was when he spotted something on the TV inside a small grocery store.

The news was about a doctor at an island hospital who privately transferred a dozen or so patients to another hospital. The excuse was that the doctor wanted to give the patients a better place to treat their illnesses—of course, all family members were notified and agreed to the transfer. Another side condemned the doctor for violating professional conduct and engaging in a secret negotiation with another hospital. The result was a heated debate on the internet and the news channels.

Xie Lanshan didn't have the time to check the news lately, but he didn't expect to see his mother in this situation.

Regardless of where the news was being reported, all cameras had gotten a shot of a beautiful but thin woman. Gao Zhuyin seemed to be unable to accept being transferred into another hospital and cried on camera, saying, "I want to see my son! Where's my son? Where's my A'Lan?"

Xie Lanshan paused before the TV in the store and saw his mother breaking down in front of the camera. She was tied up like a criminal and then forcefully taken away by medical staff.

He heard that these dozen patients were now placed inside Puren Hospital's psych department.

Zang Yifeng didn't dare to hurry Xie Lanshan. He could see clearly the latter clenching his fists tightly, the veins on the back of his hand popping until his whole body trembled.

Every shrill cry from Gao Zhuyin was like a knife slicing into his heart. Xie Lanshan was enraged at the hospital's careless actions, but his gaze couldn't help but soften as he looked at his mother. Those dried and cold eyes finally looked to regain a bit of light and moisture.

He told himself that he may never return, that he needed to pay her one last visit before he left.

The police searches had been more frequent lately, so the hotels around Gantangzi weren't safe. Thankfully, Zang Yifeng had a wide network of connections, and after two phone calls, he borrowed a place that was rather quiet. It was a standard two-bedroom unit. The furnishings were very minimal, but at least there was now a place they could stay and hide for a while.

Xie Lanshan had been suffering from a low fever these last few days due to minor infections from his injuries. After getting his finger bitten by that woman, he finally reached his limit. He didn't even stop to wash himself and headed straight into the bedroom. He walked by the bedside and dropped onto the mattress.

He was tired both physically and mentally and fell asleep the moment he closed his eyes. Yet he didn't even breathe heavily and looked as if he was dead.

"Huh? Xie Lanshan? Officer Xie?"

Zang Yifeng left the room after receiving no response and walked into the kitchen. He pulled out a knife and stepped beside Xie Lanshan once again.

Zang Yifeng held the knife with two hands above his head, eyes locked on Xie Lanshan lying on the bed. That smooth-talking demeanor from earlier vanished. His expression was unhinged and raging; flames of revenge burned in his eyes.

Yet before the blade could drop, a loud police siren blared outside.

Xie Lanshan instinctively woke up as soon as he heard the sound and jumped from the bed. He didn't notice the panicking Zang Yifeng with the knife and instead turned to look out the window.

It was already 2 in the morning, but the red lights of the police cars blazed through the night sky like a torch of fire. One after another, police cars began ringing their sirens in the middle of the night and darted out from the quiet streets toward the direction of the Hanhai City Municipal Bureau.

The police cars in the Hanhai Bureau were modest Chevys, but these were heavy Land Rovers that were clearly from the Provincial Branch. Aside from the usual blue and gold emblem of the police, they also had a unique fox symbol painted on the side.

Nobody had ever seen a mass deployment like this.

Xie Lanshan quickly realized these fancy police cars

weren't here for him, which meant something game-changing must have happened within the Blue Fox.

(iv)

This was supposed to be an average night in winter, with strong winds and a cloudy sky. Hanhai City Bureau Officer Xiao Zhang just brewed another cup of coffee for himself during his shift and returned to his desk. Just as he was about to sit down and continue playing solitaire, he realized the computer froze.

Xiao Zhang panicked as he set the coffee down and saw a window pop up on the frozen screen after a minute. Beneath the screen were two times—one was the current time, and another was a countdown to 72 hours.

Xiao Zhang immediately realized that someone had hacked the municipal bureau's internal network. Cyberattacks happened every so often in the city, but they mostly targeted businesses and other non-governmental agencies. It certainly was a first for a hacker to be so brave and shameless as to attack the public security department. Xiao Zhang stared at the video on the screen; the camera was filming in a place that looked like a storage unit, dark and empty. At the center of the screen was a heavily injured young man tied to a chair.

Xiao Zhang paused the video while it was facing the man on the chair, zoomed in, and opened his eyes wide in shock. The man was the missing Blue Fox team member, Ling Yun.

He immediately contacted the chiefs of the Municipal Bureau. The chiefs then made a call to the provincial branch and shook the entire Blue Fox team with this piece of news. All members were called on duty at that instant. With Captain Sui Hong personally leading the team, all vehicles drove out to the Hanhai City Bureau.

The hacker came prepared and set safety measures to protect himself. The technicians in the bureau attempted to track down the IP address, only to discover it led them to a foreign website's server. Ever since Mu Kun overtook Guan Nuoqin's territories, he also extended his reach to the latter's old businesses as well.

At 4 A.M., something new finally appeared in the video. A handful of men armed with weapons walked into the storage room. The leader of the group ordered a subordinate to bring a chair over so that he could sit down beside Ling Yun.

"Zoom in on that man." The Blue Fox officially took charge of this case, so Sui Hong ordered the tech expert Sun Jian from his team to analyze the video.

The screen was cropped to leave only the man's face visible. This handsome face was menacing, mad, and evil. His eyes even glowed with a demonic light that did not belong to this world.

Sui Hong recognized him, every member of the Blue Fox recognized him. This was the drug lord the team had been chasing after for three years: Mu Kun.

The drug lord lifted a faint sneer on his face as he moved his mouth to say something.

There was some background noise in the video, so it was difficult to hear what Mu Kun was saying. Sui Hong frowned and said, "Reduce the background noise."

Mu Kun seemed to have known he was finally the center of attention and once again spoke up slowly, "Long time no see, Captain Sui."

He stood up, took out a knife from his pocket, and walked behind Ling Yun. The man grabbed onto Ling Yun's throat while he sliced down the young man's ear with the hand that held the knife. The blade was sharp, but almost as if he was doing it out of malice and revenge, the drug lord slowly dug into the flesh to drag on this torturous process.

Ling Yun knew his captain and comrades were watching over him through the computer screen right now. He was afraid to make them worry and withstood the urge to cry out, beg for mercy, and shed tears. Yet he was still trapped in a flesh body; the agonizing pain was difficult to withstand. It was too painful. Hoarse growls came out from his throat as he trembled and twitched until the chair beneath him shook with his body.

It didn't take long for Ling Yun's ear to be cut off. The freshly cut ear was still twitching on Mu Kun's hand as the drug lord laughed out loud.

Even the video seemed to reek with the bloodied smell through the screen. All of the Blue Fox members were stunned and shaken by this scene. Tu Lang's eyes reddened as he pounded on the table in frustration. Sui Hong closed his eyes as his body trembled in anger.

Chi Jin stepped away from the crowd, nervously shaking behind his teammates. He could almost feel the agonizing pain that Ling Yun was going through right now. He was one second away from exposing his pain and regret but managed to quietly shoulder it all as soon as he laid eyes on Sui Hong.

"Captain Sui, didn't you say the Blue Fox leaves no member behind? Why hasn't anyone come to save your teammate yet?" Mu Kun's mood lifted after the torturous act as he perversely licked the blood on the knife. He then turned slightly toward the camera and said coldly, "Let Xie Lanshan come find me. Or else I will kill your man by the time the countdown reaches 0."

As soon as he finished, Mu Kun slashed the knife across Ling Yun's face, leaving another bloodied mark. The blood rolled down his cheek into the corner of his lips, then down his chin. This vibrant and handsome young man was already completely destroyed inside and out. His kneecaps had shat-

tered; flesh and blood glued to his pants. The young man knew
that he was at his limit, and even if he managed to survive, he
would be disabled for life.

Yet his eyes were still filled with a bright and determined
glow that showed no sign of yielding to evil from start to finish.

Mu Kun told Sui Hong that he will be live streaming Ling
Yun's torture throughout the entire countdown. After 72 hours,
he will slice Ling Yun's throat and kill the young man.

The drug lord despised all members of the Blue Fox, with
Xie Lanshan being the only exception.

Now that the case had elevated to the scale of foreign diplo-
macy, the Thai police could no longer sit back and finally investigated diligently. After another round of negotiations, the Thai
police forces finally sent in all relevant evidence, including the
cab driver's testimony to the Hanhai City Bureau. In addition,
they also mailed the physical evidence discovered at the scene
of the car crash. Amidst the piles of evidence, Tao Longyue
recognized the bullet necklace that Xie Lanshan always carried
around.

He was the one who gifted this necklace to Shen Liufei.

The testimony from the cab driver was clear and organized.
He took Ling Yun to trail another short-haired young man on
the day Ling Yun went missing. After checking the timestamps,
they confirmed it was the same time Ling Yun had sent Tu
Lang his last text message right before he disappeared.

However, the evidence from Thailand was still too little to
be decisive. Tu Lang said in frustration, "Don't they do forensic
sketches or something over there? The guy said they were
trailing a young man with short hair. Just how are we going to
find him without any other clues?"

The one thing that was certain was that because Xie
Lanshan's hair grew out now, he clearly didn't fit the description of the driver's testimony. Judging from the way Mu Kun

spoke about him, the man also never betrayed his teammates to join with the drug lord.

Sui Hong recalled that Xie Lanshan had once questioned in tears: *Why is everything I do wrong, why don't any of you ever believe in me?*

He also remembered Xie Lanshan admitting once from the bottom of his heart: *The Blue Fox will forever be my home, and you will always be my captain.*

Sui Hong coughed a few times and closed his eyes in pain, regretting that he never gave his most beloved subordinate his full trust. He allowed the appearance of a murderer to become the irredeemable sin of the young man, and he allowed it to wipe away all the hard work and honor Xie Lanshan once had.

"We were wrong about A'Lan," Sui Hong sighed in between his coughs and said, "we were all wrong about A'Lan."

Yet Chi Jin was still afraid that he would be found out. He was living his life on the edge lately, only hoping to get by every day as long as he could. He said, "If the message he gave Tu Lang is fake, then what Ling Yun said about one of us being a traitor must also be a part of Mu Kun's plan to make us suspect each other. Perhaps Ling Yun discovered Mu Kun's hideout and trailed him but was found out and fell into the hands of the enemy."

Sui Hong opened his eyes and looked at the young man with a rare and inexplicable expression on his face. With that gaze on him, Chi Jin could feel his heart thump from guilt while attempting to keep himself calm.

That was when someone knocked on the door to the meeting room. Tao Longyue walked in and reported, "We have a plan to lure Xie Lanshan out."

(v)

Shen Liufei finally woke after hearing a whisper calling him. He opened his eyes to be met with a bright light from the window.

He held up a hand to cover his eyes and then reopened them after he grew used to the bright light. When his eyes had adjusted, he looked over at the familiar face beside him and said, "It's you."

Duan Licheng smiled and asked, "Finally awake?"

Even before his memories were transferred, Shen Liufei had always treated this man as his brother. His phone number was the first on Shen Liufei's caller's list, making them very close friends. Duan Licheng rushed to Thailand as soon as he received the news from the hospital. After spending some extra effort and money, he quietly took the injured man from the hospital and found a peaceful, rural place to treat Shen Liufei.

The air was thick and warm. Dust danced like sharp pieces of metal as he breathed. Shen Liufei felt dazed as he stared at the ceiling that spun and reached a hand up to rub on his temples. He asked, "Was the surgery with that young man successful?"

Duan Licheng's smile froze momentarily. He asked, "What?"

"The young man who got into a car accident and suffered brain damage, wasn't his name Bai Shuo?" Shen Liufei lowered his head and looked at those strange hands as he mumbled to himself, "I'm sorry for suddenly taking your body like this."

Duan Licheng pondered a bit and asked, "Do you remember what today's date is?"

Shen Liufei responded after some thought. He gave a date that was over a year ago from today.

Nobody knew the side effects of the very first brain transplant surgery or what situations would trigger an unexpected reaction. After that deadly car accident in Thailand, Shen

Liufei's memories returned to the time he had just completed his surgery, forgetting everything he had been through in Hanhai with Xie Lanshan.

Duan Licheng was stunned, but quickly held it back in and said with a smile, "Yes, it looks like the surgery was a success. You seem to have successfully retained your old memories."

He wanted to keep Shen Liufei in hiding, even if it meant imprisoning the latter for the rest of his life. He didn't want this young man to risk his life anymore.

This location was quiet, like paradise. Outside the French window was a field of grass with flowers that looked as if they extended to the horizon. Shen Liufei stood topless in front of the mirror and turned his head occasionally when the floral scent made its way into the room. He could also see small animals gleefully chasing each other out in the grass field.

This young man called Bai Shuo was much taller than him and had a strong, built body with smooth skin and powerful muscles. He was said to be a fan of extreme sports and was particularly good at martial arts and car racing. It was precisely this dangerous interest that caused him to fall into a vegetative state during an accident. The young man's only family left were second cousins who weren't willing to pay for his medical bills, so they accepted Duan Licheng's offer and donated the young man's body to him.

Duan Licheng looked at this new Shen Liufei with immense kindness in his eyes. He walked over and took out a photo he carried with him in his pocket, then said to the man in the mirror with a smile, "Here, have one last look at your old photo so you don't forget how you looked before."

Shen Liufei took the photo and glanced over it. There were two men in the photo, one standing and one sitting. The man standing was Duan Licheng, handsome and tall as usual, while the man sitting in a wheelchair was distinctively thinner. His facial features weren't particularly pretty, but there was an air of refinement and elegance to him. His melancholic gaze was almost sympathetic to look at; even the clean white shirt on him seemed to add to this unique attractiveness.

The Shen Liufei in this photo was plagued with a severe illness that slowly paralyzed his body. The young man might have been introverted, but he was optimistic and always kept a faint smile on his face. He refused to meet with anyone in person and only communicated through email or mail. Because of his condition, he often spent his free time reading books or drawing. If he didn't intend to investigate the truth behind his family's massacre and mother's disappearance, he would never have accepted Duan Licheng's offer to participate in this ethically controversial surgery.

After a near-death experience, Shen Liufei could feel that his memories were still foggy. Vague images of people floated before his eyes, but he couldn't clearly see the faces, as if he was stuck behind a curtain. He felt as if he had dreamed of something that didn't belong to him, but he recalled some memories that were sealed deep in his past.

His head hurt. His whole body hurt. Chaotic imagery churned in his mind. These thoughts quickly exhausted Shen Liufei, and he laid back on the bed with Duan Licheng's help.

Shen Liufei placed a hand on the doctor's face and said, almost sentimentally, "It seems like I'm always giving you trouble."

Duan Licheng chuckled and touched the hand on his face. "You know that I will always be there when you need me the most."

Duan Licheng's deep voice was calming, like a lullaby. Shen Liufei closed his eyes briefly, then opened them up again and stared back to say, "That's strange, I suddenly remembered something."

Duan Licheng asked, "What is it?"

"I remember I was woken up by a strange sound when I was very little. I walked down the stairs to see my mother being locked inside the kitchen. She was like cattle waiting to be butchered, there were even shackles on her legs... then I heard my father ask her, 'You still want to leave while you're pregnant? If you try to leave again, I'll kill your son.' I wanted to listen in more, but that's when my grandmother suddenly appeared behind me. She covered her hands over my eyes and then whispered into my ear, 'You're just dreaming, this is a dream...'"

Aside from the wicked father and strange grandmother, his uncle—a thug who loved stealing women's underwear—would visit their house every so often. That man would always stare wildly at his mother like a stray dog drooling at a fine meal of fresh blood.

These scenes were too difficult to comprehend at his young age, to the point where he instinctively hid them in the depths of his memories. If he wasn't on the brink of death, perhaps he would never have remembered any of this.

"I've always had a feeling since I was little that she was too unhappy and that she will leave one day... so I have a guess right now that perhaps my parents were not married out of love. She was a woman who was constantly being abused and insulted." Shen Liufei closed his eyes as his fingers unnaturally rubbed on his left wrist. There was nothing there, but he had a strange feeling something very important used to be there before he lost it.

Fatigue overtook him, but before he once again fell asleep, he suddenly remembered something else. The two things he remembered seemed to be connected, but he wasn't sure.

His father always used the method of 'family connections' to punish the disobedient wife, using violence and abuse to force her into submission. He had once been hung on a tree outside their yard and whipped by his father. He cried out loud for help until he fell unconscious, but nobody came to help him. In a daze, the rope that tied him up suddenly broke off and he fell to the ground like a sandbag. By the time he woke up, he discovered that the rope had been sliced by a knife, but there was nobody around him.

Someone was helping him in the shadows. Shen Liufei told his grandmother about this, but the latter only laughed and said it was most likely a thief who wanted to steal something.

Only he knew that wasn't true. He had never actually met the person, but he'd seen that person's eyes before.

The person was around the same age as him and would often look at him through the metal gate, exposing only half a pair of his pretty eyes. Those eyes were a rare light brown that wasn't common among Chinese people. Perhaps the child was of mixed ethnicities.

As soon as their eyes met, the person behind the door vanished. Those eyes only appeared and vanished that one hot summer night. That night was like the countless nights during the season; the cherry apples were in full bloom in the yard, the red flowers became more vibrant while the pink shimmered brighter in this quiet time.

The little tricks Xie Lanshan learned from Han Guangming finally came in handy. After disguising himself, he went to pay his mother a visit to the hospital.

He braided his hair, stuck a fake mustache on his face, and put a pair of sunglasses on. He turned on his phone again as soon as he was finished and studied the photo on the arrest warrant. This quiet but stringent cop looked nothing like his disguise as a smooth womanizer. Xie Lanshan turned off his screen and lifted a mocking smile as he thought, *the smallest change is often the biggest difference. We're completely different people, and these fools only just realized it.*

He was now a wanted criminal, but his demeanor was still elegant and flashy, as if he wasn't the one being chased down by the authorities right now. However, perhaps it was precisely this confidence and boldness that didn't make him suspicious.

Xie Lanshan called the psych department just before arriving and managed to get the newly admitted patients' room numbers through his frivolous lies.

After checking there was nothing strange outside the hospital room and that Song Qilian was the only one inside, Xie Lanshan walked in without hesitation.

"A'Lan—" Song Qilian noticed someone walk in, but before she could call out, a swift hit from behind knocked her out.

Xie Lanshan carried Song Qilian to the bed and then walked toward the window. Gao Zhuyin's wheelchair was beside the window. She sat alone under the sunlight, expression calm and her gaze fixed outside, and didn't seem like she noticed the commotion inside the room.

He walked toward his mother and got down on one knee before her.

Gao Zhuyin finally turned around and glanced down at her son.

He was walking in the fire, struggling in purgatory. He fought with everyone, including himself, along the way. He had always thought he was strong enough to withstand anything through these trials, but he didn't expect that he was still weak against this gentle gaze. Xie Lanshan's eyes reddened as he buried his face in his mother's lap. Like a lost child who finally found a home, he gently whispered with sincerity, "Mom."

Gao Zhuyin also seemed to be moved by this voice, immense kindness and love in her gaze as she reached and touched her son's face. Suddenly, her eyes widened as she pressed her hands on Xie Lanshan's shoulders and cried, "Officer Tao, get this bad guy! Come arrest this bad guy who's pretending to be my son!"

Calls of "come get him" pierced through Xie Lanshan's ears and pained him. He quickly struggled out of his mother's grip and attempted to escape the room.

But it was too late. The Blue Fox members that were quietly waiting outside broke into the room and blocked the exit. Xie Lanshan reacted quickly and leapt right out the window. Seven stories wasn't too high for him. He climbed on the AC vents outside and jumped down, quickly making his way to the ground.

This body was extremely well-trained to handle sports, which was almost like a gift from the heavens. Xie Lanshan turned around and looked up at the two Blue Fox members that stuck their heads out from the window. He waved two fingers around his forehead and gave a mocking salute back at them. His lips lifted, and he said to himself, "Thanks, Officer Xie."

Aside from the Blue Fox, several people from the Municipal Bureau's violent crimes unit also hid around the hospital. Xie Lanshan took down three police officers in a row, which also hindered his footsteps a little. He darted to the streets, but Tao Longyue was already behind him. The latter held up a gun and called out, "A'Lan, come back!"

There were no children he could use as a shield this time, so Xie Lanshan had no choice but to stop. He was prepared and wasn't as shocked and hurt this time seeing his brother hold up a gun at him. Xie Lanshan turned around slowly and said with a smile, "You're the boss with a gun here. I'll do as you say."

"I don't want to point my gun at you. I just want to talk." Tao Longyue said earnestly, "A'Lan, we were wrong about you. Please come back."

This comment about being wronged was even more painful than being suspected of being a criminal. There was nothing reassuring about this. Xie Lanshan almost laughed. He lifted an eyebrow and studied Tao Longyue as if he was looking at a complete stranger, seemingly unamused.

Tao Longyue continued, "We received the latest update from Thailand. You're no longer a suspect in this case. The Blue Foxes were all stationed in the Municipal Bureau; one of their members was captured. You know, that really optimistic one who was also very kind to you, Ling Yun. They all want you to go back right now so that you can help bring Ling Yun back—"

"Hold up, Captain Tao, hold up. A Blue Fox member was kidnapped. What does that have to do with me?" As if he was uninvolved with anything mentioned, Xie Lanshan interrupted Tao Longyue and shrugged mockingly. He lifted the corner of his lips and said, "I'm Ye Shen, not Xie Lanshan. Besides, Xie Lanshan isn't even part of the Blue Fox anymore. You guys were so quick to abandon him and now you're coming back to ask him to save someone from your team? Don't you think this is a bit funny?"

"This... is something that we received from Thailand two days ago." Tao Longyue knew he was in the wrong and put his gun down after some thought. He pulled out the necklace with a bullet from his pocket and held it up before Xie Lanshan to return the item and said, "I'm assuming this is what you gave Shen Liufei."

The blood on the bullet was dry. This used to be a memento from his father that he later gave to Shen Liufei, which also contained his heart.

Xie Lanshan's eyes narrowed as he looked at the necklace; something certainly happened to Shen Liufei.

"You know that there's merit commutation for a sentence.

Even if you... you're Ye Shen, you can..." Tao Longyue couldn't continue, even he knew that this negotiation sounded too weak as a persuasion.

"Oh, really?" Xie Lanshan finally seemed to show some interest and retracted his stony gaze. He glanced slightly around and then curled up a finger to gesture Tao Longyue to walk toward him and said, "Come here and explain it clearly to me, just what exactly is going on."

"Mu Kun kidnapped Ling Yun, who was tortured. That drug lord hacked into the Municipal Bureau's internal network and sent a live stream of the torture. He said that if you don't go find him within three days, he'll slice Ling Yun's throat and kill him."

Tao Longyue explained as he walked toward Xie Lanshan. He let his guard down, only to be met with a sudden attack as Xie Lanshan shoved him away—

Just as that happened, a truck drove down the street. If Tao Longyue didn't react fast enough and hadn't rolled to dodge the vehicle, it would have crushed him at that instant.

By the time he sat back up from shock on the ground, covered in mud, Xie Lanshan vanished again. He noticed that not only did the man disappear, that necklace and his gun had been taken as well.

(vi)

Xie Lanshan escaped, and Ling Yun still needed to be rescued. Time passed brutally quick; there was only a day and a half left until the countdown ended. Ling Yun was on his last breath and couldn't even speak, but thankfully Mu Kun never once appeared on the screen again, nor did he send others to continue the torture.

But the watchers were still around. There was nothing in the storage unit aside from Mu Kun's subordinates. They were all armed with deadly weapons and spent all day and night in the storage unit, eating and drinking inside.

After the technicians cleaned up the background noise from the video, they noticed that they would often hear the sounds of ferry whistles from the outside over the last two days.

Sui Hong said, "Ferries have different whistling sounds, each with unique meanings. We've heard the ferries send out the same long whistle for two days in a row, which means that the ship is ready to take off from the port or arrive at the dock."

Tu Lang nodded in agreement and said, "There's only a handful of ports here. There's no way they will all have ships leave the dock at the same time. We'll investigate right now and see if we figure out where the storage unit might be."

Chi Jin stood on the side without a word, then turned his attention to the screen and said, "Something dropped."

A piece of paper dropped beside a drug dealer's foot on the screen. Even though he quickly picked it up, the technicians were still able to capture that brief moment and discovered it was a convenience store receipt.

While they couldn't see the address on it, being able to locate a berth made up for the lack of information. Tu Lang said gleefully, "We can narrow in on the storage unit where Ling Yun is locked!"

Chi Jin let out a small sigh, then felt Sui Hong tap on his shoulder. The latter said, "Follow me."

Sui Hong walked silently in front, coughing every so often while Chi Jin was behind with his head down like a shy new recruit. The spirit of the entire team was down, so the Captain took him to the municipal bureau's physical training room.

Chi Jin saw Sui Hong walk toward a bench press and hold up a barbell piece to study. Assuming the Captain was about to get on the bench himself, Chi Jin quickly called out, "Captain, your body..."

It wasn't a secret in the provincial branch that Captain Sui Hong was not as fit as before, which was why he had slowly moved to work on the backend these last two years and no longer led the team on the frontlines. Luckily, Sui Hong had no plans to act rashly and gave Chi Jin a faint smile. "I haven't seen you train with this in a while. Try it out."

The rare personal time with his captain lifted Chi Jin's mood a lot as he obediently laid on the bench. He reached his hands up to hold on to the bar above him and laughed. "80 to 90 kilos is still a piece of cake."

After completing a set, Sui Hong began adding on the weight of the barbells, quickly reaching Chi Jin's normal limits.

"Hey, Cap," Chi Jin begged, "can you slow down a bit?"

"Don't stop," Sui Hong said as he added another piece of weight. "Remember our motto?"

Chi Jin bit down on his teeth and answered as he pressed, "Of course."

Sui Hong added one more piece, which was completely over Chi Jin's personal limit, and breathed, "Recite it."

Chi Jin could feel his muscles pull to a point of discomfort as he said through his reddened face, "Fear no enemies, leave none behind."

Sui Hong added another piece to the other side of the bar and, while frowning, said, "Louder."

Chi Jin could feel this immense pressure weigh down on his muscles as he howled in pain, "Fear no enemies! Leave none behind!"

Just before he let out a breath, he felt his hand slip while the bar was right above his head.

He was still laying on the bench, unable to dodge in time. If he were to be hit, his rib cage would shatter in an instant.

Chi Jin's eyes widened in panic; his hands were still on the bar but could no longer muster enough energy to press up. He watched as the bar dropped toward him, but just at that moment, the man beside him reached over.

Sui Hong grabbed tightly onto the bar with great force, veins on his forehead popping. Unlike his normal demeanor as a commander who does not use force, the Captain mustered up all of his energy to hold up the bar for his subordinate.

Chi Jin caught a breath and pressed up, helping the bar back to its default position. He sat up from the bench and panted heavily, "Cap'n... that's why I said to slow dow—"

A hand pressed onto the back of his neck before he could finish. Chi Jin instinctively struggled and couldn't even lift his head. Sui Hong held him there with substantial force.

Then, he heard his captain say one line. This one sentence contained a weight so heavy that the barbells couldn't compare and struck even more harshly into Chi Jin's heart.

He said, "You're dismissed from participating in this rescue mission."

Sui Hong left the training room, and Chi Jin sat frozen on the bench. There was some new equipment in the bureau; the fresh smell of leather filled the room, but right now it was nothing but the rotten smell of corpses to him.

Emotions poured down like a waterfall inside him as he

agonized. He knew he was already being suspected. His captain didn't expose him, perhaps out of lack of proof, and didn't want to make the same mistake he did with Xie Lanshan. Or maybe it was out of a little sympathy for their decade-long friendship.

He certainly still kept in contact with Tang Qinglan, but it wasn't for the bit of red ice; it was to beg the latter to show Ling Yun some mercy. Of course, his definition of showing mercy was to give Ling Yun a swift and painless death. He couldn't bear to see his comrade suffer through this endless torture.

Mu Kun seemed to have taken his words into account and stopped the abuse on Ling Yun, but Tang Qinglan said the drug lord needed him to do another favor. The last bits of forces under Guan Nuoqin hadn't been cleaned up, and the Golden Triangle was still not fully stabilized. The drug lord wanted to exchange some goods with a Brazilian arms merchant for massive amounts of weapons to wipe out Guan Nuoqin's subordinates. Because of the strong anti-drug efforts in China right now, this was a job only a Blue Fox member could help accomplish.

Chi Jin didn't say yes, but he didn't reject the offer either. In fact, he had no idea where he should go from here. He sat quietly in the training room reminiscing about the past but didn't dare to think about the future.

Ever since the moment he touched red ice, he had stepped foot into this massive network of conspiracy that only led him down one wrong step after another. By the time he turned his head around, mountains of trials and danger already blocked the paths. He was both regretful and angry.

After returning to the temporary hideout Zang Yifeng prepared, Xie Lanshan logged into the municipal bureau's

internal network using a VPN. Right after he entered the pass-
word, he also saw the live stream video of Ling Yun being
tortured. That once handsome and bright young man
completely vanished in the video as he hung his head down
almost lifelessly. His hands were tied, his mouth stuffed with
dirty clothes, his whole body covered in bloodstains.

Xie Lanshan could feel his head throb in pain. He remembered the time this young man took him back on a helicopter,
how this young man smiled and said to him, "Comrade,
Captain asked me to take you home."

Zang Yifeng stood behind Xie Lanshan as he slurped on the
freshly cooked instant noodles. He peeked at the screen from
behind and almost choked in shock. He coughed a bit and then
said through his mouthful of noodles, "Ouch, man, that's some
horrific torture!"

Xie Lanshan moved the laptop to the side and hinted that
the man shouldn't be looking at this.

Zang Yifeng took a few courteous steps back but still asked,
"What are you watching that for? Didn't you say it had nothing
to do with you?"

"Eat your food." Xie Lanshan scolded him coldly, eyes still
fixed on Ling Yun on the screen.

After staring for another ten minutes, Xie Lanshan
slammed the laptop shut, walked toward the bed, and fell onto
the mattress.

He closed his eyes and tried to convince himself, Ye Shen,
this has nothing to do with you.

The nap didn't even last twenty minutes, and he sat back
up once again. He walked over to the desk and opened the
laptop. Xie Lanshan's analysis followed the same method as the
technicians in the bureau, and despite spending a little more
time than necessary, he also found out where Ling Yun could
possibly be held.

While he couldn't pinpoint the exact unit, having a general direction was good enough. Xie Lanshan had confidence in the abilities of the Blue Fox, but he couldn't shake off a bad feeling.

From his understanding of Mu Kun, it was suspicious for any investigations to go so smoothly.

Yet time waited for nobody; even if Ling Yun didn't get killed, the young man might die of blood loss at any time. Xie Lanshan laid back down on the bed, frustrated. He put a mint-flavored cigarette in his mouth but didn't light it up. He ground the tobacco between his teeth, fingers rubbing on the case.

The room was too small, and the luring smell of instant noodles quickly filled the space. Zang Yifeng spoke as he ate and drank the soup. "I'm sure you're just determined to act like a villain, but you really want to save your teammate deep down."

Xie Lanshan grabbed a pillow on the bed and threw it at the man. He turned and feigned sleep, but his heart was anything but calm. An eerie sense of concern seemed to grapple his heart—what was the source of his unease?

He once again opened his eyes after some unrest and rushed toward the desk.

Zang Yifeng was already done eating and stared strangely at Xie Lanshan.

In order to monitor Ling Yun, Mu Kun's subordinates lived two whole days inside this storage unit and would only occasionally come in and out of it. Xie Lanshan replayed the whole video from start to finish and took in all of the details. Finally, he noticed that someone arrived in the unit this morning with slightly damp trousers and mud beneath their shoes. They left little visible stains on the flooring.

Xie Lanshan felt a cold sweat and checked the weather immediately. He then noticed that there was no rain at the port this morning.

That's when he discovered the 72-hour countdown was a dangerous and crafty trap. Mu Kun set up two identical storage units; one was where Ling Yun was locked; the sounds of the ferry whistle and dropped receipt were all fake. This live stream was bait to lure everyone in.

And the storage unit by the port was perhaps the most dangerous trap of them all, waiting patiently for revenge to be served.

The oblivious Blue Fox members formed a ten-man team for their rescue mission at the port. They were quickly able to locate the unit Ling Yun was locked in. Tu Lang held his phone and studied the live stream carefully; he saw a masked man holding a gun enter a storage unit, and the same thing showed up in the live stream as well.

He didn't think this was an act that Mu Kun had set up, a massive trap waiting for them to enter. Tu Lang turned around and held up his thumb at his teammates, indicating that they found the right place.

They quickly analyzed the firepower these guards held, and after confirming they could take people down, they acted immediately. Tu Lang's sharpshooting quickly took down the snipers hiding on the roof of the storage unit. The drug dealers had no chance to fight back and dropped to the ground one by one.

Three members barged into the storage for rescue, the others surrounded the unit under Tu Lang's orders to prevent the enemies from gathering for a counterattack.

They saw Ling Yun on the chair as they entered the unit, facing against them. Tu Lang put his gun away and rushed forward, calling out, "Ling Yun, we're here. Just hold on a little longer!"

Yet he was shocked to find that it wasn't Ling Yun sitting in the chair. It was a plastic mannequin.

Soon, the entire Blue Fox team recognized that this wasn't the same storage unit as the one in the live stream. There was nothing inside the storage on the video, but this place had a handful of large blue paint cans in the corner.

At the same time, the municipal bureau received an anonymous call. A Blue Fox member said to Sui Hong after hanging up, "Captain, this anonymous call told us to retreat immediately and said it's Mu Kun's trap. The voice sounded like Xie Lanshan—"

But it was too late. A shadow appeared at the entrance of the storage room that was on the live stream. A man walked toward the camera.

Those lackeys who fell under the hands of the Blue Fox were pawns he was willing to sacrifice. Even they were in the dark about the true face of this conspiracy. Mu Kun faced the camera and waved at Sui Hong through the screen, then said with a devilish smile, "I win, Captain Sui."

Sui Hong realized his teammates had fallen into a trap and called out to Tu Lang, his voice trembling as he roared, "Retreat, quick—!"

There were thousands of kilograms of explosives inside those paint cans.

It was a massive explosion that shook the heavens. The explosion consumed everything within an instant, taking the lives of all the Blue Fox members who went on the rescue mission.

(vii)

Xie Lanshan went through a stressful night of little rest. He couldn't sit still and got up restlessly before the sun came up.

He turned on the TV and saw the news reporting the event that occurred earlier this morning. The camera didn't pan to the bloodied scene and only showed the rescue team helping injured civilians around the area. The image of corpses being carried out only flashed briefly.

But Xie Lanshan still saw it; there was a bloodied corpse with broken limbs lying beneath the broken metal pipes and cement. A hand stuck out from the ruins; a spirited image of a fox appeared on the blackened sleeves.

The rescue efforts were in vain. Corpses were carried out one by one from beneath the collapsed unit. Mu Kun installed enough explosives to take the lives of every single Blue Fox member that entered.

Xie Lanshan glued his eyes to the screen and felt chills and disgust. This uncomfortable feeling crawled into his bones, freezing his limbs and warm blood. He took a backpack to organize some luggage, packed a knife, and then hid the gun he stole from Tao Longyue on his waist.

Zang Yifeng was sleeping on the sofa; he turned and saw through his half-awake eyes the gun and jolted awake.

Having heard the news and able to piece together what happened to the runaway, he shook his head and said sympathetically, "What a shame."

He noticed Xie Lanshan was finished packing and ready to leave, then asked in shock, "You're going out this early?"

"I'm going to visit that A'Xia person you knew. If she did hang around Miss T for a while, it wouldn't be hard to get some intel out of her when she's awake."

"Want me to go with you?"

"No."

"Are you looking for that drug lord?"

"My partner may have fallen into his hands. I need to go find him." The rejection from his dark pupils was visible as he warned, "Don't get yourself into things you shouldn't be involved with."

"That goes to—" Zang Yifeng stopped himself as he noticed the malice on the young man's face. He was a thug who had spent his life around dangerous people and knew when to keep his mouth shut. He then explained, "I got you some antibiotics last night; they're on the stove. You can't go to the hospital right now for your injuries. At least take care of yourself first."

Xie Lanshan was about to leave when he stopped and turned to look at the man on the sofa. He tried to give a friendlier expression and said, "Thank you for your care these last few days. I'll pay the money back."

Zang Yifeng finally realized after sharing the same space these past few days that this young man was indeed full of contradictions. He would sometimes be the epitome of evil, but other times the most benevolent saint. It was almost as if he was constantly being pulled between one extreme and another; it was tiring to watch, even as a bystander. Xie Lanshan opened the door as a refreshing gust of wind blew by. Zang Yifeng nearly jumped at this cold air and finally asked, "If you're just gonna get revenge for your teammates, there really isn't a need to risk your life. Don't you think they deserved it for how they treated you?"

This question stunned Xie Lanshan for a few moments. He then walked back into the kitchen, took the medicine, and left.

Conflicted, Zang Yifeng watched the man leave. After the figure long disappeared, he suddenly punched the bed frame and let out a deep sigh.

After receiving the information he wanted from A'Xia, Xie Lanshan took a bus and left Hanhai toward the city where the explosion occurred. The place was very close to the border of China and Myanmar. Based on his knowledge of Mu Kun, this perverse man loved watching his prey struggle in pain, so he must be hiding somewhere within the same city. The man was likely in the dark, grinding his teeth and drinking the blood of his enemies as he pleasured himself with the victory of revenge.

Xie Lanshan had already guessed that Shen Liufei was likely not in the hands of the drug lord, otherwise, he would have already appeared on the screen as bait to lure Xie Lanshan.

But he needed to put an end to everything between himself and Mu Kun, and death was the only ending to this story.

The ancient city was a river away from Myanmar, but the streets were clean and peaceful. Small restaurants and shops lined the streets; colorful signs painted the scenery.

Like a magnet being attracted to the opposite pole, Xie Lanshan showed up in the most run-down bar in the city as soon as night fell. He was an undercover officer once and knew all the hidden signs and codes used by drug dealers, quickly able to determine who had the goods.

Xie Lanshan walked into another joint and purposely took the center seat in front of the bar. He placed his heavy backpack down which almost shook the ground of the establishment.

The owner behind the bar reached out, attempting to help put the customer's personal items into storage. Yet before he could even touch the bag, Xie Lanshan interrupted coldly and warned, "Hands off."

The owner chuckled and gestured that he had no ill intent and even tried to strike up a conversation with him.

"You're new here, aren't you? I've never seen you before."

"Yeah."

"A local? You don't look like one."

"I'm not."

"Just came?"

"Just came."

"From where?"

"Somewhere up north."

"Which city up north? Your Mandarin is too good, I don't got a clue."

"Hanhai."

Every response was short and succinct, also cold and expressionless. Even if the owner prided himself on being a social man, he could not pry out more information.

But everyone was looking at him. He was a handsome man that could earn himself the envious looks of the same sex and lustful desires from the opposite sex. With his open and flashy demeanor, it was natural that all eyes in the bar fell on him. Xie Lanshan was satisfied with these stares; someone would let Mu Kun know that he's here.

Combining the information he received from A'Xia, Xie Lanshan found out the source of the red ice from a local drug dealer and deduced Mu Kun's hideout.

He acted at night only to search the area but surprisingly discovered Ling Yun.

Inside a small wooden hut that reeked of mold, Ling Yun was still wearing the same bloodied shirt. A black bag covered his face as his head hung by one side of his shoulder. The light inside the house was dim, but it was enough to make out the injuries from torture on his body. Scars of whipping, grisly knife wounds, and countless areas where flesh and blood mingled revealed visible white bones.

Xie Lanshan had seen Ling Yun on the stream; the young man indeed went through an agonizing time.

After carefully studying the surroundings, he confirmed Mu Kun and his main guards weren't around. Xie Lanshan held up the gun in hand and knocked out the guard outside the house. He snuck into the house and walked toward Ling Yun.

"Ling Yun?" Xie Lanshan called out gently. He saw Ling

Yun move slightly, then quickly whispered, "I'm here to bring you home."

He reached a hand forward to take down the mask, but Ling Yun suddenly woke up and headbutted him right on the forehead.

Xie Lanshan fell back at this sudden impact that also triggered his low fever and infected wound on his shoulder. He attempted to crawl back up but moving only increased the pain in his shoulder and head. During this moment of hesitation, Ling Yun stood up and pointed a gun at him.

"A'Lan, I know you too well. You take the whole 'leave none behind' part more seriously than anyone else."

The person took down the mask—Xie Lanshan didn't expect that this beaten-up "Ling Yun'" was actually Mu Kun himself.

All the injuries on him were real. In order to lure Xie Lanshan in, Mu Kun self-inflicted those wounds.

He had already received intel by the time Xie Lanshan stepped into the second bar that night.

That was why Mu Kun was happy to give out all this free intel. He knew that Xie Lanshan would knock on his door eventually. He already got his revenge on the Blue Fox, but why didn't he keep Ling Yun in that storage room filled with explosives? Waiting for the ashes to disappear, it was all to lure Xie Lanshan. Mu Kun had been waiting for this for so long.

A figure that was hiding outside the door appeared and knocked Xie Lanshan out from behind with a heavy blow to the head.

The figure was Mu Kun's subordinate, who turned to his boss. "Job's done."

To his surprise, Mu Kun gave him a heavy slap on the face and scolded menacingly, "I didn't tell you to hit so hard."

(viii)

In order to treat Shen Liufei properly, Duan Licheng took him to a quiet and rural place that was far away from the rest of the world. There was no internet inside this massive mansion, but Shen Liufei seemed to not mind it. He temporarily kept his mind out of worldly matters and focused on his rehab.

There were a handful of physical injuries all over his body that he assumed were from Bai Shuo's car accident, and his head would spin and throb in pain every once in a while. If he wasn't attempting to search for the truth of his family's massacre, he would never have risked crossing the lines of ethics and laws to take part in this surgery. Of course, boredom was a nature of humanity. Rehab was one thing; he still asked Duan Licheng to bring in his old notebook to pass time.

There was a folder inside the laptop that contained a massive database of files regarding crimes against women. Duan Licheng was out for business today, so Shen Liufei sat by the desk and carefully read through the files while he subconsciously rubbed on his wrist. He had been repeating this motion for the last few days and felt as if something was missing. Perhaps a watch or bracelet? He looked down and stared for a moment, but nothing came to mind.

There was a cup of coffee, a desktop calendar, and a newly published weekly life magazine on the side of the table. The desk faced the window, which exposed the bright sunlight that shone above the gardens outside. A reddish and green bird flew by like vibrant colors that painted the world; the scene was almost ethereal like an oil painting.

He shifted his gaze back onto the screen. In this case numbered 002, the victim's name was Zhuo Tian, who was the second woman killed by Ye Shen after his mother. Her body was also never found.

It wasn't easy to gather all of this data. Most came from him leveraging personal connections across different channels. Even the public security department might not have information as detailed as these files. Shen Liufei read Zhuo Tian's profile thoroughly and discovered that this young woman had a boyfriend. The man was a drug addict who had a string of misdemeanors on his record. Just before Zhuo Tian was murdered, this man had also been arrested for hiding narcotics and served two and a half years.

He quietly noted the man's name: Zang Yifeng.

There was no other additional information from this name, but he felt fatigued and a headache struck again the more he pondered. Shen Liufei turned off his laptop and took a quick break. He held up a hand to check the magazine; the cover story was bland. He had no interest in celebrity columns, and only the news of an animated series called Land of Aeolus airing caught his attention briefly. Though that quickly got boring as well.

He placed the magazine back onto the table and flipped through the calendar. He soon noticed that the calendar for the next month had been ripped out. Who would rip out the pages for months into the future? He couldn't comprehend.

He studied it further and noticed the calendar rack was a little old, as if it had been taken out of storage. Shen Liufei grew suspicious and his fingers once again rubbed his left wrist.

Suddenly, the face of a man flashed across his eyes. In the fleeting image, he saw the person smile at him. The curl on his lips lifted at a beautiful angle; his eyes filled with immense adoration and love, like a warm light within the darkness.

Shen Liufei recognized it was Ye Shen's face. It was supposed to be a face he despised from the depths of his heart, but he didn't feel any hatred—instead, he could feel his heartbeat increase like a bullet ready to shoot out from a gun.

Shen Liufei grew more puzzled as he looked out the window; a girl on a bicycle rode by the stone pavement beside the mansion. A rain shower had just passed by earlier this morning. The paved road was still slippery from wetness. The girl's bike wobbled as it snaked on the road, looking as if it was ready to fall at any moment.

Shen Liufei jumped from the window toward the girl and caught her handlebars just before she fell to the ground. His brain might have been implanted into a new body, but Bai Shuo's muscle memory remained, which meant that he inherited the young man's sporty reflexes and physical traits.

The girl gave him a bright smile as she thanked him.

There was a movie ticket that poked out of her purse pocket. Shen Liufei lowered his gaze and asked gently, "Movie in the city, Land of Aeolus?"

The girl's eyes widened as she said, "That's a movie from last year. I'm watching something else."

Shen Liufei frowned and asked, "What's today's date?"

The girl responded without hesitation.

This unexpected answer stunned Shen Liufei.

The girl tried calling out to him a few times but didn't receive a response, so she got back on her bicycle and left to watch her movie.

Familiar scenes poured out like a waterfall in his mind; Ye Shen's handsome face once again reappeared before his eyes and jabbed him in the heart. He saw the man kneel before him, take the necklace around his neck off and wrap it around his wrist.

He saw the man kiss his hand and heard him say gently,

Remember that I love you.

Remember to always remember this.

Duan Licheng returned less than an hour later. But he was too late. Shen Liufei had already left.

Sunset's glow embellished the garden outside the window while the curtains danced in the breeze. He sat in the empty room and shook his head as he laughed bitterly.

He couldn't help but admit that those two were bound by fate. No matter what one of them turned into, the other would instinctively follow, as if their destinies were tied.

A Door Behind the Sun

Xie Lanshan slept for three days, so Mu Kun watched over him by his bedside for three days.

He ordered his men to clean up the young cop, changed his clothes, and even got a doctor to treat the wounds on his body. The lightly treated shoulder injury was already infected, so they needed to cut it back open and disinfect the wound. His pinky finger was also broken; they treated that as well. Mu Kun's heart ached at these injuries, but anger was the stronger emotion. He felt as if an outsider had trampled his purest and holy land. Mu Kun had never thought his plan to set the cops against each other was that brilliant, but it was precisely this rough plan that successfully turned his A'Lan into a wanted criminal. This pushed him down a dead end with the price of blood to pay.

The weather had been fine in this small town near the border of China and Myanmar. Fresh flowers bloomed every-where as their scents filled the air. The room was decorated so warmly and elegantly that it was impossible to imagine it was the hideout of an evil drug lord. Mu Kun sat beside Xie

Lanshan's bedside and sniffed the smell around the room. The more he took in the scent, the stronger he felt that Xie Lanshan's scent was more luring than the most tempting desires in the mortal world.

Xie Lanshan was exhausted. He felt as if he had walked too far for too long, and finally found a place to rest. He quietly sank himself into the soft mattress, breathing evenly while his eyes remained closed.

A pair of eyes were locked on Xie Lanshan's face. Mu Kun sat quietly by the bed for a long while; like a bee unable to withstand the tempting scent, he reached out a hand and gently brushed it across the young cop's forehead. Almost as soon as his fingers pressed along his forehead, Mu Kun felt the heat from his skin. He immediately called the doctor over and questioned why Xie Lanshan still had a fever.

The doctor injected another dose of antibiotics into the IV for Xie Lanshan, who was then shooed out of the room by an angered Mu Kun. The doctor turned back slightly by the door and was shocked to discover that the fearsome and evil drug lord who held no regard for human life was staring at his sickly lover with immense love and adoration beneath those eyes—it was almost horrifyingly romantic.

"Get lost already," Mu Kun scolded. The doctor didn't dare upset the man anymore and ran out the door.

It was less obvious when Xie Lanshan still had short hair, but a careful eye could see this face was indeed ethereally handsome like a fairy that existed in storybooks, completely unlike any of those damned cops with guns. Mu Kun leaned in close toward Xie Lanshan and traced the latter's face with his fingers. As if always yearning for more, his finger glossed past that fine skin and delicate features.

He finally leaned down and pressed a kiss on Xie Lanshan's

eyelids. The latter's eyes seem to move slightly beneath his lips at that moment.

"Shen... cuz..." Xie Lanshan finally woke from this commotion and pulled his eyelids open in a daze. As soon as he recognized the face in front of him as Mu Kun, his expression dropped, and he struggled to get up.

But his limbs were completely still; he couldn't even move an inch. Xie Lanshan sat up briefly and then fell back onto the bed.

"I asked the doctor to add some sedatives in your IV so that you can rest up." Mu Kun smiled. He lifted Xie Lanshan's chin and said as he leaned in, "Don't waste your efforts, or I'll be worried."

Xie Lanshan let out a sigh and gave up the struggle. He asked coldly, "What do you want?"

Mu Kun stared at him and asked, "That should be my question. What do you want?"

Xie Lanshan didn't know how to respond. He only stared at the man wordlessly.

"Your captain, comrades, and even those people that sacrificed for you, nobody ever really trusted you." Mu Kun turned and asked him sternly, "Just what are you holding onto so stubbornly, Xie Lanshan? You've never given up on your career and comrades, but they didn't hesitate to abandon you. They would willingly let you die with an unconfirmed suspicion, so why do you still care for them?"

Xie Lanshan still didn't respond. But his eyebrows pressed slightly, the light in his eyes faded. Mu Kun didn't understand the story behind that surgery, but those words were true. It was just as he said; his most trusted comrades abandoned him.

"Come back to the Golden Triangle with me. I won't question your betrayal in the past; we can forget about what happened and look only at the future." Mu Kun grew more excited as he spoke of their future and bloated conceitedly as the immovable king of the Golden Triangle. He said, "You would be the queen... nobody will ever harm you again. We can make love every day atop gold."

Xie Lanshan let out a mocking and cold laugh as he listened to this drug lord talk like a perverse billionaire.

"Is this not an ideal life?" Mu Kun was kneeling by the bedside like a loyal follower of Buddha. He held Xie Lanshan's hand between his palms as he begged, expression filled with adoration, "A'Lan, if you return to the Golden Triangle with me, I'll do anything you say."

"I want you dead," Xie Lanshan said flatly at the latter, unamused.

"Sure," Mu Kun responded without a hint of rage. His expression shifted as he smiled. "I'll die on your body."

A spark of inspiration appeared at that instant. He crawled onto the bed and took off his shirt, stripping off that black button-up from his body. The man was fit, all the injuries on his body were self-inflicted like a beast who wasn't fearful of murder.

"You..." Xie Lanshan was shocked to see that the man was serious. He tightened his muscles in anger and clenched his fist, hoping to wear off the effects of these sedatives and pain relievers.

But he still couldn't move.

Mu Kun tried to lean down and kiss him, but Xie Lanshan moved his head and refused to comply. Mu Kun laughed, then grabbed onto Xie Lanshan's chin and pressed their lips together.

Xie Lanshan could feel the man's invasive tongue in his mouth. Unable to resist otherwise, he suddenly bit down heavily with his teeth.

At the end of a long and bloodied kiss, Mu Kun lifted his

face, unfazed. Instead, he licked the fresh blood that rolled down from the corner of his mouth and laughed.

Xie Lanshan knew he couldn't hide and begging for mercy wasn't his style. He said as calmly as he could, "I swear I will kill you, I swear."

"I've been waiting years for this day. Even death is a good price." Mu Kun only got more excited as he unzipped his pants and pressed his body down on Xie Lanshan. He leaned into the latter's ear and whispered, "I'll make you feel better than that Shen artist ever could..."

He buried his face into Xie Lanshan's neck and bit on the latter's throat like a thirsty dog, then extended the kiss down his collarbone and chest.

He held up one of Xie Lanshan's legs and attempted to take off the man's underwear, but the action stopped abruptly.

Mu Kun noticed that there was no birthmark on this man's tailbone.

Xie Lanshan wasn't someone who cared enough about appearance to remove his birthmark, and this was finally when he accepted the truth. That ridiculous rumor was real.

His A'Lan was already dead.

(ii)

Mu Kun was shaken by the truth displayed before him and sat up stiffly. His expression was that of disbelief as he fell off the bed, as if the whole world broke down.

He was kneeling on the floor as he howled in despair; he covered his face with his hands and cried in agony.

Xie Lanshan finally caught his breath. He felt no remorse for this man; from the moment he learned of the truth, everyone he had once known and cared for had turned their backs on him in fear. Nobody had even spared a moment to consider the cop who rested peacefully in a foreign land. But he had never imagined that the person who was most affected by his death would be his mortal enemy. This bloodthirsty demon was now crying and agonizing in grief. It was so sincere that it almost seemed like he would shatter at a touch.

"Where is he buried... Where..." Mu Kun finally stopped the horrific cries and repeated the same question, "Where's my A'Lan buried?"

The question was strange; Xie Lanshan didn't know whether to answer. After a moment's hesitation, he said, "I don't know."

Mu Kun stood up, still shaking, after a disappointing response, and turned to look at Xie Lanshan.

Xie Lanshan could feel from a glance that the blow to this man was heavy, looking almost as if he had aged overnight. The usual handsome face scrunched up in a strange and twisted manner that was almost pitiful.

In striking contrast to staring adoring at a lover earlier, the man only shed a silent tear, then allowed the coldness and madness within him to emanate from his gaze.

He looked like a monster or creature of the dead—nothing like a human.

Xie Lanshan was covered in a cold sweat. He could feel some energy returning to him as he glanced around to find something to guard him.

"I'm going to kill you... I'm going to kill you, bastard. How dare you take his memories and live on with his identity..." Mu Kun walked toward Xie Lanshan, bloodshot eyes fixed on the latter. "You dirty mutt who opens his legs at anyone on command, I'm going to take you to his grave. I will shoot you dead in the head and return everything you stole from him back to him so that he can fully rest in peace under the earth."

Rage and madness quickly filled the man. He started

walking around in circles like a madman and began talking to himself, "But where is my A'Lan buried? I don't know where he is..."

He didn't think this nasty serial murderer deserved to use Xie Lanshan's identity, but also couldn't let go of this body that looked almost identical to his love. Unable to find his love's corpse, Mu Kun had a sudden idea. He couldn't allow this man to live on but didn't want to bury this body, so the best option was to keep him inside formalin solution.

There were still some empty rooms inside this house that contained massive glass containers used to make red ice. Mu Kun's lackeys took Xie Lanshan over to a room and tossed him into one of the empty containers.

A diluted formaldehyde solution could be used to create the preservative formalin. Mu Kun ordered his men to find the organic compound, and they began pouring water into the container.

Xie Lanshan was quickly drenched in cold water inside the tank. He pressed a hand on the glass and stared coldly at the man outside.

Mu Kun was rejoicing madly with his ingenious idea. He danced as he waited for his subordinates to come in with the formaldehyde to complete this masterpiece.

Yet before they returned, Tang Qinglan entered the room. She announced gravely that Chi Jin betrayed them. The young officer used his own spies to intercept a huge portion of the goods they were planning to use to trade with the Brazilians; the arms merchants were extremely displeased and sent in their men to renegotiate.

Every step of his plan was perfect, but he could not have known this foolish kid would dare destroy his goods. Mu Kun had no choice but to follow Tang Qinglan out to deal with this troublesome matter.

The container wasn't completely filled with water by the time the subordinates reappeared, but the man inside seemed to have drowned already. He was floating inside the tank with his eyes closed.

They assumed he was already dead judging by the time and turned off the water. A subordinate pulled a small stool over to climb toward the opening of the container. He opened up the bottle that held the formaldehyde and prepared to pour it. A strong scent rushed toward his face as soon as he opened the bottle. He teared up as he cursed, "Fuck, shit stinks!"

Just as he was about to pour the solution into the container, the man inside suddenly opened his eyes. That habit of holding his breath underwater saved Xie Lanshan's life; he jumped up using the buoyancy from the water and grabbed onto the man's neck with one hand and the chemical bottle with another, then shoved the bottle into the man's face.

The bottle went inside his mouth and Xie Lanshan lifted the bottle up, pouring that acidic solution down the man's throat.

It didn't take long for the man to knock out. Xie Lanshan pushed him down to the ground and jumped out of the container.

He took a gun from the unconscious man's pocket and began his massacre.

They were still within China's borders and not in Mu Kun's territories. A group of people usually guarded the place, but most followed Mu Kun to see the Brazilian merchants. The ones left in the house were virtually useless fries. Xie Lanshan shot down one man after another like a demon from hell, stealing new guns when one ran out of ammo. He didn't even bother to think about if the servant was innocent while he killed everyone else; he saw the servant beg for her life on her knees. Holding up his hand, he pulled the trigger, piercing right through her skull.

He didn't find Shen Liufei nor Ling Yun. Xie Lanshan finally escaped the house, disheveled and alone.

Mu Kun's house was in a rather rural land, so he trudged down the trail like a walking corpse. He walked from day to sundown. He wasn't sure how long he walked, but he finally saw the scene before him change and noticed he made his way to where people were.

There were young couples on the streets, all eyes filled with love and adoration. This sweet atmosphere filled the air of this strange street. Xie Lanshan looked up in a daze and then realized today was February 14th, Valentine's Day.

The adrenaline from murder vanished under this romantic and festive atmosphere. Xie Lanshan trudged forward, footsteps hesitant. His clothes were still wet, the foul smell of the acidic chemical still lingered. His wounds stung again after his heavy exercise and the pain reeked into his heart. All the couples that passed by him covered their noses in disgust and hurried away.

He attempted to blend in with the crowd, but the crowd instinctively avoided him. He felt isolated from the rest of the world.

He was alone. He was walking on wires where the sky hung above him and earth beneath him; but heaven did not welcome him, and the doors to hell never opened for him.

The festive atmosphere was heavy on this street; a store even hosted a limited discount campaign to lure in customers. Almost as soon as they made their announcement, flocks of loving couples swarmed in like bees and caused a commotion. A young couple was so engrossed in their own little world during the rush that they didn't notice they knocked a blind girl down to the ground.

The girl's walking stick also dropped, which then kicked away by the crowd that walked past it. The auntie that took her out was not beside the girl right now. Nobody noticed this blind little girl amidst the commotion and noises on the street. She was sitting helplessly by herself, almost being stepped on a few times by pedestrians.

Only the same lone man noticed her. Xie Lanshan walked over, picked up the walking stick, and then helped the girl up.

There was a foul scent on this man, but the blind girl didn't mind it. She held the man's hand gleefully and said thank you.

Xie Lanshan noticed there were injuries on the girl's hands and knees from the fall and helped her to a little flower bed on the side of the street to rest.

The girl looked to be around seventeen years old and had a round face; it wasn't conventionally attractive, but it certainly was pretty. She couldn't see but smiled brightly as she looked forward despite some injuries on her, swinging her thin legs as if she was in a good mood.

Out of an inexplicable feeling of interest, Xie Lanshan asked, "Did you come with your friend?"

"No, I came with my auntie," the girl responded truthfully, still with a smile on her face. "I asked her to take me out."

It certainly must not be voluntary for a middle-aged woman to take her niece out to shop during Valentine's Day. Xie Lanshan shook his head and commented nonchalantly, "There's no need to come out on a holiday."

"Even a blind girl like me doesn't want to be alone and wants to experience love," she said bluntly, "I became blind from taking the wrong medication when I was young. I don't remember seeing a beautiful world, nor did I ever have anyone to celebrate Valentine's Day with."

During the conversation, another young couple walked by.

The boy was tall and thin, the pretty girl beside him was barely to his shoulders even with heels on.

The girl held a bouquet of roses in hand, complaining to her boyfriend as they walked that flowers are useless, that there was no need to buy such a large bouquet on Valentine's Day.

The blind girl quickly could tell from the tone of voice that those complaints were jokes, as it was certainly heartwarming to receive flowers on a day like this.

That couple with a significant height difference walked off. The blind girl sniffed hard in the night as if she wanted to take in the fresh smell of roses through the breeze. Suddenly, her expression dimmed as she said to Xie Lanshan with great envy, "I also want someone to give me flowers, better if the person is a pretty boy. But what kind of pretty boy would ever fall for a blind girl? Don't worry, I'm just talking to myself..."

Xie Lanshan looked up and saw some street vendors selling flowers across the street. There was a little boy among the sellers who had flowers that looked a lot less vibrant than his competitors, making his business much slower than others. He seemed as if he didn't want to stay in the cold for too long for the next far off customer.

"Give me a second." Xie Lanshan stood up, walked swiftly past the crowd, and made his way toward the boy selling flowers. He had no money on him now. The only thing that might be worth something was the bullet necklace that hung around his neck.

He took his necklace off, walked toward the boy, and said, "Can I exchange this for just one rose from you?"

"Is this a real bullet?" The boy said, eyes beaming.

"As real as it can get." Xie Lanshan nodded.

The boy seemed to be interested in it. He figured he wasn't going to make more money today and accepted the offer. Then he picked up a withering flower from his basket and handed it to the man.

Xie Lanshan took this withering red rose and gave it to the girl waiting by the street.

As if he intended to fulfill all the girl's wishes today, he knelt before this blind girl, held up her hand, and placed it on his cheeks. He smiled gently at her and said, "I'm the most beautiful wandering lover of this world. You can touch me, if you don't believe me."

The girl held the rose in one hand and touched the man's face with her other trembling hand. Her fingers brushed against his deep eye socket, tall nose bridge, the sweet lips that lifted into a smile, and down his handsome chin. She had no doubt this man was good-looking, as if from a beautiful dream.

"You're really... really pretty..." Light blushes surfaced on the girl's cheeks. Her blind eyes also seemed to glow for an instant and she said, "You're also... a really good person."

Xie Lanshan's heart jumped at this comment. He wanted to say something, but nothing came out of his trembling mouth.

The girl's aunt finally walked out of a discount store at this moment and saw this bloodied and disheveled man. She screamed in horror.

After Xie Lanshan ran off, the aunt took the girl to the nearest police station to report the man.

Because the Hanhai City Municipal Bureau was the first location that handled Ling Yun's case, the violent crimes unit was allowed to conduct investigations outside of their standard territories. Captain Tao just so happened to be at the local bureau in this area with his team members. A portion of the remaining Blue Fox members and local police officers were also at the station.

In front of these cops, the middle-aged woman said with confidence, "I've seen this man on the arrest warrant already. He looked to be quite civilized, but I didn't think he was such a perverse man! Thank goodness I found out early. Otherwise, I can't imagine what he would do to our little Zhenzhen."

The woman's voice was sharp and high. Tao Longyue and Xiao Liang exchanged a glance. They couldn't explain the situation to the public and could only listen to the woman complain loudly.

The Xie Lanshan now had already been deeply influenced by Ye Shen's character. Nobody knew how far down the man had fallen and whether he would lay a hand on an innocent girl.

After the woman was finished, Tao Longyue squatted down and faced the blind girl. Despite knowing that she couldn't see anything, he remained respectful and asked her gently, "Did that person harm you?"

The girl felt the heavy air and clear animosity within the bureau the moment she stepped in. The atmosphere puzzled her, but she also felt strangely annoyed. She stared forward with her hollow eyes. Before all the adults who could see more clearly than her, this blind girl said with absolute confidence, "He's a good person."

(iii)

After learning that nearly half of his teammates lost their lives in that storage unit, Chi Jin had thought about taking his own life to repent.

They were all young men around the same age. They had just been joking around and chatting joyously yesterday, but now they had all vanished into dust today—only remembered by their heroic souls. Chi Jin didn't return to the Blue Fox's headquarters, but he knew even without having to go that his captain must have shed tragic tears for his comrades.

Chi Jin sat in a room with lights off and took a sip of that burning white wine. He clenched the gun in his hands and cried. His cry was silent, but tragic and full of regret.

He withstood that burning sensation of the alcohol and allowed all the regret and hatred to evaporate from his body. Realizing death would not solve anything, he set the gun down. He finally decided to face his fears and stop running.

Chi Jin stood in the dark and carefully packed a few bottles of the familiar cough syrup through the dim glows of the moonlight outside the window. He filled out the delivery slip and set the package in front of his door for the delivery person. He left a message and waited for the package to be picked up.

He put the guns and explosives he took from the team into his backpack and then packed some more personal items. Chi Jin locked his door and left. He stepped on the shadows of the trees cast by the moonlight and walked forward without hesitation. He prepared himself to complete his own revenge and prove his courage.

Mu Kun kept massive loads of red ice to trade with the Brazilian merchant Mariano, so he decided he would act first and intercept the red ice the day of the trade.

The bosses on both sides wouldn't show their faces easily, so Mariano ordered his men to contact Miss T first. Chi Jin was well aware of this beforehand. Mu Kun had already labeled him as a coward who would betray his own teammates and relied on him to open up the roads to export the goods.

As the Vice-Captain of the Blue Fox, Chi Jin had outstanding physical abilities that kept him at the top of the pack in close combat. In addition, Mu Kun's subordinates didn't watch him too closely at first, which made it easy for him to kill the lackeys without trouble. He quickly took the truck filled with red ice and drove it away.

It enraged Mu Kun when he received the news. He had thought the kid was under his control after the acts of betrayal and forced consumption of red ice, that the kid was merely a puppet they could play in the palm of his hand. But this young cop still surprised him.

He looked back and noticed even Xie Lanshan managed to escape. Mu Kun's anger boiled, flames of hatred burned violently as he swore to kill Chi Jin using methods even more torturous than he had done to Ling Yun.

But the trouble Chi Jin left was quite a handful. Mariano had already paid a massive deposit and was demanding to receive his goods right away. The entire province was under heavy lockdown to fight against the drug trade. It was already difficult to stock raw materials. There was certainly no time to remake the goods. This situation extremely frustrated Mu Kun. He hadn't fully controlled the Golden Triangle yet and couldn't afford to face another powerful enemy.

So he promised the merchant that he would find the intercepted goods as soon as possible.

Of course, Chi Jin knew the plan.

He arrived at the city where the storage unit was, called Miss T, then demanded, "Send Ling Yun to St. Gor Hospital."

St. Gor was the best hospital with state-of-the-art equipment in the area.

"Where are the goods?" Miss T laughed as she saw this kid attempt to play nice after a betrayal. "You need to tell me where the goods are first before you can make negotiations."

"The goods are in my hands right now. You're the one who can't negotiate with me. Send Ling Yun to the hospital, or I will burn all of your goods." Chi Jin hung up the phone after he tossed this cold ultimatum out.

His attitude was stern and unambiguous, so the drug dealers had no choice but to act as he said. They tossed Ling Yun in front of the St. Gor Hospital during the night. The entire provincial branch was shocked when they heard the news. Despite being covered in injuries, the hospital promised to treat Ling Yun and help the best they could, and that it was very likely they could at least save his life.

Chi Jin let out a long sigh of relief as soon as he heard that Ling Yun passed the critical stage from the news. He could now continue his plan without any more burden on his shoulders. Of course, the plan he had in mind was simple, yet effective. He jotted down Mariano's contact information from the man's subordinate. He contacted the Brazilian merchant and requested to make a trade. Chi Jin told him he will give the entire truck full of red ice to the man if he could give Chi Jin some money to run.

The young officer knew humanity's greed; Mariano may have paid Mu Kun a hefty deposit, but it couldn't compare to the value of that much red ice. There was no reason for him to decline paying out a little extra to take the entire truck away.

After settling on a time and place, Chi Jin gave Miss T another call to meet up at the same time and place he had promised Mariano.

Chi Jin already picked out a good place for an ambush. There were two plans he had in mind. If Mu Kun showed up, he would just kill the man right on the spot. If Mu Kun was a careful man who didn't show up personally, he would kill Mariano or a key subordinate of the drug lord. Both sides developed a rocky relationship over this transaction, so one bullet through a skull could easily become the trigger to warfare between two parties—which would then give him an opportunity to eliminate the drug lord.

Yet reality differed from expectation. This plan was hoping to fit the key into the right keyhole, but these perfect scenarios could only occur in movies. As Chi Jin had expected, Mu Kun didn't show himself even when it was time to meet.

Chi Jin hid in a place about 30 meters from the exact location of the meeting place. He saw from afar that Mu Kun was sitting inside the car, observing the outside.

It was too far away for a precise aim from a handgun; Chi Jin changed his plan and waited for Mariano to come, ready to take down the first person to show up.

Unfortunately, he underestimated Mu Kun's slyness. Ever since the first phone call, Mu Kun had already guessed that the young man had a plan to take them all down at once. He soon gave Mariano a call to indicate that he will accept the offer to lure the traitor in and take back his goods.

The person who Chi Jin took down was only a lackey and not Mariano himself. The bait might have looked flashy, but his real identity was a nameless person under the Brazilian merchant.

Thus, Chi Jin exposed his location at that moment. Both sides turned their guns toward his direction and began firing rapidly.

Bullets rained down at that instant; even with Chi Jin's dexterity, he wasn't able to dodge the deadly shower and ate a bullet in his leg. Picking a fight with the fierce lions meant he had to prepare for a bloodbath. Unlike his Type 64 pistol, the weapons used by the arms merchants were much deadlier. One shot through his leg was enough to blow open a fist-sized hole that pierced through his bone.

Mu Kun finally walked out and showed himself when Chi Jin was dragged out from the ruins with his broken leg.

The young man was pushed to the ground like a defeated stray dog before him, limbs still bloodied.

"You think you can take my life with a silly trick like this? Fool!" Mu Kun's nose crinkled as he sniffed the fresh smell of blood from the young man. He then lifted a leg and stepped heavily on the broken limb and said, "Tell me, where did you put my goods?"

Mu Kun was a perverse man who enjoyed personally interrogating his prey. Chi Jin was aware of this and knew he couldn't escape after causing such a ruckus.

Chi Jin was beaten until blood covered his face, and just when everyone thought he was on his last breath, he suddenly lifted his head and grinned. Blood mingled with his saliva and dripped from his mouth at that almost horrendous smile.

He pulled out a hand grenade from his pocket.

Mu Kun realized what was happening, cursed out loud, and quickly retreated. He didn't think that this seemingly foolish child could have kept another card up his sleeves in face of his meticulous calculations.

The truth was, Chi Jin had planned everything intending to give his life. While the best-case scenario was to kill the drug lord as he sparked a fight between the two parties, he knew he had to at least find a chance to get close to Mu Kun if it didn't work out.

He could only repay his sins with his life. He had planned to take Mu Kun to the afterlife with him from the very start.

Everyone backed up in fear as Chi Jin lifted and pulled the safety pin. At the instant his flesh exploded into pieces of confetti, he closed his eyes. He saw that man appear within an illusionary world of light. The man carried a young Chi Jin out through the burning fire; his figure was tall, shoulders wide and strong. From then on, the young boy saw a world full of possibilities and found the holy grail he would follow for the rest of his life.

The illusion before death was almost soothing. Chi Jin chanted silently with a smile in the end:

For my captain.

(iv)

Aside from Chi Jin's shattered corpse, there were other dead bodies at the scene of the explosion. But Mu Kun was nowhere to be found. The evil and mad drug lord hadn't met his end and once again escaped.

According to the analysis of the local police department, Mu Kun was likely injured from the incident. The several hideouts he had within the city were completely cleared out after the explosion, and according to reliable intel from Myanmar, Mu Kun was now in the territories of the Golden Triangle.

Ling Yun was saved, and Xie Lanshan was still on the run. Tao Longyue didn't receive any new orders and took the train back to the Municipal Bureau to report his findings.

Spring Festival had passed, and the weather was sunny for once. White clouds were visible in the clear blue sky that seemed like beautiful lace behind clean silk; even the greyish roads were shimmering beneath the light. Tao Longyue left the train station and rushed toward the Municipal Bureau without stopping by his house.

There was nobody inside the chief's office; he was supposedly meeting with a guest right now. Tao Longyue knew this was the perfect opportunity and walked right into the reception room. As expected, Director Peng from the provincial branch and Captain Sui from the Blue Fox were both sitting in the reception room, discussing important matters with Liu Yanbo and Tao Jun on the side.

Tao Longyue slammed down his gun on the table before the Director, and said, "I can't do this anymore."

This kind of attitude was frowned upon during formal occasions. It was even as serious as a capital offense in ancient times. Of course, while rules were more lax today, it was still inappropriate to pull out a gun before a direct supervisor in this manner. Tao Jun scolded frantically, "What kind of attitude is this? Nonsense!"

Unlike his normal explosive attitude, Tao Longyue only glanced at his own father with a surprising calmness in his eyes as he said, "I can't continue this job of arresting Xie Lanshan."

Director Peng's expression grew cold, but he didn't speak. Beside him, Sui Hong looked up to face Tao Longyue and said, "Please explain."

Tao Longyue was grieving, not for himself but for Xie Lanshan. His lips trembled slightly; the bright sun that always shone in the bureau finally broke down before his own father and boss.

"Even a blind little girl said he was a good person. But look at us, we have so many people who could see clearly but have such blind hearts; why are we so insistent on forcing him down this deadly path? Just what has he done wrong?" Tao Longyue clenched his fist. His eyes reddened as he said with overflowing emotions, "Li Rui messed with his car, but he would rather crash himself into the ER than harm a single innocent pedestrian on the road. If he wasn't on the ship during the cruise case, do you think any of those girls would have survived? Aren't these all cases that he solved after that damned surgery? I know A'Lan was a quiet and almost stern person in the past, so maybe that part did change, but his heart never changed. His heart was always for his country, for his people, and it's always burning more passionately than the warmest iron stoves in the world!"

Director Peng didn't speak, and Captain Sui remained wordless. Even Liu Yanbo's stern face seemed to soften up a little. Tao Longyue's usual deep voice rang even more powerful and strong amidst this silence. He continued with this same scolding energy, "His body may have died in the Golden Triangle, but his soul lived on. A'Lan is still A'Lan, we can't let him give his life honorably once and then strip that honor away from him and demand a second death." Tao Longyue waved his tensed-up arm as he reached his limit, and tears finally rolled down his eyes as he said, "Do you all think this is fucking something we can and should do to him?!"

Director Peng remained in the same position, with his hands overlapping as Tao Longyue spoke. His eyebrows furrowed, gaze cold and hard like ice.

After another long and breath-taking silence, Director Peng finally let out a long sigh. His icy eyes also seemed to have melted and reignited with warmth. He slowly opened his mouth, but every word he spoke was powerful and stern. "Let's put Xie Lanshan's arrest aside for now. Young Xie... has certainly been through too much lately."

This 'too much' comment had a certain weight to it. Two words were not enough to capture the inhuman treatment Xie Lanshan had dealt with these past days, but because they came out of Director Peng's mouth, that at least meant neither Xie Lanshan nor Ye Shen would have to fear the gunpoints of police from now on. A mix of emotions poured into Tao Longyue as he choked up a little. The bittersweetness after releasing his pent-up frustration finally caught up to him as he lowered his head and wiped away the tears on his face.

He even cursed at himself. *Damn, stop being so fucking sentimental!*

Sui Hong watched this crying, headstrong captain and also let out a sigh as he shook his head. He said to Tao Longyue,

"Captain Tao, I spoke with Director Peng about this case, and we still believe there is a spy within this special task force. Judging from Mu Kun's reaction, he seemed to have a good grasp of our rescue plan. But Xie Lanshan is no longer in the bureau. I believe the real spy must be someone else. Do you happen to have anyone you suspect?"

Tao Longyue stood back upright and pulled himself out of mourning. After some thought, he responded, "Chi Jin is already dead, but judging by his intention of taking Mu Kun down with him, I don't think he gave out any information about this rescue mission. As for members that have participated since the start of the mission, aside from the Blue Fox, there was only myself and Chief Liu from the Municipal Bureau." Tao Longyue gave two names but shifted his gaze slightly toward Liu Yanbo.

Liu Yanbo returned the glance without hesitation but still felt uneasy at Tao Longyue's gaze. After serving as a police officer for more than half of his life and facing retirement soon, he had never betrayed his profession and beliefs, even at his high rank. However, this was certainly an odd occurrence. The Blue Fox lost almost half of its members on the mission; it was unlikely the spy came out of them. Tao Longyue may be rough and rash at times, but he was still a passionate man with a good heart of justice. He looked nothing like a spy.

A little ray of sunlight slowly vanished from the window. The shadow cast over the cellphone also disappeared and exposed the item like the claws of a beast. Liu Yanbo's gaze suddenly fell onto his phone following the disappearing shadow. He quickly thought of his son and came up with a horrific assumption based on the young man's recent strange acts.

Sui Hong stood up as he left the seniors to continue

discussing the matter and said to Tao Longyue, "Captain Tao, I have someone I'd like you to meet."

Captain Sui of the Blue Fox was a commander of words and elegance. Unlike the leaders of the judicial departments, who often gave off a stern air of authority or intimidating force, he was a courteous and classy man who carried exceptional merits. Thus, even if Tao Longyue could show resistance against other leaders, he was always very respectful to Captain Sui.

It had only been a short while since they last met, but Tao Longyue noticed the man had changed a lot. Despite his relatively young age, Tao Longyue already saw white hair on the roots of Captain Sui's fringes.

Tao Longyue sympathized with the man; losing even one member of his team was the heaviest blow to a captain, however, the man still walked with his head high and tall like a warrior who refused to bow down. But his eyebrows never fully lifted in relief. His forehead creased slightly even when he smiled; the melancholic color seemed to be painted on his face.

Tao Longyue followed Sui Hong out the door and walked down the staircase to the reception rooms located in the lower levels.

Sui Hong coughed violently once again as they arrived in front of another reception room. Tao Longyue was worried about his body and asked, "Captain Sui, do you want to go to the hospital?"

"It's been going on for a while, don't worry." Sui Hong gave a faint smile as he pulled out a bottle of cough syrup from his pocket. He didn't open it up to take a sip and simply played around with the bottle in his palms, looking down at it.

The small brown bottle was easy to carry around. Sui Hong had grown used to having the bottle around him over these years.

"I've never seen this brand. How is it?" Tao Longyue didn't know where the cough syrup came from and asked nonchalantly.

Sui Hong didn't answer and kept his gaze on the small bottle in his hand. He would still cough every once in a while as his eyes grew red—not the blood-thirsty kind, but as if they contained years of sorrow.

Tao Longyue couldn't understand the grief behind that gaze, but he knew he shouldn't interrupt the man. However, Sui Hong was a man of discipline, so he simply shook his head with a smile and then quickly placed the bottle back into his pocket. He explained everything to Tao Longyue, "We've received intel that Mu Kun is currently negotiating a trade with a Brazilian arms merchant to exchange red ice with heavy weapons. He wants to forcefully take over the Golden Triangle and clean up Guan Nuoqin's old subordinates. Yet even though he prepared a little over one ton of red ice, Chi Jin stole it all."

"Over one ton?" Tao Longyue gasped in shock. "If we look at the current market price of red ice, that's at least seven to eight billion yuan!"

Sui Hong nodded and said, "The entire country is currently launching a strict anti-drug policy right now. Not only is it difficult to obtain raw materials, but it would also take at least two to three months to produce over a ton of red ice even if they found materials. The Golden Triangle is a dangerous place right now; Guan Nuoqin's followers still want to find a chance to regain power, and because Mu Kun is injured, he needs to find the missing red ice as soon as he can. This man would never give up at a time like this—and we can use his desperation right now to lure him out of his den."

"But with how sly Mu Kun is, I'm afraid he won't fall for a bait that easily. If A'Lan was still here..." Tao Longyue stopped himself. He knew they owed the man too much now and had no reason to ask Xie Lanshan to risk his life again.

"We can't rely on Xie Lanshan alone. Chi Jin hid the red ice he intercepted. Neither us nor Mu Kun knows where it is." Sui Hong's eyes would dim a little at every mention of Xie Lanshan's name, but continued after clearing his throat, "If Mu Kun is in a rush to find that one ton of red ice, we should prepare what he wants and send someone out to trade with him."

Tao Longyue asked, puzzled, "We can get some bits and pieces of red ice on the market, but where are we going to get a whole ton of completely pure ice?"

Sui Hong smiled and said, "We don't need one ton, only a bit of real ice to lure him in. The rest could be fake, as long as it's enough to make Mu Kun's men believe it's real."

Sui Hong opened the door to the reception room as they spoke. A young man that looked quite like a thug was sitting inside casually with a leg up on the table.

Tao Longyue recognized the man's face. He was the one that Xiao Liang arrested. He scolded on instinct, "Zang Yifeng, what the heck did you do now?"

"I didn't do anything. You guys want me to cause trouble and I can't even refuse."

"Explain yourself clearly and put your leg down!"

"Captain Tao, I'm the one who invited him over." Sui Hong walked into the room and closed the door behind him. He explained, "I recalled that your unit had once captured someone who made fake red ice. We can use him to fight against Mu Kun."

Zang Yifeng squinted his eyes and quirked up the corner of his mouth, then said as if he had no intention of getting involved, "I said I ain't gonna do it! Don't give me all that about merits and laws. What makes you think a bastard lowlife like me would work for the country? You've gotta be kidding me!"

Sui Hong smiled at him and said, "Why put yourself down like this? We've tested the red ice you made in the labs. There's a substance inside very similar chemically to drug-relief medicine that can help suppress narcotic effects and be used to help rehab. So, you're no bastard, you're a genius chemist and a good person."

"Stop, stop it right now, don't give me those praises! I hate drug addicts and drugs, but that doesn't mean I'm a good guy!" Zang Yifeng cried out loud in anger, then quickly calmed down. His eyes dimmed until his pupils looked to be two black stains on his body that contained a painful scar. He continued to speak at a lower volume. "It's just that someone close to me got killed after taking drugs. I also got jailed for selling drugs and couldn't protect her at the time she needed me most... Anyway, go find someone else. Can't believe you guys think a murderer is a cop! I won't work for you guys!"

Sui Hong was a little surprised at these words; he was certain this man had seen Xie Lanshan and perhaps had some history with Ye Shen as well.

Tao Longyue said angrily, "Do you not want to clear your records?"

"Now that's open bribery!" But Zang Yifeng insisted on not helping and continued to sit with his legs up on the chair, staring right at Sui Hong and then glancing repulsively toward Tao Longyue on the side. "You look more reliable. I'm not talking with that big ol' bear guy beside you!"

"Hey, you—"

The door opened once again, and a man stood against the light.

Tao Longyue turned to look and could almost feel his jaw

drop to the ground. He called out, stuttering, "Shen, Shen Liufei? You're alive!"

(v)

Zang Yifeng didn't recognize Shen Liufei, but the latter certainly recognized the man. His gaze scanned the entire room, from Sui Hong to Tao Longyue, and then finally focused on Zang Yifeng's face.

Tao Longyue rejoiced as soon as he saw Shen Liufei, because that meant Xie Lanshan would no longer wander off outside anymore. He rushed up and gave the artist a warm embrace and said, "Mr. Shen, I'm so glad you're back!"

Faced with an overly excited Tao Longyue, Shen Liufei took a step back to dodge the hug and only responded with a gentle nod. Pieces of his memories had returned, but the scenes that flashed before his eyes still seemed too unrealistic—like they were hidden behind a silkscreen or fog. Even this passionate Captain Tao was still a stranger to him.

Yet Shen Liufei remained calm and collected, so Tao Longyue didn't notice the change in the man. He stopped himself in time and scratched his head as he said, "A'Lan... I'm sure you heard about Xie Lanshan's situation already, huh?"

Only at the mention of the name did Shen Liufei's eyes lit up a little, like a small but graceful candlelight behind the shadows.

Zang Yifeng was a guest here, and if he insisted on not cooperating with the case, even Sui Hong couldn't force him to comply. The thug had never been able to stand tall in front of these police officers and was enjoying this minor victory in his mind. Under the angry glares of Captain Tao, he strutted out of the Hanhai City Municipal Bureau.

Zang Yifeng only walked a block out when he noticed someone was tailing him.

He hung out with criminals before and was quite alert to danger, so he acted as if he was glancing nonchalantly at a store window and carefully checked his surroundings, but didn't find anyone.

His heart was still restless, even if there wasn't anyone around. He wrapped his jacket tighter around himself and sprinted back home.

He opened his door to see a large backpack resting inside.

Before heading off to the Municipal Bureau, Zang Yifeng contacted A'Xia and learned that Xie Lanshan was still in contact with her. So, he purchased a train ticket and packed all of his luggage as quickly as he could. Afraid the people from the Municipal Bureau would continue to pester him, he grabbed the bag and rushed out of the house without even stopping to sit.

The streets were empty after a holiday. Zang Yifeng walked on the quiet roads and once again noticed someone tailing him. The person also didn't intend to hide. The footsteps behind kept a respectful but confident distance from him. Zang Yifeng's heart sank; he knew he got into big trouble.

He began taking bigger leaps forward and ran. Near the end of the street, Zang Yifeng turned to the right side and then quickly attacked the incoming stalker.

Shen Liufei reacted swiftly, dodging the attack.

"Why are you stalking me?" Zang Yifeng was used to fighting his way out of trouble, so the missed ambush didn't bother him. He quickly lifted his fist and threw it toward Shen Liufei. His idea was to beat the man down with force first, then interrogate to find out the man's intentions.

After seeing the man successfully dodge the second punch, Zang Yifeng riled up all of his energy to throw more punches, one heavier than the next. Yet he couldn't have imagined that this exquisite Mr. Shen was actually an expert in close combat.

Finding an opening, Shen Liufei lifted a hand after dodging all attacks and twisted Zang Yifeng's wrist. He pulled up his other arm and then locked the latter's throat in his hand.

Shen Liufei pressed the man onto the moldy wall and said courteously beside Zang Yifeng's ear, "We can continue this pointless fighting game or sit down and have a peaceful talk."

Zang Yifeng knew he couldn't fight back with the hand locked on his throat and nodded.

Shen Liufei glanced at the backpack that was tossed to the side and asked, "Are you going on a trip?"

Zang Yifeng waved his sore arms and could only answer reluctantly, in fear of being beaten. "I'm looking for a friend."

Shen Liufei asked, "Xie Lanshan?"

He explained after seeing the latter's eyes grow wide, "I've checked the train ticket you purchased as soon as I entered the bureau. If you're heading near the China-Myanmar border, I'm assuming you're going to visit Xie Lanshan over there."

"H-he's a wanted criminal and I'm just a gangster," Zang Yifeng stuttered as he tried to give an excuse. "We might have met out of pure coincidence, but I have no reason to go outta my way to find him."

"Of course you have no business looking for Xie Lanshan," Shen Liufei said as his eyebrows furrowed, expression grave, "but what if the person you're looking for is actually Ye Shen?"

Zang Yifeng couldn't believe his deepest secret was exposed like this. Like a snake that was grappled at his weak point, he froze and closed his mouth.

Shen Liufei continued, "I know that you've already recognized that the Xie Lanshan now is Ye Shen since the first time you met him. I also know that you assumed he killed your girlfriend, Zhuo Tian."

Zang Yifeng recovered from his state of shock and fired back, "I didn't assume; I know he's the murderer! A disgusting man!"

It was certainly quite nasty. The data showed that Ye Shen never ran after Zhuo Tian called the police. By the time the police entered his house, the suspect was properly sitting by the window. The entire floor and his whole body were covered in blood. Only the moonlight showered on his long hair as he caressed a piece of fresh human skin in his hands gently and lovingly. He faced the cops pointing their guns at him with a smile and said, "I've been waiting for you all."

They discovered more than one person's DNA and skin in his house, as if he was someone who had a perverse hobby of collecting such items.

And the piece of skin he was holding in his hand was from Zhuo Tian.

Ye Shen didn't explain the other human skins in his house but confessed fully to two particular cases. He admitted to being the culprit of the family massacre ten years ago and the one who murdered Zhuo Tian.

According to the police investigation, he was the neighbor of the family that was murdered when he was young. He was able to give a detailed account of the crime, admitting to some aspects even the police weren't aware of. They also discovered the murder weapon at the crime scene with only Ye Shen's fingerprints found on the knife handle. Since the testimonies and evidence matched up, the case was solved without trouble.

Shen Liufei asked, "Have you met him before?"

Zang Yifeng responded, "I've never met him and he doesn't know who I am. But A'Tian fell for him like she went mad before her death, telling me every day that she met a very attractive man. I followed her a few times and saw Ye Shen that way."

"Attractive?" Shen Liufei asked, He could tell she didn't simply mean his good looks and said, "Please explain."

"A'Tian said that he isn't interested in women but respects them a lot. He told her that women are symbols of beauty and kindness, that they're like spring buds of flowers. But he also said that some women are not aware of their own powers and allow themselves to sink into the abyss of drugs and violence. They don't know how to escape and don't dare to fight back—he even said that he wants to save these women and help them recognize the inner beauty they have inside them like some sort of delusional hero. A'Tian was head over heels with this nonsensical logic and even tried to break up with me. But how could I have known this guy was just a damned crook!"

Shen Liufei fell into silence; the occasional hints Xie Lanshan had shown in fighting poison with poison while solving cases seemed to have a clear explanation now.

"I've been tracking down Ye Shen's whereabouts ever since I got released from jail, and heard that he was sentenced to death, that he even donated his body right before he died. That man was an orphan, so no family even came in to check his body. I always assumed he was really dead until I saw him one day on the news. I think it was some mass kidnapping case on a cruise. They said he saved a ship full of high school girls... I first thought it was just someone who looked like him because it wasn't impossible to find similar faces, especially with a huge population in China. But I double-checked just in case, and after I saw him with my own eyes, I confirmed he was that twisted murderer who committed his first crime at fourteen. I will never forget those eyes of his, those arrogant, cocky..."

Shen Liufei nodded in agreement with those words. Vengeance could turn people's eyes sharp; he knew from experience. He also recognized upon first glance of Xie Lanshan that there were traces of Ye Shen in him—that kind of arrogance that treated mortal life like toys was not something that could easily be hidden.

"So I decided to stay in Hanhai, purposely caused some trouble near the Municipal Bureau just so I could be arrested. I wanted to get close to him and confirm my suspicion with my own eyes. And then he became a wanted criminal soon after. I walked in and out of the Municipal Bureau so often that I'm practically on a first-name basis with that Officer Xiao Liang. I overheard a conversation about some 'memory transplant' and that's how I confirmed my suspicion was correct. This guy really is Ye Shen." Zang Yifeng paused at that moment and cried with his face behind his hand, "Why did they allow this sinful murderer a chance to be reborn? And even turned him into a national hero? And my A'Tian, my A'Tian's lying alone beneath the earth. I don't even know where her body is right now."

Shen Liufei empathized with the man's agony and waited until the man vented out all his frustrations before saying, "The local police acted immediately after Zhuo Tian reported the crime; Ye Shen didn't have enough time to hide a body. The police already searched all possible locations around his house that could hide a body but found nothing. Have you considered the possibility that Zhuo Tian wasn't killed, nor had her body dismembered, and instead ran away on her own?"

"How is that possible?" Zang Yifeng growled. "Even if she had plans to run and hide, why would she still run away after the police came?"

"That's a question for you." Shen Liufei's sharp gaze locked on the man and asked, "Does Zhuo Tian do drugs?"

"S-she doesn't!" Zang Yifeng denied in shock.

"I've asked someone to investigate your background privately, so I have more information on her than the cops do. You two lived together for a long time; since you used to sell and do drugs, doesn't that mean she was likely doing drugs with you?"

"So what if she did!" Seeing that he could no longer hide, Zang Yifeng admitted and asked, "Does that mean she deserved to die because she was a druggie?"

"The police captured you for drug dealing at the time and didn't expose your girlfriend, but that doesn't mean the police wouldn't investigate her. I have a guess. Because she was also involved in the drug trade with you, there was no way she could show her face before the police, so she chose to go missing after calling the police."

Zang Yifeng instinctively defended Zhuo Tian and said menacingly, "Your guess is baseless! You're just trying to say that the victim is guilty!"

Shen Liufei said, "My assumption is based on the fact that we've found Zhuo Tian's body. It wasn't in the city Ye Shen lived in, it was near the border of Thailand and Myanmar thousands of kilometers away. She was tossed into a mass grave; all the victims inside were female prostitutes from the red-light districts. These young women were sold off, kidnapped, or had their own reasons to sell their bodies."

Zang Yifeng's expression was bizarre; he opened his mouth as if he was breathing in water, his eyeballs rolled around in different directions. Shen Liufei caught this strange and negative emotion on his face.

Shen Liufei narrowed his eyes and asked, "If you two are a drug dealing couple, is it possible that you two have talked about moving to the Golden Triangle to escape the stricter laws and shrinking market here in China?"

Zang Yifeng choked on his own spit for an instant, then finally let out a sigh and nodded his head. He said darkly, "We did talk about that right before she was murdered."

He lifted his voice once again and cried out in anger, "And

so what if we did? Even if A'Tian died in Myanmar, that doesn't mean that man could torture her like that. Why did he let her bleed out so much and even rip off a piece of her skin? And why did he admit to killing her? Can you imagine how big this man's ego is? He didn't even run when the cops came. It's like he was waiting to be arrested!"

If Zhuo Tian never died in his hands, why did Ye Shen choose to shoulder the blame for her murder?

Shen Liufei couldn't find a reasonable answer—Zang Yifeng's question was also his question. After a long while, he finally said, "I don't think he actually killed any of the women he ripped the skin off of. Perhaps his actual intent was to save them. If Zhuo Tian never sold herself off in the Golden Triangle, perhaps she would have had the same fate as the first victim from the family massacre; that young mother who suffered through years of abuse and harassment who couldn't stand up for herself is still living peacefully somewhere in this world."

Zang Yifeng's eyes widened. "How could you be so sure?"

Shen Liufei looked at him calmly and said, "I'm the survivor of that massacre, the son of that young mother."

Zang Yifeng's shocked expression froze. His body trembled for a long while until even he felt his world shattered, only repeating the words, "I don't believe... I can't believe..."

"If you don't believe me, then bring me to the man you're looking for. I'll prove it to you."

Zang Yifeng finally said that Xie Lanshan was keeping in contact with an old friend of his, A'Xia, in order to find Mu Kun. A'Xia had hung around Miss T and knew the people in the organization well. Zang Yifeng could ask her for potential places where Xie Lanshan might hide.

(vi)

Xie Lanshan sat alone in front of the dinner table at sundown, the corners of the table worn over years of use. There was nothing on the table, no food or water.

Night fell quickly. The last ray of light escaped through the window and shone on his face.

This was a place A'Xia told him about. Every city seemed to have a blind spot where the police could not reach, and many drug addicts gathered in these places like bacteria growing in a mossy corner.

His whole body felt heavy, as if lead filled his veins. Xie Lanshan's face was wet, his fringes also wet, unsure if it was from sweat or tears. The reopened wound still hadn't been treated and his fever continued to burn, a much more serious one.

Xie Lanshan stared blankly ahead of him—there was nothing and nobody there.

The 'good person' comment from that blind girl touched on his weak spot. These two words were like a sandstorm in his mind. He tried to fight against it, but felt his soul continuously being tugged and pulled by different forces in agony.

One inch, two inches—the ray of light shifted like the last remaining spark of fire grasping onto an extinguished stove. Another one inch, two inches—the room was finally left in darkness.

His eyes had grown used to this despairing blackness. Yet the moment he lifted his heavy eyelids, a strong light shone through. The light expanded like threads on a fabric, and he saw a man within this blinding light. It was a man who looked identical to himself. Or perhaps it was more accurate to say the man was himself.

Xie Lanshan never imagined he would face himself under

these circumstances. For an instant, he thought he was either on the brink of madness or having a hallucination from the fever, that everything was just a dream.

Yet the world told him that he was sitting right in front of himself right now. Xie Lanshan was sitting in front of Xie Lanshan.

Xie Lanshan's wet hair fell onto his shoulders, his white shirt was covered in bloodstains and dust, completely disarrayed. But the man sitting in front of him was wearing a police uniform; beneath the cap was a clean short haircut and deep eyes. His gaze was confident but kind, his expression highlighted by the warm light around him like a saint of purity.

Xie Lanshan let out a snarl at this ironic scene which tugged at the corner of his lips as he said, "It's you."

The man across from him said, "It's me."

Xie Lanshan leaned in to stare at this identical face. He clapped his hands together like a beggar and asked, "Can you tell me who you are, and who I am?"

The latter smiled. "I'm you."

"No, you're not..." Xie Lanshan's eyes widened as he shook his head, "They said that I'm not you. I don't even know who I am."

According to most people in this world, good and evil were separate sides, heroes and villains were never synonyms in any language.

To drug-enforcement officer Xie Lanshan, he should have successfully completed his mission and returned in victory if it wasn't for that deadly accident. If he didn't go through that ridiculous surgery, he should have returned to his home as a martyr. His coffin would have been covered in that red flag, fresh flowers decorating his tombstone. Perhaps many years later, people would sing the song of his heroic deeds to their children.

As for a criminal on death row like Ye Shen, he was a sinful murderer who should have been rejoicing at this chance to live on. He was reborn through this surgery and received all the abilities of a special forces officer—he could have easily used this newfound knowledge and physical abilities to escape the shackles of the law.

But he was still in pain.

The man before him looked gently at him and said confidently, "Then follow your heart."

What was his heart? Xie Lanshan thought about it for a moment before he shook his head and mumbled to himself, "But... it's too painful..."

He looked at the man in front of him with a cowardly, muddled gaze fixed on this familiar yet strange part of himself. A tear rolled down Xie Lanshan's face. He really didn't understand and was desperate for an answer, so he asked, "Don't you think it's too much? Nobody remembers what you've done, even your sacrifice was taken for granted. You continue walking down a solitary path with such a heavy burden on your shoulders, unable to complain or find someone who could understand you... it's too painful to be a good person... it's too much..."

The latter gave him a smile and said, "But isn't this our fate?"

Xie Lanshan frowned and looked at the cop before him, puzzled.

"From the moment we are born from our mother's womb until the end of our time where we return to the earth, this is how life is from start to finish. Solitude, helplessness, unable to be understood, unable to make decisions... All the mortal lives that are intertwined on this earth share a similar experience." Xie Lanshan saw the gentle smile on the other's face and a hand reached out to him. The latter said, "I chose to live this unique way of life myself, as a way to honor and respect the concept of life itself."

A ray of light flashed in the midst of chaos and darkness. All the memories from this drug-enforcement officer reappeared more clearly in his mind. Xie Lanshan also reached out a hand and attempted to touch these illusions.

We are all born alone until we overcome solitude.

We are all born with egos until we overcome our own limits.

We see through the purest evil in humanity until we overcome the abyss of darkness and share benevolence with the world around us.

Without me, there would be no you.

Xie Lanshan closed his eyes and could almost feel the warmth on his hand.

And then he heard a voice. A familiar voice called to him by his name, "Xie Lanshan!"

It was Shen Liufei's voice.

He opened his eyes in the dark like two revitalized sparks of fire, glowing more fiercely by the second.

Shen Liufei rushed over with Zang Yifeng's guidance. He wanted to knock on every door to search but grew more anxious until he finally gave up and began crying out the man's name.

Xie Lanshan heard his voice and walked out the door to greet the man that came for him.

Zang Yifeng stood still before his enemy and removed the friendly facade. He stared coldly at Xie Lanshan and said clearly, "I'm Zhuo Tian's boyfriend."

"I remember her." Xie Lanshan nodded and didn't explain further. He took a step toward Zang Yifeng and knelt before the latter.

Both men standing were shocked. This sudden action meant the man admitted to who he was. Rage filled Zang Yifeng as he lifted a leg and stepped violently on Xie Lanshan's injured shoulder. Fresh blood once again stained his shirt as the wound reopened.

Despite the pain, Xie Lanshan didn't cry out at this violent gesture and crawled back up, once again kneeling before the man.

"I'm gonna kill you! I'm gonna kill you! How dare you treat her that way! If it wasn't for you, she wouldn't have died!" Zang Yifeng had the intent to kill this man, so he wouldn't let go of this opportunity to avenge his girlfriend. He kicked Xie Lanshan and then stepped heavily on the latter's stomach after Xie Lanshan fell to the ground multiple times.

Xie Lanshan vomited stomach acid and crawled up once again. Out of a guilty conscience to repent, he never returned a punch and allowed Zang Yifeng to beat him over and over.

Hatred fueled every punch and every kick, but Xie Lanshan didn't feel pain. Instead, he felt relief.

Shen Liufei still had mixed feelings about this man. He stood silently on the side and watched the beating. He watched as Xie Lanshan was beaten down, then crawled back up again and again to the same kneeling position. He watched as blood rolled down the corner of Xie Lanshan's lips, leaving a trail of crimson down his skin.

Those shared memories he had with this man reappeared in his mind.

Beneath Shen Liufei's dark eyes, sparks of fire melted through the coldness and shone through the silk screen of memories. Finally, those forgotten emotions were rediscovered, and the fog dispersed.

"I'm gonna kill you! I'm gonna—"

"That's enough." Xie Lanshan was still kneeling on the ground when he suddenly clapped his hands together, catching Zang Yifeng's fist between them. He slowly lifted his head and gave the man a playful smile behind his disheveled look. "Keep your hands off the face. Don't you feel bad for trying to attack my handsome face?"

Shen Liufei's lips curled up at this scene; he knew that along with his own memories, his Xie Lanshan had also returned.

Xie Lanshan's mind was clear and awake at this moment. He turned and pushed Zang Yifeng down to the ground. Before the man could get up, he leaned down and stared at the man in the eye, promising sincerely, "Stop the beating for now, put it on my tab. I promise I'll return it to you after I finish my job."

This gaze differed completely from the first time Zang Yifeng met the man; it was clear, bright, and confident. Zang Yifeng was startled by this gaze and subconsciously nodded.

Xie Lanshan pulled himself up after letting the man go. He wiped off the blood from his chin and then wobbled toward Shen Liufei.

He leaned his forehead onto the man's shoulder and called out gently, "Hey, cuz."

Shen Liufei lifted a hand and placed it on Xie Lanshan's back, then pulled the man into a full embrace.

This powerful but warm embrace finally calmed his heart. Xie Lanshan closed his eyes and repeated softly, "I want to be a good person..."

I want to be a good person.

Homecoming

Xie Lanshan returned to the Golden Triangle on a spring night of light rain.

The once blooming opium fields had vanished, like the place had completely transformed. After Mu Kun's group was annihilated, the governments around the Golden Triangle set strict policies banning the growth of opium flowers. Among the countries involved, Laos was the first to invest in recreation. The Laos government stationed national guards around the area and began implementing new policies to replace narcotics with more economic agriculture.

Yet the Golden Triangle was still the biggest source of illegal drugs in the world. Many locals suffered from addiction as traditional and new drugs continued to grow in the market. The underground ice labs beneath the Mekong River were powerful factories, and the dying heroin market could also easily revitalize if precautions were not taken. As the neighboring province in China, Hanhai was an important checkpoint in intercepting the cross-national drug trade.

The Jinlong mountains were like a fearsome dragon resting

beneath the dusky sun, the Mekong River shimmering red like blood. The banana forests beneath stretched past the horizon while the kapok trees stood tall against them. Xie Lanshan stared for a long time at the scene and closed his eyes, feeling his heart beat heavily and senses stimulated.

Six years of being undercover passed like a horrific dream.

Xie Lanshan knew where Mu Kun and his men liked to hang out in the Golden Triangle. He had seen some familiar faces when he was captured by Mu Kun, and perhaps out of his own bias, every face was unforgettable and damned.

After a few days of investigation, Xie Lanshan successfully tracked down one person. He tailed the man carefully until he went into an isolated location, then forced the man down and shoved him against a wall.

Xie Lanshan handed the drug dealer a USB drive and told him to bring it back to Mu Kun. He said, "He will reward you heavily if you do as I say, but if you don't give it to him, I will chase you down across the globe until you're dead."

Mu Kun soon received the USB drive that contained a short video. The video was filmed in an entire room full of red ice with his beloved Xie Lanshan on camera.

There was one pack of red ice beside Xie Lanshan. In the video, he took out some of that beautiful crystal-like substance and slowly ground it into powder with his fingers. The purple powder fell between his fingers almost artfully.

A small portion of the drugs was bought off the market, but most of it was fake, made by Zang Yifeng—though Mu Kun couldn't possibly tell the difference from just a video. Xie Lanshan lifted a luring smile in the video and said, "I'm still a member of the Blue Fox in the end. I know my teammates better than you. So, sorry, but all the red ice that Chi Jin stole from you is in my hands now."

That damned bastard! Mu Kun cursed in his mind; he had searched everywhere the kid could have hidden the goods but could not find anything.

"These goods are worth at least seven billion to you, but for someone who has no intention of selling drugs, they're completely worthless to me. So, I'm going to ask you to give me some money. Those damned cops are still after me. I need to get out of the country."

In order to lure Mu Kun in, Xie Lanshan kept his arrest warrant up.

At the end of the video, Xie Lanshan gave a satellite phone number and then gave Mu Kun a smile, saying, "You know how to find me."

Chi Jin's grenade may not have killed Mu Kun, but it did gravely injure him. Just before the explosion, Mu Kun grabbed onto a lackey to use as a shield, but it wasn't enough to spare him from some injuries. Aside from severe burns and scratches on his left arm, there was also a serious avulsion on the same side. He went through three surgeries back to back after returning to Myanmar.

Mu Kun's bandages were being changed when he called Xie Lanshan through the number; the doctor was cleaning his wounds with iodine and preparing to rewrap with clean bandages.

The sharp pain during this process made cold sweat roll down his face. Mu Kun leaned against the soft tatami and waited for Xie Lanshan to pick up the video call from the other line. Almost as soon as Xie Lanshan's face appeared when the call went through, his eyes beamed. He almost forgot about his injury and struggled to sit up.

Unlike the playful style in the recorded video, now Xie

Lanshan had cut his hair short and exposed his clean features; harsh bruises were visible on his face. He sat on the ground before the camera, one hand holding a sculpting knife and another hand holding a half-sculpted wooden elephant. Beside his feet were chips of wood varying in sizes. His expression was calm and tranquil, like a peaceful body of water, reserved and quiet.

This man who had been undercover for years beside the drug lord had worked harder than anyone else and suffered the most injuries than any of his men. Mu Kun still remembered that Xie Lanshan would always sit in the corner with small wounds all over his body, quietly sculpting a piece of wood in his hand.

For a moment, Mu Kun felt as if he was in a dream, as if that A'Lan he once knew had returned.

Xie Lanshan saw the injuries on Mu Kun's exposed upper body. The sharp cuts were still untreated, blood was still visible through the white bandages.

"I remember you were also injured that time you were ambushed by Guan Nuoqin's men," Xie Lanshan recalled at a strange time like this and said calmly, "it was in a forest near the borders of Thailand and Myanmar. I told you back then that I would get you out of there."

The drizzle over the last few days finally stopped, but the weather remained foggy and moist for the sprouting greens. A gust of wind shook off a floor full of raindrops, making the place look even more like a rainforest from a fairytale. The stony expression on Xie Lanshan's face brought all the memories back. Mu Kun remembered how Xie Lanshan took out the poison from his leg and how this young man carried him out of the forest on that same rainy night.

He half-jokingly said that he wanted to tattoo his name on Xie Lanshan, to which the latter finally responded after shaking his hand and promising earnestly that they will forever be brothers.

The rush of memories only made Mu Kun feel agonized and dazed, even more than the physical pain he felt on his body. He covered his face in his hands and begged through his lips, "Stop pretending to be him, you're not him... you're not him..."

Xie Lanshan stared at him pitifully and silently for a few moments, then suddenly chuckled. At that moment, his expression changed; his gaze was aloof and cocky. He tossed the little wooden elephant in hand aside and pressed the back of the knife's blade against his red lips, then smiled. "Alright, let's talk business."

The man shifted smoothly between two vastly different states. Mu Kun's mind was still foggy from his injury and almost couldn't tell if this man on the call was a drug-enforcement officer or a wanted murderer.

"Seven billion worth of red ice; I only want one billion worth of diamonds from you. I think it's a pretty fair trade." Xie Lanshan shifted the camera angle and gestured toward the helicopter outside of his hideout. He then moved the camera back and said, "I rented out a helicopter with some of your red ice. Once you give me the money and I hand off the goods, I'll leave this place and never show up before you as Xie Lanshan again."

"How are you so sure that I can pay out one billion worth of diamonds right now?" The doctor pressed a little harder while changing his bandages. Mu Kun bit down his teeth and glared at the man, then turned back and snarled at Xie Lanshan. "Besides, what makes you think I'll agree to this trade-off?"

"Diamonds are a girl's best friend," Xie Lanshan said pretentiously and lifted an eyebrow. He then laughed and said, "Didn't you say I'm the queen of your dreams? What's wrong with winning the affection of your queen with some diamonds?"

The smile vanished almost instantly as soon as he finished the line. He held up a hand at the camera and then said sternly, "We're brothers who have been through life and death together."

When Xie Lanshan entered the state of a drug-enforcement officer, everything from his demeanor down to the tone of his voice seemed to have transformed. That stiff and stern look was strangely enticing to Mu Kun. The drug lord was enchanted by this image and said, almost without thought, "Why do you even need to escape overseas when you can come back to my side?"

The passion from this man was almost laughable and pitiful. Xie Lanshan once again pulled himself out of this stern state and said cockishly, "I'll decide the place we meet. You decide the time—just to be fair."

They set the location, the third military zone near the border of Laos. The Laos government had established a special Golden Triangle economic zone and specifically stationed a group of militia in the area, supervised by a Laotian Colonel named Xayachack.

Guan Nuoqin was able to overtake Mu Kun's territories within a short time because he had connections with government officials in all countries surrounding the Golden Triangle. The investigation behind Kang Tai also dragged out some dirt among high-ranking officials. Most of them in Thailand had already lost power, and rumors had it that Xayachack was the double agent for the drug lords in Laos.

Mu Kun couldn't possibly buy the Laotian off in such a short time frame, and because he often worked with drug traders, there was hostility between Xayachack and the Chinese forces.

Mu Kun would therefore not dare to act too rashly in this theoretical neutral zone. The Chinese forces also had no jurisdiction over this piece of land, making it a safe space for both sides.

"If you're scared, you don't even need to show up yourself and just send your men in with the diamonds." Just before hanging up the call, Xie Lanshan said lightly:

"I'm the cop, you're the bandit."

Tang Qinglan, who had been waiting outside, walked into the room holding the hand of a young girl that looked to be only seven or eight years old. She was Guan Nuoqin's granddaughter, Naga. She was a pretty girl with a round face, eyes big with long lashes, and had soft natural curls in her hair. Mu Kun raised her in order to keep Guan Nuoqin's old subordinates under control.

Tang Qinglan knew what the man was thinking, seeing him ponder silently in the room and took the little girl out to play. Before she left, she warned, "Xie Lanshan clearly has an ulterior motive for proposing this trade. I don't trust him."

His bandages were fully rewrapped with a new medication, but Mu Kun's muscles still twitched in pain. The glare in his eyes was flickering like a ray of cold moonlight in the black night.

"We heard from Liu Mingfang's branch chief dad through the bug on his cellphone that Blue Fox Captain Sui Hong is in Myanmar right now. It's clear that they're trying to lure you out with Xie Lanshan and this one ton of red ice." Tang Qinglan grew anxious after receiving no response from the man. Her pretty face twisted as she said, "Has that little mutt from the Blue Fox not caused you enough trouble that you're willing to risk your life once again?"

"Come here." Mu Kun finally spoke after panting heavily, his voice deeper than normal.

"Don't try to swallow what you can't digest. Are you saying that the red ice is more important than our business and your life?"

She walked toward the man on the tatami, only to see the latter enraged. He picked up a medical scissor the doctor hadn't taken away from the side and lashed out.

Tang Qinglan couldn't react in time; a deep cut sliced across her face.

She screamed and attempted to run, but the man quickly pulled on her hair.

"You fool, do you really think I care about that seven billion red ice?" An injured beast was the epitome of madness. Mu Kun pulled Tang Qinglan toward him, leaned in, and growled into her ear, "The only thing I want is Xie Lanshan."

A subordinate opened the door during the conversation and Mu Kun finally let the woman go. He closed his eyes lazily and said, "If it's not something I want to hear, then don't say it or I'll kill you."

The report was exactly what he wanted to hear.

After listening in to Liu Yanbo's cell phone, he learned that Captain Sui Hong had secretly arrived in Myanmar. However, the man didn't rush to carry out a mission and instead went to a small town east of the country called Mongton.

Mu Kun sent out massive forces to search for Sui Hong's whereabouts in Mongton and finally discovered that the man would visit a small temple in the village every year.

Myanmar was a Buddhist country with countless temples across the land. This temple was on the top of a small mountain, which made it quite deserted. It was dusty and old, as if nobody ever came to pay respects.

Aside from some old monks that still lived there, the broken temple was a lone tower that stood silently for centuries facing northward.

It wasn't likely that a drug-enforcement unit captain would be a religious man, and even if he was, he wouldn't secretly visit this insignificant temple in the middle of nowhere. Mu Kun thus guessed that his A'Lan was buried there.

(ii)

Xie Lanshan suggested a few locations to meet up within the military zone, and Mu Kun happily accepted to meet up at a small bar.

Members of the Blue Fox were already hiding around the bar. Xie Lanshan's plan was carefully calculated. The first step was to make sure Mu Kun showed up and let either snipers or the Blue Fox take him down by force.

Xie Lanshan was certain that Mu Kun would come personally to the meeting; the man would never give up his twisted obsession with the young cop.

Mu Kun certainly arrived on time with three bullet-proof cars in front of the bar. A little girl with curled hair jumped out as soon as the door opened, followed by Mu Kun, who then held her up above his shoulder.

Armed drug dealers also stepped out of the three cars outside and guarded the front door of the bar, while others stayed in the car as if they had other plans. Mu Kun carried the girl into the bar with a loving smile.

He had his reason for choosing this location.

There weren't many places for snipers to hide during the daytime. In addition, the environment made it difficult to find good angles to aim. As expected, the Blue Fox lost their opportunity to snipe and barge in with force. This drug lord was cruel and sly, allowing a seven-year-old girl to be his hostage and shield.

The bar was still open to the public to hide from the eyes of the authorities. A few young men sat and drank at the bar table while a singer serenaded the patrons with her deep voice.

Xie Lanshan arrived earlier than Mu Kun and sat beside the window. He didn't roll up his sleeves nor unbutton his white-collared shirt; its tails were tucked into his black pants conservatively. The shimmering sunlight showered on his profile through the window. He was deep in thought; his whole figure emitted a sense of purity and cleanliness.

Mu Kun stared carefully at Xie Lanshan for a while before placing the little girl on his shoulder down. He walked over and sat before Xie Lanshan.

The latter looked up, saw the little girl beside Mu Kun, and frowned.

The girl was more reliable than a bullet-proof vest, and Mu Kun knew that very well. He gestured for Naga to stand by the window and said gently, "Be a good girl and sing a song for me here, okay?"

The girl did not know her grandfather died under this man's evil conspiracies, treating him as her real uncle. She gave a sweet smile, stood beside the window, and began singing.

Mu Kun clapped for her with a smile while her clear vocals rang inside the bar. The drug lord also seemed to enjoy playing the role of a good uncle. Mu Kun counted the beats for her as he watched the girl, but said to Xie Lanshan, "Let me search you. I don't think you would want this little girl to become an innocent sacrifice."

Xie Lanshan let out a small sigh, stood up, and held out his arms in front of Mu Kun.

"Turn around."

Xie Lanshan obeyed the order under the curious gazes of a few customers inside the bar.

Mu Kun walked behind Xie Lanshan and began searching carefully.

Against the thin fabric, his fingers traced down Xie Lanshan's fit body from the shoulder, underarm, even down to his thin waist. Mu Kun kneeled to check if there were guns hidden beneath Xie Lanshan's pants, his face practically glued onto Xie Lanshan's butt.

He couldn't stop himself from yearning for this body. He attempted to find traces of the other person's existence on this man. From that gaze, the movements, even down to the tone of voice and smell, every similarity he could find enticed him but also pained him.

Soon, Mu Kun found a listening device and small hand grenade—an identical one that Chi Jin had before.

"Do you Chinese people all enjoy suicide bombing or something?" Mu Kun laughed as he tossed the two items on the table. The few young men at the bar saw the items and ran out, screaming.

Only the little girl by the window who didn't recognize these items continued singing and asked Mu Kun with a grin, "Do you like my song, uncle?"

"I do. Sing another one for your uncle." Mu Kun grinned back at her and then turned to Xie Lanshan in anger. "They've used you, wronged you, and even harmed you like that. Why are you still willing to die for them?!"

"I'm not doing it for them. I just want you dead." Xie Lanshan sat back down and responded calmly, even after being exposed, "I've said it already, I'm the cop and you're the bandit."

Mu Kun was almost shaken up by this familiar stern demeanor of Xie Lanshan. The next moment, he clapped and laughed. "Good, a lesson learned today."

His eyes fell outside of the window as he said, "These cars outside are all filled with explosives. If you dare do anything fishy or attempt to take me down with you, the area within a radius of a few hundred meters will burn into ashes. You, me, and everyone else will be crushed in an instant." The man was insane. He lowered his head and spoke into that listening device on the table with reddened eyes. "Captain Sui, I don't know what your government did to pressure Laos to allow special forces like your team to arrest someone in their territory. But I know that the rest of the Blue Fox is here and waiting outside the door. Do you want them to die too?"

Sui Hong's expression darkened outside the bar. He glanced at his teammates and gestured for them to back off.

Soon after, Mu Kun began ranting about the Cuban missile crisis at Xie Lanshan. He rambled about how Kennedy and Khrushchev's battle was to prove who was the maddest man on earth, and who was willing to be the cruelest dominator. He said that the crisis almost a century ago mirrored the turbulent situation today. Even if he dared to blow up the entire military zone in Laos, that would mean he was digging his grave to let the military crush his organization.

"You sure are crazy." Xie Lanshan's eyes widened for an instant, but he quickly regained his posture and sneered.

"Just some occasional madness for you... no, not you..." Mu Kun corrected himself and said with a painful expression, "Not for you, it's for my A'Lan."

Mu Kun took a bottle of wine from the table and crushed the listening device with a heavy slam.

A sharp noise came out of the earphones of the officers. Sui Hong, who was drifting back toward a safe zone, could no longer listen in to the conversation inside the bar.

Mu Kun looked at Xie Lanshan and said coldly, "There must be another tracking device on you. Take it out."

Xie Lanshan rolled up his left sleeve, grabbed a knife on the table, and sliced his arm to pull out a small GPS chip from beneath his skin.

"Do you know why I agreed to meet here?" Mu Kun looked quite pleased as he pointed at the latter and forced Xie Lanshan to stand. He then took out a rope and tied Xie Lanshan's hands in the back. He shoved the man to walk in a certain direction and said, "War exists alongside the people living in the Golden Triangle. All bars and clubs here are connected to each other through underground passages."

They left the little girl in the bar and walked down into a tunnel, then got into a car that was parked and waiting underground.

"Where are we going?" Xie Lanshan frowned and asked as he got into the passenger's seat, then laughed. He licked the corner of his lips and brushed his tongue across his white teeth, saying, "Just you and me, not too bad of a scenario."

The difference between this man and his A'Lan was only millimeters away, but this comment completely set them apart. Unamused by this flirtatious attitude, Mu Kun's eyes dimmed down and knocked Xie Lanshan unconscious with a heavy punch.

Mu Kun turned on the engine as he glanced at the unconscious man on the side and drove out before the Blue Fox could chase them down.

He whispered to the man beside him gently, "Don't you want to know where you're buried?"

(iii)

Amidst the conspiring plots woven by truths and lies, every step leading up to the small temple on the mountain top had advanced just as Xie Lanshan and Shen Liufei planned.

Yet neither of them could have expected that Mu Kun would send his men to guard the temple and dig up Xie Lanshan's ashes from the side of the tower.

Xie Lanshan's expression changed slightly as he realized the danger of this situation. Aside from Mu Kun, there were another dozen or so drug dealers fully armed with weapons. Some guarded outside the temple while others were stationed inside. Perhaps from Mu Kun's orders, they were forced to chant mantras with the monks in the temple to send off Officer Xie's soul properly.

After four hours of driving, the sky became grey. Xie Lanshan could see the plain but clean structure of the sacred temple through the dim light. Flames from a row of red candles swayed in the breeze, and that blue and white urn rested quietly within this circle.

Four Blue Fox members who had already shaved their heads and donned the crimson monk robes sat quietly with their heads down, suppressing the rage within them and the temptation to pull their guns from beneath their robes. They continued to chant with the masters of the temple as they waited for an opportunity to strike.

"You're about to die here. Any final words?" Mu Kun held up a gun against Xie Lanshan's head and forced him to walk toward the empty ground before the temple gate.

"You said you want me to die before Officer Xie's grave. Can't you at least show me where he's buried?" Xie Lanshan attempted to bargain with Mu Kun, but he knew it was in vain. If the urn was already dug up, the gun hidden beside the tower must have already been taken away by Mu Kun's men as well.

That was originally his backup plan, but it didn't seem like it would work now.

"There's no need anymore." As expected, Mu Kun pointed his gun toward Xie Lanshan on the empty field, past the group of monks still chanting on the ground. "You disgusting mutt. You don't deserve to live on with A'Lan's identity—I'll send you to hell in front of him right now."

The monks all witnessed this scene, and the chanting paused for a second. Mu Kun immediately hollered, "Don't stop! Keep chanting, louder!"

"What are you talking about? I'm A'Lan..." The chanting continued rhythmically by his ears. Xie Lanshan's hands were still tied, facing Mu Kun's gunpoint as he carefully took steps back.

The small blade sewn into his sleeves was close to cutting through the rope, but the situation was still dire.

There were a dozen drug dealers at the location and four special agents disguised as monks. The difference in manpower wasn't the problem, but the fact that almost half of the drug dealers carried submachine guns was worrisome. Sui Hong had already set up plans to send out helicopter backup at any moment, but they still needed to take down Mu Kun first and take control of the situation or they would risk the lives of all the monks in the temple.

Xie Lanshan's face grew pale and he bit down on his lips. He wasn't fearful, he simply hated his uselessness and that he allowed himself to be prey in the hands of a predator. Despite promising Shen Liufei that he would take care of himself and not die with Mu Kun, he refused to let this chance be in vain under the man's gun.

"You aren't, stop trying to pretend you are!" Mu Kun's gun was pointed at Xie Lanshan as he glared evilly. "I remember I told you that I will kill you in front of A'Lan."

Xie Lanshan's sweat rolled down his face as Mu Kun's finger was about to pull on the trigger. His throat rolled unnaturally at the comment. If he hadn't forgotten what Mu Kun said, he would have planned everything differently and not allowed the man to bring him over here.

But alas, no plan was perfect, and he was one step behind.

The instant before the trigger was pulled, a little Sami stood up amongst the monks in red. He called out to Mu Kun, "Wait."

The Sami wasn't that tall, his face clean and elegant, looking to be about thirteen or fourteen years old. He faced the gunpoint fearlessly and said to Mu Kun with his palms together, "There's an old saying in Chinese that said 'the sinner who has wronged the heavens shall be beheaded. Another saying is 'the gravest sins cannot be liberated by prayers'. These two sayings prove that all prayers and transcendence rituals for the dead who saw their ends in foreign land will never reach the heavens. And even if they do reach the afterlife, it could affect their fortune in the land of gods."

Xie Lanshan certainly was in a foreign land right now; his body had been buried for years, but his soul and memories continued to live on in another body. Mu Kun was angered. "How dare you curse him, monk!"

The Sami sighed and shook his head, "Sending off the soul is to allow the dead a peaceful afterlife after agony, also a way for us to cultivate and practice goodness. I cannot and will not persuade you to not kill a person, so instead, I will vow to carry this urn at the end of this man's life. Borrowing Buddha's powers, I will help return the body to where it belongs so that the dead can escape the torturous cycle and return to reincarnation."

Mu Kun's expression was wistful. Chanting, transcendence, and vows—everything he had done was for his A'Lan; his grief was sincere and genuine. His lips trembled as he said, "Bring A'Lan... bring his urn over here, to me."

The Sami held up the urn, stepped out of the temple, and walked slowly toward the two men.

Lights were dim inside the temple, and Xie Lanshan only saw clearly under the sunlight that the urn wasn't made of fanciful white marble or sandalwood, nor did it have any intricate carvings.

It was a plain and basic ceramic urn, blue and white pottery designs with only cleanly painted mountains and rivers on the exterior.

A few steps away from Mu Kun, the Sami suddenly tossed the ceramic urn toward Xie Lanshan.

Within an instant, the urn shattered beside Xie Lanshan's foot. Beneath the white ashes was the gun he had hidden beside the tower.

While Xie Lanshan broke out of the rope to grab the gun from the ground, Mu Kun cried out loud, "A'Lan!"

The drug lord didn't even notice the gun and only saw his A'Lan shattered on the ground, about to be blown away by the winds on the mountaintop.

"Ah! A'Lan!" Mu Kun snapped and turned his gunpoint towards the Sami, firing a few rounds without even aiming.

Fresh blood splashed out as the bullets pierced through his body. The Sami fell to the ground with a smile.

Xie Lanshan grabbed onto the gun at this moment, narrowed his eyes, and aimed at Mu Kun's head. The next moment, he pulled the trigger.

At almost the same time, Mu Kun twisted his head and also fired back.

Both men dropped to the ground after being shot; the bullet pierced through Mu Kun's head while Xie Lanshan was shot on the right in his chest. The four Blue Fox members in disguise got up amidst the chaos and quickly took down two drug dealers holding submachine guns.

Every member was a brave soul; some still stood up after taking bullets and brawled with the drug dealers.

The Sami was on his last breath, his limbs twitched in pain. Xie Lanshan, who was still on the ground, stared at him. He wasn't sure why the child decided to do this.

The large robe pressed onto the Sami's body, exposing some feminine curves. The Sami reached a bloodied hand out toward Xie Lanshan. Her hands trembled like a withering flower as she moved her lips, coughing out blood as she said, "Do you... remember me...?"

Unlike the clear and calm voice earlier, this weak and gentle sound was that of a little girl.

Xie Lanshan attempted to recall where he'd seen this Sami as blood rolled from his injury. He tried to crawl up but fell back down due to lack of energy. He thought she was familiar.

"Are you..." Xie Lanshan traced his memories and finally found the source of this familiarity. His eyes widened in surprise and disbelief as he said, "You're... Annie?"

"Annie's my sister..." The girl blinked as tears rolled down her eyes, and she smiled. "I'm the little girl you saved from the brothel."

Xie Lanshan could never forget that beautiful and brave woman. He almost exposed himself from saving the brothel full of children, and she gave her life to protect his comrade in return.

He also remembered what Annie said before her death; *Buddha is not supposed to commit murder, so I will do it for him.*

And the nine-year-old girl from that time, he also remembered. A high-ranking government official violently abused her in the brothel in Myanmar. The official was over 50, portly and ugly. Just as she was drowning in despair, it was almost as if the heavens heard her prayers when she saw the man arrive. He struck down that heavy man who was pressing on her small body with a gunshot. He then took off his jacket, kneeled before her, and gently wrapped her naked and wounded body with it. The warmth was real, as if he was wrapping home-made dumplings during a family gathering.

He burned down that damned place. He took her and all the girls who shared the same tragic fate as her out of the endless abyss into a new life.

Her sister Annie was too deep in the drug trade and could no longer act on her own; she had nowhere to go once she escaped and so hid herself in this temple. Never could she have imagined she would meet that man's captain in a place like this. She eavesdropped on the conversation between his captain and the master and learned that the man who saved her was a Chinese drug-enforcement officer named Xie Lanshan. Then, the evil drug traders knocked on their temple door. In order to prepare for the worst, she silently hid that gun she found in Xie Lanshan's urn.

The girl would never forget how this handsome man named Xie Lanshan warmly saved her from that torturous life.

"Sis..." She was willing to give her life for this man, just like her sister. She closed her eyes with a smile and said, "He really is... a kind person..."

The backup helicopter arrived almost as soon as the battle broke out. The propellers raised a gust of sandstorm, the sharpest but warmest gale of spring.

This gust of wind carried the ashes of a hero into the air, higher and higher, further and further away.

Xie Lanshan's injury was still bleeding. He was too exhausted to move. He could only watch as a ground full of snow-white ashes floated into the air. This was a peculiar feeling; it was like seeing a part of himself ride the wind and fly to the horizon.

He refused to stay for the blossoming flowers, the sky-soaring mountains, or the streaming rivers. He returned with the winds, flying northward, northward; past the 4060 kilometers of the international borders, until he reached the beautiful Xishuangbana prefecture. Further in was the Hanhai City he was born and raised in—the vast country of China he had served.

Because of the unique geographical location, the Chinese drug market was the most rampant in Hanhai. Ever since the formation of the first anti-drug force, over 2000 tons of illegal drugs had been blocked outside of the country. Dozens of police officers sacrificed for these efforts, over hundreds were severely injured.

Shen Liufei came, Sui Hong came; many people came. They all looked up and watched the gale travel further away.

Xie Lanshan smiled as he watched the earth from above. This was the land he protected with his blood and bone; this was the peace he had loyally sworn to watch over for the rest of his life.

He was finally home.

Finale

"I hereby swear to become a police officer of the People's Republic of China, to give myself to the honorable career of protecting the civilians of my country. I pledge my allegiance to the government, to serve the people, abide by the law, and uphold discipline..."

In the warmth of spring, the Hanhai City Municipal Bureau welcomed twenty new officers into their department. Traditionally, every officer must give their pledges on the first day of the job, but as the Municipal Bureau was heading the troubling anti-drug efforts throughout the whole province, they temporarily held off the requirement.

The Golden Triangle finally settled after cleaning up the storm left by Mu Kun and his remaining forces. That was when the Municipal Bureau remembered that they still needed to host the orientation for newcomers. After delegating tasks to the appropriate departments, the branch chief asked human resources to arrange a tour for the newcomers who recently entered the Municipal Bureau. The plan also included an orientation for pledges, open for both veteran and new officers.

June was the beginning of summer, the sky was exceptionally clear. In the martyr's hall inside the public security's education department, a staff member was summarizing the most heroic deeds in the history of Hanhai City's anti-drug operations. The veteran officers were all standing in their navy blue uniforms in a straight row, listening to the speech with grave expressions on their faces.

Even the leaders from the Provincial Department of Public Security showed up. The person who escorted the guests in these events was no longer Liu Yanbo. Ever since he discovered his son had installed a listening app on his phone, he cooperated with Sui Hong in setting up the trap to lure Mu Kun in. After Mu Kun was shot dead and Tang Qinglan was arrested, he personally reported Liu Mingfang to the public security department. After this heartless cut-off between father and son, he grew tired of staying in Hanhai and found an excuse to be transferred to another city.

The representative from the bureau now became Tao Jun. Director Peng scanned the row of cops standing in the hall and then leaned in toward Tao Jun, asking, "Where's Xie Lanshan?"

Tao Jun followed Peng Huaili's gaze and noticed that the little rascal evidently didn't show up.

After greeting the senior officers, Tao Jun walked toward Tao Longyue. Unable to scold Xie Lanshan in person, he had no choice but to release his anger onto his son and asked, "Where's Xie Lanshan? Didn't you call him?"

Tao Longyue explained, "I told him, but he..."

Tao Jun's expression darkened. "He what?"

Seeing the old man's face grow darker, Tao Longyue could only confess, "He said he'll come if he feels like it."

"If he feels like it? He just got promoted to Vice-Captain, how can he still act so undisciplined?" Tao Jun roared in anger at his son, "Give me your phone, I'll give him a call!"

"Hey ol'Tao, didn't I tell you I'll come if I feel—"

"Feel what? Feel like my ass!" Tao Jun was ready to reach through the phone and drag this rascal over to the orientation as soon as he heard Xie Lanshan's voice. He held the phone and howled, "Get over here right now!"

"My... my wound reopened..." The energetic voice earlier disappeared as Xie Lanshan put on an act and explained to Tao Jun sickly, "I wanted to show up, but I can't..."

Xie Lanshan was certainly on his last breath that day they carried him up to the helicopter from the mountaintop. He was in critical condition for seven whole days before his life was finally saved.

This time, he didn't spill blood in vain and earned himself another second-class merit, allowing him to be promoted to the rank of Vice-Captain in the homicide and violent crime unit as soon as he returned.

"Stop acting in front of me. I'm warning you now, hurry over—"

"I think the signal's bad here. Ah, my head hurts, can't see, it's morning sickness... I'll hang up now."

"Xie Lanshan? Xie Lanshan, how dare you hang up! You—"

"Hello... Wow, what's with this signal? Hello?" Xie Lanshan called out a few more times to fake a poor signal and then hung up the phone. He let out a breath of air and turned off his phone in case of more unwanted harassment.

He had just gotten off the airplane and was sitting on a bus, heading toward a southern town called Guitang with Shen Liufei.

"Already a disciplinary warning just when you got promoted." Shen Liufei commented, "That's not good."

"Hey cuz, don't you know how boring those stupid patriotic orientations are?" Shen Liufei wasn't a cop, of course he never had to sit through it, but Xie Lanshan couldn't stand a second of that. He pulled out a canned beer from the backpack and leaned back on the seat with a grin. "It's one thing to listen to those old men giving speeches and telling stories, but everyone has to sing that bland national anthem. I swear it's the most boring thing in the world."

The bus drove straight down the uneven roads. Xie Lanshan was ready to open the can of beer when Shen Liufei reached an arm over and took the can from him.

Shen Liufei carefully tapped the bottom of the can with his fingers to reduce the carbon dioxide in the beer and stop it from fizzing upon opening.

It was a simple trick that even Xie Lanshan knew, but of course, he was too lazy to do it himself. He stared at Shen Liufei with a warm look and full heart, thinking: *My cuz really is handsome and kind.*

Shen Liufei pulled on the ring and opened the can, then handed it back to Xie Lanshan.

"Thank—"

Before the 's' sound could drop, Xie Lanshan saw the man pull his arm back and took a sip of the beer as if to tease him.

As the taste of barley rolled down his throat, Shen Liufei said coolly, "You can't touch alcohol."

"Why not?" Xie Lanshan didn't understand; it was already summer.

"Didn't you say you wanted to puke earlier?" Shen Liufei turned to him and said sternly, "Pregnancy vomiting. For the sake of my future son, you should drink some water instead."

"Hey, that was just a joke..." Xie Lanshan's gaze fell onto Shen Liufei's throat as he saw the latter take another gulp down and said, "Hey cuz."

Shen Liufei turned around and pressed his lips against Xie Lanshan's before the latter could react and fed him the beer mouth-to-mouth.

The alcohol danced between their tongues, some dripped down from the corner of their lips. Xie Lanshan tasted the booze and returned the kiss passionately as he drowned himself in this intimacy. The bitterness of the beer intertwined with this sweet kiss into a spiral of madness. Xie Lanshan could feel his body melting as he sank deeper into his seat while Shen Liufei reached an arm over and held his waist.

The two generally kept a good distance in the Municipal Bureau and didn't get too close in front of people. But it was different when they were away from their hometown; they didn't need to worry about their job roles nor the eyes of others. Shen Liufei lifted Xie Lanshan's chin up and gently pressed his lips against the corner of Xie Lanshan's mouth where the beer dripped out.

A passenger nearby them on the same bus clicked their tongue in disgust. Xie Lanshan didn't mind and glanced to see a middle-aged man staring in judgment. He gave the man a snarky grin and then turned back to bite Shen Liufei's tongue.

The kiss lasted for about ten minutes before they finally separated.

Shen Liufei turned to look out the window after letting his hands down from Xie Lanshan's waist. There was a small rural town with no tall buildings outside. The sky was a clear blue, grass emerald, the small boats on the river all carried traditional red lamps. The small town only began a tourist business within the last two years, but it wasn't a popular tourist destination and was rather quiet compared to the city.

The two men arrived at Guitang today not for vacation, but to search for Shen Liufei's mother.

Duan Licheng's guess was correct, and the aftereffects of the surgery were complicated. One of them was that people who had gone through the surgery would sometimes trigger deeper memories when they were near death. Just like how

Shen Liufei recalled being abused as a child, Xie Lanshan regained all of Ye Shen's memories.

Shen Liufei waited by Xie Lanshan's bedside for seven days and nights, and Xie Lanshan told him two things as soon as he woke up.

The first was: "I love you."

The second was: "Your mother isn't dead; I remember everything now. I know where she is."

(ii)

Two decades later, Shen Liufei finally saw his mother again. He could no longer see the rest of the world; his eyes were fixed on that woman dressed in a peach-colored qipao.

Twenty years had passed, and that woman now past 50 had certainly aged. Her hair was white, her body and face rounder than the old photo he had in his memories. Fine wrinkles covered the corners of her eyes. But as Shen Liufei stared at his mother from afar, he could still see the beautiful young woman from many years ago. The woman in his dreams combed her hair up like a fine serving lady in ancient paintings. The wrinkles on her face were more beautiful than paper-cut flowers.

The woman sat in front of her little shop, which sold local handmade crafts just like the many other stores in the town. The woman's shop wasn't particularly competitive and rather slow compared to others, but she remained calm. Her eyes narrowed as she enjoyed the slightly moist air and gentle sunlight unique to here, occasionally fixing her qipao to be smoothed out more comfortably under the light. Her clothing was intricate; the skirt was open on one side, the peach-colored fabric was decorated with black lining, the collar and sleeves all had hand-embroidered details. She was like a blooming lotus flower resting elegantly beneath the sky.

In order to not make his visit too sudden, Shen Liufei brought his sketchbook along with him. He pretended to be a tourist and walked over to strike up a conversation with the woman.

Xie Lanshan waited outside the shop quietly, allowing this precious time for the mother and son.

The woman didn't recognize her son due to the change of his appearance through the surgery. She could tell from the way the young man dressed that he must be one of those tourists with good money. So, she smiled a little brighter as she happily marketed her little crafts from the store.

"Here, this one would be a great accessory on clothing. You can buy some more to gift your girlfriend or classmates." The woman assumed he was still in college, judging by his looks.

"We also have these handmade little bags. They're a local specialty, hand-embroidered. Look at how artful they are..."

"And this, cloisonne silver bracelets. Buy one for your mother..."

Shen Liufei nodded and took everything the woman tried to sell without complaints. He ended up with a handful of bags, bracelets, and local articles of clothing that a man like him wouldn't wear.

Even the woman was a little embarrassed by the end of it and gave Shen Liufei a slightly awkward smile. "Oh dear, you have to learn how to say no even if you have money to spare. Don't just buy everything people try and sell you."

Shen Liufei's expression was still empty as usual, but in the face of his mother, there was a light of warmth and love beneath his gaze. He said, "It's fine, these are all for my mother. I don't mind as long as she's happy."

"Your mother sure is fortunate to have such a caring and handsome son."

A young girl called out from afar amidst their conversation, "Mom!"

Shen Liufei looked over to see a girl of about fifteen or sixteen rush over toward them. The girl had a fresh lotus seedpod in hand as she called the woman in qipao "Mom".

Shen Liufei quickly realized that his mother remarried and formed a new family with new children.

The girl donned a pretty and intricate long hairstyle with slanted fringes on her forehead. Her big eyes gave her youthful face bright energy; her features looked very similar to her mother and even a little like himself. Shen Liufei could almost recognize with a glance that this was his little half-sister.

The girl wasn't shy and seemed quite interested in this tall and handsome young man. She saw him carry a drawing board and asked, "Are you here to draw? A lot of art students come here to paint sceneries; I also want to become an artist."

Shen Liufei nodded. "I am."

The girl asked, "What do you draw?"

Shen Liufei responded, "Scenery and people, I draw everything."

The girl grinned and asked, "Am I pretty enough, then? Can you draw me?"

Shen Liufei nodded.

"Come here, look at yourself. Your hair's all messed up now for running off. Let mom re-tie it for you."

The woman called her daughter over with a smile. She took the hair tie off and braided the girl's hair. Shen Liufei didn't recall his mother being so skilled with crafts, nor did he ever remember her smiling so sweetly and earnestly.

"Wipe off your sweat and put on some lip gloss." The woman took out a small lip gloss from her pocket and gently brushed a thin layer on the girl's soft lips. She held the girl's shoulders, looked up and down, and after seemingly being satisfied with her daughter's looks, she smiled even brighter. She then said, "Draw down by the bridge. The scenery is much better there."

Green moss covered the red sand rock bridge near the area where the water flowed in. This strange contrast of colors created a unique visual in this peaceful little town. The river streamed gently beneath the bridge; the pencil brushed onto the paper. Shen Liufei sketched carefully as Xie Lanshan quietly stood by his side.

An adolescent girl at this age couldn't sit still. She wasn't able to move as the subject of the artwork, but her mouth was always open for conversation as she asked Shen Liufei questions like she was from the national census. Finally, she got to the most curious question she had and asked, "Are you two... a couple?"

Shen Liufei didn't answer and Xie Lanshan responded, "What do you think?"

"Sure looks like it." The girl studied both men again; the two were tall and handsome like a painting when they stood together, like the most perfect couple in her eyes. She then asked, "There's a lot of places that are open for same-sex marriage now. Will you guys go somewhere to get married?"

The question was a little too much to consider. Xie Lanshan laughed and said, "You sure are a brilliant girl."

"Marriage is a very important part of life to many people, and you need to find the right person. It has nothing to do with gender." The little girl certainly was a progressive soul who opened up, even without anyone asking. "My mom used to suffer a lot when she was younger. Her old husband would beat her all the time and the husband's family even tried to trap her in the house. She used to just take it all in at first until she realized she couldn't continue and rebelled; now look at her, she's living so well! She always told me that if I ever get into a bad marriage, yell back if he yells at you and divorce if he beats you. She said that it's never too late for a woman to stand up for herself, just don't die like a helpless frog in a warm pond—get up even if you're in a pool of blood."

Perhaps out of a natural familiarity with the two men, she kept repeating her mother's words until she suddenly covered her mouth and then giggled. "Oh man, what am I saying?" She stretched her neck and attempted to look at that drawing board she couldn't see, asking, "Are you done? Did you make me pretty?"

Even without Xie Lanshan telling him the truth, Shen Liufei already had a good guess of what happened after seeing the vibrant light on his mother's face. He lifted a faint smile, finished the last few strokes on the paper, and said, "It's done."

He gave the portrait to the little girl, left the items he paid for in the shop, and said he would come to pick them up tomorrow. After they bid this happy family farewell, Shen Liufei and Xie Lanshan found a small tavern to stay overnight.

The town of Guitang was a very close community that preserved many traditional cultures. Houses were virtually glued next to each other in this town, like the residents saw each other as family.

Night fell as the river fogged up beneath the moonlight. All of the families loved hanging lanterns in front of their houses. Red glows lit up at nighttime, like a peaceful starlight of happiness that could be obtained within a hand's reach.

But only those who wished for it would grasp that light.

Shen Liufei stood before the window and watched the quiet scenery outside.

Xie Lanshan asked him, "Are you going to visit her tomorrow?"

"No," Shen Liufei said. "It's enough to know she's living well. There's no need to bother her anymore."

"Maybe it's not bothering her, maybe she would be willing to accept you."

"I wasn't born out of a loving marriage for her, neither was my brother. That's why she didn't leave him out when she tried to rebel."

"That's not true," Xie Lanshan said, "I think your brother's death really was an accident."

The woman was raped by the uncle who had his eyes on her for a while, Zheng Chenlong. Yet her husband blamed her and believed she was in the wrong for seducing the man. After another painful beating, the woman finally couldn't withstand it anymore. She poisoned their drinking water in hopes of taking down the entire abusive family.

Yet she didn't put in enough toxins. Her tough and strong husband didn't die, and instead grabbed an axe and threatened to kill her.

The woman grabbed the axe in the end while the poison weakened him. At that moment, years of pain and hatred finally poured out of her as she dismembered the whole family that was struggling on the ground. The fourteen-year-old eldest son was studying art outside. The strange commotion woke the eight-year-old younger son, and he stepped down the stairs to find his mother.

The woman's eyes were bloodshot; madness consumed her. She heard a sound behind her and turned, axe in hand, ready to butcher.

When a fourteen-year-old Ye Shen heard the sound and arrived at the woman's house, the massacre was already in place.

The young boy was an orphan whose legal guardians didn't care for him, but he enjoyed roaming around freely. He was smart enough to know he'd never feel at home anywhere he went, as if he was a bird that could always fly off at any moment.

The only time he ever received any bit of warmth and care was from this timid, quiet woman.

He saw the woman on the brink of breakdown. The young boy stood up and gave her a way to escape. He quickly rearranged the crime scene and pinned the blame on Zheng Chenlong, who was lying unconscious on the ground.

In order to create a facade of the woman being dead, he made her spill some blood and ripped off a piece of her skin.

The young boy drove off Zheng Chenlong's car and took the man's body away. He buried him deep in the mountains that nobody knew of—until ten years later, when the area began developing and the Dongchuang incident occurred.

Shen Liufei had been searching diligently for his mother over these years, and the weight in his heart finally rested now that he saw her. This was a strange sense of relief that he'd never felt before.

"You're the kid that kept looking in my house when I was young, right?" The two men laid on the bed after a shower. Shen Liufei was still puzzled and asked, "The Hunting Net Operation allowed for cold cases to be reopened. You were afraid the truth of my mother still being alive would be exposed, so you harmed Zhuo Tian, but ended up letting her escape in the end so that you could be arrested on purpose. But I still don't understand. Why are you willing to shoulder crimes that you never committed?"

"Who knows? Maybe I'm tired of this materialistically fulfilling but mentally exhausting and empty life. Or maybe I just pitied them for having to suffer because they were born a different gender."

Shen Liufei almost wanted to laugh at this twisted savior mentality. He turned and embraced Xie Lanshan, then said,

"We're certainly two unique oddballs unlike any others in the world. For the sake of world peace, let's not cause others trouble and just trouble one another."

Xie Lanshan laughed and bit Shen Liufei's nose playfully as he joked, "Didn't you say you wanted a son on the bus? C'mon, give me some trouble."

They kissed and stripped the clothes off each other. The lights were off in the room, only the red ambiance shone through the window. It was a romantic atmosphere that sparked their desires. Like budding flowers in spring, their limbs intertwined until Shen Liufei took the upper hand and pressed Xie Lanshan down.

"I'd rather have a daughter. They say daughters always take after their fathers more." In contrast to Xie Lanshan's bright and large eyes, Shen Liufei's eyes were sharper and colder but had unique attractive curves.

Xie Lanshan raised a hand up and brushed his fingers against the corner of the man's eyes, then said affectionately, "All beauty and romance in this world are like you, but nothing is as good as you."

"No rush," Shen Liufei said. His lower body was already burning up, but his face was still cold and stoic. He turned over and kissed Xie Lanshan's finger, then said, "Work hard and I'm sure one or two children is no big deal; I'm sure you can bear even ten if you wanted." He leaned down and kissed Xie Lanshan's lips.

Whether it was Bai Shuo and Xie Lanshan or Shen Liufei and Ye Shen, their fates had been connected even before they realized. Their love brought them together and as Shen Liufei deepened the kiss, he said, "I love you too."

Their bodies passionately tangled together for the entire night. It was near sunrise when the two men finally fell onto the bed in exhaustion and slept. Xie Lanshan woke up first this time.

He had always woken up to an empty bedside without Shen Liufei. Perhaps the man always had some reservations about this relationship with Ye Shen, but he maintained the contradiction in his mind well. Now that the burden had been lifted, he could finally rest in peace with his lover in his arms.

Shen Liufei lay on the bed; Xie Lanshan rested his head on the man's firm chest, one hand playfully tracing down his body. Yet his phone was in a rush and rang loudly in the next instant.

"I shouldn't have fucking turned on this phone." Xie Lanshan complained as he saw the sound woke Shen Liufei and picked up the call. "Hey Tao, didn't I tell you I'll come in when I feel like it? I know the orientation isn't done yet."

Tao Longyue insisted on killing the mood and called from the other line, "Orientation my ass. There's another murder victim. Get back here and help with the investigation!"

As a newly promoted Vice-Captain, he could skip out on welcoming ceremonies but couldn't leave behind a case. He quickly got up to pack his luggage and rushed back to Hanhai. They tossed their luggage into their house as soon as they got off the plane and headed to the crime scene.

The body had already been taken back for an autopsy, but the search at the scene still continued. Xie Lanshan took a photo of the corpse from Tao Longyue and studied it carefully.

"A civilian was working out in the park yesterday morning and saw a man suspiciously burying something. They later heard the sound of a car driving by and called the cops after. The victim was an adult man around 30 years of age, cause of death a heavy blow on the head from a large object. There were multiple broken bones in his body. We're initially suspecting that his body was tossed after a fatal car crash." Tao Longyue summarized the case for Xie Lanshan and then turned to Shen Liufei. "Mr. Shen, the witness who called the cops is still around. We need you to help with the sketch of the suspect."

Tao Longyue took Shen Liufei to see the witness while Xie Lanshan stayed at the location where the body was dug up to search for more clues.

He picked up the photo of the body once again, but this time he wasn't looking at the strange man in the photo. Through a familiar death scene, he saw another familiar face— he'd seen this man twenty years ago. He was Shen Liufei's uncle, that sinful and disgusting man who even assaulted his cousin's wife—Zheng Chenlong.

Zheng Chenlong had always boasted about wanting to rape a young woman once but didn't pin her down in time and made her fall and drown in a pond while she attempted to run. The girl's family knew that he was the murderer but didn't have evidence to prove the crime. The mother grew sick from anger and died the second year.

That same year, the fourteen-year-old Ye Shen drove the man up onto a deserted mountaintop. Yet just as he was digging the hole, the man woke up.

Zheng Chenlong was only injured, none of the wounds fatal. Because he had lost too much blood, he couldn't move temporarily and could only beg the young boy in front of him. He said that it was just a spur of the moment, that despite being a serial rapist, he didn't want to die...

But no matter how much he cried and begged, the young boy only stared at him with a blank face like a snake eyeing a prey.

Perhaps there really are criminals who were born evil in this world; they were people who judged through murder, allowing the stimulation of blood and flesh to gain the simplest peace of mind.

"That girl drowned on her own. I didn't kill her..."

Irked at the man's talking, the young boy lifted a finger and hushed him up, then gave a faint smile.

"A'Lan, the branch chief just called and said we need to settle this in three days."

Xie Lanshan lifted his eyes and saw Tao Longyue walk over. That devilish smile on his face once again appeared, but then vanished before the latter could notice.

"Did you find anything?" Tao Longyue asked.

"Look here," Xie Lanshan pointed at a dent on the victim's skull and said, "this was a blow by a spindle-type object, perhaps a long stick with a sharp edge. The surrounding parts of the injury bled badly, which means he was struck before his death. As for the rest of the injuries on the head, the bruises are almost unnoticeable. Aside from potentially covering the injuries beneath the hair, it could be that these injuries were made after death."

"We'll know once the autopsy reports are in," Shen Liufei said as he walked the witness over and continued Xie Lanshan's analysis. "Hiding a body after a car crash is both a crime of escape after a traffic case and crime of removing evidence. However, if they intend to create a fake car accident to cover up the truth, then it's a homicide."

"The case isn't that easy." Xie Lanshan nodded toward Shen Liufei and then lifted an eyebrow proudly. "But three days is more than enough time to solve it."

The clouds in the sky jumbled up on this bright June day. A ray of sunlight hastily pierced through the cage of clouds, shining onto the vast lands and water.

Xie Lanshan watched his lover continue to walk toward him as they exchanged a glance.

There was a flash of uncertainty beneath Xie Lanshan's eyes for a moment, yet as Shen Liufei walked closer, the fog disappeared. Just like their first meeting, his heartbeat raced as he saw the man.

Shen Liufei told him through that clear and affectionate gaze:

All roads lead to Rome, even for gods and demons; yet my yearning for you is like the lone flame in the dark, yearning for eternity.

ChiSui Extra: The Unwavering Innocence

The rain shower lightened up the moment the train engine started; for a moment, time seemed to have stopped.

Sui Hong sat by the window. The buildings and trees outside seemed to all move in slow motion as they backed off against the loud sounds of the train trudging away on its tracks. Shortly after, the scenery blurred before his eyes. Sui Hong wasn't in the mood to appreciate the view outside. He took off his heavy coat and pulled out another cough syrup bottle from his pocket.

His melancholic gaze fell onto this small brown bottle as he stared silently.

Chi Jin mailed him a package just before the incident, a whole package full of cough syrup. Captain Sui finally had time to return home and clean up his belongings after annihilating Mu Kun's organization. He discovered that one bottle seemed to have been opened. He found a small piece of paper hidden inside the bottle. On it was an address he didn't recognize.

This was also the destination of the train.

In the border areas of the Hannan Province, there was a small village that people often forgot the name of, but rumors said that Loquat flowers bloomed across the whole mountain range.

Sui Hong was only 25 when he saved a young Chi Jin from the fire. Back then, he was still a member of the main special force team in the city's municipal bureau. It was a time just after the last congressional convention of the nation. All public security officers were called to take part in civil activities to help their communities. Only the frontline anti-drug forces were not required to join in.

But Sui Hong always had an inexplicable interest in this poor but brave young boy. After the fire, he would often take time off to visit him.

Noticing how the parents often neglected this child and he lived in a run-down house, Sui Hong would sometimes invite the boy over to stay for a few days so he could study for school.

One young man and one boy shared the same living space for a while. These times were relaxed and fun. The two would often play basketball together or watch some films in the afternoon at home. Chi Jin was still young and small, so he would often lean over and fall asleep on Sui Hong's shoulder while watching TV. The boy was quiet and innocent when he slept, unlike his normally rowdy demeanor. Sui Hong turned to look at the boy and found his sleeping face silly. He reached out a hand and squeezed those cheeks; Chi Jin didn't open his eyes, but moved his head and buried his face in Sui Hong's chest.

Sui Hong wanted to tease the boy more but didn't want to wake him up. Soon, he also leaned his head back and slowly closed his eyes.

Hot June weather had arrived, white clouds floated above

the blue sky. The boy rested on the man's knees as they both slept peacefully on the sofa.

A few years later, Sui Hong solved a major case and became the youngest Captain in the history of the Blue Fox Commando. The job of a cop was filled with difficulties, but even personal issues became a headache. As soon as he reached 30, Sui Hong's family began pestering him about marriage. The parents were waiting to play with their grandchildren, only to see their son completely dormant in the area of relationships, almost as if he had no interests. Therefore, they began searching their networks to introduce potential partners and force him into arranged dates.

Sui Hong was a respectful son who couldn't fight against his parents, so he naturally accepted the request to see a young woman.

The girl's name was Mi Mai, her appearance pretty and clean, just like her name.

The young woman from a good family almost fell for the Captain of the Blue Fox at first glance, and Sui Hong's impression of her was quite positive.

The good beginning could have led to a happy ending if it continued, but he made the fatal mistake of telling that young boy about it.

It was glossed over almost like a joke, but Chi Jin, who had just entered his last year of high school, was stunned. He then immediately told the Captain no—don't see her anymore.

"Why not?" Sui Hong was shocked.

"Because you can't. If you see her again, I-I..." The young teen stuttered and then yelled, "I won't take the university entrance exam anymore."

"Now that's too harsh. That girl is quite nice. She's very

passionate and smart too. Besides, I like the shape of her eyes." Sui Hong teased him, then said, "People need to be with one another and have a home to survive in this world."

Chi Jin's face froze immediately and felt his heart crushed as he heard those words. He scrunched up his eyebrows and pondered for a bit, then placed a hand on his heart and said as if he was making an oath, "Then I'll be with you."

Sui Hong was taken aback and stared wordlessly at this young man.

"Can you wait a few more years? Five, just five more years should be enough." The teen pressed a hand on his chest as if reciting some cheesy soap opera line, then held another hand out with his pinky up. His gaze was blazing, but his tone was warm and firm.

Wait for me, wait until I can fight. Wait until I can kneel before him, hold my head high and tell him, for my home, my country, and for you.

Sui Hong's heart softened at this bright gaze and finally said, "Are you... really not going to take the exam?"

Chi Jin lowered his gaze shyly and said, "I still have to take it because I promised I'll get into the police academy. Then I can become a special forces officer like you."

Sui Hong stared at the boy's face, eyebrows furrowing slightly as if he was pondering an extremely serious matter. After a long silence, he finally smiled and said, "Alright, I won't see her anymore."

Chi Jin's eyes beamed in surprise. "Really?"

"Yes, but let's make a bet." Sui Hong smiled wider as he pinched Chi Jin's arm slightly and said, "These arms are too skinny, no special forces officer looks this thin."

Chi Jin jumped like he was on a springboard and said, "I'll go out to run right now!"

Sui Hong laughed and said, "Don't forget to keep your grades up in other subjects!"

He admitted the boy didn't have many assets, thin like paper as soon as he took his clothes off. But Sui Hong quickly realized that Chi Jin seemed to have taken this bet seriously. The teen began eating a lot more and worked out intensely. Not including other exercises, he would run over 10,000 meters every day.

The boy gained some muscle, but the training was getting a little too hard. The boy's family almost pitied him and tried to blame Sui Hong for setting an unrealistic example, but that still couldn't shake the boy's determination to become a special forces officer. By the last semester of his last year in high school, Chi Jin moved in with Sui Hong instead of going home.

Thankfully, Sui Hong was also a rare full-time officer with postgraduate degrees from prestigious schools. He could help Chi Jin train in the day and tutor the boy at night.

Once, Sui Hong caught this young adult hiding something from him, which was exposed as soon as Sui Hong called him from behind. The boy revealed a bottle of some indie-brand protein powder.

Sui Hong was angered, but also wanted to laugh. He pulled on Chi Jin's ears and said, "You're not even that old. Why do you need to eat this?"

Caught by the tail, the boy's face flashed red at that instant. Even his ears heated up in embarrassment. He stuttered and said, "This bodybuilder in my class told me about it. He said it works like magic."

"You're not bodybuilding, besides, we don't know what's in these indie brands and it could end up harming you." Sui Hong let go of the boy and took the bottle of powder, then turned away with it. "I'm confiscating this!"

"Huh? No, that was expensive! I ditched class to pick up a part-time gig—" Chi Jin chased behind and quickly closed his mouth after he realized he outed himself.

"Oh, and you're skipping class in your last year of high school to work?" Sui Hong stopped and turned around.

The teen knew he screwed up and stood frozen. Only those pretty eyes stared like a poor puppy at him, clearly still attempting to fight back a little.

Sui Hong's temper dropped at those eyes as he sighed. "Alright, if you promise to not skip class anymore, I'll make steak for dinner tonight."

"I promise! I swear!" The boy's face beamed as he cheered and promised to not skip class anymore.

Sui Hong laughed at this silly gesture.

This place was originally a two-bedroom unit he rented, and after the boy moved in, it finally became more like a home.

Going into winter, even the sun seemed to shiver in the cold. The icy light cast onto the railways like two streams of black rivers stretching to the far ends.

Sui Hong opened up the cough syrup bottle after letting his thoughts run free and took a sip. The slight bitterness hidden behind the sweet syrup swirled in his mouth.

He pondered, just when did their close relationship change?

He recalled back to when Xie Lanshan died in the Golden Triangle. The surgery was a decision Sui Hong made on his own, and to this day, he wasn't sure if he had made the right choice.

Now that he thought about it, Xie Lanshan's personality wasn't fit to be an undercover agent. The young man almost had no flaws. The only exception was that he could not withstand seeing others in pain, even if he had to walk into fire himself.

Of course, Director Peng also noticed this about him. Xie Lanshan wasn't the only one who was sent undercover—but nobody else made it back alive.

In the face of a living hell, even Xie Lanshan had thoughts about giving up. Yet the young man was easily convinced back after a simple comment about prosperity and peace.

Afraid of any troubling aftereffects and how that bloodthirsty and dangerous persona might still linger within the body, Captain Sui had specifically instructed Liu Yanbo to not promote Xie Lanshan.

Most participants of that multinational effort to corner Mu Kun that year returned with promotions—except Xie Lanshan. The young man returned home in great glory, only to fall into a helpless and isolated situation. He was kicked out of the Blue Fox with an arbitrary excuse; even his days in the Municipal Bureau weren't particularly fulfilling.

The emblem on his shoulder never changed. When the Hanhai City Municipal Bureau promoted the captain for the violent crimes unit, Tao Longyue couldn't believe they selected him for this merit and felt wronged on behalf of his best friend.

Xie Lanshan wasn't pleased either, but it wasn't about the promotion. He just didn't understand.

Sui Hong still remembered when he saw Xie Lanshan during a training event; he was shocked at how quickly the surgery had its effect on the man. This once reserved and almost brick-like young man could now smile brightly around others and chat sociably.

Yet when nobody else was around, he would return to being his most beloved subordinate. Xie Lanshan stood before him like a deflated balloon, helpless and weak. He moved his trembling lips and asked, "Captain, I don't care if I can't get promoted, I just don't understand...J-just where did I go wrong?"

Sui Hong analyzed himself and decided that perhaps he had some slight masochist tendencies. He couldn't face the changing "Xie Lanshan" after surgery, but also couldn't help but keep an eye on the young man. He knew the young man was troubled by rumors, discriminated against by his leaders, and even plagued by nightmares. Sui Hong was deeply regretful of his actions and often spent nightless hours sitting in the dark, mourning for every piece of bad news that came up.

Chi Jin already moved out by this point. Even if he still tried to cling on and ask to stay overnight, Sui Hong would always kick him out mercilessly.

One day at home, Sui Hong's attention was seized by the news of Xie Lanshan shooting down a suspect on the news while he was drinking casually with Chi Jin. He dropped into another long and mournful silence.

The boiling alcohol rushed through his veins; Chi Jin always hated seeing his captain show such wistful expression and asked, "Do you like Xie Lanshan?"

"Yes," Sui Hong responded, "I also like you and every one of my teammates."

"Not that kind..." Chi Jin took in a breath of air, desperately trying to hide the envy inside him, and said, "I meant, the kind that speaks to the soul, the kind that makes you desire skinship, the kind where it must only be you. Like love."

Sui Hong looked at him in silence. His feelings toward Xie Lanshan certainly weren't romantic love, but he couldn't understand why this young man in front of him was so hung up on the topic.

"Then why? Why do you always look at him so painfully?" Chi Jin's expression was also in agony; his voice trembled along with his clenched fist. "If you don't like him, then something must be wrong with Xie Lanshan! I've seen with my own eyes how Xie Lanshan let Mu Kun go at the last minute, and even how Mu Kun would rather kill his sniper than take Xie Lanshan's life... I didn't even see bruises on his hands when he returned. You said he's gone through a lot during undercover, but to me it seemed like he was enjoying his six years there. Even I could tell something's wrong, why couldn't you? If you don't like him, they why don't you tell Direct Peng about all of this—"

The high-ranking officials in the provincial branch could no longer get in touch with Xie Lanshan in the Hanhai City Municipal Bureau. Yet Sui Hong was still afraid that Chi Jin would report it to his boss; there were too many loopholes with Xie Lanshan right now. He would not stand a chance if the provincial branch searched him.

So, he decided to tell a lie.

Sui Hong told the young man earnestly, "Yes, I like him."

Chi Jin was stunned; he froze up for a while before he finally cried out in despair, "But doesn't he like Song Qilian? He likes girls."

"It doesn't matter who he likes. What's important is that I like him." Sui Hong suppressed his mournful attitude and said, "Trust me, Xie Lanshan never betrayed the Blue Fox. I don't want any unwanted investigations to affect his life and career."

Like a severely injured beast, Chi Jin suddenly growled and jumped toward him.

After an unrestrained brawl, Sui Hong realized that his little boy had really grown up. Chi Jin was tall and strong, his muscles toned over years of training, and skilled in physical combat. Finally, Chi Jin won and pinned the captain down.

The two men panted heavily after the brawl.

Chi Jin used up all of his energy to pin Sui Hong down beneath him. His gaze filled with desire as he pulled the belt from his pants violently. The alcohol and lust boiled inside him; his eyes were burning as he stared at the man beneath him, breathing heavily.

He couldn't stand listening to this man say that his heart belonged to someone else; those words triggered the suppressed emotions in him as madness consumed his consciousness.

Chi Jin's hand fell onto Sui Hong's crotch, which was quickly gripped by the latter. He leaned down and gently pressed his lips to the other man's but didn't dare to pursue it further.

He hoped for the one he loved to give a response, but his feelings and desires were crushed by unwavering coldness.

While maintaining this awkward position, Sui Hong said gravely, "Chi Jin, I'm your captain."

At that next instant, Chi Jin buried his face in Sui Hong's neck and cried for his unrequited and hopeless love.

Chi Jin sat up. The moment he lifted his head, a single teardrop rolled out from his eyes, down his nose, and dropped onto Sui Hong's face.

This single teardrop burned through Sui Hong's heart. Even many years later, he could still remember the heat of that moment. Perhaps he would never forget it for the rest of his life.

The next day, Chi Jin knocked on his door with a Nim Jong Cough Syrup box as an apology. He smiled and tried to lighten up the mood, saying, "I know Cap'n isn't a stingy man. Just forget everything I said yesterday when I was wasted."

Sui Hong coughed and pulled out a small brown bottle inside the box and laughed. "I also had a bit too much last night and forgot it all."

Chi Jin's eyes dimmed for an instant, then he looked up once again with clarity as he grinned. He left the box of cough syrup in the house and left.

Perhaps that was when the seeds of tragedy were inevitably sewn. From that day on, Chi Jin saw Xie Lanshan as a rival in love. Envy grew within an imaginary bed until it finally blinded the young man, consuming his heart.

Sui Hong sat on the train and recalled the times when Chi Jin was still young. They would sit side by side on the sofa and switch channels to watch a movie when they got bored with documentary films.

As always, the boy couldn't sit still and leaned his head down on the man's knees, curling up like a big puppy on his master's legs. The television was playing Brokeback Mountain, and the little boy suddenly started crying when he saw the two men on TV embrace each other tightly.

Sui Hong tapped Chi Jin's back and asked gently, "What's wrong?"

Chi Jin looked up at him with teary eyes. "Are you... okay with this kind of relationship between two men?"

Sui Hong might not have had much experience in the field, but he never doubted his sexuality and didn't think he would be asked to respond to a question like this. He answered without thinking, "Only if a fire can light my day, and that fire can last for eternity."

. . .

It wasn't until the day he felt those lips brush across his own that Sui Hong realized there had always been hints of Chi Jin's feelings for him. But he refused to take it seriously and always assumed it was just a mistaken emotion, that the child must have confused admiration with love.

And perhaps he really did. After that night, Chi Jin brought a girl back. When asked by his teammates, he only said it was a childhood friend and he wanted to try dating her.

Ling Yun was the one who told Sui Hong about it.

Sui Hong was obviously shocked and suddenly felt empty in his chest. After a long while, he pulled himself back and asked, "How's the girl?"

"Pretty, really pretty!" Ling Yun said that just from looks alone, the girl was a good match with Chi Jin. She had a pair of pretty eyes and a tall nose; her personality was also bright and bold.

Sui Hong's heart settled as he lifted a faint smile. He quickly tossed the memories of that night away and continued living on peacefully with his little boy.

Chi Jin turned 25 in a blink of an eye, and a 38-year-old Sui Hong once again faced the pestering of his relatives as they urged him to settle down with a family.

His gaze fell on the bottle of cough syrup resting on the table as he explained to his family how dangerous his work was. Their lives were always on the line, and it wouldn't be fair to a young wife to have a husband like this. Of course, his family didn't believe him. They shot back with the fact that drug enforcement officers have gotten married before, so what was he waiting for?

Sui Hong also wanted to ask himself sometimes, just what was he waiting for?

He had certainly thought about that joke-like bet, but it had already been too long. Captain Sui of the Blue Fox no longer wanted to maintain a relationship beyond boss and subordinate with his teammates. His friendship with Xie Lanshan had already enchanted him to make a decision he still wasn't sure was right, so what would a deeper bond like love potentially do? Sui Hong couldn't imagine it. Maintaining an acquaintance relationship was much better for him; like a gentle stream of water that wouldn't hurt even if they separated.

He would forever owe a lifetime's worth of guilt to Xie Lanshan, whether it was to the one who gave his life in a foreign land or to the one now who lived in a different body.

Besides, his little boy had already decided to fix his mistakes. Even though he no longer saw Chi Jin bring the pretty little girl over anymore, he always received positive news whenever he asked about their relationship. They were together peacefully and perhaps would get married in another two years.

Sui Hong was happy for his little boy. Love was like a dream, especially to drug enforcement officers like them who lived on wires. Having a fulfilling love that was accepted by society was the only thing that could heal their damaged souls.

The train arrived at its destination. Sui Hong found a hotel near the station, placed his luggage down, and followed the address on the paper to the small village.

Every household here had their own loquat trees in the yard; the grand view was stunning. Sui Hong learned quickly from the locals that everyone here seemed to know Chi Jin. They praised the young man at every mention, saying that he was a dependable man.

An old farmer who looked very spirited and young for his

age told Sui Hong that even though it looked like there was an abundance of loquat trees here, only a few households had been engaged in this trade since the beginning. The cough syrup brewed from the loquat trees was not the same as the ones that could be bought from stores. The locals insisted on using old recipes passed down over generations and handmade them, so the syrups were especially good for helping coughs. Their business relied on word of mouth over generations and only had a local market until that young man discovered this village.

The old farmer explained joyfully as he gave Sui Hong a tour around the farm, "Officer Chi is very kind. He taught us how to market our products on the internet, saying that we need to change our methods of selling exclusively in person. I don't understand it very well, I just did as he said and now there's a huge business here. Cars drive in and out every day from distributors all over the country."

Seeing how the first two families began making bank with the business, other families followed along. Some started specializing in making syrups with leaves, others made loquat honey, and some even made jam out of sweet fruits. In short, they began building a business around the loquat fruit. One after another, the mountains were quickly filled with loquat trees and every household began to make money.

Many in the village would stop to greet the old farmer as they passed by. Their eyes would turn to the tall and handsome Sui Hong, then ask the farmer who this sophisticated man was.

The old farmer laughed and said, "That's Officer Chi's Captain! Certainly, only a man like him is fit to be Officer Chi's Captain!"

The villagers grew revered as soon as they heard Sui Hong was Chi Jin's captain and joined in to converse with him.

A villager held Sui Hong's hand and shook it wildly,

thanking him. "We don't really understand these commerce and business things in the village. Officer Chi was the one that helped get patents for our food!"

Another villager chimed in, "It was impossible to sell ripe loquat fruits in the past, so we just let them rot on the ground. Officer Chi helped film me brewing these ripe fruits into jam and uploaded the video on the internet, then added a lot of interesting words to the video. That quickly got many clicks on the internet, and my business also grew thanks to him!"

Every comment was a praise for Chi Jin. Sui Hong smiled as he listened to them, sometimes coughing a few times, but didn't interrupt anyone.

The old farmer later said that Officer Chi drove a truck over here just before the year's end and never took it back. There were plenty of cars and trucks driving in and out of the village every day. The villagers all knew that Chi Jin was a busy police officer and would come to take it someday, so they didn't really pay much attention to the truck. It wasn't until Sui Hong paid a visit today that they realized Chi Jin hadn't shown up in a while.

Sui Hong frowned slightly and asked, "Where's the truck?"

The old farmer said, "This way."

A blue and white truck was parked alongside the other trucks filled with cough syrup.

Sui Hong followed the old farmer and asked someone to open up the doors.

Just as he thought, the truck of red ice neither Mu Kun nor the Blue Foxes managed to find was hiding quietly inside this place.

Sui Hong made a call back to the provincial branch immediately, gave an exact address to his current location, and said, "Send people over. We finally found Mu Kun's red ice."

The mountains covered in loquat trees surrounded the village on all sides. It was almost the blooming season for the loquats, but the trees on the mountaintops all seemed to procrastinate.

By the time forces came to take the truck of red ice, Sui Hong was sitting behind a tree facing the mountains. He looked up at the sky and suddenly recalled the times he was training with Chi Jin in the mountains.

Just before Mu Kun returned, their captain took the group of young Blue Fox members up to the mountains for their usual half-month seclusion training in the wild.

The training followed the same tradition; no digital products or any entertainment items were allowed during the training period. There was no signal up there, anyway. These young 20-year-olds were thus locked in the mountains during a burning hot season in August for ten days.

On the second to the last day of training, the young men could clearly see their improvements. The leaders in the provincial branch celebrated the successful training and brought in boxes full of beer and white wine.

Everyone drank a little more than usual during this celebration.

Only Sui Hong remained sober. He wasn't a man who touched alcohol or tobacco, and his countless injuries over a decade of working as a cop affected his body's immunity, so he graciously stayed away. He also wasn't a fan of parties. After grabbing some food to eat, he sat alone beneath a locust tree.

Night fell, but the party continued. Ling Yun was still in high spirits as he dragged Chi Jin over to offer a cup of wine to their captain. Sui Hong didn't drink wine, so Ling Yun happily downed the cup for his captain and then rushed back gleefully to his teammates.

He left a helpless Chi Jin, who stood stiffly in front of Sui Hong, with a large glass in hand. The liquor in the container was only half-filled. The young man looked to be tipsy already.

Sui Hong laughed and called him over, "What are you standing around for? Come sit over here."

Chi Jin sat down beside his captain as he was told but didn't speak and only drank. The two hadn't spent time together alone in a while. Even if everything looked to be the same on the outside, some things certainly changed after that night.

Sui Hong silently watched those young men not far away from him play around with a faint smile on his face.

He wasn't sure how long he sat, but all team members had been knocked out from the alcohol. Sui Hong turned around and noticed Chi Jin was already sleeping by the tree as well. The young man's face was still reddish, his breathing even, lashes trembling slightly in his sleep. This innocent image looked just like how he was when he was younger. The flies in the woods circled around him; a few even landed on his eyelids.

Sui Hong leaned in and saw Chi Jin's face beneath the moonlight. He looked at those long and thin lashes, that tall nose, and raised a hand to brush off the fly from the young man's face.

This small gesture woke Chi Jin, who suddenly grabbed onto the man's wrist while his eyes remained closed, as if it was a reflexive action in his sleep.

Sui Hong didn't pull his hand away and allowed it to be placed on Chi Jin's face gently.

Chi Jin repeated through his dreams, "I miss you a lot."

Night fog descended as the moisture in the air thickened.

Sui Hong assumed the young man was thinking of his fiancée and said softly, "One more day, and you'll see her soon."

Chi Jin didn't open his eyes and instead slyly pursued further with the excuse of alcohol. He kissed Sui Hong's fingers gently, allowing a single teardrop to roll down his cheek.

He then bit lightly onto Sui Hong's fingers as he continued pressing them on his lips, then mumbled through his lips, "Let's bet on something. When the white flames of the day can reach eternity, you'll let me love you."

Sui Hong's body temperature was lower than the average person's due to his chronic sickness. He could feel the warmth at the tips of his fingers, which also warmed his heart. Enchanted by that moment, he leaned down to comfort his little boy with his lips.

A bug bite woke Ling Yun. He looked up and saw two shadows leaning closely together from afar. He rubbed his eyes and called out, "Captain?"

Their lips were only a hair strand away, and the call broke the spell of the moment. Sui Hong felt apologetic for his actions, even more so for Chi Jin's fiancée. He coughed twice, pulled his hand away from Chi Jin's face, and walked away.

Sui Hong only found out at Chi Jin's funeral that there was no fiancée at all.

He saw the pretty girl at the service and learned from her that she was Chi Jin's cousin. Perhaps Chi Jin was afraid of making things awkward for both parties; he decided to not make Sui Hong worry.

A powerful gust of winter wind blew by. Sui Hong felt the icy air and stood up. The local police officers arrived quickly.

Now that the missing red ice was found, he could also leave this place.

The old farmer walked over and noticed the man was ready to leave, then called out, eyes beaming, "Oh Captain Sui, great timing! The loquat flowers are blooming!"

Sui Hong turned around and saw the moment the flowers were in full bloom.

Perhaps that gust of wind earlier reminded the flowers of the season; all the flowers bloomed at once. The petals were snow white, torus crimson red, and stamen golden yellow. The small flowers consumed the trees as if they were dominating the mountains.

Sui Hong stood frozen at this grand scene of nature.

Bud after bud, petal after petal, the loquat flowers bloomed proudly as they elegantly decorated the entire mountain range; even the sunlight of day couldn't compare to the shimmering white of these flowers.

At this very moment, he felt it. He felt his little boy embrace him from behind, his lips pressed by his ear.

Sui Hong's hands trembled after this long-awaited and realistic touch, then a tremble spread through his whole body. He tried to lift a smile, but could only close his eyes quietly, allowing a teardrop to fall down to the ground.

He heard that boy say:

"Captain, look at this mountain blooming with loquat flowers, just like the eternal flames that can warm and light your day."

End.

About the Author

Jin Shisi Chai is a renowned and popular webnovel author in China, graduate of Tongji University in Shanghai, and a member of Shanghai's Writers Association. Famous works include Lip Gun, In the Dark, and Gentries of the City. She is known for her sharp writing, deep insight into social topics, and unique style of prose that earned her a loyal following of readers on social media. Many of her works have sold adaptation rights in China from film to webcomics.